FIRE IN THE NIGHT

He stood over her, black cloak whipping like the spread of dark wings, his eyes a match to the night. She stared up, her gaze as open as a flower.

He tipped her chin up with a finger. Shivers coursed through her body. She stood there, not powerless to stop him, only unwilling. Her own need held her there, and when his tongue etched a delicate path along her upper lip, she arched her throat, her small gasp lost beneath the cover of his mouth. Each kiss became deeper and fuller than the last, heady and sweet. She drank them in like fine subtle wine.

"Elspeth," he murmured, his breath soft on her brow. "I had not thought that this would happen."

"Nor did I," she said, trying to pull her ragged thoughts into coherence. Then she said with the strength of desperation in her voice, "Leave now, Duncan. Please. Leave me, leave the Highlands."

But his burning gaze and the fire within her told her that it was already too late for anything but desire at its height and passion at its darkest. . .

ANNOUNCING THE

TOPAZ FREQUENT READERS CLUB
COMMEMORATING TOPAZ'S 1 YEAR ANNIVERSARY!

THE MORE YOU BUY, THE MORE YOU GET

Redeem coupons found here and in the back of all new Topaz titles for FREE Topaz gifts:

Send in:

◆ 2 coupons for a free TOPAZ novel (choose from the list below);
  ☐ THE KISSING BANDIT, Margaret Brownley
  ☐ BY LOVE UNVEILED, Deborah Martin
  ☐ TOUCH THE DAWN, Chelley Kitzmiller
  ☐ WILD EMBRACE, Cassie Edwards

◆ 4 coupons for an "I Love the Topaz Man" on-board sign

◆ 6 coupons for a TOPAZ compact mirror

◆ 8 coupons for a Topaz Man T-shirt

Just fill out this certificate and send with original sales receipts to:

TOPAZ FREQUENT READERS CLUB-1ST ANNIVERSARY
Penguin USA • Mass Market Promotion; Dept. H.U.G.
375 Hudson St., NY, NY 10014

Name_____

Address_____

City_____State_____Zip_____

Offer expires 5/31/1995

This certificate must accompany your request. No duplicates accepted. Void where prohibited, taxed or restricted. Allow 4-6 weeks for receipt of merchandise. Offer good only in U.S., its territories, and Canada.

The Raven's Wish

by

Susan King

A TOPAZ BOOK

TOPAZ
Published by the Penguin Group
Penguin Books USA Inc., 375 Hudson Street,
New York, New York 10014, U.S.A.
Penguin Books Ltd, 27 Wrights Lane,
London W8 5TZ, England
Penguin Books Australia Ltd, Ringwood,
Victoria, Australia
Penguin Books Canada Ltd, 10 Alcorn Avenue,
Toronto, Ontario, Canada M4V 3B2
Penguin Books (N.Z.) Ltd, 182-190 Wairau Road,
Auckland 10, New Zealand

Penguin Books Ltd, Registered Offices:
Harmondsworth, Middlesex, England

First published by Topaz, an imprint of Dutton Signet,
a division of Penguin Books USA Inc.

First Printing, May, 1995
10 9 8 7 6 5 4 3 2

 Topaz is a trademark of Dutton Signet,
a division of Penguin Books USA Inc.

Printed in Canada

To my mother Anne—
for Fraser ancestry,
and laughter, and memories.

ACKNOWLEDGEMENTS

I am deeply grateful to Drs. Mary and Edward Furgol, historians, scholars, and friends, who gave generously of their time and knowledge, and read the text for authenticity. Thanks also to their son Malcolm for some wonderfully gruesome details about the Edinburgh dungeons. Sharing tea and history—and trading kids—with the Furgols is always a privilege and a delight.

To Dr. James Douglas Farquhar, art historian and professor, I owe profound thanks: If my work is carefully done in any way, it is due to his superb example and guidance during my graduate years.

Alden O'Brien, costume historian, gave me information and her approval when I let my heroine run around in a belted plaid; my brother-in-law Jimmy Vita read the golf scene with an expert's eye; my sister Paula Longhi shared her books and photographs of Scotland; Tony McGrachan and Mary Furgol let me listen to their wonderful accents; and Gwyn Webb gave me some last-minute horse advice.

My friends and family deserve many thanks for many reasons. I am particularly fortunate because there really are too many to list here, but I am especially grateful to Rachel, Joanne, Janet, Andy, Diane, Kurt, Barbara, Paula, Karen, Norma, and my Dad.

And lastly, thanks are due to my own loyal, patient, and handsome heroes, David and our sons Josh, Jeremy, and Sean, who have graciously accepted that I like writing and research far better than cooking and cleaning.

Prologue

Bridles brack, and wight horse lap,
And blades flain in the skies,
And wan and drousie was the blood
Gaed lapperin down the lays.
        —"Katharine Jaffray"

Scotland, the Highlands, 1552

"That was the day of our greatest betrayal," the old *seanchaidh* said. Among the fifteen small faces upturned toward his, a few of the children nodded solemnly. Their bright and dark heads gleamed in the low light of the peat fire.

"And all our fine, brave Fraser men," he told the children as he bent forward, "rode in a great body, that day of betrayal, to meet the MacDonalds. In faith they rode forward, with a full host of Grants and Macraes at their backs. The Fraser chief, the MacShimi, he was called, as are all our chiefs—" The old bard paused to nod to a small boy with dark hair and serious hazel eyes. The child nodded gravely in return, already showing the dignity of a clan chief.

"Well, the MacShimi, our own Hugh's brave father, meant to support a MacDonald's claim to the chieftainship of that clan. This MacDonald had been fostered in the MacShimi's own house and had wed his niece. But the MacDonalds refused him as their rightful chief and called him *Gallda*, the stranger, for having fostered with Frasers, and sent them all away.

"The Frasers rode off in peace, though there were near four hundred of them, strong warriors with broad-bladed claymores and sharp dirks, and keen, swift arrows for their bows. They could have insisted that the MacDonalds accept the *Gallda* as their rightful chief. But they rode away in

full trust." A little boy grew restless at his feet, and the
seanchaidh spoke a soft Gaelic word to him, smiling indulgently until the lad settled again.

"On this fine summer day, the Frasers left their allies
and rode home through the glen of Loch Lochy. And there,
beside the shore of that long loch, they were ambushed by
over five hundred MacDonalds. The summer afternoon had
grown so warm that the men soon became blinded by
sweat, and dizzy with the heat. So the warriors threw off
their hot, heavy wool plaids and cast them down on the
grass by the loch. And they fought on, Fraser and MacDonald alike, wearing only their long linen shirts.

"The sun blazed like the fires of hell, they say, a heat
such as comes only once in a while to the Highlands. And
though the Frasers were far outnumbered by the MacDonalds, they did not run but stayed and fought. Half clad they
were, and exhausted, struggling hand to hand along the
swampy shore. By late afternoon the boggy, muddy banks
were scattered with hundreds of discarded plaids, and hundreds of bodies, discarded by their souls." The old man
drew a breath and looked at his audience.

"The MacShimi was killed, and his son, the young Master, with him. And the MacDonald *Gallda* died, too, fighting beside our chief, for he would not desert his foster
father. And though they lost most of their own, the Frasers
wielded as much death with their claymores and dirks as
they got. Just as much and more."

The children waited breathlessly for the end of the story,
though they had heard it countless times since they had
been born. One or two fidgeted, but the rest sat transfixed,
lulled by the soft, hot crackle of the peat fire and by the
spell the *seanchaidh* wove as his voice swelled and softened,
finding every nuance in the story.

"Nearly nine hundred men fought that day. Yet five Frasers, and no more than eight or nine MacDonalds, survived.
And though the bodies are buried now and the blood has
been absorbed back into the earth, we will always remember what happened on the banks of Loch Lochy eight years

ago today. And we call it Blar-na-Léine, the Field of Shirts."

"Blar-na-Léine," a few of the children repeated softly. The old man nodded.

"Indeed, little ones. But remember that the might of the Fraser clan cannot be reduced so easily. Before that battle, eighty and more of the Fraser women, who became widows, were already with child. And all those women, so our legend says, birthed fatherless sons." He looked solemnly around the group of male children. Each one sat a little taller as the storyteller's gaze passed over him. "You were all born then, eight years ago, into a clan filled with sorrow, but gladdened by your births, every one."

"Every one," he said softly, reaching forward with a gentle hand to touch the small, bright head nearest his knee. The child's glossy locks were the warm color of flames reflected in gold.

"But the legend has a secret, eh?" The boys smiled, and some of them nodded eagerly. "One of those widows birthed our little Elspeth here, and then died in her woman's battle, and went to heaven to join her brave warrior husband."

He lifted his hand from the small girl's head. Making a fist, he thumped it against his heart.

"Na dèanamaid diochuimhn," he whispered to the group of little Fraser cousins. *"Na dèanamaid diochuimhn:* let us not forget. You are the hope and faith of the Frasers, a new generation of warriors, born from ashes and sorrow. Like the yew tree, my children, which grows a new tree within the ruin of the old one"—here he plucked a green sprig from his bonnet, which lay beside him—"like the yew, which we Frasers wear as our own proud badge, the Fraser clan is reborn out of strife and woe. And as the yew survives and grows, so we too will overcome, through our pride and our strength, whatever the will of God or man may bring to us."

"Na dèanamaid diochuimhn," the children murmured.

"And so be it," the *seanchaidh* said.

Chapter 1

Betwixt the hours of twelve and one
A north wind tore the bent,
And straight she heard strange eldritch sounds
Upon that wind which went.

— *"Tam Lin"*

Scotland, the Highlands, August, 1563

"Aaarrghh! Missed him, the son of a snake!" Splashing wide-legged through the water, scrambling over slick rocks, the girl gained steadier footing. Staring intently into the stream, she swore softly. The airy Gaelic oath sounded like a prayer.

Ignoring the raucous chorus of male laughter that floated out from the bank, she shifted her fingers along the stout stick gripped in her hand. A silvery flash teased past her bare legs, and she struck downward, then cursed loudly. Cold water surged over her knees, saturating the hem of the plaid wrapped about her slim hips and slung over her shoulder.

"That fish won't wait for you! Strike faster, cousin!"

"Elspeth! Use your Sight, girl! Find yourself another fish, just as you find the cattle when we go raiding!"

Scowling, Elspeth glanced toward the bank. Four young men, her cousins, stood on the slope, two or three guffawing heartily as they watched her efforts. Sunlight brightened the deep blues and greens in their plaids, echoing the colors of the grassy moors and distant hills beyond. A quick, cool breeze lifted and dispersed their laughter.

"Hush, now, Ewan Fraser," Elspeth called, addressing the redheaded cousin who had last spoken. "Loud as the pests of hell, the lot of you, and scaring the trout too. How can the Frasers boast of their own way of fishing, striking

fish with rods, if the Frasers themselves cannot do it
proper?"

"Ah! Fraser *men* can do it proper! Look here, girl!"
Ewan gestured toward the slithery and substantial pile of
trout that already lay on the bank. Her cousins looked back
at her, grinning blithely.

Her own laughter bubbled out. "Men? *Gillean gòracha.*"

"Foolish boys, is it?" Magnus said, his blond hair like a
golden beacon in the sunlight. "Foolish girl, you should be
home preparing our supper, and not out here playing with
the lads!"

"Hah! My cakes would be burned, and I would make a
mess of your fine fish," she called back. At this, Ewan, and
her cousins Kenneth and Callum after him, bent forward
playfully, clutching at imaginary bellyaches.

"A fine wife she will make for Ruari MacDonald," Ewan
said to the others.

"Do not dare say that name!" Elspeth called angrily.
Ewan flushed and shrugged as if to offer an apology.

"Fraser men, is it, and acting like babes," she grumbled,
turning away. "Now be silent, all of you."

Deepening her frown and balancing her club between
her hands, she bent forward to scan the glinting, rapid shallows. "Ah, there you are, back again, old fish. Flora Mac-
Kimmie wants you for her cooking pot, and won't take no
for her answer."

At supper the night before, Flora, the housekeeper at
Castle Glenran, had stood to her full height of six feet and
fisted her hands on her wide hips, declaring hotly that she
was like to die of beef every day and had to have some
fish. Fresh trout it should be, not salted or smoked like
the fish the Frasers exported out of Inverness, Flora had
added imperiously.

Magnus, the eldest of the Fraser cousins still living in
the stronghold of Castle Glenran, had marshaled an early
expedition to catch Flora's trout. Fishing was always enjoyed by the cousins, though none of them, Elspeth
thought, much enjoyed eating fish.

Slipping through the water, fast and elusive as a shadow,

the fish wended its way closer to Elspeth's still, steady legs. Slowly, like a bloom unfurling, she lowered her arms as the trout approached through the bright, dappled shallows.

She struck hard and fast. Reaching into the water, she lifted the fat, gasping trout with both hands.

"Oh, gillean! Lads!" she called, tossing the fish toward the bank. "Cut your teeth on this!"

Ewan caught the large fish easily and flipped it onto the pile. He and the others turned toward her and, with much ceremony, bowed graciously.

Elspeth laughed out loud at the picture they presented: four Highlanders in wrapped and brooched plaids, bare-chested and bare-legged, long hair in shades of brown, gold, and red. Wild, wind-tossed, and wet from a morning's fishing, they bowed as politely as if they were in Queen Mary's court at Edinburgh.

Still grinning, moving through the cold, swirling water, Elspeth pushed back a curling strand of coppery hair that had slipped from its sagging plait. Her cousins stood on the bank, one or two watching her, the others talking among themselves.

Kenneth stepped down into the stream and came toward her. His legs cleaved the water rapidly, and his wide, bare shoulders gleamed in the sunlight. His dark hair was longer than hers, hanging down in wet strings and braids. He shoved it back impatiently and grinned at her.

"Well done, cousin," he said, and clapped her on the back with a long, flat hand. "That was a big fish, and old, and stubborn. You are as good as any lad among us. And always have been," he added.

"That I know," Elspeth said, stumbling a little from the enthusiastic back-slapping. "But thank you, Kenneth."

"You have grown up a little wild," he said, "but you are a fine woman all the same." She slid him a curious look. He cleared his throat. "And a fine wife you would be to Ruari MacDonald"—he held up a hand as if to ward off a blow—"if you would but consider it."

Elspeth sighed in exasperation. "Brave man to tell me that," she said. "I have given the MacShimi my refusal. But

he is as stubborn as a goat, as are all of you. None of you
will listen to me."

"We understood your reasons for refusal, girl. The Mac-
Shimi does too. But as clan chief he knows that some good
could come of such a match."

"Good? Surely none for me!" She stared incredulously
at him. "Kenneth, would you truly see me wed a
MacDonald?"

He looked away. "There's talk of fire and sword from
the crown unless we stop feuding with Clan MacDonald.
You know that the queen's council is sending a lawyer here.
He will likely demand an end to the feud. Perhaps we
should make our own effort to do that, without the interfer-
ence of the crown."

"We could no more cease feuding with the MacDonalds
than we could cease breathing," Elspeth said. "Let that dry
old lawyer come and spout his rules at us. Such threats
mean little in the Highlands."

Kenneth smiled impishly. "Ah, but we would not raid on
some of the MacDonalds if you were living in one of their
castles and eating their beef." His warm brown eyes glinted
at her.

Usually his smile could charm Elspeth out of any dark
mood, but she resisted now. "There has been too much
talk of this lately," she grumbled. "Marry that MacDonald,
you say, and save the clan from fire and sword. I will not
wed Ruari MacDonald. The day is cursed that the offer
was ever made!"

He regarded her somberly, then sighed and turned.
Sloshing away from her, he scanned the water for other
trout.

Elspeth waded through the cold shallows, her temper
gradually cooling as she watched the undulating flow of the
water. She had continued to staunchly refuse the marriage
offer that the MacDonald chief had made to the chief of
the Frasers a few weeks earlier. As her cousins had expressed more often their tentative approval of the match,
she had begun to wonder how much meaning her refusal
held.

She and her cousins had grown and played and learned together since they had been babes. Elspeth and these four, along with several other cousins, had fostered together at Castle Glenran under Lachlann Fraser. One of the few survivors of the battle that had taken so many Fraser men, Lachlann had been a generous, educated laird, beloved by his fosterlings. After his death last year, his son Callum, who stood now on the streambank with the others, had become the laird of Glenran Castle.

Elspeth had more than eighty cousins, all lads. But these few Glenran cousins, along with her cousin Hugh, the Fraser chief, she loved as deeply as if they were her brothers. She frowned sourly, thinking of her own half brother, Robert Gordon, who had never shown much interest in her beyond whatever might benefit him. Doubtless he would approve of this marriage.

Looking at her cousins now, she saw four strong, handsome Highland warriors and felt a swell of pride. The Glenran Frasers were part of a legend that had flourished in their childhood. The astonishing number of boys born in the months following the battle of Blar-na-Léine had become the core of that legend, which spoke of the strong, hopeful future of Clan Fraser.

She had been the only girl born that year. Lachlann Fraser had once said that Elspeth had been born as a special gift to Clan Fraser, with her God-given ability to see what others could not. She had always been proud to be a part of the hope and faith of her clan, to be part of the legend.

But now the lads were men, with the responsibilities of men. As the closest kinsmen to the Fraser chief, and as his personal bodyguard, they must consider the needs of the clan as a whole. Elspeth knew that she should follow that lead, but she could not do so. Not in this matter of marriage to Ruari MacDonald.

She sighed gustily. She was a woman, and her cousins were men who could decide her fate. Though Highland women had greater freedom and more rights than Sasunnach women, she knew that her cousins could force her to marry against her will. They could even allow Ruari to abduct her to get the matter done. But she did not want to marry a MacDonald. Above all, she did not want to leave her cousins and her home.

Slicing through the water, she gazed at its sparkling, rippled surface. "I will never marry Ruari MacDonald," she muttered. "Never, as long as the streams run in the Highlands!"

The water swirled about her ankles. A shiver rushed through her that had nothing to do with the chill of the stream. As a Highlander she was used to wading through cold water. This shiver was very different: she recognized the inner shudder that often preceded a vision.

She stood still. Subtle but compelling, the gathering power within her deepened her breath. A haze, tinted bright gold, gave her eyesight an unnatural clarity.

As if some unseen hand turned her head, she looked over her shoulder. Her gaze traveled upward, past the cousins who watched from the bank, and beyond, up the long slope that rose beside the stream. She looked at the top of the hill, crowned with a stand of pale birch trees. The wide, odd expression in her eyes caused her cousins to look up there also.

Silent and swift and dark, two ravens glided above the birches. Elspeth drew in her breath sharply: ravens were a sign of death and misfortune. Then a movement among the trees caught her attention.

Along the high ridge a man rode a dark horse, passing between the pale birches at an easy canter. Sunlight dappled his black cloak and glinted off his dark hair.

As Elspeth watched, he turned his head. Even from this distance she felt his gaze on her, keen and intelligent and focused. His eyes were the sharp, clear blue of a Highland sky, and his face had a stern beauty, like a dark angel. He lifted a hand to her in salute, as if he had come there only to meet her. She blinked and looked again.

The man was gone. Branches waved gently in the breeze, moving in the empty space where the man had been. But the fine, shivery bumps along her arms, and the golden haze, told her that he had never been there at all.

He had not been real.

Heart pounding in a fierce rhythm, she fisted her hands and steadied herself against the light-headedness that swelled briefly through her. She saw her cousins turn their perplexed glances from her to the empty hilltop and back to her again. Only a moment, a few breaths of time, had passed since she had raised her gaze to the top of the hill.

Her cousins watched her, silent and somber. Ever since Elspeth had been a child, her family had accepted that she was a *taibhsear,* a seer. Her cousins seldom asked what a vision had shown her, but respectfully waited for her to speak of it. She knew they would do the same now.

Rubbing her eyes, she took a slow step forward through the cool shallows. Some visions, she knew, were of little consequence, like the flashes of light from tiny blinking stars, their mysteries never quite discovered. Perhaps, she thought, the stranger on the hill had been the time-drifted shadow of a real man, one who would ride along that hill in the future.

Or perhaps he had been one of the *daoine sìth,* the people of peace, the fairy people who dwelt in the hills and caves. Such beings, it was said, could take the shape of the most beautiful of humans, and could be seen only by a *taibhsear.*

But the ravens, the messengers of death, had preceded the man. He had worn black, riding a black horse. Yet she had no sense of her own death being foretold by his appearance. What could the vision mean? Shivering again, she rubbed her arms.

She had felt a strange tugging at her heart when she had looked at him, and a strange yearning to ride with him. Somehow she felt no fear, no dread of this man. The odd, brief vision perplexed her greatly as she moved toward the bank.

The water, she thought: sometimes it was so with water. Gazing at the glistening surface of a stream or a lake could be the same as looking into a bow of rainwater used for divining. Spontaneous visions could happen unexpectedly. She blinked rapidly, and the lingering haze began to dispel.

Drawing a breath, she looked at her cousins. They had resumed talking quietly among themselves, and one or two glanced toward her with covert concern. Squaring her shoulders, shaking back her loosened braid, she stepped forward.

Though the vision had left her knees and hands trembling, Elspeth stubbornly advanced toward the bank as if she had nothing more on her mind than a few trout.

Where a steep hill rounded up to a rocky peak, two men reined in their horses and gazed out at the broad view. The cool, damp snap of the summer breeze billowed the wrapped and brooched plaid of one man, and tore at the black cloak worn by the other rider.

Spread out below them, the long surface of a loch gleamed like a mirror of dark steel, reflecting the surrounding forested hills and azure sky. The Highlander nodded in satisfaction and glanced at his companion.

"Ye've nae seen such a sight in years, I think, Duncan Macrae." Making a sweeping gesture with a large, leather-gloved hand, he grinned. Thick blond hair glinted beneath a dark, flat wool blanket, into which were thrust a few sprigs of fresh yew. Looking around with a broad, toothy smile, the burly Highlander inhaled the fresh air as if he breathed in pride.

Duncan Macrae looked westward along the great loch. A rugged line of hills faded from blue into lavender, marching and soaring into distant mists. Silent, staring ahead, he rested long, lean, neatly gloved hands on the saddle bow. The tall black stallion shifted beneath him.

" 'Tis true, Alasdair," he replied quietly after a moment. "I've nae seen the like for sixteen years and more." An instant of breeze lifted his black cloak from wide, powerful shoulders, revealing a carefully tailored black doublet and trews tucked into high boots of ebony-dyed leather.

"Isn't enough to stir the Highland blood in ye, then, Duncan Macrae of Dulsie?" Alasdair said. "Remember, ye are now the laird of Dulsie Castle in Kintail."

"Alasdair Fraser, *bràthair*," Duncan said, "brother I will

call you, for you fostered with my family and you are wed
to my sister. Call me laird of Dulsie Castle if you will,
though I've nae seen the place since I was seventeen." His
tone became grim. "As for my Highland blood, well . . ."
He paused to shove back a windblown drift of his dark
brown hair. "Perhaps blood such as mine shouldna be
stirred up."

"Bah," Alasdair protested. " 'Tis good ye've been sent
north by the queen's council. I did wonder if ye'd ever set
foot in the Highlands again." Duncan did not reply, and
the two men sat silently.

As he looked out at the bold, beautiful line of hills and
loch, Duncan's heart surged almost painfully. Far in the
western Highlands, well beyond those blue mountains, lay
Dulsie Castle, which had passed to him on the death of his
last remaining brother two months ago. He had not sent
word to the rest of his family there that he had returned
to the Highlands. He was not certain when—or if—he
would do that. Perhaps he would ask Alasdair to carry a
word of greeting to his grandmother and his two sisters.

For now, Duncan's immediate destination lay closer, a
ride southwest along Loch Ness, whose waters flowed
below them. At the lower tip of the great loch lay Castle
Glenran, the home of Alasdair's kinsman, a laird called
Callum Fraser. There Duncan had been told that he would
find Hugh Fraser, the MacShimi, the chief of Clan Fraser.

As one of the queen's lawyers, Duncan Macrae had been
sent by the Privy Council to journey into the Highlands
with an important document for Clan Fraser. The necessary
signatures would take but a day or two to collect. Then he
would return to Edinburgh. He did not intend to stay long
in the Highlands. If he remained here too long, he feared
that he would never want to return to the safe, ordered life
that he had made for himself in the Lowlands. He had
stayed away from the Highlands for all these years, convinced that it was best.

A breeze ruffled lightly through his hair, bringing the
blended scents of pine, heather, and water. The smell of
water was everywhere here, from the great loch, from myr-

iad streams and rivers, even out of the very dampness of the air. He was keenly reminded of the tangy scented air of Dulsie.

He thought of his family there. "And how is my sister Mhairi, auld man?" he asked.

"Auld man? I may be married now, and a father, but ye're the same age as me. Auld is it, at two and thirty," Alasdair muttered. "I hear men in England dinna marry afore the age of thirty. Is it true?"

"I ken little of English ways. I lived with my mother's people for years, on the Scots side of the border, and never crossed over."

"Hah! Ne'er crossed by light o' day, ye mean to say, and ne'er crossed legally."

Duncan pinched back a smile. "My cousins, the Kerrs, are fine correct citizens of her majesty Queen Mary Stewart."

Alasdair laughed out loud. "That Highland Macrae blood of yers, lad, found its merry niche with the Kerrs. Yer cousins rank with the most fearsome border reivers who ever haunted the line between Scotland and England."

"Well," Duncan drawled, "I admit that occasionally a few cattle and sheep would wander over the border. Someone had to fetch them back again."

"Yer solemn duty, man. Wi' lances and swords, no less."

"Just so," Duncan said. "Those cattle can be dangerous beasts at night." He paused. "Ye started to tell me about Mhairi and your three bairns. And how is my wee sister Kirsty?"

"Wee Kirsty?" Alasdair smiled. "She is fine, as is Mhairi. We called our eldest Douglas, after yer father. He's dark like the Macraes, but will be broad and bonny as the Frasers." Alasdair slid him a careful look. "Mhairi took the wee ones north to spend time with yer grandmother and Kirsty at Dulsie. I'll be going there soon. Will ye nae come?"

"I have duties in Edinburgh when I finish wi' this task."

Alasdair, watching him, sighed. "They would welcome ye."

Duncan shook his head. "I have made a life for myself

in the south. I will send documents north to turn Dulsie over to my sisters, I think."

"Well. Ye've been a Lowlander for a long while, with all those years spent on the border, and at St. Andrews University, and then lawyerin' at the courts in Edinburgh," Alasdair said. "But dinna fool yerself, lad. No such tame life could discourage that wild Macrae blood." He tipped a shaggy brow. "Ye shouldna be ashamed of it. 'Tis long past time ye became a Highlandman once again."

Duncan shook his head. "The wild Scot in me is gone, Alasdair. And I canna mourn his passing." Truly, he mused, he no longer felt that burn deep within. The wild inner spark in him was extinguished, and he was glad; it had nearly ruined him once.

"Hah," Alasdair said. "The Macraes are legendary in the Highlands for recklessness, and for strength and darin', and for tempers that would make even Frasers quake. That blood tells in a man, no matter where he goes wi' his life. And ne'er was a lad as bold as ye were, Duncan Macrae."

Duncan smiled mirthlessly. "I once meant to be the wildest Macrae of all, the boldest o' the lot. Long ago."

Alasdair looked at him for a long moment. "Let it go, lad," he said softly. "Ye were sixteen when they died. Must ye carry the guilt of that day forever?"

"Aye," Duncan said curtly. "I must." Shutting the familiar regret out of his thoughts, he set his lean jaw and fixed his gaze on the far mountains. He was a lawyer now, disciplined and scholarly, no longer the wild, angry lad who had left these hills behind.

As a lawyer, he had been successful enough to earn the respect of Queen Mary Stewart's Privy Council. Ironically, that same capability had gotten him sent back into the Highlands, by royal order, to deliver a legal document to the Frasers.

He glanced at Alasdair as he thought of his assignment. And some called the Macraes wild, he thought. The Frasers' feud with the MacDonalds had been fierce enough to catch the attention of the crown. He had been sent up here to quell it.

"Alasdair," he said, "nae more talk of wildness, I think, unless ye wish to discuss the Frasers." Gathering his reins, he urged his horse forward.

Alasdair laughed as he rode alongside. "Aye, wild they are, every one o' my cousins. Including Elspeth, who has likely ridden on every raid into MacDonald territory. Ye'll hae some challenge there, discouraging this feud."

"Elspeth Fraser?" Duncan frowned, not recognizing the name. Likely one of the Fraser widows, he thought, to be so adamant about the MacDonalds. "What, does she stir her sons into battle fever?"

"Hardly. In the thick o' it herself, weapons and all."

Duncan raised his brows in disbelief. "A warrior woman? A matronly Athena? A Boudicca in your midst?" He laughed. "Well, if she shares your brawn and your mean looks, my friend, 'tis no surprise to me that she wields a claymore wi' the best o' them."

Alasdair laughed outright. "I'll say nae more on that, man. I'll say nae more." He kneed his sturdy horse into a fast canter. "Come ahead, then, lawyer, do ye dare. Castle Glenran is only a few leagues from here!"

Chapter 2

*"Late, late yestreen I saw the new moone
Wi' the auld moone in hir arme;
And I feir, I feir, my deir master,
That we will com to harme."*
                    —"Sir Patrick Spence"

"Fish are no fit food for warriors," Callum complained. Sitting down beside Elspeth on a sun-warmed boulder by the stream, he looked disdainfully at the day's catch. He tilted a brow at Elspeth, and when she laughed softly, Callum smiled as if pleased, thrusting his fingers through his light brown, woolly hair.

"All is well with you, Elspeth?" he asked.

She looked away, determined to say nothing of her strange vision of the man dressed in the raven's color. "All is well."

He nodded. Out in mid-stream, Kenneth struck suddenly at the water and leaned down to bring up a large brown trout. The fish sailed through the air in a flash of golden brown and landed on the slithery pile with a soft plop.

Callum watched the flight of the fish. "Flora MacKimmie may have had her fill of beef, but I have not," he grumbled.

Looking at the brawny muscle on her cousin's tall, broad frame, Elspeth smiled. Callum could outeat any warrior she had ever seen. Tall and solid as an oak, he had always seemed to desperately need every morsel of food that Flora provided him. But he ate very little fish whenever it was offered.

Ewan moved toward them and folded his lanky legs on the ground. He shoved back a glossy fall of hair, a rich russet color, out of his brown eyes, and flashed a devilish smile. "Flora's wish for trout sits hard with Callum," he said, clapping him sympathetically on the shoulder. Callum grunted in miserable assent.

Watching, Elspeth pinched down a smile. Callum truly hated fish, but since childhood he had adored Flora. Elspeth knew that he would eat the trout at supper tonight out of utter devotion.

"Flora wants fish, Flora shall have fish," said a calm, deep voice above them.

"Ah! Magnus will eat the fish without complaint," Ewan said, stretching his arms as he yawned. "Me, I may pass."

"You will eat the fish and like it." Magnus, standing tall over them, fisted a hand toward his cousin Ewan.

Ewan grinned. "Ah, a threat? Would you spoil a finer face than your own, then?"

"The devil is often handsome," Magnus said. "As are you."

"Hah, I give handsome to you, then," Ewan returned.

Elspeth listened, knowing that Ewan's quick tongue could evoke laughter as often as annoyance. But whenever Ewan sang, his deep, rich voice entranced anyone who listened.

She looked up at Magnus, who towered over her, his long golden braids hanging down like silken ropes. He was only a few years older than the others, but Elspeth sometimes thought that Magnus was like an ancient Celtic god, all golden strength and beauty. When she had been a child she had adored him.

But often when she looked at Magnus now, her heart surged with sympathy. She sensed the pain and the anger that flowed through him like a dark, silent river, and knew that he still carried deep hurt from the death of his wife two years earlier. She had watched him harden, most of his rare gentleness reserved for his little daughter, who lived with her grandmother.

Kenneth had come out of the water as they spoke, and sat down to rub his feet dry with an untucked end of his long plaid. "Well, I will eat fish gladly rather than risk Flora's vengeance," he said.

Laughing, Elspeth looked up at Magnus. "If we do not

have enough fish to please Flora, we can go down to the loch. Angus Simson will give us some of his net-catch, I think. He is always generous to his laird."

Magnus looked grim. "Angus lost several cattle the other night to reivers," he said. "His son came to Glenran early today and told us that Angus was sore beaten when he came outside, hearing a noise. But they could not see the men that did the deed for the murk and the rain."

Ewan nodded. "We were surprised to hear of reiving so soon. Summer nights are too short for it, with sundown coming so late."

Listening, Elspeth felt the heat rise to color her cheeks. She frowned and toed one bare foot along the rocky ground.

"MacDonalds," she said softly. "I know it was them."

Magnus watched her for a moment. "Perhaps you do, for you see things that others cannot. But we must act with some caution now, and not attack the MacDonalds without good cause."

"I see that making a marriage with Ruari will not end this feud," Elspeth said crossly.

"And I, for one, do not think it wise to marry Elspeth into that clan of wolves," Callum said.

Elspeth nodded vigorously. "I agree."

"This feud has brought the wrath of the crown on our heads," Magnus said. "The queen's lawyer, when he arrives, will likely tell us to end it quickly. The marriage might do that."

"I will not sacrifice myself to end this feud for you," Elspeth muttered.

"Well, the marriage is not made, and the lawyer is not here, and cattle reiving is always repaid in kind," Ewan said. "We must at least take back Angus's cattle, and a few more head for our trouble."

Callum nodded. "We've done it often enough before, and they to us, and so it goes."

"They'll expect a counter raid," Kenneth agreed. "Would we disappoint them, then?"

"One small raid," Elspeth said. Her cousins nodded but for Magnus, who shrugged.

"The nights are yet too short for reiving," he said.

"We could take back the cattle and leave the fish," Callum suggested.

Chuckling at his hopeful tone, Elspeth glanced up. What she saw in the distance brought a quick frown. She straightened, alert and watchful. "Hold," she said sharply. "Look there, across the stream."

As one they turned their gazes northward. The burbling chant of rapid water filled the sudden quiet.

Crossing the grassy moor that spread away from the far side of the stream, three horsemen galloped toward them and halted their mounts by the bank. Bright multicolor plaids, red over blue, fluttered in the breeze. The sturdy, shaggy garron ponies snorted restively, and the three riders glared across the sluicing boundary that separated them from the Frasers.

Kenneth bounded up and stepped forward. One by one the Frasers rose in silence. Elspeth stepped between Magnus and Kenneth. Magnus put up an arm to hold her back.

"MacDonalds," Kenneth muttered.

"What the devil do they want here?" Magnus said.

"Take no fish from our waters, Frasers!" The cry boomed across the stream. "This land belongs to the MacDonald clan!"

"By hell it does!" Callum called back. "This stream is on Fraser land, and well you know it!"

Ruari MacDonald, his hair bright as rust in the sun, snarled and rested a hand on the long sheathed dirk stuck in his belt. Callum, Ewan, and Kenneth stepped back swiftly to pick up their own dirks, which lay piled on their dry shirts heaped on the bank.

Elspeth stepped forward suddenly. "Leave here, MacDonalds!" Veins corded on her slim neck as she yelled. "Ride on, or I will be the first at your throats!" The MacDonalds laughed loudly.

"No proper way to treat your betrothed!" Ruari called back.

"Elspeth," Magnus barked out. "Stop!"

She glanced at him. "They would not dare to cross the stream to our side," she hissed. "Ruari MacDonald is but a bully and a craven coward. And one curse from me would send him home weeping for his *màthair*."

"His *bràithrean* are with him," Kenneth said. "They will not hold back from a fight. And marriage plans will not stop them."

"Elspeth Fraser, hold your temper," Magnus said. Moving forward, he reached out to curl his fingers around her arm.

The grim current that ran beneath his words made Elspeth pause. A shudder of dread, slow and heavy, slid through her, and she knew that Magnus was right.

"My thanks, Alasdair, for meeting me at Inverness," Duncan said as they rode side by side toward a grove of birches.

"When ye sent word to me of yer visit, I thought ye might need a companion to Castle Glenran," Alasdair said. He eyed Duncan critically. "Ye war nae plaid or plant badge. Ye look like a Lowlander, and ye could even be taken for a Sasunnach. Though I admit yer Gaelic, when ye speak it, is as pure as any Highlander's."

"The Fraser chief agreed to meet me at Castle Glenran. Apparently he is there on a fishing holiday."

Alasdair chuckled. "Holiday? The MacShimi does little else but fish and hunt and raid, I think."

"MacShimi—'tis what you call your chief?"

"Aye. An auld title, after the first Fraser chief, Simon. And so *MhicShimidh,* son of Simon, ye ken." He cast a sideways glance, brown eyes curious, at Duncan. "I vow the MacShimi doesna ken the why of yer visit."

"Queen Mary and her Privy Council desire peace throughout Scotland. They wish an end to the feud between the Frasers and the MacDonalds."

"Hah! Such a request, even from the queen, will fall on deaf ears among Highlandmen."

"Perhaps. But the crown wants the bloodshed and the

cattle thieving between the Frasers and MacDonalds to cease. I simply act as the royal lieutenant in this."

Alasdair let out a loud breath that suited the volume of his lungs. "So they sent ye in George Gordon's place."

"They did. The Gordon clan is in disgrace now, and their titles and lands are taken by the crown. Nor can they continue to serve as the royal lieutenants in the northeast."

"The cocks o' the north, the Gordons are called, but they hae been brought low."

"Aye, low enough. Gordon's plan to abduct Queen Mary and marry her to one of his sons was an embarrassment to the whole of Scotland."

Alasdair nodded. "A beastly affair, wi' a gruesome end."

Clenching his fists around the reins, Duncan recalled the trial months earlier in Edinburgh, when a grotesque tradition had been obeyed. George Gordon, the earl of Huntly, had died of an apoplectic fit months before the trial, during a battle against the queen's troops. Nevertheless, his corpse, once obese but by then hideously sagged and discolored from salting and embalming, had been propped up in the courtroom for the trial and the solemn pronouncement of his guilt.

Sitting as one of the lawyers on the Gordon case, Duncan had watched in sympathy as the young queen, obliged to be present, had struggled to overcome illness brought on by sheer horror.

"Aye," Duncan sighed, "a cruel thing indeed." He drew a fresh breath as if to cleanse the tainted memory from his brain.

"The council sent ye, then, as queen's lieutenant, to talk of peace wi' the chief of the Frasers," Alasdair said. "I know ye hae a document, but what is its purpose?"

Duncan leveled a sober glance at Alasdair. "I am sent to make a bond of caution with the MacShimi and his kinsmen."

"Bluid o' Christ. A letter o' caution, is it. And so soon. The feud's nae twenty years old yet, nae much by Highland measure. And who is named as the cautioner? Yerself?"

Duncan nodded.

"Och. Ye may well regret that obligation, man."

"I anticipate little problem. I will witness the signing and take the document back to the Privy Council. The long friendship between the Frasers and the Macraes will see me safe through the cautioning period of one year."

Casting him a wry look, Alasdair shook his head in disgust. "Luck go wi' ye, then. A Highlander cherishes a good feud."

"I know that well," Duncan said.

"And better than most," Alasdair said. Taking up the reins, he kneed his horse forward. "Come ahead, then, cautioner. There's some o' the Frasers, below there, on the bank o' that stream." He pointed down a long slope.

Spurring his black horse, Duncan rode between the slender, pale birches. Squinting in the sunlight, he peered down the grassy, rock-studded slope, and saw a few Highlandmen, wearing plaids of the dark blue and green often favored by Frasers. They stood beside a wide, rushing stream. Nearby, a boy with glinting flame-bright hair stood ankle deep in the water.

As he saw the boy, a sudden chill crept up Duncan's spine. He glanced around uneasily. His black cloak floated out on a quick breeze, and he almost smiled at his foolishness. A disturbance of the wind, he thought; he had forgotten about the forceful, nearly constant presence of the Highland winds.

"We're close to Glenran here," Alasdair explained. "I heard shouts from this direction. Nae surprise to find some o' the cousins here fishin'. Though I dinna see the Mac-Shimi among them."

"Fishing?" Duncan peered ahead. He saw no poles or nets, though he noticed that some of the men carried large sticks. "Ah, I see. The Fraser way."

"Knock the fishie on the head," Alasdair said. "We're famous for it, right enough. But these lads are done wi' fishin'. Look. The riders across the stream hae red rowan in their bonnets."

"Aye." Duncan swore softly. "MacDonalds."

"Your clan's greatest enemy," Alasdair said. "Did the Privy Council ken that when they sent ye north?"

"Aye, 'tis why I was sent to caution the Frasers and nae the MacDonalds," Duncan said. "The Council is not foolish enough to send a Macrae with a bond of caution for Clan MacDonald. There would be blood instead of signatures."

Alasdair huffed a grim laugh and guided his horse down the tufted, rocky slope. Duncan followed. They reined in their horses a few yards from the stream.

"Hail and good day to you, cousins," Alasdair called out in fluent, airy Gaelic. "Callum, Magnus! A fine catch of fish, there. Ewan, Kenneth! Greetings," he said.

Duncan watched in confusion as the names were reeled off. He could not, at first, sort one lad from another, with their similar faces and big, sturdy builds, wearing blue and green plaids. Only their heads were different, like a blazing autumn forest of gold and russet, copper and dark chestnut.

Two of them stepped forward, one tall and broad, with hair like lamb's wool. The other was strikingly handsome, with dark hair in four or five long plaits.

"Well met, cousin," the burly woolly-haired young man said to Alasdair, then turned to Duncan and introduced himself as Callum Fraser, the laird of Glenran.

"What goes on here, lads?" Alasdair asked.

The one with the long dark braids pointed at the far bank. "MacDonalds."

"That I see, Kenneth. What do they want?"

"Only trouble," Kenneth answered with a shrug.

Some kind of commotion was going on down near the water, Duncan noticed. The MacDonalds were shouting across the stream to the Fraser boy who stood in the water. The lad was obscured from Duncan's view by the brawny Frasers who stood on the bank.

Watching, Duncan could not clearly hear the words that were being exchanged, but the angry tones were obvious enough. He studied the scene with interest. Here were some of the very trouble stirrers that he had come to reprimand.

He frowned suddenly, realizing what these Glenran Frasers had in common. "Alasdair," he muttered low, in Scots English. "These lads, and the laird too are more bairns than men."

"They are," Alasdair agreed softly. "Many o' the Fraser males are but lads. Because o' the losses at Blar-na-Léine nineteen years ago, there are few Fraser men left in this part o' the Highlands over the age o' majority. D'ye not recall the legend?"

"Sweet Christ," Duncan murmured with sudden comprehension. "Of course. The legend. All those male babies born to Fraser widows. If 'tis true, they'd all be eighteen, nineteen by now."

"If 'tis true? Ah, ye've been in the south too long. A Highlandman friendly to Frasers couldna doubt such a thing." Alasdair sighed, sounding disappointed. "Duncan," he said, peering toward the stream, "that legend—did ye ken that one o' the bairns born after the battle was a wee lassie?"

Duncan frowned. "I dinna recall that."

"Well, look then. There, in the water, stands one o' the wildest Frasers. My cousin Elspeth."

Duncan looked toward the stream and saw then that the lad was no lad after all. Standing in the water with her back turned toward the bank, Elspeth Fraser shouted again in Gaelic. The words were lost on a breeze, but the angry reactions of the MacDonalds on the opposite side attested to the insult she had delivered.

The thick plait of fair hair, sheened like Celtic red-gold, was neither longer nor tidier than the braids of her cousins. The plaid, worn over a linen shirt, was thick and enveloping, and revealed no clue to age or gender. But her bare legs, long and smooth and tightly muscled, planted firmly in the water, had, he plainly saw now, all the grace and strength of a woman grown.

Kenneth spoke to her and she glanced up at him, the quick turn of her head a motion of simple grace. Sunlight danced over the crown of her head and the fine bones of her face. Reflected light from the stream touched her eyes.

Duncan thought their color was very like the water, or like a stormy sky.

Hardly an aging Diana, he thought, remembering his earlier words made in jest. Boudicca, perhaps, young and pretty, and copper-haired like the ancient Celtic warrior woman was said to have been. Fascinated, he stared, admiring her form and face even as he was mildly surprised to see a female here, half clad and in an obviously dangerous situation.

He knew women in Edinburgh who would faint at the thought of what this girl did; he knew others, however, who would applaud. The queen herself, for one, he mused: Mary of Scotland and her ladies often dressed in men's clothing for an evening's supper and entertainment. He smiled a little, thinking how women, particularly in England, were beginning to argue for intellectual rights with men. Yet here in the Highlands, regarded as backward by southerners, this girl assumed complete equality as easily as she assumed male clothing.

Duncan saw that she appeared to directly invite the threat of danger. Certainly she did not shrink from the spectacle of three angry MacDonalds, mounted and armed on the opposite bank. She was shouting, leaning forward with the force of her fury. When the wind shifted, Duncan could hear her more clearly, and understood the Gaelic easily.

"Do not think to come over here, MacDonalds!" she yelled. "Reivers and thieves!" One of her cousins, the tall blond whom Alasdair had called Magnus, spoke urgently to her from the bank, but she waved him away. "Leave me be, Magnus!"

"A chick among pups," Duncan remarked wryly in Scots.

"A wha'?" Alasdair looked at him, puzzled.

"My sisters once had a wee fluffy chick that they raised wi' the pups. Grew into a fine hen, but she ran wi' the dogs, ate under the table, and slept on the hearth. She was totally wild and nae great egg layer. But most o' the dogs accepted her, and she thought she was one o' them. That one there," he gestured toward Elspeth, "is a chick among pups."

Alasdair nodded sagely. "What happened to yer wee hen?"

Duncan shrugged. "She was bested by a larger hunting hound and eaten."

Alasdair blinked, eyes wide, and looked toward Elspeth.

"Dare to cross the stream, Ruari MacDonald!" she shouted. "And if you reived the cattle that went missing from Angus Simson's land, and if you laid a hand on an old man, a kinsman of the MacShimi, then you will have your due payment here and now!"

Magnus stepped down into the water. "Enough, girl."

"Angus was beaten that night," she hissed loudly. "Would you have him go unavenged?"

"We may cross the water when we please!" one of the MacDonalds shouted then. "Such is not possible for you, witch!"

"Witches cannot cross a running stream!" came another taunt. The young MacDonald who had shouted made a gesture as if to shield his eyes. "Watch her *Droch Shùil,* her evil eye!"

"Hold your wicked tongues!" Kenneth hollered angrily. He and the others, sparked by the insults, splashed down into the water ready to defend their cousin.

"Fools!" Callum shouted angrily. "Elspeth is a *taibhsear,* and you will treat her with the respect she deserves!"

"Respect a seer? Hah! Clan MacDonald wears the rowan in our bonnets as protection from witches such as her!" yelled a rusty-haired MacDonald. His companions laughed unpleasantly.

Elspeth surged forward, clearly infuriated. "I will cross, and you will need protection from my dirk!" She charged through the water with a phalanx of cousins at her heels.

Unsure if the boys meant to stop her or support her, Duncan dismounted and ran to the bank. Alasdair must have been of the same mind, for he was close behind. Such disputes easily drew blood in the Highlands. Duncan knew that too well.

Reaching the water's edge, he stepped in, the chill taking his breath for a moment as it struck his legs, even through his woolen trews and high boots. When he was nearly within arm's distance of the virago, she ceased shouting. He lurched forward between her brawny cousins, ready to lay a hand on her and haul her unchivalrously back to the bank.

Quite abruptly, as if they had all struck a stone wall, the young men in front of him stopped. Carried by his forward momentum, Duncan knocked into the broad back of a Fraser. Tall enough to measure with the tallest of the lot, he looked over Magnus's shoulder.

Elspeth had halted suddenly and stood still, the water swirling around her legs. Though her cousins stepped slowly away from her, she appeared not to notice them. She neither spoke nor moved as she looked up at the sky.

Duncan looked up at the sky too, expecting to see some awful sight. Only a few fat clouds drifted over the sun. What the devil was going on here? He glanced over his shoulder. Alasdair was as still and watchful as the rest.

"What—" Duncan began.

"Quiet," Alasdair murmured.

Duncan turned back. The girl stared upward, her eyes a crystalline gray, as if filled with silvery light. Incongruously, he thought of a painting he had once seen, a depiction of an angel who had the same limpid, beautiful eyes as this girl, wide and innocent and holy.

Hardly angels for this brawling wench. He glanced around him. All of the men, including the MacDonalds on the far bank, were as still as if they waited for the Host to appear at Mass. The jaws of the MacDonalds, he noted, hung open stupidly.

A perfect time to seize the girl and stop this nonsense, he thought. Such incidents, after all, were the reason that Queen Mary had sent him north. Duncan moved forward, shouldering between the lads who stood nearest Elspeth. Hearing a murmur beside him, he looked up.

Elspeth had turned and now stared full at Duncan. Her eyes, luminous above her pale cheeks, were fixed intently on his face. Tears sprang onto her lashes, and she reached out a trembling hand to him. As her lips moved, he strained forward to hear her.

"The raven," she whispered. "Are you the raven come to earth? Or are you one of the *daoine sìth,* the fairy people?"

Confounded by her curious words, Duncan stretched out his hand to her, partly following his original intent to grab her, and partly in hesitant response to her proffered fingers.

Alasdair grasped his shoulder from behind. Another Fraser, Callum, he thought, threw out an arm to stop Duncan's advance.

"Do not touch her!" Callum hissed. *"Dà-Shealladh!"*

The Second Sight. Duncan turned to stare at Callum. He recalled some mention of seers and witchery earlier, when the MacDonalds had shouted at the girl. He had thought it merely an insult. Apparently it had been said in earnest.

"Touch a *taibhsear* at the moment of a vision, and ye will see the same sight," Callum said urgently. "Stay back!"

At the whispered reminder the Fraser cousins stepped farther away from Elspeth. Alasdair pulled again on Duncan's shoulder.

He did not move. He held his hand up, palm out. A powerful sensation, strange and irresistible, had begun to fill his body, as if two strong lodestones pulled between the girl's hand and his. A deep, desperate ache swirled through him. He wanted to touch her. He stretched his hand closer to hers.

"Do not touch her!" someone said.

· The girl's eyes were wide and silvery. She seemed to watch something near his left shoulder. Then she looked at him and held out her hand.

As his fingerpads brushed hers, as his long fingers closed over her hand, he felt only cool flesh over small, slim bones. Fragile and vulnerable, not fearsome, he thought.

But an eerie golden mist seemed to gather over his sight. He blinked and could not clear it. Neither could he separate his gaze, or his hand, from hers.

"Your death. Your death will be mine," she whispered,

so softly that only he could hear her. He frowned, gazing at her.

Lower lashes floating in tears, her eyes rolled up to disappear beneath fluttering lids. As her body went limp, she lost consciousness, knees buckling into the water just before Duncan caught her. He shifted her weight in his arms. In that moment the cold Highland breezes seemed to blow the golden mist from his sight, and his thoughts cleared.

Stunned, breathing as hard as if he had been running, he looked around at Alasdair, who stared in astonishment at him. Then they both glanced up as they heard the rapid thunder of hoofbeats.

The MacDonalds fled as if hell's own hounds pursued them.

Chapter 3

"What news? What news, bonny boy?
What news hes thou to me?"
"No news, no news," said bonny boy,
"But a letter unto thee."
          —*"Bonnie Annie Livieston"*

"No more of that foul stuff, Flora," Elspeth complained, putting up a hand to refuse the wooden cup held out to her. She sat up gingerly on the feather bed. "My head is sore, and another drop of that posset will heave my belly quick." Her head felt crushed, and her stomach roiled dangerously. Thankfully, the chamber was dark; even the dim glow of the peat fire in the hearth hurt her eyes. She placed a trembling hand over her brow.

"Tch," Flora said calmly, placing a large, warm hand on Elspeth's shoulder. "Drink it down. It's an infusion for a sore head and a poor stomach. Need be, I will hold a basin for you, as I did when you were a babe." She handed the cup to Elspeth.

Accepting the cup again, Elspeth sipped it and made a face. "It's bitter."

"Tch," Flora said again, unsympathetically. Tapping one large foot expectantly, she lifted dark eyebrows over deep brown eyes and looked at Elspeth with absolute authority. Elspeth sighed and finished the contents.

"Such headaches are part of the burden of *Dà-Shealladh*," Flora said. "Bethoc MacGruer has the Sight, and is plagued with a sore head every day. Every day, poor woman." Her voice was husky and deep, and as large as the woman herself. She clucked her tongue as she turned away to set the cup down.

Elspeth smiled, knowing how Flora exaggerated: Bethoc

had visions, and sometimes headaches with them, but hardly every day. She moved her legs slowly over the side of the bed.

"Slept for hours, you did, poor bird," Flora said. "And you missed dinner."

Glancing at the one small window in the bedchamber, Elspeth saw a deep twilight blue streaking the sky beyond. "I missed the fish?" she asked hopefully.

"You did," Flora answered, and gave a loud grunt of effort as she bent down to rummage in a wooden chest near the wall. One fat iron-gray braid slid over her broad shoulder to dangle off the shelf of her generous bosom. "Delicious, those trout, rolled in oats and butter, and fried. The lads ate like they were starving. I did not know they liked fish so well." Coming back to the bed, Flora looked down at Elspeth. "None for you just yet. A bit of *fuarag* would be better."

"Oats in milk?" Elspeth was relieved that she would not have to contend with fish for dinner. Her stomach lurched, and her head thudded painfully as she shook it. "Not now, Flora," she answered, running a hand through her bedraggled, loosened braid.

"Well, if you are feeling better, the MacShimi and Callum asked that you come to them as soon as you woke." Flora held out a folded tartan cloth and a clean shirt.

Elspeth nodded her thanks, and stood to change the rumpled linen shirt she wore for the fresh one. Flora carefully arranged the long length of the plaid on the bed.

"A pretty cloth, this," Flora remarked as she pleated the wool into neat folds. The tartan pattern was mostly white, crossed with dark blue, green, and purple. "Suitable for a young woman it is, with the lighter colors."

"Bethoc wove this length of plaid seven years ago, I think," Elspeth said, fingering the lightweight wool, soft and warm against her cool fingers. "I helped her to set the purple yarns and made an error, here—see this break in the pattern."

"I see it. No matter, when it is folded. Though why you keep to the wrapped plaid, I do not know. Any girl your age wears gowns. But then, you're a bit wild and always have been, with only those lads for companions."

"I love the lads, and running wild," Elspeth said.

Flora sighed heavily. "Your aunt had a soft heart always, and after she was gone, your uncle Lachlann had no good idea what to do with one girl in the midst of all those lads." She shrugged. "Well, we all learned early on to let you go your way. You will do as you please." She raised a brow, but humor sparkled in her dark eyes.

Elspeth settled the long linen shirt around her hips and sat lightly on the plaid, which Flora had pleated flat on the bed. Quickly gathering the cloth around her waist, she nipped the long shirt and plaid together with a wide leather belt. Standing to drape the remaining length of the plaid over her left shoulder, she tucked the end in at her waist and pinned the cloth to her shirt with a brooch that Flora handed her, a wide bronze circle studded with a polished cairngorm, a piece of smoky quartz.

As she stood, she noticed that the pounding in her head had begun to lessen. She wiggled her bare toes against the rushes on the wooden floor planks, intending to go shoeless, as she often did in summer. Reaching up, she slipped her fingers through her hair to undo her tangled braid.

Flora handed her a wooden comb and tilted her head. Her wide mouth pursed as it did when she was thinking about something. She heaved a great sigh. Flora used words sparingly, Elspeth thought, but her sighs were exquisitely expressive. This one indicated concern. "You swooned with this vision. That's not happened before," Flora said.

"Never, though I've felt faint with them."

"Ah. Well, swooning with the Sight is not uncommon, or so Bethoc says." Flora shook a finger, thick and knotted at the knuckles, at Elspeth. "You go soon and talk to Bethoc, now."

"I will," Elspeth agreed. "I visit her every week." She worked her fingers through her braid. "Who was the man with Alasdair at the stream today?"

"Duncan Macrae of Dulsie, brother to Alasdair's wife. He is the lawyer sent by the queen and her council." Flora laughed, short and breathy. "I thought all long-robes were old men with long beards. But not this one, not at all. A fine man. Even has a ring of gold in his earlobe."

"He's here?" Elspeth looked up.

Flora nodded. "He's brought a letter from Mary the Queen, about the fighting with the MacDonalds. Callum and the MacShimi are meeting with him now. The queen should send that letter to those fool MacDonalds and not to the Frasers." She folded her arms over her large bosom.

Elspeth sat on a stool near the hearth, her hair glowing bronze in the low light. As she combed it out, she thought about Duncan Macrae, who had worn the raven's color and had been clothed like a Lowlander, without a plaid, in a black doublet and high boots. His hair was a deep, glossy brown, nearly black with an auburn gleam. And his eyes were a flash of blue like a bright sky. He was handsome, she thought, with a calm, sure look to him. No unearthly messenger. Only a man, the queen's own lawyer.

The lawyer had not been frightened by the touch of a *taibhsear* in the midst of a vision, though by the time she had felt his hand the vision had passed. He could not have seen it.

She recalled his touch, dry and warm, and his arms around her, like firm iron bands. Just as she had fainted, she had felt his hard chest beneath her head. A deep tingle swirled suddenly in her belly at the memory, and a quick, fierce blush heated her throat and cheeks.

She was certain that he was the man who had appeared in that brief vision on the hill, like an odd glimpse into the immediate future. Two visions of this Duncan Macrae had appeared to her today, both so vivid that she was still shaken by the experience.

She sat up and tugged the comb through her hair with trembling fingers. No vision had ever had such an impact on her. She had swooned, had slept like the dead, and had awoken with a crushing headache, quivering like an aspen.

Even now, hours afterward, she felt a strange yearning, as if she struggled with a deep, hurting loss. She felt a glaze of fear as well, like a chill mist over green earth.

She would visit Bethoc soon. Surely Bethoc, with her knowledge of such things, would have some insight for her, and could tell her why this had happened. But before that she must warn the man to leave the Highlands.

"Duncan Macrae," she repeated softly. The Macraes, she knew, formed a small clan farther north and west. The Frasers and the Macraes had been loyal friends for generations. Some earlier MacShimi had once had an inscription carved over his castle doorway, faded now but still legible: *If a Macrae ever stands without, he will always find lodging and welcome within.*

Not so easy, then, for a Fraser to ask a Macrae to leave. Between the generous nature of Highland hospitality and the friendship between Macraes and Frasers, the lawyer might stay at Glenran indefinitely.

But he must leave, and soon, she thought. He must.

"What did you see at the stream?" Flora asked.

Elspeth looked up, having nearly forgotten that the other woman was with her. Flora's imposing height and large build were deceptive: although she gave the impression of overwhelming power, and indeed had a temper like a dark, fierce Highland storm, Flora could be quiet and calm, a soothing companion.

"The lads have not asked, but it clearly has upset you. Tell me what you saw."

Elspeth stopped combing her hair and looked away. A simple turn of her head could not dispel what she had seen at the stream. Though she squeezed her eyes shut, the memory of the visions remained clear.

First a pair of ravens overhead. Then the man on the hill. And then the ravens again, when she had turned to see the lawyer behind her in the stream.

Then, through a golden mist, she had seen the lawyer, unshaven, fierce-looking. His shirt had been pulled away from his neck, and a cloth hid his eyes. She gasped to see it again. The wooden comb slipped from her fingers.

"Ravens," she said. "I saw ravens. The lawyer's life is in danger unless he leaves the Highlands."

"And what else, then?" Flora sat down on a stool, her gaze unwavering, her silence patient.

"I saw him in a plain shirt, open at the neck. I saw a cloth bound about his eyes. I saw a wooden block."

"By the cross," Flora murmured. "You saw a heading block."

Elspeth nodded. There was more, so frightening to her that she could not mention it aloud. Clenching her fist tightly, she bowed her head, and her hair swung around her shoulders like a copper-tinted cloud, soft and cool, hiding the sudden tears that stung her eyes.

She had seen her own image standing beside Duncan Macrae as he had stood in the stream, as if she had looked into a mirror.

And in that instant, as she had looked into his startled blue eyes, she had known with a shock of certainty that his fate was tied to hers. Because she had seen him blindfolded and about to die, and because she saw herself somehow linked to him, she feared that she would bring Duncan Macrae to the heading block.

That was why she was so determined to warn the lawyer to leave the Highlands. He would die on the block if he stayed here with the Frasers, with her. She felt the cold truth of it.

Your death will be mine, she had whispered to him. She did not know why she had uttered those words. Guilt perhaps over knowing that she would somehow bring him tragedy. Standing in the stream with his hand in hers, she had felt a chill glaze of fear, and a deep, mournful, passionate regret.

Overwhelmed by her thoughts, Elspeth lowered her head and began to cry, silent and soft, into the palm of her hand.

"Do you weep for the lawyer, then?" Flora murmured. "You cannot change what you have seen. If the man is to die on the block, that is between him and his queen and his God."

"I am cursed, Flora," she whispered. "Why do I see these things? I have no wish to see the ravens hover, waiting for this man's death. I did not want to see my aunt's death, or my uncle's, before their time came. I did not want to see that Magnus's wife would die." She pressed her eyes shut, and tears slipped down her cheeks.

Flora touched her hand gently. "The Sight is a gift from God. You see joyful things as well. You have seen marriages to come, and you have seen births. You have told others of happy things in their lives."

Elspeth wiped her cheeks. "But why do I see death? I have kept silent each time I have seen a death vision. A warning would not have saved any of them."

Flora shook her gray head. "God arranges fate. Seers only catch a glimpse of it. You did the proper thing, holding your silence. You could not frighten or hurt someone that you loved."

Elspeth covered her eyes with a trembling hand. "This Sight only hurts me, Flora. These death-knowings help no one."

Flora stroked her fingers over Elspeth's hair, a light, loving touch. "I have no wisdom for you, my little bird," she said. "Only God knows why you have been given the Sight."

"What is this lawyer Macrae to me? Only a visitor to the MacShimi. Yet I saw his death."

"Perhaps you should tell him that it is dangerous for him to stay here."

Elspeth nodded. "Warn him, but not tell him the truth of his death." She shuddered. "This gift is a curse, Flora."

"Hush, you," Flora said. "You are tired and fretful. Poor little bird. I would help you if I could. Hush, now."

"A bond of caution! May as well be iron fetters," the MacShimi said. He leaned back in his chair, his lanky length haphazardly arranged. Torchlight flickered over his stubborn frown. "We will not sign such a promise."

The MacShimi, Duncan thought ruefully, was no older than his cousins. In fact, he mused, the MacShimi looked the youngest of all the Fraser cousins. Barely eighteen, strikingly handsome with glossy dark hair and hazel eyes, his chin was sparsely whiskered and his voice had not yet

settled. Hugh Fraser, laird of Lovat Castle and chief of all
the Frasers, had been born the last of the legendary crop
of Blar-na-Léine babes.

Duncan silently cursed the ill luck that had given him
this assignment. No member of the Privy Council had mentioned that the Fraser chief and most of his bodyguard were
well under the age of majority, and disposed to argue any
point. Originally he had thought to present the letter, collect the signatures, and depart quickly. Judging by the stubborn resistance he had met in the past hour, he had a
disturbing feeling that he would be at Glenran for a long
time in pursuit of those few signatures.

He sighed heavily and glanced out one of the windows
that pierced the thick walls of the great hall. The sky, which
held summer light in the Highlands until very late, was
growing decidedly dark. He was tired, and it had been a
very long day.

At supper he had felt as old as Zeus in the company of
the Fraser cousins; but for Alasdair, he was the oldest male
here. Castle Glenran was like some odd Highland nursery,
he thought wryly, a noisy haven for lads—and one girl who
acted like a lad. He imagined a score of plaided bairns
teething on dirks. Alasdair had mentioned to him that
Lachlann Fraser had fostered all of these orphans, and
more, under his own roof.

"The bond is a promise between your clan and the
crown," Duncan said carefully. His usual patience was beginning to wear thin. They had been discussing this for
hours. At least the young chief could speak Scots, but his
cousins could not, and so Duncan used the Gaelic.

"Your signature marks your promise to cease feuding for
one year," he said, and held out the document, written on
stiff new paper in his own precise legal hand. A copy for
the Fraser chief to keep, which also required signatures, lay
on the table. "There is a fine of seven thousand pounds if
you break the bond. Since I am named the cautioner, and
the human pledge for this agreement, I will be held responsible if the bond is not honored."

The MacShimi did not take the page. "If we do not sign,

then you will not be held responsible for us." Restlessly, he turned away and addressed the laird of Glenran, his cousin Callum. "Where is Elspeth?"

"Flora has gone to fetch her," Callum replied quietly.

"Duncan takes a great risk in being named the pledge, Hugh," Alasdair said. "He can be charged with treason if the bond is broken. But as a Macrae he trusts the Fraser clan to honor his welfare."

Duncan did not comment on that. "Your signature and those of your advisers are required," he said. "They are . . . ?"

The Fraser chief sat straighter in his chair. "My Glenran cousins form part of my personal bodyguard, and as such they are my closest advisers. You have met Callum, Magnus, Kenneth, Ewan, and Elspeth. There are several others as well who are at Lovat Castle now."

Duncan nodded. "Your advisers here at Glenran will do. Their signatures, and yours, will be enough to seal the promise."

"And that promise is to cease fighting with the MacDonalds."

"Certainly. The queen and her council expect it."

"And do they expect us to sit here and watch the MacDonalds reive off our cattle and our sheep?" The MacShimi frowned. "If we sign the bond, what guarantee do we have that the MacDonalds will not ride in and take all we have, knowing we dare not fight back? I will not put my kinsmen in that position, Macrae." His eyes, a deep hazel green, were filled with concern. Duncan realized that despite his youth, the MacShimi took his responsibilities as chief very seriously.

"The MacDonalds are being given a similar letter," Duncan said. "Clan Campbell are the royal lieutenants in the western Highlands. One of them will negotiate with the chief of the MacDonalds."

The MacShimi snorted a quick half laugh. "I would like to see that! The Campbells have been feuding with the MacDonalds longer than the Frasers have. Well, then. When the MacDonalds sign their bond, we will sign this one. And not before."

Duncan sighed and rubbed his temples, keenly aware of a dull headache and a creeping fatigue. Reaching for a pewter jug, he poured foamy, pale heather ale into a cup. He tried, as he drank, to hold his temper as steadily as he held the wooden cup.

He had been in this room with the MacShimi, Alasdair, and Callum Fraser for hours now. After dinner had been cleared away and the other cousins had left, the four of them had stayed here to discuss the letter of caution.

Setting down his drink, he glanced around the long hall. Rushlights flickered over the high walls, turning the bare gray stone to gold in places. A tall iron basket anchored in the center of the stone floor held glowing peat bricks, orange and black. The peat fire gave off little light, but sent out waves of strong heat and a musty, comforting odor. Smoky tendrils wafted toward the open arrow-slit windows. Since it was summer, the two large fireplaces in the room were not in use.

Bronze-studded targes and a few beautifully crafted swords and axes hung on the walls as the only ornaments. The furniture was solid and plain, and the floor was scattered with clean rushes and fragrant petals. There were no tapestries, fine hangings, or even painted decorations. Yet the effect did not hint at lack. The room's straightforward simplicity spoke of strength and pride.

On the long table were jugs of ale, cups, and two rotund flasks made from sheep bladders. Those flasks had been passed freely from hand to hand all through dinner, and *uisge beatha,* the Highland water of life that the Lowlanders called whisky, had poured out like liquid amber to fill cup after cup.

Duncan's head was spinning now from the drams that he had consumed; he had not had true Highland *uisge beatha* for a very long time. He had, rather wisely, he thought, switched to the pale heather ale a short while ago. Grateful that the stuff was watered, for it could have a heavy kick, he sipped it slowly.

Alasdair leaned against one edge of the table, arms folded, legs crossed, his usual bright, toothy grin replaced by a stern frown. Near him, Callum Fraser rested in an elaborately carved wooden chair, holding a pewter cup between his large fingers. He waved it in a slow bell-like motion, his woolly head bowed.

Tugging in idle habit at the tiny gold earring in his left earlobe, Duncan was mustering his thoughts to try another angle on the discussion when the door, set in one long wall, opened. Elspeth stepped into the room, closing the planked door behind her. She moved softly across the rush-covered floor in bare feet, her plaid swinging gently.

"Ah, girl, there you are!" Callum said, sitting up suddenly. He waved a hand and introduced Duncan as the queen's lieutenant. Elspeth nodded curtly in Duncan's direction, avoiding his eyes, and returned a bright smile and a soft greeting to the others. Sitting on the far end of the bench that Duncan occupied, she pointedly ignored him.

Alasdair leaned toward Elspeth to murmur a brief explanation of the letter of caution. Watching them, Duncan lifted his cup and drank. Settling one elbow lazily on the table, he suddenly felt very loose and comfortable, a result of the good amount of liquor and ale he had downed that evening. As he waited for Alasdair to finish talking, he studied the girl.

Elspeth listened, nodding in understanding and asking a few questions in soft Gaelic. Never once did she glance in Duncan's direction, although he heard his name mentioned.

He, on the other hand, had centered his gaze wholly on Elspeth from the moment she had entered the room. Although earlier he had puzzled over the strange incident at the stream, he had forgotten about it during dinner with the Fraser cousins and their generous drams and stubborn resistance. The girl had not entered his mind at all until now.

As she tilted her head to listen to Alasdair, Duncan studied the rich red-gold sheen of her hair. Her eyelids lowered, and he saw her cheeks pinken, as if she was aware of his gaze.

He recalled, with startling clarity, the vulnerable, frightened look in those gray eyes when she had turned toward him in the cold stream. He could almost feel her small, cool hand in his, and heard again the strange words she had whispered to him: *Your death will be mine.* A tiny chill spiraled up his neck at the memory.

Like any Highlander, Duncan knew about seers. There had been one near Dulsie Castle when he was a boy, an old crone who had prattled on about death visions and nonsensical predictions to anyone who would listen to her. That woman had warned him against riding after the Mac-Donalds, so long ago, predicting tragedy and death.

Anyone could have seen that outcome, but Duncan had been too young and hot-tempered to see it himself. He had long ago decided that seers and prophecies had no power, no reality.

From what he had seen today, Elspeth's cousins certainly believed that she had some true ability. However odd the incident had been, Duncan was convinced that his own peculiar reaction had been affected by those around him. Scientific studies, he knew, had lately proven that the brain was a remarkable storehouse for a variety of sensations. And any lawyer knew that complete nonsense could be made to seem factual with the proper argument.

As for that strong, irresistible urge to touch the girl's hand at the stream—well, he thought, looking at her now, she had a simple, appealing beauty. Obviously he had been swept up by some sudden male impulse. That would not happen again. If the MacShimi chose to allow a wee, pretty lass to be part of his personal bodyguard, it was no matter to him. He would collect her signature with the rest and move on.

He was curious, though, as to what the girl had seen, or thought she had seen, at the stream. Elspeth Fraser had a vulnerable, ingenuous quality. He would not have thought her a fraud. He narrowed his eyes in the flickering light. Perhaps, he thought with sudden dismay, she was a little mad. Certainly she dressed and behaved out of the ordinary.

Mad or not, he was fascinated by the curious mix of bold, brash adolescence and gentle femininity in her. He was aware too of a strong physical attraction to her. Sitting up straighter, he realized with chagrin that he was more than a little drunk.

Then Elspeth lifted her head and stared directly at him.

Just as he had felt at the stream, an odd sense spun through him when her gaze touched his, like a fall from a height this time. He looked openly at her for a long moment, seeking something in her gaze that would illuminate this new sensation. He was not accustomed to confusion.

"Hugh," Alasdair said, looking at the MacShimi, "this bond of caution will be a good thing for our clan."

"We need no action from the crown that binds our hands so that we cannot defend ourselves," Hugh Fraser answered.

Alasdair sighed. "If you refuse the bond of caution, worse will follow from the crown. Tell him, Duncan."

Clearing his throat, Duncan sat up, nodding briskly. "A letter of fire and sword will follow if you refuse to sign. Your clan will be outlawed, your homes destroyed, your warriors killed."

Hugh Fraser looked directly at Duncan, his gaze straight and steady, his hazel eyes gleaming. "And who," he asked softly, "would carry out such orders? The crown has no army, and not enough coin to waste on hiring soldiers to come up here and rout us out. It would take years to accomplish it. Highlandmen cannot be found in these mountains and glens unless they want to be seen. Fire and sword may work for the crown in the Lowlands and in the Borders, but it is not effective in the Highlands." He sat back, chin lifted proudly.

"The MacShimi has a point," Callum said quickly.

"That is true, but—" Duncan began.

"We have no need of this bond," Hugh said. "There is another way to stop the Macdonalds from raiding our land."

"What do you mean?" Duncan asked.

"Indeed. Tell us what you mean, cousin," Elspeth said. She gave her cousin a grim look. Even Duncan felt its chill.

"John MacDonald, chief of that clan, has made an offer

to ease the feud with a marriage," Hugh said. "He has asked that Elspeth marry his nephew Ruari."

Duncan frowned slightly as he considered this. "Certainly the idea is a sound one," he said. The girl's eyes were on him, stormy now. Marriage ties were, in essence, family ties, and he knew that clans generally avoided feuding with family. "Until you sign the bond, perhaps this will suffice," he said.

"Suffice!" Elspeth snapped, standing. Duncan felt the bench they shared rock. She glared at him. Then she looked at Hugh. "Have you given them an answer?"

"Not as yet," Hugh said. "I was going to refuse, but now that the crown has sent this letter of caution, I need to think about it further. It would ease the feud, Elspeth."

"Would you have me marry into the MacDonald clan to save you from signing a bit of paper?" she cried angrily.

"Elspeth—" Hugh began.

"I will not do this! I have said so again and again. But have you listened? I care about the clan as well, but I will not be sacrificed to it!"

"Elspeth—" Hugh and Callum said together.

"And you!" She swung to face Duncan, her chest heaving beneath the diagonal swath of her plaid. "You come here with a letter that dooms our clan, and then say this marriage is a good thing?" Her voice rose indignantly as she glared at him. "If you are wise, long-robe, you will get on your fine black horse and be gone from here. There is nothing here for you but your own doom!"

Stepping around the bench, she strode toward the door, leaving Duncan and her kinsmen with their mouths slightly open in surprise.

Duncan cleared his throat in the silence that followed the slam of the door. "I do not think that she will marry this Ruari MacDonald," he said.

Chapter 4

So slowly, slowly, she came up;
And slowly she came nye him;
And all she sayd, when there she came,
"Young man, I think y'are dying."
  —*"Barbara Allen's Cruelty"*

Elspeth ran steadily up and around the turning staircase, past the bedchamber levels, until she reached the roof. Pulling open the door, she burst outside and moved along the wall walk, skimming her hand over cool, rough stone, feeling the brisk wind whip her hair. As she walked, the tumult of anger and apprehension inside began to lessen. Drawing a deep breath, she looked up at the wide night sky, where stars glistened like diamond slivers on black velvet.

She thought of the golden rushlights in the great hall below, and thought of the queen's lawyer who sat in their light. Duncan Macrae should have politely declined to give his opinion on the subject of a marriage between her and Ruari MacDonald, she thought. Such would have been more acceptable behavior for a guest.

But his direct, steady gaze, while she had listened to Alasdair's explanation of the queen's bond, had lacked the polite veneer of new acquaintance. A hot blush stained her cheeks, and the rhythm of her heart quickened. He had looked at her, she thought, as if he knew her quite well.

Tall and broad-shouldered even beside her brawny Fraser cousins, Macrae was a handsome man, older than her cousins. He had lean, precise features and a firm, clean-shaven jaw; his dark hair, long enough to brush his shoulders, had gleamed deeply against his black doublet. Elspeth remembered that his eyes had flashed an intense blue at the stream, their color piercing in sunlight.

But deep in his eyes she had sensed a shadow, a depth
of silent feeling, like a well of private hurt. She remembered too the gentle, firm touch of Macrae's hands on hers,
and his hard strength when he had lifted her into his arms.

She closed her eyes and leaned her forehead against
gritty stone. The inexplicable yearning that she had felt
earlier that day returned with sudden force. She wanted to
see this Duncan Macrae again, wanted to hear his voice
skim over her senses like velvet, wanted to feel the touch
of his hand once more. And yet she wanted him to leave
Glenran. A confusion of emotions rippled through her. She
felt anger toward him for approving of that cursed marriage
arrangement to Ruari MacDonald, and she felt a wash of
fear, not of the man, but for him.

Never in her life had she known such a pull to anyone.
She sensed his presence in the castle, like the low, steady,
compelling drone of a bagpipe. She was keenly aware that
he was here, yet he should be nothing to her. As Flora had
said, if the man's destiny lay on the heading block, it was
not her concern.

Resting her hands on the parapet, Elspeth told herself
that the Sight, for the first time in her life, must be wrong.
How could she ever cause a man to come to the heading
block? Such a death was political, and her involvement
seemed ludicrous. She had no knowledge of such matters.

The chill wind caused her to shiver. Moving away from
the wall, she went back into the castle, her quick, sure
footsteps on the stairs echoing the decision she had made.

She would wait until all had quieted for the night, and
then she would warn Duncan Macrae. She would urge him
to leave the Highlands. Once he knew that he was in danger, he would listen.

She had never known anyone to ignore the warning of
a *taibhsear*.

Strong ale, far too many sips of *uisge beatha*, and travel
fatigue had plunged Duncan into a deep and dreamless
sleep. The soft sound that woke him brought him to a sudden but groggy awareness. Blinking in the dark, propping

an elbow on the deep feather mattress, he slowly pushed aside the heavy bed curtain.

Thick stone walls and a solid oak door muffled outside noises. He heard only the faint crackle of the stacked peat fire in the hearth. Not eager to bed on straw in the hall after days of riding, he had been grateful when Callum, who had consumed a massive quantity of liquor with little effect, had shown him to this tiny bedchamber before saying good night.

Perhaps the room was infested with mice, or with ghosts. What else, he wondered, would be about at this hour, well past midnight? His eyes scanned the black shadows. The faint orange glow in the hearth revealed little, and nothing worrisome.

Letting out a slow breath, he forced himself to relax back against the pillow. Closing his eyelids, he rolled onto his side to welcome a quick slide back into warm sleep.

A touch, like a feather, brushed his head and bare shoulder, a warm and gentle caress that drifted and left him.

"Who's there?" he hissed, opening his eyes to darkness.

One of the black shadows detached itself from the bed curtain. Duncan bolted upright and reached for the dirk that he had earlier placed beneath the pillow. The blade was not there. He groped about, then cautiously slid one leg out of the bed, trying to focus his eyes in the darkness.

"I have your dirk," a soft voice said in Gaelic. "Stay where you are."

He peered at the shadow. "Christ," he muttered in relief and surprise. "I thought ye were some awful haunt."

In the dim light he could see the outline of her body swathed in a plaid, the golden curve of her face, and the glint of her bright hair. She motioned to him with his own dirk; he could faintly see the inlaid-pearl handle of the blade.

"Stay there," she repeated, "and do not move."

Puzzled, mildly amused, he leaned back against the high wooden headboard and kept one leg extended, his foot on the cold rush-covered floor, ready to pounce if need be. His nudity, if it was apparent to her in the darkness, did not seem to bother the girl. She watched him warily, like a warrior waiting for an opponent to strike.

"What do ye want?" he asked.

She only slanted a cautious glance at him and shook her head slightly. He realized then that she did not understand Scots English. He rephrased the question in Gaelic.

"I owe you an apology," she answered.

"Frasers apologize with drawn blades, do they?"

"I meant to give you a warning. But I did not mean to say it so sudden, in the hall." She drew a long breath. "Listen well to me, lawyer. Leave this place, and quickly."

Duncan glanced down at the blade of the dirk. "Is this your sweet farewell?"

"I needed to speak to you. This was the best way to do that," she answered. Her tone was so simple, so honest, that Duncan almost laughed.

As she spoke, he noticed that her loose hair flowed just past her shoulders, colored with a warm light of its own. The gentle beauty of her face and hair contrasted oddly with the brave fix of her stance: legs spread wide, head raised defiantly, dirk gripped with fierce caution in a remarkably steady hand.

"Bold, even fearless," he said, "to come into a man's bedchamber and steal his own blade."

"I needed to speak to you alone. I did not want you to mistake me for an enemy and use your blade on me."

The girl dressed like a man and kept company with a pack of wild cousins, he thought, but she was a lass after all, and no match for a grown man a head taller and nearly her weight over again heavier. He leaned forward, assessing the distance between them, watching the way she gripped the blade.

"Do you threaten me, Elspeth Fraser?" he asked coldly. "And what of the trust between guest and host? In the Highlands no guest, even an enemy, can come to harm in his host's castle. Murder under trust is a very serious crime."

"Spoken like a long-robed lawyer," Elspeth snapped. "I know well the trust of hospitality. And I will not break it. Only listen, and I will go. There is great danger for you here."

He laughed, curt and soft. "From a spit of a girl with my own dirk?"

She took a step toward him, brandishing the blade. *An incautious move, warrior maiden,* Duncan thought. He eased one hand forward in the shadows.

"I will not harm you," she said, "but you must take heed. Be gone at first light. We have no need of Lowlanders here, or long-robes."

"I am no Lowlander, nor am I what you deem an unworthy intellectual. I am the queen's lieutenant, and a Highlander born and bred."

She narrowed her eyes. "You do not act or dress like a Highlandman, though your Gaelic is truly spoken. Go into the Highlands, then, or go south, it is no matter to me. But leave here." At the earnest note in her voice, Duncan sharpened his gaze.

"I will leave when my task is finished," he said. "Now, Elspeth Fraser, if your apology and your warning are delivered, leave me in peace and let me get back to sleep."

"You must listen to me," she said. "I saw tragedy for you if you stay. Leave, and perhaps you will be safe."

"Tell me what you think you saw today, at the stream."

She lifted her chin. "As I said, tragedy. I will not speak of what I saw. Only know that you must leave here."

Duncan was rapidly losing patience. "You mentioned death at the stream. If you speak of my death, believe me, girl, you had better say what you mean." His voice was a low, dangerous rumble.

"Only a fool asks the truth of his own death," she said.

"I do not believe that you, or anyone, can see a man's death." He narrowed his eyes in sudden suspicion. "Surely you knew that a lawyer was to come here. If this is some scheme between you and your cousins to scare me away from my duty, it will not work."

She cursed softly in Gaelic and leaned forward. Duncan reached out quickly, so fast and strong that her defense, lifting the dirk, came too late. Grabbing her arms, he flung her down on the bed and fell deliberately on top of her.

As they went down together, Elspeth exploded with movement like a shot from a cannon. She kicked out and pushed against his grip with such strength that he could barely hold her down. Squeezing her wrist until she let go of the dirk, he finally pinioned her hands to the bed, above her head. Twisting fiercely, hair flying, she tried to bite his arm, while her strong, slender legs coaxed a few good bruises from his shins. Somewhere in the midst of the commotion, he thanked God she was barefoot; thick Highland brogues could have inflicted some real damage.

Gripping both her wrists with one hand, he snatched up the dirk with his free hand and tossed it away; it fell onto the pillow. Realizing that she might have another weapon, most likely a little *sgian dubh,* he slid his hand along her torso.

Though she bucked desperately beneath him, he found the thin, sharp blade tucked into a small scabbard at the back of her belt. Extracting it, he flipped it away to land near the dirk. Barely holding her down, he took her wrists in each hand again.

Panting like a runner, he collapsed his full weight onto her. Though unwilling to crush her slim body with his greater weight, he was more unwilling to give her the least chance to get free. He flung his upper leg heavily over both of her thighs. Keenly aware of the heat that emanated from their bare legs pressed together, feeling the gentle swell of her breasts beneath him, he tried to think about more immediate concerns.

Breathing heavily, she lay still, glaring at him through the shadows. A faint crescent of light fell across her face. Noting the snapping furor in her eyes, he remembered that an important part of his nude body was unprotected. He angled his groin away from her squirming legs.

"Now," he said, holding her hands and arms flat on the bed with his own, "tell me about this danger you see for me." He lay nose to nose with her, his dark hair weaving into the bright amber flame of hers. His heavy breaths mingled with each breath she took.

"I cannot," she huffed.

"How is my life forfeit?"

She shook her head. "Get off me."

"I will not." He grunted with the effort of keeping her still while she struggled beneath him. "Likely you scheme a plot on me yourself. Any threat on my life comes from you."

Halting her attempts to get loose, Elspeth stared up at him with an expression of horror. "Never!"

He blinked, surprised at the vehement answer. He had rather expected her to agree with him. "And what should I think when a blade is pulled on me in my sleep?"

She scowled then, looking disgusted. "I will not harm you, and I said it clear. Now get off me." She pushed upward, arching with her whole body.

Beneath him, her legs were smooth, taut muscle. He could feel the soft, alluring curves of her body, even swathed in the bulky plaid. Her breath on his face was light and sweet. Firm, lush breasts rose and fell beneath her shirt, the linen grazing the hairs on his bare chest.

She was warm and strong and wildly beautiful, Duncan suddenly thought, and somehow belonged here in his bed. He blinked in distracted surprise at his own impulsive desire. When she arched again, the imitation of a more delicious thrust sent a hot shiver through his body. No longer struggling beneath him, she only pushed in an attempt to shift him off her. Since he held her down securely, she was unable to move his greater weight with only her hips.

Her mouth was only a breath away from his. As he inhaled, he seemed to take in her air; as he exhaled, she took in his. The exchange seemed to lengthen and extend the moment. He moved his head forward slightly. Her eyes, cool and deep, slanted down to fix on his mouth.

Luscious heat gathered wherever their skin met. He could feel the warm, yielding length of her along his body. He sensed each breath she took, each small movement that she made.

Earlier that afternoon, standing in the stream with her, he had wanted desperately to touch her, to hold her. Now that same yearning flowed through him again, with greater strength and urgency. When she had ceased to struggle, the nature of their contact had altered and gentled. Now he looked at her mouth, at her full bottom lip, and moved forward infinitesimally, unable to stop himself. His lips touched her cheek

A little slide of his mouth, and his lips brushed hers. For the briefest moment her mouth softened beneath his.

Then she gasped and turned her head away. Her cloud of hair was soft and fresh; he inhaled mountain air and heather. She lay still, tense as a drawn bowstring. He stroked a thumb gently along her wrist, his heart thumping a heavy rhythm in his chest.

"Elspeth Fraser," he murmured, his breath against her cheek, "you touched my hair while I slept."

"You must have dreamed that," she whispered.

"No dream, but a soft, sweet touch." He looked at her and nearly smiled at her scowl. Even in this light he saw that she blushed like a fresh-bloomed rose.

He had relaxed slightly, lying atop her, and though he had been solicitous on behalf of his most sensitive area, it was beginning to betray his care with a solid arousal. He was too greatly aware of her warm body beneath his, of her hands curled in his palms, of her soft lips half open a breath away. Best the girl be gone now, he thought, before he lost the precarious hold he had gained over his urges. He sighed audibly.

"Without a doubt," he said, "I will forfeit my life, just as you predict. And it will happen this very night, at the hands of several angry Frasers, if you do not quit my chamber. Now." He released her hands and sat up, pulling up a corner of the fur bedcover to drape over his lap.

Leaping away from him as if he were made of flames, she whirled around. "Never force your hand to me again!" she spat angrily.

"Well," he drawled, drawing up the rest of the covers, "do not threaten me with your sweet hand again." With

quick movement he reached out to capture both his dirk
and her *sgian dubh,* and pushed them firmly beneath his
pillow. Then he lay back on it, positioning his hands casu-
ally behind his head.

"Is there something else?" he asked, tilting a brow at
her.

She stood there for a moment, looking at him through
the dark. He could hear her breathing, soft and quick.
"You see this as some jest," she said. "It is not. I am a
taibhsear, and I have given you a warning. Will you heed
it?"

"If you let me get a night's undisturbed sleep, I will consider any warning, even one that comes from a crazed, dirk-
wielding seer." He watched her for a moment. "But remember that I have a task here, and will not leave until it
is done. And remember as well," he added softly, "that I
intend to learn the truth of that vision you claim to have
had." Then he rolled over, presenting his broad back and
shoulder in dismissal.

She muttered something inaudible, and Duncan heard a
soft sliding sound. He held his breath, waiting for the slam
of the door. But he heard only the quick, muffled sound of
her barefoot steps padding away.

Puzzled, he turned over. The inside bolt was still in place
across the oaken door. Frowning, he looked around the
room. There was no other door. Where the devil had the
lass gone?

"Christ," he muttered, realizing that she must have gone
through a secret doorway. Many castles had them, sliding
panels of wood or turning stone blocks that led to narrow,
dark tunnels and stairways. "By the holy rood," he grumbled irritably, turning over and yanking up the covers. "I
wonder how many of these mad Frasers know about the
damned thing."

Chapter 5

The first an step that she stepped in,
She stepped to the queet;
"Ohon, alas!" said that lady,
"This water's wondrous deep."
— *"Clyde's Water"*

Darkness enveloped her, a black so deep that Elspeth could not see her hand in front of her face. A soggy, heavy burden tugged on her arms, and she could hardly move her legs. Opening her mouth to scream, she spat out wet, cold stuff that tasted vaguely of decay and mold. Then, with a jerk of horror, she realized that there was no air in this black density. Her lungs burned as she struggled frantically against the cloying darkness.

Elspeth awoke with a start, her heart pounding in her chest. Breathing hungrily of the cool night air, she sat up, grateful to see the banked orange glow of the hearth. Flinging off the bedclothes that had become tangled around her arms and legs, she shoved away the last traces of the vivid, horrifying nightmare.

A soft rustling sound, followed by a light tapping, came from a corner of the chamber. Drawing a woolen blanket around her nude body, she got out of bed and crossed toward the sound.

Half hidden in the wall behind a hanging length of tartan wool, a tiny wooden door opened, its frame hardly large enough for a child to pass through comfortably. Kenneth poked his head around the doorjamb. A rushlight flickered behind him, held in Callum's steady hand.

"Tonight?" Elspeth asked softly, blinking against the bright yellow light that silhouetted Kenneth's head. He nodded.

"Let me dress, then, and I will meet you," she said.

"Hurry, then." He ducked down and closed the door.

Laying out her plaid, she turned to first yank on a long linen shirt; tying a leather cord around her waist, she tucked the shirttails between her legs and up into the slender belt to form snug breeches. Then she sat to wrap her long plaid around her, tossing the free end over her left shoulder and fastening her wide belt. Reaching for her little knife, she cursed softly as she remembered that her *sgian dubh* was in the possession of the long-robe, the queen's lawyer, Duncan Macrae.

And that one, she thought, would surely disapprove if he knew that the cousins were riding out tonight. Certainly he would have no understanding of the Highland system of borrowing good cattle in the dark of night.

Elspeth smiled grimly as she pulled on high, soft deerskin boots and laced them up to her knees. Best that Glenran's honored guest remained soundly snoring in his chamber, where she had left him only a little while ago.

Pulling open the hidden door, she ducked low and stepped into the musty darkness of the stairs that led away from her room. Although the narrow space was barely large enough to accommodate her cousins, it was roomy enough for her. Carved from the thickness of one of the castle's broad, sturdy outer walls, the secret stair spanned five levels, leading past one of the chambers on each level down to the kitchen that backed up to the great hall. Elspeth and her cousins often used the hidden stair, which was hardly a secret at Glenran.

Nearing the narrow doorway that led to the second-level bedchamber where Macrae slept, she hurried past, continuing downward. Outside, in the castle yard, she knew her cousins waited with the horses.

For the second time that night, Duncan was roused from sleep by a rustling noise. His first thought was that the girl had returned. Thrusting his hand beneath his pillow, he closed his fingers around both his dirk and her little knife.

As he sat to stare around the empty room, he heard a soft scraping sound.

Bounding out of bed, he went to the outer wall and began to probe gently. His ears were keenly aware of the slightest sound as his fingertips moved over the hard, cool stone, looking for the opening that he was certain was there.

There, again: a faint brushing noise, below his room now. He smiled in triumph as his canny fingers found the low door in the darkness, well hidden in the shadows, behind a heavy high-backed wooden chair deliberately angled to conceal the corner and its small wooden door.

He found the ring latch and pulled the door open. Bending to peer into the dark stairs beyond, he wondered how generations of tall, burly Frasers had ever managed to negotiate the stingy dimensions of the secret stair. Being easily as large as any of the Fraser males he had seen, he would not eagerly enter that space. But the Fraser girl, slim and lithe as she was, obviously passed in and out of here like a cat.

Leaning into the doorway to peruse the darkness, he listened carefully and heard the unmistakable sound of a door closing softly somewhere below. A moment later, he backed out of the little space and rose to his feet. Rubbing his whiskered jaw, he wondered who might leave the castle in the middle of the night—and why.

There were few good reasons to use a secret stair at this hour. Somehow he did not think the girl had gone to meet a lover.

He made a sour grimace. As the queen's lieutenant, he was obligated to investigate this. Sighing, he pulled on his trews and shirt, wondering if he would get any sleep this night. He laced up a sleeveless jack of quilted leather, and then groped around in the thick, obscure darkness for his black cloak and high boots.

If anyone knew a reason to venture out on a cool dark night, it was Duncan Macrae. He had ridden with his own brothers, long ago, to raid on Clan MacDonald. And when he had lived with his cousins in the Lowlands, he had ridden with the best of the border reivers. They had gone out in silent packs through the darkness to steal cattle and sheep, to burn a manor house or a barn, or to kill if a feud, or the moment, demanded it.

With a certain chill, he knew that something of the sort was happening here tonight. His senses were keenly tuned to such palpable stealth and tension. He knew well the lure of a quiet, clear night; he had followed, many times, the beckoning glimmer of the moonlight.

Pulling on his gloves, he went to the little door and opened it. With a muttered oath that mentioned mason workers, he bent and wriggled through the narrow doorway.

Over hills springy with deep summer heather they rode, the moonlight silvering their way. Crossing the stream that bordered Glenran, the Frasers guided their sturdy horses with purposeful rhythm, slipping silently into territory that belonged to Clan MacDonald.

Riding beside Ewan, Elspeth glanced ahead, where her cousins Kenneth and Callum cantered steadily onward. She had been a little surprised to find that only these three rode out tonight. A raid often involved several riders, Fraser kinsmen gathered from the homes and shielings around the countryside. She had gone out in raiding parties as large as thirty riders, mostly Fraser cousins all of an age, and she had ridden out with as few as five or six. Tonight, then, was meant to be a quick, small raid, a sharp comment on the MacDonald attack on Angus Simson's land a few nights past.

The night wind blew soft and fresh, whipping their hair and refreshing their lungs. Elspeth smiled into the wind, loving the cool snap of it, the scent of heather and moss and pine in it, reveling in the way it shook her braid loose and played with her hair. She laughed aloud and Ewan, riding beside her, turned.

"Elspeth," he said, "tell us what you think."

She closed her eyes briefly. After a moment she could feel the presence of the cattle, like a dull congestion on the wind. Consciously she heard only the wind, smelled only heather and pine. But her keen inner senses detected a bovine dullness, without human presence. Unguarded cattle grazed to the east.

"That way," she said, pointing. Kenneth slowed his horse to ride beside her.

"To the east, lads," he said. The others nodded and turned their horses' heads to follow him.

They rode through rolling landscape, hills and burns and forests lushly beautiful in the moonlight. At the crest of a grassy hill, Elspeth halted her horse.

She glanced around the unfamiliar valley, though she had ridden through MacDonald territory on other raids with her cousins. "Here," she said. "Somewhere near here."

"MacDonald cattle," Kenneth remarked after a moment. "Just listen: lowing loud and rude like their owners. Look there." He gestured. Peering through the soft milky light, Elspeth saw the black dots of an untended herd of cattle, at least fifty head, moving slowly over the hillside far below them.

"You were right, girl, as always," Callum said.

"The MacDonalds no doubt snore just as loud and rude, snug inside their castle, more than a league from this place," Ewan said. He grinned. "Simple this will be. Come ahead, then."

Rounding up a part of the herd was quick work. Kenneth and Ewan, fast and certain on their mounts, and Callum and Elspeth on foot, split off a group of fifteen cattle from the larger herd. Silent and swift, the reivers followed an unspoken Highland tradition of courtesy in raiding, which ensured that a full herd was rarely taken.

Small, black, shaggy, and impossibly dumb, the cattle went wherever they were shooed. Soon the Frasers were all on horseback again, guiding the animals between them. Grinning widely, they rode back toward Glenran.

Riding behind the herd, Elspeth kicked out now and again with her foot to remind one or another of the short-horned steer to stay with the group. When her boot lacing came loose, she fell behind, pausing to retie the thongs.

As she did so, she heard an odd sound and lifted her head. For a wild moment she thought that a baby cried nearby, then recognized the plaintive bleating of a lamb. Dismounting, she walked cautiously toward a cluster of bushes that sprang up beside a rocky outcrop on the moor.

She knelt to reach toward the knotty base of a thorn bush. Tangled in the prickly branches was a lamb, no more than a few months old, bleating furiously, its wobbly voice barely audible over the wind and the muted thunder of the passing herd.

"Oh, little one," she crooned, "come here!" She freed its soft, thick fleece from the thorns. In another moment she had disentangled one foreleg from the clinging branches. Cradling the lamb gently, she discerned that no bones were broken, though the little creature trembled like an aspen leaf under her touch. Murmuring softly, she gathered it in her arms and stood, laughing as the lamb lifted its head to nuzzle her cheek.

She ran back toward her pony, which grazed contentedly in the rough grasses. Ahead, her cousins had paused to wait. Sensing their impatience, she hastened to remount, settling the lamb in her lap.

"MacDonald shepherds are as lax as their cowherds," Callum said as she drew near him. He looked tolerantly at the black-faced lamb, which bleated and struggled for a moment.

"We shall reive this little one from them as well, then," Elspeth said, laughing.

Callum grunted indulgently and rode ahead.

Riding along, Elspeth patted the lamb's soft white fleece, its body warm against her. Bony legs and tough little hooves restlessly kicked her, and she finally tapped its rump. "Stop that, now," she murmured. "I will not harm you."

For a brief instant she recalled saying something similar earlier that night, when the lawyer Macrae had pinioned her to his bed as if she were a hare caught in an eagle's talons. Blushing furiously at the memory, she ducked her head and urged the horse onward. Twice today she had felt the strength of Macrae's arms: when he had caught her in her swoon, and when he had trapped her in the bed after her attempt to warn him away.

Her blush deepened. She felt foolish now. How could she have thought to frighten him off with a blade and a vague prophecy? He had nearly laughed outright. Apparently he did not accept the power of a seer to foretell the future.

Remembering how he had thrown her down to the bed, she told herself stiffly that she did not care if he lost or kept his handsome head. But in truth she knew that she had to convince the man to leave.

The lamb shifted and kicked inside the swath of plaid that covered her chest, and she stroked it with one hand. A whistle from Kenneth up ahead brought her out of her thoughts and reminded her that she had a task to perform. She nudged with her toe at the nearest shaggy cattle rump. Obligingly, the animal stepped away, though it responded with a grunt, followed by a loud, round lowing that startled Elspeth with its volume.

The lamb was startled as well. Struggling and kicking, it managed to slide halfway out of her lap. Then it leaped from Elspeth's arms and went downward with a plaintive bleating.

A wild commotion erupted. Screaming for the lamb, afraid that it would be trampled to death by the cattle, Elspeth leaned down from her horse and reached frantically. The lamb disappeared between the cattle's hooves, a rapid, zigzagging blur in the moonlight.

Terrified by the white creature that bleated and cried in their midst, the cattle took off in several directions, lowing and grunting and shoving with their heavy heads in their haste to be gone. Elspeth leaped from her horse, pushing to veer him off in a safer direction. Glancing at her cousins, who were now chasing the runaway animals, she dashed off on foot after the tiny white blur. By some miracle the lamb had not been trampled underfoot.

As the lamb disappeared over a hill, Elspeth pounded with booted feet through thick clumps of heather. Behind her, she heard someone shout her name, but she did not stop. The moonlight was clear enough to show her the white shape of the lamb and the long slope of the hill that she rapidly descended.

A dark, glistening plain spread out at the foot of the hill. Myriad burns sparkled there, like silver threads woven into nubby black wool. She ran on.

The heather thinned out and her feet struck raw, soggy ground, tufted with mosses. The lamb bounced and bleated, leading her forward. The ground grew softer, and Elspeth slowed her pursuit, suddenly wary of her surroundings. All around her black water gleamed. Intent on catching the stray lamb, she had not heeded the warning of the moonlight reflections ahead of her, had not thought about the softening ground beneath her feet.

When the lamb stopped and turned hesitantly, its tiny black face merging with the darkness, Elspeth pounced ahead, arms out.

And sank into a sucking, cloying peat bog. One leg, and then the other, disappeared in the thick black mire. She sank to the waist and fell forward, arms out, thrusting her hands into the oozy stuff. Struggling only sucked her deeper into the bog. Straightening as best she could, she stilled her movements.

With the toe of one boot she felt solid ground beneath the deep layer of dense, wet peat. Gasping, she fought for balance and glanced around her.

She was surrounded by a marshy sea of peat. The black, treacherous surface foamed with mosses and grasses. Watery stretches glistened brightly in the moonlight. In the dark, the safer passes of firm ground were nearly impossible to distinguish.

Ahead, the white blur of the lamb was smaller now, its frightened bleating grown more excited. Elspeth moved toward the lamb, laboriously lifting and dragging her legs through the rich, odiferous mire. Touching the fragile, trembling head at last, she gained a firmer grasp on the little animal's slithery back and drew the lamb toward her.

Leaning forward, she slipped deeper and nearly went facedown. Coughing and gasping, she righted herself and

inhaled the repulsive odor of rotting vegetation, of dank
molds and muck.

Then, with a chill of horror, she remembered her nightmare, and began to scream for help.

Duncan had found it easy enough, in the bright moonlight, to follow the Frasers and their tough garrons. He had
seen them occasionally, once in black silhouette as they had
topped the crest of the hill, another time as they had entered a long stretch of pine forest. Once he had heard the
girl's light laughter float back on the breeze. Although he
had kept a discreet distance, he had no desire to lose them
altogether and be left riding through unfamiliar MacDonald territory.

A grim thought. If the MacDonalds were to discover a
Macrae riding through their land, he would not survive the
night. The animosity was generations old between their
clans. Frasers were not the only ones who had known trouble from the MacDonalds, he mused.

Shifting the reins of his stallion, he scanned the darkness
ahead. He had, in truth, lost the Frasers not long ago, but
only temporarily, he was sure. Now he sat, deciding
whether to follow the valley to his right or keep to the
river. He was inclined to go into the valley.

The river, were he to follow its northwestern angle,
would eventually lead toward the western sea and the distant mountains that edged Kintail, a journey of a few days.
His own home, Dulsie Castle, was nestled in those hills.

He watched the silent curves of the dark moors, aware
that most of the land between here and Kintail belonged
to the MacDonalds. The territory of Clan MacDonald was
extensive. Here, they disputed borders with the Frasers;
farther west, they fought the same disputes with Clan
Macrae.

He breathed a sigh. He had no desire to meet up with
MacDonalds again. As for the Frasers, he need not follow
them farther this night. He now knew what he had set out
to discover: the Frasers had indeed ridden out on a midnight cattle raid.

Tightening the reins, he urged the horse to turn back toward Glenran. God knew he craved a soft bed more than a hard ride over Highland moors just now. As he turned, the first sounds of a stampede rose on the wing. He paused to listen.

And sighed in exasperation. The Frasers must have gone into the valley. And either they had met with some very angry MacDonalds, or they had totally lost control of their night's booty. He sat for another moment, then spun his horse to ride toward the sounds.

After another half league, he clearly heard the distressed bellowing of cattle and the thunder of hooves. Rounding the top of a grassy knoll, he saw a scattered group of riders and cattle, chasing crazy patterns of pursuit and flight through moonlit heather.

If this was the Frasers' approach to Highland cattle reiving, then he was glad to have learned the skill elsewhere. Sighing gustily, he rode forward, his horse cleaving an easy path through pandemonium.

He noticed the bright gloss of Ewan's red hair, dark in the moonlight, and waved a cheery greeting as he passed. Next he saw Callum—the fellow's broad shoulders were unmistakable—and nodded pleasantly. Kenneth, his dark braids flapping, stopped his garron and gaped. Duncan raised his hand in a relaxed salute.

"Greetings," Duncan called out. "Enjoying the night air, are you, lads?"

Kenneth continued to gape. Callum turned his horse and rode directly for Duncan.

"Why are you out here?" he snapped.

"I had some trouble sleeping," Duncan answered affably, reining in his horse. "There were some rather large mice in Glenran's hidden stair."

Callum looked at him for a moment, then nodded slowly. He turned to survey the commotion behind him as his cousins chased after the cattle. "We mean no harm out here. Go back to Glenran."

"I know you mean no harm," Duncan said. "Just a little cattle exchange. But the beasts can be troublesome at

times, far past their value. Round up your cousins rather
than the herd, and get back to Glenran before the Mac-
Donalds hear this happy night song." He looked around at
the moor, peppered with lowing cattle—or what few remained after most had run off—and turned back to Callum.
"What frightened the herd?"

"Elspeth and her—*Dhia*, where is the girl?" Callum
twisted in the saddle, looking around. "Elspeth!" He rode
away, calling his cousins.

"Quietly, please," Duncan muttered. "This is a raid." In
the distance he saw a riderless horse grazing in the long
grass. He rode toward it, cursing softly when he realized
that it must be Elspeth's horse. Without her horse, in the
middle of a stampede, the girl could be in serious danger.
Seeing no broken body lying out on the moor, he rode
farther along the ridge of a long hill.

A terrified scream drifted up from below the ridge. Turning his horse, he rode down the slope. When it grew too
steep, he dismounted, threw the reins over a low bush, and
walked down.

The scream came again. Duncan narrowed his eyes but
saw no obvious threat. No MacDonalds, no wolves or wildcats, only a maze of glittering watercourses in the
moonlight—

"*Dhia*," he breathed, "the girl's gone into the bog!" Calling out a whoop to summon her cousins, he threw off his
cloak, then his doublet and shirt as he began to run.

Reaching the spongy surface of the quagmire, he began
to tread more carefully. Only the locals would know the
safe passes through the peat bog. In the moonlight he could
not tell firm from boggy ground.

"Elspeth!" he called softly. "Elspeth Fraser!"

"Here" came the tremulous reply. Duncan saw only slick,
oily stretches of black water and acres of tangled grasses.
Then a dark, amorphous shape rose and fell, and he heard
a mournful bleating sound. Poor girl, he thought; she was
nearly incoherent with terror.

Pulling off his boots, he tossed them up the hill toward
his other garments, and lunged forward in trews and bare

feet. He curled his lip in disgust as the cold muck began
to envelop him. Moving slowly through the ooze, which
licked and bubbled around his waist and lower ribs, he
made his way toward Elspeth.

"Stay where you are," he told her. She nodded, a brief
moonlit glint of bright hair and face above blackened
shoulders.

Another careful step, and another; he felt with his toes
for the firm ground beneath the deep pudding of peat mire.
Close enough to see Elspeth clearly, he stretched out his
hand and eased nearer.

Earlier today—it felt like a lifetime ago—he had waded
through crystal-clear water for this girl, and had reached
out his fingers to her in just this way.

"No visions, now," he chided gently, "and no blades either, and I will take your hand."

He thought she smiled in the cool blue light. "No visions
and no blades," she agreed, holding out her blackened
hand. A tremulous cry emerged through the darkness, poignant and tender. His heart gave a curious lurch of
sympathy.

"Do not be frightened, girl," he murmured. Wrapping
his fingers over hers, feeling slippery slime, he tugged her
toward him. "The bog is only so deep—you will not drown
in this."

She laughed, a quick, light trill, as she came closer. He
circled an arm around her and drew her along through the
soupy mire, wondering at her humor. When she pressed
something soft and slithery and cold against his bare chest,
he was startled.

He caught and held a squirmy, solid creature, so covered
in muck that it was nearly unrecognizable. Then it bleated
out weakly. Duncan blinked in surprise. "A lamb?"

She nodded. "She was trapped in a thorn bush, and I
meant to carry her home, but she jumped away and scared
the cattle—"

"And you ran after her, and found yourself in the bog."
With one arm he curled the lamb against his chest.

Elspeth nodded. Duncan wrapped his fingers around her

arm. "Come, then," he said. "We must be out of this muck
quickly and back to Glenran. You and your lamb and your
cattle-reiving cousins have made enough noise this night to
wake the dead." He waded through the heavy mire, pulling
Elspeth with him.

"Hush," she said. "Do not speak of such things even in
jest." The lamb gave a pitiful bleat, and Duncan jiggled its
scant weight awkwardly.

Elspeth stopped to look up at him. "How is it you are
here?" she asked suddenly. "Though I thank you for it,"
she added. She placed a hand on his bare chest for balance,
the press of her slippery fingers cool and pleasant.

Duncan gazed down at her. The black wallow clung to
her breasts and shoulders, and darkened her slender throat
and her hair. Flexing his hand on her arm, he suddenly and
ridiculously wanted to gather her closer, but he only smiled
and shrugged.

"Noisy walls has Castle Glenran," he said.

"Oh," she said in a small voice.

They neared the edge of the bog, rising out of it as horrible as any pair of water monsters. Ewan and Callum
stepped forward to pull Elspeth out of Duncan's grasp. He
would much rather have relinquished the lamb, which
bleated in an unhappy rhythm, safely held in the crook of
his arm.

Climbing the hill behind the Fraser cousins, listening to
their concerned murmuring, he bent down to gather up his
discarded garments. Kenneth obligingly took up the reins
of Duncan's horse and led it upward.

At the top of the hill, Duncan thrust the lamb at Ewan
and then handed Elspeth his white shirt, with which she
removed some of the mucky peat from her limbs and torso.
Feeling the chill of the night air against his wet skin, he
threw his cloak around his shoulders, tossing the jack and
boots behind his saddle.

Turning to Elspeth, he grabbed her around the waist and
boosted her up onto his horse. Mounting behind her, he
wrapped them both in the wide folds of his thick black
cloak.

"I have a garron," she protested.

"You do. And you will feel the night's chill if you ride it in that wet plaid. Your cousins will lead your garron back with them. Ewan," he said, "hand up that bothersome thing." Duncan gave the bleating bundle to Elspeth. "Here is your bog beast, my girl," he said. She cuddled it, wrapping a portion of Duncan's cloak around its blackened, slimy pelt.

"I am owed a linen shirt for this night's work," he drawled, watching, "and now I think a cloak as well."

"A length of good plaid would be much less cumbersome than this great black cape you wear," she said.

Grunting unenthusiastically, Duncan wrapped one arm around her and kneed his horse forward. The horse's momentum caused Elspeth to lean back against Duncan's chest. Warmth gathered in the damp stickiness between their bodies. They rode toward Glenran over the quiet, moonlit moor, surrounded by the soft pounding rhythms of horses hooves as her cousins followed.

Elspeth yawned. Duncan smiled and shook his head. "Does no one ever rest in Castle Glenran?" he asked.

She stifled another yawn, and Duncan touched her shoulder to urge her to rest against him. After a moment of stiff resistance, she complied, leaning her head against his chest.

In spite of his exhaustion, in spite of his irritation with these Fraser cousins for their ridiculous raid, he felt relaxed and exhilarated. Perhaps the feeling was born of the midnight ride, he thought. Even a reiving gone awry was an invigorating, thrilling thing.

Somehow, though, he realized that the soft, sweet pressure of the girl's head on his chest brought an excitement and a contentment unlike any he had ever felt before.

Without quite knowing why, Duncan smiled softly to himself as they rode on through the night.

Chapter 6

And see not ye that braid, braid road,
That lies across yon lillie leven?
That is the path of wickedness,
Tho some call it the road to heaven.
—"*Thomas the Rhymer*"

"*Dhia*, Alasdair, the Council has tossed me into a devil of a pit here." Duncan yawned and sipped cool watered morning ale from a cup. "I had hoped you would help me convince these lads to sign the bond. The Earl of Moray and the Privy Council want the matter seen to quickly."

He poked a wooden spoon into the steaming bowl of porridge that a serving girl had brought from the nearby kitchen. Such close proximity guaranteed hot food, but this was amazingly hot, and the girl had forgotten the cream to cool it.

Alasdair gingerly blew on his spoonful. "I leave for Dulsie Castle this morning," he said, slipping easily into the Gaelic that Duncan had used. "I have not seen my wife, Mhairi, for three months and more." He took another mouthful, gasped from the heat of it on his tongue, and quickly sipped his ale. "Ouch. Be patient but a few days more, man, and your bond will be signed."

Duncan tipped a brow doubtfully. "A few days more will see only more argument, and no signature but mine on that page."

"Truly, I did not know that the MacShimi would refuse like this. He is an intelligent lad, and stubborn. But you are a fine lawyer, and you will convince him of the need for the bond."

Duncan sighed. "I had planned to talk to the MacShimi this morning and make certain he understood the dire importance of this document. But he and his cousins went out hunting just after dawn."

Alasdair nodded. "And on foot. They will be gone most of the day, if they come back at all before tomorrow. Your bond will wait yet again on the Frasers."

Duncan shook his head in discouragement. He had arrived here expecting the bond to be signed without fuss, wanting only to deliver the documents to the Privy Council and return to his quiet rooms in Edinburgh. The council would have other legal cases that would require his attention.

So far the Frasers had shown him only frustration and delay. In spite of their good humor, they had sorely tried his temper. He was normally strong on patience, having taught himself years ago to keep a careful rein on his emotions. His temper had nearly ruined him in his youth, and he would never again let it overtake him.

Yet these Fraser lads—not to mention the lass—raised an urge in him to shout until the veins stood in his neck. He wanted to wave the cursed document in their faces and get those signatures if he had to use the dirk to do it.

"These lads have a strong disregard for the law, and for lawyers," he muttered.

"Only typical for Highlanders," Alasdair remarked, pouring a little cold ale into his porridge and stirring it.

Duncan grunted assent and watched with distaste. He had not yet ventured to try his own cooked oats. Tiny swirling clouds of steam wafted up. He blew at them.

"True," Duncan said. "Highlanders ever will ignore the rule of the law. That raid the other night went against the letter of caution, but no signatures have been set. And the Frasers show no remorse for that night's work. They only regret losing the cattle they had cut out of the herd."

"My kinsmen will not trouble themselves with rules. They leave that for the long-robes and the Lowlanders."

Duncan huffed a laugh. "Am I to slap their hands, then, like babes, and put the pen in their fingers to get the bond into effect? I have no desire to send for the sheriff's men at Inverness. Though James Stewart, the Earl of Moray, would have me do that, I think, since he is now the titular sheriff of Inverness. Though he will not soon come up into the Highlands."

"*Ach,* no need for sheriffs or for forcing the lads. See them on their own ground. They will sign when they come to trust you."

Duncan groaned at such spare reassurance. "A lawyer who acted like a wild Scot would better gain their trust, and those signatures, I think," he grumbled, stirring his porridge.

"I think so, man," Alasdair said. "Do that, then."

Duncan slid him a wry look and tasted the thick cooked oats. Hot, but hearty and good, sweetened with honey and liberally salted. He ate a few mouthfuls and considered Alasdair's words.

"You are a Highlandman," Alasdair said. "They trust their own kind. You come from a clan that has fought Mac-Donalds for longer than the Frasers have done. Macrae is not just the name you bear, it is your legacy as well."

Duncan ate another mouthful. "You may have a point."

"I do. You take a challenge well, Duncan, and always did. Here is one for you. See these lads on their own ground."

Duncan smiled ruefully as he thought of the other night's raid. "I think I did that already," he said.

"Hunt with them, or fish with them—"

"Or raid with them."

Alasdair looked curiously at him. Duncan smiled. The idea that was taking shape in his mind had a pleasing irony. "They are a bit inept at the raiding, from what I saw."

Alasdair lifted a shaggy brow. "Riding so many times with the Macraes, and then the Kerrs, you would know a poor raid if you saw one."

"I would."

"And you might know the way to improve the raids."

"I might."

"Until the bond is signed, the raids will continue."

"They will," Duncan agreed. "And if the lads will ride against MacDonalds, they may as well do it proper."

Alasdair grinned. "The MacDonalds might suffer the loss of quite a few cattle by the time this bond is signed."

Duncan shrugged. "The thought of a displeased Mac-Donald has never kept me awake at night. I do not wish to see the Fraser lads killed trying to take the cattle by their own unique methods."

Alasdair laughed as he poured ale into both cups. "There is hope for you, Duncan man," he grinned. "The law and the Lowlands have not made you stale all through just yet. That wild Macrae is still in there."

"Only a spark, Alasdair. Enough to light a fire under the Frasers and get them to sign the cursed document."

"Well done, then," Alasdair agreed. "You will get your bond made, and amuse yourself a bit in the process. Your own father could not have thought up a better scheme."

Duncan glanced away and nodded. "He would have enjoyed this scheme. He was a good man, my father."

"He was that." Alasdair watched him for a moment. "Well. I wish I could be here to see this, but I leave within the hour."

"God go with you then, *bràthair*."

"I will ask you once again to come to Dulsie Castle when you finish your task here."

Duncan shook his head. "Give my grandmother and my sisters my greetings."

Alasdair looked at him. "No other message?"

A muscle jumped in Duncan's cheek. "None other."

Climbing into the hills that rose behind the castle, Elspeth turned to whistle softly to the leggy lamb that cantered behind her. She laughed as the lamb bleated, as if asking her to wait.

Her own strides were quick and strong, though she moved carefully through deep grasses and over rocks slippery with mist. Her leather brogues were protection enough from the wet ground, though she had not pulled on woolen stockings or full trews. Even for a damp day, the late summer weather required no extra layers beneath her plaid.

She began to sing as she walked, her clear, light voice

and steady step weaving in pleasing rhythm. Tapping her fingers lightly, she enjoyed the brisk pattern of the words and melody.

Clearing the crest of the last hill, she descended toward the moor, hastening her stride now, aware that Bethoc would be expecting her. For the past several years Elspeth had gone every week to Bethoc MacGruer's home, only missing a visit when winter snowdrifts had prevented travel.

Far off to her right lay the long, smooth surface of the great loch, like a shard of a dark mirror fallen between the forested hills, reflecting dull grays and deep greens. The lamb scampered ahead of her, its fleece only a shade or two lighter now than its dark face.

"Bog beast indeed," she said. She thought again of that ride home from the raid, leaning secure and warm against Duncan Macrae. She must have fallen asleep as they rode, for the next thing she recalled was being lifted down into his arms. She had been so tired, and the feeling had been so pleasant, that she had let him carry her into the castle before she had jumped down and run up the stairs.

She watched the little lamb as she strode over the heathery hills. Elspeth and Flora had scrubbed the lamb's pelt with soft wet cloths and even a bit of precious Flemish soap, but the peat had stained the lamb's fleece to a muted gray-brown.

Elspeth had scrubbed the slimy peat from her own skin and hair easily though. So had the lawyer, appearing in the hall the next day with his hair still wet from a bath, dark and glossy as raven wings, his freshly shaved face lean and handsome. He had handed over to her, silently and discreetly, the little *sgian dubh* that she had lost in his bed. When she had blushed fiercely, he had smiled before turning away to speak to Hugh.

Since then she had seen little of him. He had been spending his days with her cousins, riding with them and walking out over the hills. She knew they constantly discussed the details of the queen's legal document. She had overheard a fair amount of argument, although good-natured, between her cousins and the queen's lawyer.

Shoving her fingers through her unruly hair, she squelched on through wet summer growth in the lamb's wake. The fine mist dampened her plaid and coaxed a halo of frothy curls around her head. She loved these washes of mist and light rain that rinsed the land, loved the cool, fresh billows of air, loved how the green and heather tones softened in the mist. Feeling a fine contentment, keenly aware that she loved the Highlands, she walked on, singing softly.

She saw Bethoc's croft just below her, snuggled against the foot of the hill. Elspeth halted her step, cut her song short in mid-phrase, and frowned.

Smoke curled, cozy and dark, from the chimney hole set in a roof of dried heather thatch. Vines climbed a stone wall. A goat nibbled on a block of turf that served as an outside bench, unperturbed by several chickens that pecked in erratic circles underfoot. The front door stood open, as it usually did. All was quiet and apparently peaceful.

But a heavy whispering dread gripped Elspeth's insides like a fist. She began to run.

Reaching the doorway, she paused, hearing only silence, and peered into the shadowy interior. The open door admitted a wedge of cool daylight. Scant light was provided by a little window in the back wall.

"Bethoc?" she called, stepping inside. Her brogues shushed over the dried rushes that covered the well-swept dirt floor. In the hearth, a circle of fitted stones in the middle of the floor, a peat fire crackled. The sweet, musty fragrance of dried herbs, hanging in bunches from the rafters, mingled with the peat smoke.

Elspeth blinked as her eyes adjusted to the dimness. "Bethoc?" she called.

Across the room, behind a woven cloth hung for a curtain, lay a snug box bed. Crossing the room quickly, Elspeth drew aside the curtain, and looked down at Magnus's little daughter.

Eiric slept soundly, curled on top of the fur covering, a tiny form in a rumpled white shift, her black curls gleaming in the faint light of the box bed, one thumb disappeared into her little mouth. Though she was dark like her mother had been, her eyes, when she was awake, shared Magnus's deep blue color.

Eiric's mother had been Bethoc's youngest daughter, who had happily handfasted with Magnus. But before the year and day of their arrangement drew to an end, the girl had died bearing their daughter. Not even Bethoc's considerable skill could save her.

Magnus had been making plans to marry her in front of a priest. Instead, he had buried her, and had given his infant daughter, Eiric, into Bethoc's hands for raising. He knew, as did Elspeth, that Eiric was well loved here. Elspeth also knew that in the two years since, he had secured his heart against further hurt by making no attempt to find another wife.

Elspeth reached out a gentle hand and tucked a woolen blanket securely around the sleeping child. Eiric's soft breathing caught occasionally, as if she had gone off to sleep crying piteously.

Elspeth drew her brows together with concern. "Eiric *gràdhan,* little dear, where is your grandmother?" she murmured. Bethoc, she knew, never went farther than the yard when the child napped.

The second room of the house, formed by a half wall made of a wattle screen, held Bethoc's sturdy, wide loom and little else. She saw quickly that Bethoc was not in the weaving room.

Leaving the cottage, Elspeth walked around the side of the house, past the turf bench and the goat, her quick strides parting the cluster of chickens. The small garden behind the house was deserted, its rows of herbs and vegetable plants lush and still in the damp, silent air.

But several of the green leaves were trampled and smashed. Elspeth suddenly felt as if a lump of lead sat in her stomach. Her heart beat with quick thumps as she turned away.

"Bethoc!" she called. A quick circle of the cottage yard revealed nothing but the wandering bog lamb, bleating and lonesome. She shooed it impatiently toward the turf bench, where the goat moved over without interest.

Wondering if Bethoc had gone to fetch some water, Elspeth began to turn down a little hill that led to a burn.

There, beneath the alder trees that lined the burn's banks, she saw Bethoc seated on the ground by the rapid, narrow stream.

Even from this distance Elspeth could see the darkening bruises that covered one side of the woman's face. Just as she broke into a breathless, anxious run, she saw the stiff manner in which Bethoc half lifted herself to her feet, only to stumble again to the ground.

Reaching her, Elspeth fell to her knees. "What happened?" she cried, placing a hand on Bethoc's shoulder. Looking at the woman's face, Elspeth sucked in her breath.

Purpling bruises swelled beneath Bethoc's right eye. The right side of her face had begun to swell viciously at the corner of the firm jaw. Blood seeped from a cut on her lip.

Bethoc pushed back the black and silver hair that slipped down from her wrapped braids. "Elspeth," she murmured. "Well enough I am, girl. Do not fret. Where is Eiric?"

"Sleeping," Elspeth said. Bethoc nodded as if in relief. Stepping over to the little burn, Elspeth soaked a corner of her plaid's hem in the cold water, and came back to apply the cold compress to Bethoc's face and gently cleanse away the blood.

"Tell me how this happened," Elspeth said.

Bethoc shook her head. "Help me up, *mo cuachag.*" Leaning a hand on the tree trunk, she placed her other hand on Elspeth's shoulder.

Elspeth sensed the weakness in the woman's limbs as Bethoc stood. "Your foot—" she said, looking down. "Can you walk?"

"Only as well as ever," Bethoc smiled. She stepped forward with a slight lurch, her twisted foot rocking with her weight until she put the other foot forward. Born with a club foot, Bethoc moved slowly but rarely used a walking stick.

"Lean on me." Elspeth slipped an arm around Bethoc's back.

Though lacking the sturdy bulk of Flora, Bethoc was quite tall, and solid enough. But Elspeth was strong and easily assisted her as they climbed the slope back to the cottage.

Inside the house, Bethoc sat on a bench by the table and let out a heavy sigh. Elspeth checked to see that Eiric still slept, then went to a wide cupboard and opened its doors. Bundles of herbs, wrapped and tied in pieces of cloth, and a few small clay jars were set on the shelves.

Bethoc had taught her much over the years. Now Elspeth chose comfrey for bruises, willow for pain, oak and wormwood for swelling, gathering each bundle or jar as she found it. Then she fetched the wooden bucket that always held cool water for drinking and cooking uses.

"An infusion of comfrey and willow bark would help, but would take too long just now," Bethoc said. "Just moisten the comfrey root—it is ground, there—and make a cool poultice."

Elspeth worked quickly to prepare the poultice, and listened to further suggestions from Bethoc as she began to prepare an infusion. She stirred herbs and ground bark into an iron kettle of hot water, suspended on a rod over the hearth.

Her mind worked as quickly as her hands, racing through her anger and shock and fear. Repeatedly, fretfully, she glanced at Bethoc, who calmly held the comfrey poultice to her cheek and leaned her head back against the wall, eyes closed.

Elspeth was reassured to see that calm in Bethoc, a hint of the constant serenity that seemed part of Bethoc's nature. When the infusion was steeped, Elspeth added honey and knelt on the dried rushes to hand a cup to Bethoc.

"Now tell me," she said sternly. "This was no fall down a hill, or onto some rocks."

Bethoc gazed evenly at her. "That is what you assume," she said, and took a sip. "What do you sense?"

Elspeth half smiled; even now Bethoc would be her

teacher. Obediently she closed her eyes, took a breath, and tried to clear her mind. She tried to let the knowledge come, in spite of her wildly beating heart and anxious feelings.

Nothing. Only the darkness behind her eyes. She drew another breath, slowing her chaotic thoughts by slowing her heart. Then a glimmer of an image: a shock of rusty hair, an upraised arm.

Elspeth opened her eyes. "Ruari?" she whispered. "Ruari MacDonald did this to you?" Bethoc looked at her in mute admittance. "But why? You have no herd, only a few sheep, a goat, chickens—"

Bethoc shrugged. "My house sits on the border of the land that Ruari inherited from his father." She winced and brought a finger to her swollen lip. "He told me that he has no care to share borders with—with a—" She looked away quickly.

"With a charmer and a healer?"

"He did mean that, though his words were not so kind."

"Was he alone? Did he—oh, Bethoc," Elspeth murmured, touching her arm gently, "did he—"

Bethoc shook her head. "He only hit me, and left me lying there by the burn, when one of his brothers rode over the hill calling for him. I was in the garden when he came. He rode his garron through the plants. I had just put Eiric down for her nap." She settled her back against the wall. "He drove me from the yard with the flat of his broadsword as if I were a cow. He struck me with it, and screamed vile things at me, saying that my twisted foot branded me a creature of the devil, and he would not have a witch woman living so near his land. I heard Eiric crying inside, but I could not go to her—" She drew a shaky breath and closed her eyes.

Tears came to Elspeth's eyes as she looked at Bethoc's strong-boned, handsome face distorted with bruises. After a moment Bethoc opened her green eyes and took a sip of the herbal infusion.

Fisting her hands tightly, Elspeth anticipated, with a swell of rage, the moment when she would tell her cousins the truth of the man they wanted her to marry. The moment when they would ride out in revenge against Ruari MacDonald.

"My cousins will see that Ruari pays well for this," she said. "Magnus, I think, will kill him."

Bethoc shook her head. "The lads must not go after him. I know that Magnus cares for us, but he will realize the folly in attacking Ruari."

Elspeth laughed, a hollow sound. "Folly?"

"The crown wants peace between our clan and the Mac-Donalds, I hear. Clan Fraser cannot afford such an incident just now." She glanced at Elspeth. "Magnus was here the other day to bring us some fresh trout. He told me of the lawyer who has come to Glenran, and of the queen's letter."

Elspeth scowled. "Bond of caution or not, the lads will have Ruari's head for this when they find out!"

"Then you must not tell them," Bethoc said.

Elspeth stared at her. "We cannot ignore this! Ruari MacDonald is evil to do such a thing."

"Tch," Bethoc said, her eyes drifting shut, "Ruari Mac-Donald is only simple and stupid."

"Have you no anger against him?" Elspeth asked, rising to her feet in agitation. "We will have enough anger for you, then, my cousins and I. The MacShimi will gather a tail of Frasers to march after the MacDonalds!"

"Elspeth." Bethoc fixed her with a stern glance as she pressed the poultice to her bruised jaw. "Say nothing of this."

"I cannot keep silent!"

"I want your promise."

Elspeth shook her head. "Do not ask this of me. I will not risk your safety, and Eiric's. What if he were to return and . . . do worse?"

"He will not come back here, for he will be expecting the wrath of the Frasers over this," Bethoc answered. "But say no word to anyone. If the Frasers were to strike out at the MacDonalds now in revenge, if a MacDonald were to die at their hands—" She sighed heavily. "The crown would have reason to send fire and sword after our clan. Fire and sword, Elspeth. Think what that means. Remember the queen's lieutenant and the power he has to bring disaster on our clan."

Elspeth nodded reluctantly. "Macrae could bring down swift retribution on all our clan." She sighed and shook her head in dismay. "I will keep your secret, then, so long as you are safe."

Knowing only virtues in Bethoc, Elspeth could not conceive of the hatred that must sully Ruari's mind. He had beaten Bethoc because she helped others, using her herbal knowledge and her God-given gift of the Sight. Never turning down a request from any, including members of the MacDonald clan who lived near her land, Bethoc offered her healing skills freely. Charms or augury were performed for any who asked, though Bethoc never expected payment. She was often given gifts of food or household goods or livestock. Bowls of oats or milk were sometimes left on her doorstep, a sign that if she was regarded as a witch, she was not feared but respected.

"I do not understand," Elspeth said. "Healers and those with the Sight are thought special in the Highlands. But Ruari and his brothers—" She shook her head, remembering the taunts at the stream the other day, and recalling other such insults, although Ruari had never threatened Elspeth physically.

But then, she thought bitterly, surely he knew that her cousins would butcher him like a beast if he ever made such a move against her. Elspeth fervently hoped that she would soon be able to tell her cousins the truth of this day. She would like to see them ride against Ruari; she would go with them.

Bethoc sighed. "Elspeth, *mo cuachag,* Ruari and his brothers drink fear and think it wisdom. There are some like them, who cannot understand how we see things beyond earthly sight. God has given us eyes to see into His world. It frightens some."

"They think it evil to have such a gift?"

"They do," Bethoc murmured, closing her eyes. "The

fear began in the rantings of those who would change the
Holy Church to suit their own ideas. Their teachings move
north now, out of the Sasunnach world and into the Highlands, like a foul cloud. Ruari and others like him listen to
the ideas of these fanatical men. And they think us evil,
we who have the Sight."

"But you have never done ill to any," Elspeth protested.
"You heal and help and advise. You were a good wife to
your husband, and a good mother to your daughters. When
I needed to learn about my own Sight, you became my
teacher. And you have been the only mother that little Eric
has ever known." She glanced at the curtained bed briefly.
"Who could fear you? How can anyone perceive you as
evil?"

Bethoc did not answer for a long moment, her eyes
closed. "Before the end of your lifetime," she said, her
voice flat and slow, "after I am gone, there will be wide-
spread hatred of the sisters and brothers of the Sight. They
will be hunted and accused of evil deeds. Horrible deaths
will come to them."

"We are not evil," Elspeth whispered in protest.

"Most seers are not. But some there are who look to the
dark side of the power. One or two evil ones among many
will condemn the lot." Bethoc opened her eyes.

"This cannot be," Elspeth breathed.

"In my heart I have known this will come to pass for
some time, *mo cuachag*," Bethoc said, and passed a hand
over her eyes.

Elspeth helped Bethoc to the bed, lifting Eiric out when
the child whimpered softly, waking up. Elspeth gave her a
bright smile and a soft greeting, fetched a little cup of goat's
milk, and then sat with Eiric in her lap.

Smoothing the glossy tangle of dark curls, she sang a soft
tune. Eiric listened, sipping the milk, dribbling some liquid
down her chin and onto Elspeth's hand.

Elspeth thought again about Ruari MacDonald's cruelty.
She could not imagine any man so brutal as to beat a de-
fenseless woman with his sword. Rage rose in her, and she

squeezed her eyes shut against its power. She had promised to do nothing.

Marrying Ruari was unthinkable now. She could not tell her cousins what had happened here today. But Ruari Mac-Donald would pay well for his deed. Somehow, she would see to it.

She had come here hoping to discuss her strange vision of the queen's lawyer with Bethoc, but that was not possible now. Elspeth decided to tell Bethoc soon, perhaps in a few days.

As for Bethoc's ominous prophecy regarding those with the Sight, Elspeth knew little about matters of southern thinking and Protestant ideas. Most of the Highlands, including the Fraser clan, still remained Catholic, unconcerned by the dictates of Lowland ministers.

The queen's lawyer had already made it clear that he did not believe in prophecies. Macrae had even thought that she schemed up the vision in an effort to scare him away. Perhaps he shared this Protestant distrust of the Sight, although he did not look like a man who would succumb to ideas based on fear.

Well then, she thought, let Duncan Macrae think what he would. She would say no more to him of her vision. Shifting Eiric to her other knee, she kissed the warm crown of the little girl's head.

She remembered his arms around her, and an unwilling tremor spiraled through her. Undeniably, he raised odd feelings in her. She would be glad to see the letter signed. Then he would ride away on his tall horse, and she would never hear of him again, would never know if he lived or died.

"My dark little lamb," she whispered to Eiric. "I have just remembered that I brought you a new friend today. A young bog beast. And I think your grandmother, who loves you so very well, will let you keep her."

Softly, Elspeth began to croon a song, a quiet, soothing melody. Music often brought her peace and calm; she surrendered now to the sweet, lilting rhythms.

As Elspeth sang, Eiric hummed and clapped her small hands, trying to follow the rhythm. When the lamb poked its dark, narrow muzzle through the open doorway, she cried out in delight and wriggled down from Elspeth's lap.

Chapter 7

"O waly, waly up the bank,
And waly, waly down the brae,
And waly, waly by yon burnside ..."
—*"Waly, Waly, Love Be Bonny"*

A leather ball the size of a hen's egg flew in a high arc over Duncan's head and thunked down on the ground. Bouncing once and rolling a little farther, it landed on a bare hillock close to where Callum stood.

"Well struck, Kenneth!" Callum yelled as he pointed at a small hole nearby that had been dug in the turf. Kenneth, waving, walked up the hill to join him.

Tucking his borrowed golf club under his arm, Duncan walked alongside Magnus toward another knoll. Shaking his head, he thought in dismay about his own luck that morning, which was not nearly as good as Kenneth now enjoyed. Instead, he felt as if he had spent hours knocking a fair host of those little feather-stuffed balls into tough snags of heather, boggy puddles, and shallow burns. The leather-covered featheries, as they were called, were too easily lost in the heather and bracken, and had grown soggy with water.

The way he had played this morning would not have revealed to anyone watching that he had any experience at the golf. Often enough, though, he had managed to strike close enough to the intended turf hole, tapping the featherie with the hawthorn head of the club and watching the ball roll easily across grass that had been nuzzled short by sheep. But far too many times he had swung, missed, chopped into turf or rocks, or watched helplessly as the ball had plopped into water. He had fought winds and moist grasses and the unfamiliar feel of the borrowed ashwood club—too short for his grip, he had decided glumly—until Magnus and Kenneth and Callum had begun to look at him with sympathy in their eyes.

Sighing heavily, Duncan shoved back his hair, which blew across his brow in the stiff breeze, and moved a few feet away to lean the polished head of his club against the ground. He practiced his swing while waiting for Magnus to strike his current shot. Curling his hands around the cloth-wrapped *whippen,* shifting his fingers, he tested the slight, supple give of the ashwood shaft; swinging, he felt the resistant push of the wind.

All the frustrations of this morning's game, he thought suddenly, reminded him sharply of his failure, so far, to gain signatures for the letter of caution.

For now, at least, he was disappointed on all fronts in games played with Frasers. Since Alasdair's departure, he had continued to think about how to earn the Frasers' trust. Certainly, if an opportunity came up, he would not hesitate to advise them on raiding techniques. If the Frasers were determined to raid before the bond was signed, he would do his best to ensure they did it carefully, without incurring a full-scale battle with the MacDonalds.

Although he was a representative of the crown and the law here, he was prepared to turn a blind eye until the bond was signed. He had no choice. Knowing how unimportant legalities were in the Highlands, he knew that the young chief and his equally young bodyguard needed coaxing in order to sign the document. If that coaxing took the form of raiding, hunting, golfing, and fishing with them, then so be it.

As yet he had heard no mention of raids being planned, and did not honestly expect such to occur within hearing of the queen's lieutenant. Nor had there been any retaliation for the Fraser raid last week. Possibly the MacDonalds were unaware of that embarrassing venture onto their land.

Yesterday, Duncan had gone fishing with Hugh and Ewan, and had learned how to club trout. He had thoroughly enjoyed the day, and the meal that evening. He had always had an appetite for fish, and Callum had generously

given him his own portion. No progress had been made
with regard to the bond of caution, but Duncan knew now
that he need only wait. His customary patience was gaining
ascendance again.

Duncan had been glad, early this morning, of Magnus's
invitation to play at the golf. The day was too fine to spend
it explaining and cajoling. Hugh Fraser was a clever chief,
but young and incredibly stubborn. He continued to insist
that there was no need for the bond of caution.

The MacShimi's quiet refusals were as resistant and constant as the wind that Duncan now fought with his slim
wooden golf stick. Sighing heavily, he set down his stick
and watched Magnus balance a featherie ball on top of a
small rock.

Magnus swung hard and fast, sending the ball very near
the mark. The chief's cousins had proven to be skilled, bold
golf players, who swung fine clubs made by an Inverness
bow maker and had a barrel full of expensive Flemish-
made featheries, recently traded for five barrels of smoked
fish. A sheep-nibbled moor served as their course, dug with
a crazed pattern of holes. A long course, they had called it.

Duncan almost laughed as he looked around. They had
walked so far that he could hardly see the misted outline
of Castle Glenran, a league away in the distance. At this
pace, he thought, they would be knocking featheries into
the eastern sea by nightfall.

Raw, windswept hills and rocky moorland ran toward
distant mountains dusted purple with heather. Just underfoot, the grasses were turning a late-summer gold, grazed
flat by sheep. Duncan breathed deeply of the sweet, moist
air. The spitting mist of the past few days had cleared today
to warm sunlight.

Suddenly he was glad to be back in the Highlands, even
if he was only here temporarily to negotiate the bond with
these genial but uncooperative Frasers. Standing here now,
he could not regret the journey north. He had not seen
these blue-purple hills or inhaled air as sweet and clear as
this for far too long. Looking to the west, he saw the faded
contours of the mountains that led to Kintail and Dulsie.

A pang of longing, keen and deep, twisted in his gut. Alasdair would have traversed those hills by now, and must surely be at Dulsie Castle. Duncan abruptly turned away.

He looked toward Castle Glenran in the distance. The stark tower house, a gray-walled fortress, rose solid and square on a grassy knoll, overlooking a small loch, or lochan, which lay just south of the great loch called Ness.

Squinting, Duncan noticed several tiny shapes moving along a hill behind the castle. A rider with a group of several running gillies descended the far-off slope. Gillies were male servants, a kind of bodyguard, who ran in attendance beside a chief or a laird; often delivering messages back and forth, they were loyal men and fine fighters. Duncan wondered who the mounted man might be; usually only great lairds or chiefs brought that number of gillies along. These runners' bright plaids were like red splotches against the dun and green hills, while the single rider wore somber dark colors.

He shrugged after a moment and walked on to meet Magnus. At this distance he could not even be sure that the travelers were headed toward Glenran.

"Kenneth has an eye like a hawk," Magnus said as Duncan joined him. He pointed toward his cousins, who were celebrating another of Kenneth's lucky shots. "And his aim is as good as his eye. He cannot be bested out here on the long course."

"He must be a good tracker, then, with such an eye," Duncan commented. "A useful man to have on a raid, I would think."

"He is." Magnus glanced at Duncan. "And he and Callum are both fine men to have at your back, with a lance or an arrow. Elspeth is the better tracker, though, in the black of night or in the day."

"Oh?" Duncan placed his featherie and tested his stroke.

"She seems to know just where the cattle are. Or where the deer are when we go hunting. The Sight has its uses," Magnus said. Seeing that Duncan was ready to make his stroke, he stopped speaking and stood back.

"Dhia!" Duncan swore as the wind swooped up the

featherie, which careened left, rolled down a hill, and
landed in a small burn. Duncan swore again. Magnus shook
his head in sympathy as both men descended the slope.

Grimacing in disgust, Duncan stepped into the cold burn
and angled his club, his high boots protecting his legs from
the chill. He swung, splashing widely, to launch the water-
laden ball into the air. Halfway up the slope, it fell and
began to roll down. Before it could land back in the burn,
Duncan ran to swing at it again.

"You use Elspeth as a tracker?" he asked after stubbornly beating the ball back up the steep slope.

"We do. She has a fine sense of where to find the
animals."

Duncan blinked at him in disbelief. He had never heard
of such a thing. A tracker should know the lay of the land
like the hairs of his own hand, not guess at it, or even
worse, divine the knowledge. "Well, then. I should have
asked your cousin Elspeth how my game would fare
today," he grumbled. "Perhaps then I need not have come
out here."

"If she foresaw this game, she would have kept silent out
of her soft heart," Magnus said. Duncan slid him a glance.
"But I would not have asked any favors of her this morning. She was in no mood for pleasant speech. Since she
visited with Bethoc MacGruer a few days past, she has
been snappish as a cat." Magnus thoughtfully scratched the
brown and gold sand of his beard. "None of us have had
a kind word from her."

Magnus took the next shot as Duncan watched. Then
they walked over the moor toward another small hole, and
Duncan spoke.

"Do you really believe the girl can find hidden cattle or
foretell the future?" he asked.

"If the Sight comes to her, she can indeed. She has done
it all her life, and told truly each time." He glanced at
Duncan. "She saw some vision when you arrived at the
stream, though I do not know what it was. But should the
girl say a word of warning to you, listen well to her."

"She told me some warning: leave or suffer death," Duncan said. "I thought it nonsense. She would like to see me leave here, I know." He looked up, hoping for a reaction, but Magnus was silent, his dark blue eyes unreadable.

Magnus stood back, and Duncan swung wide to send the featherie sailing cleanly, at last, toward a hole marked by a stick and a scrap of heather. As it bounced once and dropped in, Duncan laughed out loud in amazement.

"I could not have wished for a better shot," Magnus said, smiling. He gestured ahead. "There are two other holes at this end of the moor, and then we go back."

Duncan nodded. "When we get back to Glenran, I will go over the document again. Meet with me in the hall, and tell your cousins to do the same."

"You will not give up until the paper is signed, I think."

"Indeed, I will not."

Magnus narrowed his eyes as he looked up at the sky. "We will not sign until the MacShimi does. We are his bodyguard," he said simply. "There is not much good in a feud, I know that, even one with the MacDonalds. But our clans have been fighting since before we were born. We cannot stop so quickly just for a bit of paper, even one sent by the queen. Wait a bit."

"I will wait as long as it takes. But tell Hugh Fraser the sense in making the bond as you see it."

Magnus laughed, short and mirthless. A breeze gently swayed his golden braids, and he shaded his eyes with a flat hand, peering into the distance. "Elspeth's half brother may wish to comment on where her signature goes."

"Half brother?" Duncan frowned, puzzled. "Are you not all cousins? Which of you is her brother?"

"We are cousins here at Glenran, fostered together. Elspeth has a half brother, though no Fraser is he. Now and again he comes for a visit. Look." He gestured toward the slopes that lay beyond Glenran. "Just there he rides, see, with his gillies running alongside. They will reach the castle sooner than we would even if we left now."

Looking across the moor, Duncan noticed the group that he had seen earlier, the single rider with several runners, all so tiny against the rough, rocky contours of the hills that they looked like fleas crawling over the gloved knuckles of a giant.

"Well then," Magnus pronounced with a sigh, shouldering his golf club, "Hugh will be wanting a rescue from Robert Gordon."

"Her half brother is a Gordon?" Duncan asked quickly.

Magnus nodded. "He is. The Gordons are not in favor with the crown just now, we have heard."

Duncan huffed out a wry sound. "The Gordons, my friend, are in deep disgrace. Their chief's heir has been stripped of his title. I would guess that you have heard the story of George Gordon's trial for treason."

Magnus nodded. "Grim indeed. The council sent you as the royal lieutenant in place of the Gordons."

"They did." Duncan glanced again at the party of men approaching in the distance. "How is it that Elspeth has a Gordon for a brother?"

"Elspeth's father, Simon, married a Gordon's widow, who had a young son. Simon Fraser died at Blar-na-Léine, and his wife passed a few months later, after Elspeth's birth. Robert was but five or six years old then."

"He was not raised by the Frasers?"

Magnus shook his head. "Robert went with his Gordon kin. But Lachlann Fraser, who fostered us all, was Elspeth's uncle, so he raised her as if she were his own daughter." He sighed and fixed serious blue eyes on Duncan. "There were many of us who were taken in at Glenran. Fostering is a common thing—kin often raises kin in the Highlands—but Lachlann and his wife took as many as they could, mostly babes whose parents had died. They had one son of their own, Callum."

Duncan listened with keen interest. "How many children fostered at Glenran?"

"Fifteen and more we were, babes and young children. I was four when I was brought here. Elspeth and Kenneth came later, newly born. Then Lachlann took in Ewan and some others you have not met—David and Andrew, Tomas and James and Iain, Diarmid and Domhnall—all babes, most of them barely walking."

Duncan blinked in amazement. Lachlann Fraser's generous spirit toward these tiny children years ago was more than admirable. It demonstrated the love and pride within this clan. "Were there so many orphans, then, after the battle?"

"Too many. But there were also many Fraser widows, mothers struggling to care for their children without a man in the household to hunt and herd. Lachlann was not the only one to take in fosterlings. Other families did the same around Fraser lands, fostering as many young ones as they could support.

"More than fifteen babes," Duncan said. "I had four brothers and two sisters—and our home was loud enough."

"Loud hardly describes Glenran when we were small," Magnus said, chuckling. "Lachlann's wife needed help with all the children, so Flora MacKimmie came to live with us. Lachlann was her brother. Flora brought her four grown daughters with her. A formidable pack of nursemaids those girls were, and kept sharp eyes on us, until they wed and left Glenran."

Magnus bent to place his featherie ball on a little stone. In silence he aimed, then swung his club. Watching the flight of the ball, he nodded in satisfaction when it landed well, then turned to look sharply at Duncan.

"Lachlann was one of only five Frasers who survived Blar-na-Léine. He did what he could to protect the fatherless children of the clan," Magnus said. "He taught us to read and write, for he had been educated in France as a youth and had a scholar's heart. But he taught us, above all, to have loyalty and pride in our clan. Our fathers, all of them, died on the shores of Loch Lochy at the hands of the MacDonalds. Remember that, Macrae, when you ask for our signatures on a promise to stop this feud."

Duncan nodded slowly. "I understand more than you think, Magnus. My father and my brothers died at the hands of the MacDonalds. Such a loss is not easily forgotten."

Magnus turned to him in surprise. "If you have no love

for the MacDonalds, then why do you try to end our feud
with them?"

"The crown has sent me here to attend to this task. I
will do that regardless of my own feelings," he said flatly.
They walked ahead in search of Magnus's featherie ball.
Duncan looked again toward the advancing party of rider
and runners in the distance. "I know this Robert Gordon,
I think," he said.

"Do you? He is laird of Blackrigg, well south of here."

Duncan thoughtfully rubbed his jaw. "Robert Gordon of
Blackrigg was at the inns of court in Edinburgh when I
studied law there. We interned together. All I truly recall
of him was that the fellow kept much to himself. He lacked
a sense of humor too, I think."

"Ah," Magnus said. "That would be Robert."

"Even with the Gordons in disfavor," Duncan said, "I
am surprised that the council did not send Elspeth's half
brother with this bond of caution. He is a lawyer, after all."

Magnus laughed ruefully. "Robert deliver a letter of caution to the Frasers? Hah. The man would not pledge himself for us or for anyone." Shaking his head, he balanced
his club to swing. Duncan stood back again as Magnus
tapped the featherie cleanly into a turf hole. Then Magnus
scooped it up and stood to wave to Kenneth and Callum.

"Robert Gordon rides to Glenran," Magnus called, walking toward them. "Just there, see."

Duncan did not miss the grim glance that was shared
between the Fraser cousins. He turned to look again at the
party in the distance, who now skirted the edge of the little
lochan. Soon they would enter the gates of Glenran, which
rose smooth and solid beside the water.

"Well. A few shots more, then," Kenneth said.

"Robert will be annoyed that we are not there to greet
him," Magnus said affably. Duncan glanced at him.

"Ah. That he will. Good," Kenneth said, and stood back
to let Callum take the next shot.

"Annoyed? Good," Callum grunted, and swung.

Looking from one Fraser to another, Duncan saw a distinct glimmer in each pair of eyes, though whether from satisfaction or amusement, he could not tell.

"They are waiting for you, Duncan Macrae," Flora said, "on the roof."

"The roof?" Duncan asked. Setting his beaker of ale down on the table in the great hall, he glanced at his golf partners, lately returned from the moor. Thirsty from the long game that they had played, they shrugged in unconcerned response as they drank their ale. Crossing the hall toward Flora, who stood in the doorway, Duncan asked again. "On the roof, you say?"

Flora nodded her heavily jowled face and pointed upward with a long, knotty finger. "The MacShimi did say, when the long-robe returns, send that one to the roof." She directed her finger toward the stairs.

Duncan quickly mounted the spiral steps, which curved around a central pillar, his boots scuffing on the worn stone. Afternoon sun slanted through the arrow slits cut into the outer wall.

Climbing to the uppermost level, he reached a small landing lit by one arrow-slit opening. A rough-hewn wooden door led outside to the roof and parapet wall. He heard voices beyond the door, raised in argument.

Through the tiny window, motes spun along a slender shaft of daylight. He stepped toward the door and reached out to grasp the iron latch. He heard an angry curse, uttered in Elspeth's clear, light voice.

Those pure, silvery tones, in other circumstances, might have reminded him of an angel. At this moment he thought only of an avenging angel. His hand tightened around the handle.

Pushed from the other side, the door burst open. As the heavy oak planking slammed into the bridge of his nose, his vision went momentarily dark, then red and gold before the first flash of shocking pain hit him.

"Dhia!" he exploded, and pressed his hand to his nose to subdue the pain with pressure. He took his palm away,

saw no blood, and touched his face gingerly. His nose throbbed beneath the cover of his hand.

Elspeth had stopped short in the doorway and was looking up at him in evident surprise. Behind her, sunlight made a golden halo of her hair. She stepped onto the small landing and slammed the door closed behind her with a resounding, apparently satisfying crash. The iron latch rattled and fell still.

"What are you doing?" she demanded, glaring up at him.

"Holding my nose," he answered in muffled irritation. Massaging the bridge of his nose with two fingers, he frowned at her over the rim of his hand.

Ignoring his intent stare, she stepped sideways, passing through the shaft of light that beamed across the landing. For an instant as he watched, she seemed to glow, her hair turning to delicate copper, her smooth brow and cheek to creamy gold. When she looked back at him, her eyes caught the light. Their hue was extraordinary, like transparent silver, or sunlit water.

In spite of the pain he nursed, Duncan involuntarily sucked in his breath. He had earlier thought of angels when he had heard the sweet, light air of her voice; now he thought of fairy beings. The girl was sylvan and delicate, with an unearthly purity in spite of the tartaned plaid, the linen shirt, and the tousled, thick plait of hair.

"I did not know you were there," she said over her shoulder. Her clipped tone offered scant apology. "You will have a bruise for your trouble, I think. Is it listening you are doing, here at the door? Do you seek information for the queen's council? Ask my half brother, then. He lives in the same pocket that keeps you!"

The gossamer moment disappeared abruptly. Stepping toward her, Duncan shot out an arm to block her way at the head of the curving steps. Leaning his weight into his hand, palm flat against the stone wall, he looked down at her.

"I am no spy, Elspeth Fraser," he snapped nasally.

She looked up at him, her breath heaving in her throat. "Are you not?" she asked. "What is a spy but a man who lingers at doors and follows others through the dark of night?"

Narrowing his eyes at the insult, he lanced her with an angry look. Her eyes skipped away. Leaning on his extended hand, he stood a head taller than Elspeth. He felt as if he caged her in that small space. Another step, the slightest movement of his other arm, and he could trap her against the wall. He considered it briefly, for she had a bitter edge to her tongue. And his nose throbbed. He thought he deserved some apology.

Even in the midst of anger and pain, he was aware of the indefinable pull that he felt each time he saw her, as if a whirlpool swept him along its outer edge. He wondered if she felt it too. But when he looked at her again, he saw only a cool spark of anger in her eyes. His own temper began to flare.

"If I had not followed you through the dark of night on your raid," he said, lowering his voice to a growl, "—and believe me, you Fraser cousins were easy enough to follow with the noise you made—all of you might have been beset by angry MacDonalds. And you, my girl, would have been swallowed whole by the peat bog."

She lifted her chin. "What does a lawyer know of rounding up cattle? We were fine, needing no help. And I would have pulled myself and the lamb out of that bog in quick time."

"Ah, well, then, my apologies. And your apology to me—?" He rubbed his nose meaningfully.

"I am sorry that I did not know you were spying behind the door," she snapped.

Duncan rolled his eyes. "Graciously said."

Elspeth scowled. He studied with interest the delicate wrinkle between her slender brows. "Go on, then," she said, gesturing toward the door. "They wait for you. The MacShimi, my cousin Ewan, and my half brother Robert Gordon."

"On the parapet? Do they expect an attack?"

"They do not. Hugh often holds meetings on the roof.

He enjoys it there." She frowned up at him. "Go, then. You and my half brother have much in common, I think."

"And what," he said between his teeth, "might that be?"

"Robert has come here to demand that I marry Ruari MacDonald within the month. An order you would approve."

"Ah. And so you gave him the same forthright answer that you gave us in the hall the first evening I was here."

"I did." She looked up at him defiantly.

He lifted an eyebrow. "Do you always answer any mention of marriage with the help of stout doors?"

"Robert has no right to demand this of me. The Mac-Shimi, as chief of the Frasers, is my guardian. My father is dead, and Robert is not a Fraser."

"Then whatever the MacShimi decides for you, that you must do. Where is the difficulty? He and Robert both want you to wed this MacDonald. Some of your cousins do as well."

"And the queen's lieutenant approves." She scowled again.

Duncan shrugged. But an odd twist swirled in his gut. Suddenly he no longer approved of this marriage arrangement. Before he could follow his own contrary thought to discover why, Elspeth had stamped her foot in blatant anger.

"None can make me wed this man!" she burst out.

"You seem certain of that."

"I am." She spoke through tightly pinched lips. "Ruari MacDonald will not live long enough to wed."

Duncan watched her warily. A chilling suspicion occurred to him. He stepped closer and circled strong fingers around the back of her neck. Though she resisted, he tipped her head up with his thumb. Her hair slipped over his hand like cool silk. Her gray eyes sparked like flint.

"Another prophecy, Elspeth Fraser?" His quiet voice toughened with anger. "Have you warned Ruari MacDonald of his awful fate? First you attempt to frighten me away from my duty. And now you try to avoid this marriage the same way."

"Do not mock me," she whispered.

He leaned close enough to threaten, so close that his breath fluttered the soft, wild curls that edged her brow. With his restraining hand he felt the tension in her neck as she looked up at him. Delicate muscles in her throat rippled as she swallowed in the silence.

"This is a dangerous, witless game that you play," he said.

"I do not—"

"Never claim knowledge of a man's death, my girl," he went on. "Unless you have seen his death with your own eyes."

He heard her sharply indrawn breath. With a muffled exclamation that sounded like a sob, she thumped a fist against his chest and pushed. He would not let her pass. Grabbing her shoulder, he held her firmly in place. Swirling currents seemed to race unbidden through his body whenever, wherever, he touched her, but he tightened his will against them.

"Would you call me a liar?" she sobbed, pushing again at his chest. "I will tell you this, and it is no lie—Ruari MacDonald will never wed me. I will kill myself if I must! And that is no prophecy!"

"Indeed. That sounds like an angry threat," he said. She nodded. Her nostrils flared and her breath came too fast. "How does a feud cause you to hate this one man so?" he asked.

"Surely the queen's lawyer knows what a feud can do." Her voice was bitter. "Let me pass."

Keeping his gaze and his grip on her, he suddenly remembered the vile taunts that Ruari and his brothers had called out by the stream. They had very nearly accused Elspeth of witchcraft.

Certainly there was more to this refusal than she had told anyone, he thought. He would wager that her cousins were unaware of her intense anger against Ruari MacDonald. Surely they would not support the marriage offer if they knew.

With that quick understanding came a frisson of dread.

"Elspeth," he said slowly. Afraid to ask, he knew he must. "Has this MacDonald done harm to you? Has he laid a hand on you?"

She flashed her eyes away from his. "Let me go, long-robe."

"Tell me," he said. His earlier suspicion of her so-called prophecies now paled to absurdity. Fear and anger stung him as he thought of what MacDonald could have done to this girl. "If Ruari has touched you, your cousins will kill him—"

"I know that well."

"—they would kill him, and I would ride with them." He felt the sudden and total conviction of his words. She stared up at him as if in surprise. "Has he harmed you?" he asked.

"Ruari has not harmed me," she said quietly, looking away.

He bent forward to hear her. She lifted her head, and her cheek grazed his in passing.

A sensation like sudden, hot lightning shot through his body at the casual touch of cool, soft skin against the grate of his unshaven cheek. Silken hair slipped over the back of his hand at her neck. His hands on her softened to draw her nearer.

She held still, her breath a soft caress near his mouth. He shifted slightly, and her mouth met his so easily that it surprised him. Soft, dry, tentative, her lips brushed his and lifted away, more touch than kiss. A surge plummeted to his loins, intense and demanding, and the whirlpool began to spin. He took a deep breath to steady himself against the pull.

She drew back and looked at him, her eyes wide, her breathing as pronounced as his. "You would ride after Ruari?"

"If he harmed you, I would," he murmured.

Her brows drew together. She pushed his chest hard and broke away. Duncan lifted his hands and stepped aside to let her pass. He watched as she ran down the curving steps and out of sight.

Sighing heavily, he rubbed his aching nose. Once again

a few moments with this girl had thrown him into some
mad eddy of emotion and impulse.

He reached for the iron latch, opened the door, and
stepped out onto the parapet.

A breeze lifted his hair as Duncan advanced toward the
three men who stood by the parapet wall. From up here,
he noticed, the view extended for miles. Light flowed like
liquid over heathery slopes, and the lochan below sparkled.
Overhead, a few geese flew past, honking loudly.

"Aha!" Ewan exclaimed as Duncan came nearer. "Look
at you. Caught the rest of Elspeth's temper, I think. Black
as a badger about the eyes you will be by morning. And
she, the little wildcat, will still be angry at all of us."

"I bumped into the door," Duncan said.

"A door named Elspeth Fraser," Ewan said, and smiled
over at his cousin Hugh, who nodded.

"Elspeth has a disgraceful temper. Someone must control
her." Speaking Gaelic in clipped tones, a man stepped out
from behind the taller Frasers and looked coolly at Duncan.

"Master Robert Gordon," Duncan said. "It has been
long since we last met. Inns of court, was it not?"

"It was," Robert replied. "Macrae of Dulsie. Greetings."

Duncan held out his hand, and Robert grasped it. Long-
hooded eyes, a flat gray-blue, assessed him openly. Although it had been over ten years, Duncan had remembered the distinctive coppery hair and the down-turned
mouth. He now saw the vague resemblance between Robert and his half sister.

Where Elspeth's coloring was warm and delicate, like
sunlight and roses, Robert Gordon's skin had a sour, yellow
look. His lanky hair had brassy tone, and his short beard
was sparse. Unflattering but stylish, his slashed black satin
doublet, trimmed with gold-thread embroidery and a stiff
yellow lace ruff, added to the rancid impression.

Though a Highlander by birth and property, Robert wore
only a narrow bit of tartan in the Lowland manner, crossing
the front of his doublet and tossed over his shoulder like
an afterthought. Robert's slender frame seemed slight be-

side the Frasers in their wrapped plaids. Even Ewan, who
was not as tall as his cousins, was brawny beside Robert.

"Elspeth has never been encouraged to behave like a
proper young woman," Robert said, his voice nasal and
refined. "Now she has injured the queen's own representative in a fit of temper. This is shameful. Obviously I have
made the correct decision to wed her off."

Duncan raised his eyebrows. Near him, he heard Ewan
swear softly. Hugh turned to Duncan, frowning. "Robert
has taken it upon himself to accept the MacDonald offer.
He has promised Elspeth's hand to Ruari within a month's
time. He has already sent word to the MacDonald chief.
Without authority from us—"

"She is my charge by the blood of siblings," Robert said.

"I am chief of the Frasers," Hugh said, rounding on Robert to stare down at him from a height advantage of several
inches. "I am her guardian. You had no right to accept
the offer."

"You gave no answer to the MacDonalds," Robert said.
"They were anxious to seal the bargain and appealed to
me."

"That wolfpack deserves no courtesy from us," Ewan
said. "We would have answered them in good time."

"Wolves they may be," Robert murmured. "And I have
given them your best ewe to appease their appetites."

Duncan glanced at the Frasers, while masking his own
sudden anger. The MacShimi sucked in a sharp breath.
Ewan's face was suffused with a dark flush.

"No woman is a sheep," Ewan said. "And our answer,
when we chose to give it, would have been a refusal."

"But Hugh agrees," Robert said. "When I arrived today,
he told me that he was still considering the marriage offer."

"I was not aware then that you had already promised
her," Hugh said, his voice hard-edged. "Do not twist my
words. I told you that we had not decided. And I have
never agreed with you on any matter."

Robert shrugged elegantly. "Regardless, it is done, and
will be the best course for all of you. The feud will be
quelled after the wedding."

"And you mean to accept credit for that with the Privy Council," Ewan said caustically.

Robert shrugged. "I am pleased to help the council to resolve this feud." He looked at Duncan. "I understand that you have not yet collected signatures for the letter of caution."

"We are discussing the matter," Duncan said, feeling as much on guard, suddenly, as the Frasers seemed to be.

"I would hear Macrae's legal opinion," Hugh said. "What of Robert's promise to the MacDonalds?"

Aware of Robert's flat glare, Duncan looked at Hugh. "The signed bond of caution will be the only acceptable legal proof of a truce between the clans," he said. "A marriage is not a formal declaration of truce. Without the bond the council members will not care about weddings."

"I need no legal advice from you, a man who has pursued the disaffection of a Highland clan," Robert said to Duncan.

Duncan blinked at this venomous reference to his minor involvement with the Gordon trials. He said nothing.

Robert looked at Hugh. "The Frasers should have forced Elspeth long ago to learn her woman's place. I have only put her in it at last."

"You know what Elspeth is, Robert. She needs our protection, not the force of our will," Ewan said.

"We are the ones who need protection from her will." Robert tipped his head toward Duncan. "Look at Macrae's bruises."

"Elspeth deserves our respect," Hugh said. "Because she is a woman, and because she has the Sight."

"Sight or not, she holds the key to ending your feud. The key is in her womanhood. Use it."

"If any key interests you, man, it is the key that will open doors for you at court," Hugh snapped.

Robert flared his nostrils. "I only offer help to you. Take it or not."

Duncan turned away from the tension and looked out over the hills. The breeze that buffeted his head and shoulders blew away the rest of Robert's sneering commentary as he spoke to Hugh.

Duncan felt a mounting sympathy for Elspeth. Now he understood why she had been so angry when she had first knocked into him. She had too much pride and too strong a temper to accept Robert's arrogant gesture with the Mac-Donalds. Perhaps Frasers would not use women willingly, but this Gordon apparently had no qualms about using his own half sister to gain greater favor for himself. The man clearly had no interest in Elspeth's happiness.

Duncan could only approve of her adamant refusal now. Though the marriage had a distinct political advantage, he no longer thought it feasible. After hearing Robert, he regretted having ever spoken in favor of the arrangement.

He leaned a shoulder against hard stone and looked out. Skimming over the rocky shoulder of a hill, a small figure moved rapidly, her bright plaid and coppery hair catching the sun. Half listening to the bitter argument that continued behind him, he relaxed against the stone support and watched.

Elspeth ran easily, freely, taking the rocks and tufts in downward leaps. Duncan felt a strange tugging at his insides, not lust but something more subtle and poignant, as if he wanted, even needed, to be out there with her rather than here.

He remembered running like that through the hills, a long time ago. He sighed; the queen's representative should fix his attention on the legal quagmire at hand.

As he turned away, he had an impulse to defend the girl against her sneering half brother. He decided to offer his legal opinion. Whether or not Robert wanted to hear it, the Frasers should know every angle. He cleared his throat.

"This marriage promise can be retracted," he said.

Robert turned to blink at him. "What?"

"Because Robert is not the girl's proper guardian, no binding promise has been made. Send that word to the chief of the MacDonalds. Then it is still up to the MacShimi to decide."

"We will tell them that you only sent your opinion on the matter and not a binding promise, Robert," Ewan said.

"Tell the MacDonalds that I have made a mistake?" Robert asked. "Are you fools? The MacDonalds are a proud clan. They will not only take Elspeth by force, they will take my head with her!" His glance, narrow and pale, shot around the group. "And all of yours as well!"

Hugh shrugged. "Macrae is right. I will send word to John MacDonald that you have overstepped your authority. My cousin, I think, will not marry a MacDonald after all. She will be promised to another. And quickly."

"What?" Three men swiveled their heads toward the MacShimi.

"Who?" Duncan asked.

Hugh shrugged. "There are many kinsmen who would wed her. Ten lads at least who are distant cousins. Two or three in my own bodyguard at Lovat, good lads. I will find someone."

Duncan frowned at the thought of anyone else marrying the girl. A slight brush of the lips, a whirlpool spin of sudden lust and longing, was no claim to Elspeth. He had best stay out of this. Certainly the clan chief had a full right to assign a husband to her with no further comment from the queen's lawyer.

"We could send word to the chief of the Grants, or to Clan Macintosh," Ewan added. "They must have a kinsman willing to take a wife. But what man is brave enough to wed a girl who has refused a MacDonald?"

"Ruari will not forget this. Elspeth may be in danger," the MacShimi said. "If she is to be married at all, she should be wedded and bedded and taken away from here soon."

Robert snorted contemptuously. "What does it matter to us if she turns up her nose at Ruari MacDonald? She would settle down to her new hearth, and soon enough have babes to worry over. And we would have what we want from it. If we do as Macrae says, we will lose our heads in some night raid."

The others turned to stare at him. "That head of yours," Ewan drawled, "will most likely be taken by your sister."

Chapter 8

Then by it came the Elfin Queen,
And laid her hand on me,
And from that time since ever I mind,
I've been in her companie.
                                          —"Tam Lin"

Smoking torches cast golden pools of light over the table as Duncan stood and moved along the length of the bench to sit between Callum and Flora. He had risen from his seat beside Robert, leaving on the excuse of seeking another cup of the fine French wine that had been served at the supper.

In truth, he could not sit a moment longer beside Robert Gordon. A dry lecture on suitable physical punishment for particular crimes was not to his liking just now. The subject had once composed a grueling three-day exam that Duncan had endured at St. Andrews; he had no desire to sit through the experience again, especially with a tutor as obtuse and as opinionated as Robert. Although Elspeth had been seated on the other side of Robert, she had been silent so far, with little to say to Duncan or to her half brother.

Flora smiled at Duncan, her ruddy face framed by a wreath of iron-gray braids, the generous bosom of her dark gown covered by a tartan shawl pinned with a large silver brooch. Much of the evening she had scuttled back and forth between the great hall and the kitchen, which was located across the corridor. Under her direction, serving girls had brought platters of roast chickens and kettles of carrots and onions cooked in broth. Flora had reminded the girls to move *deiseil,* with the sun, around the table, in order to bring luck to those who ate.

Duncan had eaten his fill from his shallow wooden bowl,

and had tasted the hot, peat-flavored oatcakes spread with
honey. Flagons of red wine and sheeps' bladders of *uisge
beatha* had been poured out into pewter cups all through
supper. Duncan sipped wine now, his head spinning a little.
He welcomed that, for it numbed the dull ache in his
bruised nose. Ewan had been right, earlier today; his eye
was now ringed with a dark purple smudge.

He sipped the wine again. "A fine meal, Flora," he said.

She smiled and nodded her thanks. "Master Gordon of
Blackrigg found the roast chickens not to his liking, I
think."

Magnus, who sat across from her, leaned forward. "Robert was insulted when hens were served to him. He likely
thought a roast steer would have been more to his honor."

"As if Glenran would waste good beef on such as Robert
Gordon," Kenneth muttered, sitting nearby.

"*Ach*, you lads," Flora said. Duncan noted the gleam in
her eye and the grin that she pinched down.

"The lawyer Macrae of Dulsie, here, has not complained
of our hospitality," Callum said around a mouthful of oatcake. "We offered fish to him the first night he came here,
and no complaint from the man." He clapped Duncan on
the back.

"Good plain food we offer guests here, no roasted swans
painted gold, such as the Sasunnachs eat at the English
queen's court," Flora said.

Only half listening, Duncan looked toward Elspeth, sitting at the other end of the table. In the flickering light she
looked small and delicate. He watched her sip from her
cup, and noticed the flat look she sent Robert, as if anger
still simmered in her from her encounter with him earlier
that day.

Earlier, Hugh had asked Duncan to write a letter to re-
tract the marriage promise that Robert had made to the
MacDonalds. He intended to do that tomorrow, and wondered if Elspeth would still be so angry once the letter was
signed by Robert and sent.

Kenneth reached over and patted Duncan roughly on the
back, spilling his wine. Righting the cup, Duncan managed

to chuckle. Kenneth laughed too, so heartily that he nearly fell off the bench. Duncan reached out a quick hand to steady him.

"Tch," Flora commented to Duncan. "Look at that lad. He and one or two others are already whey-faced. I will be ministering to sore heads all day tomorrow." She shook her head and swiped some crumbs with her large hand.

"Hush," Magnus said. "What is Robert saying to Hugh?" With the others, Duncan leaned forward to hear.

"I am building a fine new addition to my family's castle at Blackrigg," Robert said. "I have commissioned painted ceilings, and I intend to fill the rooms with goods from France and Flanders. Tapestries and candlesticks, mahogany tables, silver cups and bowls. Glass windows too, and paneling."

"Is that not an excessive display for a disgraced Gordon?" Hugh asked, rolling his cup between his fingers.

Elspeth frowned and leaned forward. "Where do you get the money to pay for all of this?"

Robert smiled patronizingly. "Only a Highlander would ask such a question. Sheep, Elspeth. There is good money in raw wool and woven cloth. Scottish wool is in demand in Flanders and France. I buy lengths of cloth from local weavers for a pittance, and ask a high price overseas. A good profit."

"If you are doing so well," Elspeth said as she broke an oatcake in half, "why do you bother with me and my affairs?"

Robert's answer was too low to hear. Callum snorted derisively and leaned toward Duncan. "He bothers because he thinks he will gain favor with the Privy Council. He craves fortune and power, that man."

"I have noticed," Elspeth said loudly, "that you have given up wearing the wrapped plaid. Do you think Highland wool only good enough for trading?"

"If I had stayed with Highland ways, I would never have been able to afford to rebuild my father's castle," Robert said.

Elspeth frowned. "And what is wrong with Highland

ways? You were raised with them among your Gordon
kin."

Robert shrugged. "Many Lowlanders believe that Highlanders are unintelligent, incapable of a trade, and can only
run barefoot through heather chasing cattle. So I have
adopted southern ways and have found that beneficial."

"Too stupid, are we?" Callum called out loudly. Robert
and the others turned their heads. "We are smart enough
not to wear satins and laces like a woman and act like a
damned Sasunnach." Kenneth chuckled, and Magnus
looked pleased.

"Wear what you like, Callum Fraser," Robert answered
smoothly. "I dress no differently than any man in the
queen's private circle. Your lawyer friend, there, wears
southern dress as well. Macrae of Dulsie may come from
the Highlands, but he is no fool. I will wager that he has
found little value in Highland ways. But if this simple life
suits you Frasers, do not let my opinions concern you." He
smiled smugly.

Duncan could feel the tension rise in the Frasers surrounding him. Watching Robert, he was reminded of a
small wildcat, tawny and sly, patient and very dangerous.

Elspeth scowled. "You have been drinking imported
wine here, Robert." She gestured toward the pewter flagon
set on the tabletop. "And have you seen the cups of gold,
set with rubies, that have been at Glenran for three hundred years? King Robert the Bruce drank wine from one
of those cups when he visited a Glenran Fraser. Castle
Glenran was rebuilt over a hundred years ago. Surely it
took money for that," she snapped. "This is a stronghold
to be envied."

"Of course, and you are content with that. I look for
something better. For example, I have recently purchased
a set of tall candlesticks from Belgium, fashioned of
chased silver."

Hugh, who had been sitting back in his chair staring into
his cup, suddenly leaned forward and slammed his fist on
the table. "I have heard enough. You are eating supper in

the finest hall in all the Highlands," he said. "And we pos-
sess finer candlesticks than you could ever purchase."

"That I would like to see," Robert said.

"Then you shall." Hugh leaned over and whispered to
Elspeth. She looked startled, and then rose from her seat.
Running down the length of the table, she whispered a
word to each cousin. Then she went to the door, opened
it, and left.

"Are there treasures locked away, that you keep secret?"
Robert asked Hugh. The MacShimi shook his head and
smiled.

Duncan looked at Callum and raised his brows. Callum
leaned over. "Wait, and you shall see what a chief we have
in Hugh Fraser," he murmured.

Three servants entered the room then, holding blazing
rushlights; Duncan realized that Elspeth must have sent
them in though she had not yet returned. He relaxed
against the table, prepared to watch with great interest.

Hugh rose from the table and beckoned Robert to stand.
Plaided and brooched, the young chief was tall and handsome beside Robert, who, in spite of his fine black satin,
appeared slight and sour. Hugh went to the widest window
in the hall and threw the shutters open.

"Look there, Robert," he said. Robert Gordon leaned
forward to look. Duncan, seated at the table, turned to
watch, as did the others around him.

Beyond the open window Duncan could see the fading
sunset, a wash of rose and gold and indigo. Dark hills and
rocky crags were silhouetted against the tapestry.

"There," Hugh said, sweeping his hand toward the scene.
"That is a Highland hall. And that decoration is finer than
any hall you will ever see. Those designs have been painted
by the hands of angels."

Ah, Duncan thought, Hugh was clever. Anyone would
feel humbled in the presence of the natural magnificence
of the Highlands. Whether Robert appreciated Hugh's message was an interesting question.

Elspeth's half brother, Duncan noted, did not seem to

feel particularly humbled. He was sputtering. "That is a hill and rocks," Robert fumed. "You play me ill, Hugh Fraser."

"Ah," the MacShimi answered. "A hill with rocks. And living among these rocks and hills, my friend, is a privilege."

Duncan was beginning to enjoy Hugh's dramatic display thoroughly. He doubted that Robert Gordon would boast soon to the Frasers about his silk tapestries and mahogany tables.

"You have silver candlesticks?" Hugh asked. "I will show you a set of candlesticks with no equal anywhere on earth." He turned his head. "We would have light for our supper!"

Around the table the Fraser cousins rose from their seats and went to take the burning rushlights from the servants who had been holding them. Then the four Fraser cousins, Magnus, Callum, Ewan, and Kenneth, stood in a row and held the blazing torches high over their heads.

Tall and strong, in belted plaids, they stood motionless, their long hair falling over wide shoulders. The torches sparked and crackled, spilling a wide golden veil of light over the table. Duncan watched with silent approval.

"These," Hugh said, "are our Highland candlesticks, the lights of Clan Fraser. They have no equal anywhere. Do not doubt their worth."

The door opened, and Elspeth came into the room alone, carrying another rushlight. She had changed her plaid for a simple white gown and a tartan shawl. Walking toward her cousins, she took a place among them and held her light aloft.

Duncan sucked in his breath. Beneath the shining golden light she glowed with strength and delicacy, an angel come to earth. The brilliant flame turned her flowing hair and the white gown to purest gold. He stared in open wonder.

Then she took a step forward, lifted her chin, and began to sing.

The first notes rose so softly into the air that the song seemed a part of the air. As Duncan heard the rare quality of her voice emerge, he leaned forward, entranced. He had not known that she had this ability.

Her voice was clear as water, strong as silk. He listened to the Gaelic verses, all the time aware that he was listening to a true gift. This beautiful voice, then, must be why her family regarded her as a blessing to the clan.

Sitting beside him, Flora sniffed noisily and wiped her eyes. Duncan recognized the message of clan pride and loyalty in the song, and saw here the Frasers' keen pride. The music, and the wild sky and magnificent hills beyond the window, stirred something profound in him that had long been dormant.

Duncan loved the Highlands as much as these Frasers did. But he had left his home, choosing to stay away. Now the girl's sad, sweet song tore at his heart. He wrenched his gaze away as the last dulcet note of her song drifted into silence.

Hugh clapped a hand on Robert's shoulder and smiled. Robert frowned, pale and thin-lipped. "Let us hear no more from you regarding what is of value in the Highlands," Hugh said.

Duncan glanced again at Elspeth. Immediately she flicked her gaze toward him, her silvery eyes cool and direct. Then she looked away, the subtle movement proud and defiant.

As if a candle had flared in the dark, Duncan suddenly knew what the bond of caution meant to the Frasers. As the queen's lawyer, he offered no welcome solution to their feud with the MacDonalds. He offered a set of iron fetters to confine and humiliate them. He no longer wondered at their reticence to put their signatures to that bond. He understood why they resisted.

But despite that dauntless Highland spirit, he had to gain those signatures and leave for the Lowlands as soon as he could.

Looking at Elspeth, who stood between her tall cousins shining like a warm light, Duncan was no longer so certain that he wanted to leave Glenran.

*   *   *

Her cousins' voices reverberated throughout the hall. Elspeth yawned, listening to the boisterous clamor of song and laughter. She was too tired to take part and too restless to go to her chamber to sleep. Ewan's true, mellow voice rose now, deep and dominant over the others who sang with him. By the width of their grins and the volume of their song, Elspeth knew that her cousins had consumed a good many drams.

Flora came to sit beside her. "Look at that Robert Gordon. As sour a face as I have ever seen. He will not boast again soon of his fine hall, I think."

"I hope he took no true offense at what Hugh wanted to show him," Elspeth said. "Look, he smiles a little now, and seems to be enjoying himself well enough."

"Hmmph." Flora eyed Robert critically. "That lad's trouble is that long ago he did not have a good wallop to the bottom whenever he spoke like the king of France to his equals. The Highland way holds that no man is better than another, laird no better than shepherd, a woman no less than a man."

"Hugh reminded him of that this evening," Elspeth said. Looking up, she saw Kenneth gesture toward her, wanting her to sing with them. She shook her head in refusal.

She noticed that Duncan Macrae was watching her, his gaze steady and calm amid her cousins' good-natured turmoil. He always seemed to look at her as if he knew her well. Inhaling sharply against the yearning that stirred in her whenever she saw him, Elspeth glanced away and pulled her tartan shawl closer around the bodice of her white gown.

Ewan began another song, one of Elspeth's favorites, light and quick with a lilting rhythm. She hummed, tapping her foot, and then began to sing a little on the refrains, unable, finally, to keep silent. Ewan grinned at her.

Keenly aware that Duncan watched her, she had to focus carefully on the words so as not to lose her place in the rapid progress of the rhyme.

When Kenneth stood up and began to dance, she laughed and clapped while watching him. Intricate rhythms were

tapped out for him, and with quick, clever steps, arms held
high, Kenneth toed around two pairs of crossed swords laid
on the floor.

Magnus and Callum took their turns. Triumphant shouts
burst forth from the dancers, who now and again picked
up the swords to swing them around their heads and drop
them back to the floor. The pace was breathless. Rapid,
complicated, and dangerous, the sword dances continued
until all were exhausted, those who danced as well as those
who watched and clapped time.

"Pipes!" Kenneth shouted gleefully. Callum took up the
cry and then Magnus. "Pipes!" They pounded on the table.

Ewan whooped out loud, grabbed a container of liquor,
and left the hall. Invigorated by the music and by watching
her cousins' indefatigable dancing, Elspeth followed. Flora
came behind her, and then the cousins, including Hugh.
Glancing over her shoulder, Elspeth noticed that Duncan
was urged to come and did, while Robert declined to
follow.

Ewan had run into the yard to fetch an old man who
tended the horses at Castle Glenran; the man was the finest
piper in this part of Fraser territory, so fine that Hugh had
given him a servant to carry his pipes. Since tradition dic-
tated that the bagpipes were never played inside a hall,
those who wished to listen came outside.

The old piper, coaxed with a healthy dram of *uisge beatha,* set the pipes under his arm, pumped them full, and
began to blow. The plaintive sound whined and then grew
on the breeze. As the piper walked through the yard and
passed under the opened gates of the castle, heading toward the moorland that skirted the lochan, Elspeth and the
others followed.

The pipes skirled into a high, powerful sound. Elspeth
felt the familiar, beautiful music sweep through her heart,
some of its strains poignant, some exquisitely joyful. She
turned and saw Duncan just behind her. He smiled when
she looked at him, and she knew that he felt the music too,
like a cleansing wind through the soul.

The piper, with the Frasers following him, headed for a

ridge of hills. When the piper reached the top of one rock-studded hill, he stood, began to turn slowly *deiseil*, sunwise, and played to the starlit sky.

Elspeth listened, filled with the music. When it faded away on the last reedy note, the momentary silence that followed seemed profound. Her cousins began to whoop and ask for more.

The piper began another song and turned back for the castle. Elspeth, enjoying the feel of the night wind, decided to stay a little longer. She stood on the hilltop and watched the group stride back down the slope toward the castle.

The darkness was not deep, the night cool and pleasant as Elspeth looked out over the shadowed, silent glen. This rounded knoll was very familiar to her, for she had come here often as a child. Breathing out a long sigh, she sat down and propped her back against a boulder. She closed her eyes wearily and listened to the faint, plaintive skirl of the pipes.

"Are you well?"

Startled, Elspeth opened her eyes, realizing that she must have dozed. She saw long muscular legs in black boots and black trews, and looked up. Duncan Macrae stood before her, his face shadowed, his black cloak draped like a raven's wings.

"Are you well, girl?" His dark hair swung forward to hide his expression, but his tone was sharp.

"I am fine," she answered.

"I saw that you stayed here on the hill—that gown shines like a star in the dark," he added. "I wondered if you were ill, so I came back."

"I like this place," she said. "I decided to sit here for a little while. It is peaceful here."

He nodded and sat beside her, leaning his back against the large stone. Drawing up one leg, boot leather creaking, he rested an arm on his knee and looked out over the dark glen. "A pleasant place for a rest, this hill," he said.

"It is," she agreed. "My cousins went back inside?"

"They are still in the yard, sharing drams and stories now

with the piper. I had no wish to hear more." Tilting his head back, he closed his eyes with a deep sigh.

Elspeth watched his profile in the dark, and felt sympathy for him, a harmony of shared fatigue. Her anger earlier today had faded, replaced by a small twinge of guilt at her behavior in the stairwell; his left eye was dark with a bruise. "If my cousins are still telling stories and singing, then they may stay there until dawn," she said.

"They may. They are there, in the courtyard." Raising his arm to point, he leaned sideways, his shoulder brushing hers. "Do you not see them just over the castle wall?"

She squinted. "You must have the eyes of a hawk."

He leaned closer, and the warm pressure of his shoulder against hers sent an odd thrumming through her body. "There," he murmured. "Can you hear them?" His voice was velvet, deep and soft and warm.

Hearing the faint strains of a song, Elspeth nodded. A breeze skimmed over the hilltop, and she shivered, drawing her plaid more securely around her shoulders.

"That gown is a fine thing."

She looked up. "You like it?"

"I do."

Her heartbeat quickened and deepened. "Hugh told me his idea to have us hold the torches. I thought the song and the gown would add to what he wanted to show Robert."

"It was cleverly done." His glance was keen and direct. The increasing pace of her heart felt as if she were running. "And you sang like an angel. Or a fairy. Finer than—"

"Hush!" She pressed her fingers to his lips.

"Mmmph?" he asked, blinking.

"Hush," she said urgently. "Do not boast in this place." She lifted her hand away.

"I only said that you sing like—" Her hand flew up again at his words. His unshaven beard was sharp and short beneath her fingers, his skin pliant, his breath warm on her skin.

"This is a *sìthean*," she whispered.

"A fairy knoll?" His lips moved against her fingers. The

curious sensation, lush and pleasant, sent a chill through her.

"This hill is a home of the *daoine sìth,* the people of peace. The fairies. Do you know of them?"

He laughed. "Indeed," he said, lifting her hand away from his mouth. "What Highlander does not know of the fairy people?" He let go of her hand, and she missed the dry, warm touch.

"Ah. You were Highland born."

"I was. And my own castle is on just such a fairy knoll. We call it Dulsie, for *tull-sìth,* hill of the fairies."

"Your own castle?"

He looked away, out over the dark hills. "I am laird there," he said softly. "Laird of Dulsie, in Kintail." He rubbed his jaw. "So I have heard of the fairies who live in the hills. They play their music at night, and any human who hears may be lured inside to dance forever." He cocked a brow at her.

She nodded. "A fairy night may last a hundred years. And the singing of the fairies is so beautiful, it cannot be resisted."

Looking at her, he tilted his head. "Your voice," he said softly, "could lure the fairies out of their hill."

"Hush! They are very jealous," she whispered.

His smile was an elusive, joyful thing in starlight, the smile of an elfin king, clever and charming. When it faded, she longed to see it again. The weight of his arm pressed gently against her shoulder. He smelled of smoke and wind.

"And if we should fall asleep on this fairy knoll, would we be taken, as usually happens in such tales?" he asked. "What story is told of this place?"

She looked down. "Just that the fairies are here."

"Just that? Come now, I have lately been with your cousins. Surely you tell a tale as good as any of them."

She opened her mouth to speak, then stopped, afraid that he would laugh if she told him what she had believed as a child. She shook her head.

"There is something. Tell me." When she remained silent, he leaned over. His voice hummed through her chest, soft and deep, as much a lure as the fairies themselves. "Tell me, Elspeth Fraser."

She took a breath, hesitating, for the tale was precious to her. Yet his solid, warm presence was somehow comforting, patient and uncondemning. She wanted to tell him.

"When I was a small child," she said, "Robert would sometimes spend time here. We had the same mother, though he lived with his Gordon kin." She saw him nod. "He told me that our mother went into this hill and disappeared after I was born."

"He told you that she was taken?"

She shook her head. "He said that she returned to her real home through here. He said that she was a fairy lady who left her baby daughter and little son and returned to her own kind."

"Ah." He did not laugh. "Robert was very young. He told you his own fantasy."

"But when I was small, I thought it true. Robert said that our mother sang sweetly, which was proof of her fairy magic."

"Then you have your mother's voice."

She shrugged. "I never knew her. But I did come here when I was young, hoping to hear her. Robert laughed at me when he found out." She looked down, feeling a twinge of that old hurt. "I never heard a sound but the birds and the wind, and yet ..." She felt a little embarrassed but went on. "I used to imagine that her voice was in the wind, singing for me." A blush heated her cheeks; she had never spoken to anyone of her wish to hear her mother's voice out of the fairy hill.

"You wanted some part of your mother," he said. "Even if it was only the sound of her voice."

She nodded, and tears stung her eyes, startling her. She blinked them away. Surprised that she had told a childhood secret to Duncan, she realized that she felt deeply at ease with him. She knew somehow that he would guard her inner thoughts.

"If your mother was in this fairy hill, she would be happy to know that you sing as well as any of her kind."

"Do you think so?"

"I do," he said. "As well or better than any of her kind."

Elspeth leaned forward to stop his mouth at the boast. He took her hand, laughing softly. "Would you silence me?" he teased. "Surely I may say that much."

"They are old beliefs, and perhaps foolish. I have never seen a fairy, in truth."

He brushed a strand of curling hair away from her brow. "Have you not?" he asked quietly. In the deep light his eyes were the dark blue of the night sky.

Suddenly she remembered her first sight of Duncan Macrae. She had seen him—or a vision of him—riding the crest of a hill. He had resembled one of the *daoine sìth*. Now, in the shadows, he looked like a magical king, tall and strong and darkly beautiful, his features precise, his hair sheened like raven feathers.

The haunting memory of the other vision glimmered suddenly. She squeezed her eyes shut, willing the awful image to be gone. She did not want to see it, not here. Not now.

Keeping her hand tucked in the warm cocoon of his fingers, Duncan looked toward the castle, where tiny sparks of torchlight glowed. He tugged her hand gently and rose to his feet, pulling her up. His other arm came around her back. "Come, Elspeth. I will take you back to Glenran."

Elspeth looked up. Deep inside, in that instant, some vulnerable center opened in her. He stood over her, black cloak whipping like the spread of dark wings, his eyes a match to the night. She stared up, her gaze as open as a flower.

He tipped her chin up with a finger. Shivers coursed through her body. She stood there, not powerless to stop him, only unwilling; she suddenly wanted his touch, his closeness. Her own need held her there. The small voice that might have cautioned her to stay away from this man was silent.

He lowered his head. Hesitantly she moved forward. He touched his lips to hers. His eyelids drifted shut and he touched his mouth to hers again, a warm and gentle pressure. Sliding an arm around his neck, she felt his hair, smooth and cool, stream through her fingers. Her heartbeat seemed to expand, drumming through her blood, through her belly, into her knees.

When his tongue etched a delicate path along her upper lip, she arched her throat, her small gasp lost beneath the cover of his mouth. Each kiss became deeper and fuller than the last, heady and sweet. She drank them in like fine, subtle wine.

Drawing a breath, she wrapped her arms around him, feeling the rapid pounding of his heart against her breasts. He touched his lips to her cheek, to the underside of her jaw, tracing a gentle path. The sensation curled through her entire body.

His fingertips lighted on the bare skin of her throat, moving softly downward, tracing gentle arcs as the heel of his hand brushed the top of her breast. She shuddered, pressing forward, feeling uncertain, wanting more.

He kissed her again. She threaded her fingers into his hair, exploring, and found the firm shape of his ear, the angle of his jaw, the strength of his shoulders. She kept her eyes closed and only felt, keenly and without thought, the warm, moist comfort of his lips; the feather touches over her throat, her jaw, in her hair; the harsh rasp of his beard against her cheek.

"Elspeth," he murmured, his breath soft on her brow. "I had not thought that this would happen."

"Nor did I," she said, trying to pull her ragged thoughts into coherence. Her heart surged, fear overcoming wonder. "Leave now, Duncan. Please. Leave me, leave the Highlands."

He took her face in his hands. She felt the pulse of his heart in his fingertips. "Elspeth Fraser," he said softly. "Deal truthfully with me."

She nodded slowly.

"That day at the stream—"

"Hush, you," she said. Her fingers trembled as she touched them to his cheek. A swoop of dread rushed through her. "Do not speak of that."

"Listen to me. Was that vision a ruse to send me away? Surely you knew that I was coming here."

She hesitated, took her hand from his face. Her breath slowed, and she set her chin high. "It was a true vision," she said.

"I want to know what you saw." He moved his hand to her arm.

She wanted very much to tell him then, contrary to what she had decided earlier. The raw, hurtful image burned like a poison in her brain, and purging it would be a relief. But she was afraid, as if speaking of the vision would engrave the event indelibly into his future and make it irreversibly real.

She shook her head. "I will not tell you."

Then, swift and sure, his hand grasped the back of her head, his fingers clutching her thick hair, pulling back her head, not hurting her but firm, as if he controlled a wave of anger.

"You spoke of death, and a raven. You have warned me to leave or face tragedy. I have listened to it all. And now I want the truth from you."

"Leave me be on this," she whispered.

"I cannot. Speak, and I will listen, and the thing will be done between us. Seers, in my experience, are usually eager to spread their wisdom. You, however, are not."

"In your experience?"

"I have heard something of my future from a crone who lived in Kintail when I was a boy," he said. "None of it ever frightened me. None of it has ever happened. Now speak."

"What did she tell you?"

He huffed out a breath of exasperation and released her hair. "Chaff and rubbish. I have forgotten."

She looked away. "Perhaps I have too."

"You have not." He looked at her thoughtfully. "At the stream that day, you looked at me as if—" He stopped.

Elspeth glanced up at him. "As if what?" she asked.

His fingers traced a gentle line along her jaw. Her knees gave slightly, and her breath quickened.

"You looked at me as if you cared for me beyond all

others in this world," he said. "I want to know why. Tell me what you saw."

Her heart seemed to tumble to her toes and bound back up again. She wanted to reach out to him, but squeezed her fingers tightly against her sides.

"What did you see, Elspeth Fraser?" His voice was as deep as comfort, as compelling as a lure.

"You will face the heading block if you stay here. That is what I saw for you, Duncan Macrae." Released unwillingly, the words tumbled out on a half sob, a poor gift to return for his lush kisses, for his gentle touch.

He stared at her. A gust of wind lifted his hair, but he stood still as granite.

"Leave here," she said, feeling weary. "Go to Dulsie, or go to Edinburgh, but leave this place."

"Whatever you saw, girl, it will not affect me." His voice was calm. "Because I do not believe it."

She sighed and drew her plaid around her. She turned and slowly walked away from him, down the slope toward Glenran.

She had felt something between them, just as he had, ever since that first moment at the stream. Her life was fastening to his inexorably, like a weaving of silver threads. Each word, each look, each touch, was another filament in the bond. Aware that it was happening, she felt powerless against its progress.

And yet she feared now that such a bond would destroy them both. She walked on, without looking back.

Chapter 9

O winna ye pity me, fair maid?
O winna ye pity me?
O winna ye pity my poor steed,
Stands trembling at yon tree?
  —*"The Broom of Cowdenknows"*

"Here, Lasair, dip in the water," Duncan said patiently. "The cold will do you good. Stay there, now," he said, and pushed down on his horse's leg when Lasair pulled his tender hoof out of the cold, shallow burn.

Duncan sighed loudly. "Try to keep in the water for at least a moment, my friend. I have no remedy but this for you." The horse cocked one ear in confusion and snorted testily, but complied. Patting Lasair's shoulder, Duncan urged the horse's nose downward for a drink.

Having spent the morning composing a carefully worded letter to the chief of the MacDonalds, which he had then presented to Robert Gordon, Duncan had witnessed Robert's signature. After Hugh had summoned a running gillie to deliver the letter to the MacDonalds, Duncan had saddled Lasair and had ridden out alone.

A hard gallop over moorland had cleared his mind and lightened his mood, but before long his horse had caught a stone in the soft inner part of the hoof. The bruised area, Duncan knew, had to be quite painful. The limping horse would have to be led back to Glenran.

"There, *mo caraid,* my friend, the water helps, I think," he murmured. He realized then that he had been speaking aloud in Gaelic, as easily and naturally as he once had as a child, with no careful thought preceding the words. He smiled ruefully, recalling how Alasdair Fraser had urged him to allow the Highland part of his character greater freedom.

Briefly he imagined Alasdair at Dulsie Castle, seated around the table in the hall with Duncan's own family. Mhairi, who was Duncan's sister and Alasdair's wife, would be there with their children, as would his grandmother and his young sister, Kirsty. Three years had passed since he had seen Mhairi, who had once accompanied Alasdair on a visit to Edinburgh. Kirsty had been little more than a babe, willful and pretty, when he had left; he doubted she much remembered him now.

He had not seen his grandmother since the day he had left Dulsie without her blessing. He sighed again, remembering how much he had loved her as a boy. Now he wondered how much she had aged, and if her health had withstood the years; and he wondered if she was still so very angry with him.

Smoothing a hand over Lasair's glossy black withers, he waited a few minutes longer while the horse's hoof soaked. Then he picked up the reins and tugged gently to lead the horse out of the shallow stream and slowly up the shoulder of a broad hill.

Reaching the top, he saw a wide view of the great loch off to the east, its surface gleaming like dull pewter beneath the overcast sky. Pushing back the hair that whipped over his brow, Duncan turned for Glenran, barely visible in the far distance.

Then he stopped, laying a hand on the horse's neck, and swore softly. On the moor below, he saw a cluster of Highlanders on horseback. Narrowing his eyes, keeping still, he watched cautiously, wondering if these men were MacDonalds.

Eight men, plaided and dirked, rode slowly over the rough moorland past a fringe of birch wood. Duncan could see the glint of weapons at the Highlanders' waists. Their bronze-trimmed targe shields gleamed in the thin light. The mix of tartan patterns that decorated their plaids made it difficult to guess their clan. These were not any Frasers that he had seen, though they rode, armed and bold, through Fraser territory in clear daylight.

At that moment a lone Highlander emerged from the

birch wood at the edge of the moor. Clothed in dark green
and blue, the Highlander was clearly a Glenran Fraser. One
fat braid glimmered like soft copper.

"Dhia!" Duncan swore. He watched as the armed riders
moved toward Elspeth. Soon she was surrounded, her head
a bright flash in the midst of the garrons and the tartaned
plaids.

Duncan dropped the reins and ran down the slope, one
hand gripping the dirk sheathed at his waist. His black
cloak beat out in the wind behind him as he descended the
slope in leaps. Bounding with fluid strength over the swells
and dips in the ground, still unseen by the group not far
ahead of him now, he came to a rocky outcrop and hun-
kered down out of sight.

Crouched behind a boulder, he studied the distance and
the number of men, judging the best angle for his approach.
Eight mounted Highlanders circled around Elspeth. One of
them spoke to her. She answered, standing very still, her
back to Duncan.

He knew now that these men were not Ruari MacDonald
and his brothers, whom he had seen that first day at the
stream. None of the men wore bonnets, and without knowing their plant badge, he could not identify their clan easily.

Elspeth spoke, pointing and shaking her head. One of
the riders reached out an arm to her as if to lift her to his
horse, but she shook her head again and stepped back. The
man reached forward again.

Anger roiled in Duncan's gut. He stepped forward. His
approach would be no secret across the open moor. He
would have to hope that his sudden appearance would star-
tle these men into riding away. If not, then he would have
to fight his way free. Either way, he would do his best to
protect the girl.

He stalked firmly toward them with deliberate footfalls,
his gaze direct and unafraid. Never show fear to an enemy,
his father had once told him; he had remembered it all his
life, had made it a part of everything he did. Even the law
used unpredictability as a defensive element. With his hand
openly resting on his dirk, he stepped boldly into the circle.

"Greetings," he said in Gaelic.

Surprised gazes swiveled to meet his. Duncan lifted a hand in casual salute, the other resting tense and ready on the dirk. Elspeth stared at him. Cocking his head toward her, he beckoned with authority. She walked toward him.

"What are you doing here?" she hissed. Without answering, he wrapped his fingers around her elbow and pulled her to his side. One of the Highlanders dismounted. Duncan tensed and began to back slowly toward the birch wood.

The man was tall and very thin, with black hair and a wide mustache that hid his mouth. He approached Elspeth and Duncan, frowning, his large hand on his own dirk.

"Shall we kill this one for you, Elspeth?" he asked.

Duncan blinked in surprise and looked down at her. She slid a quick glance at him and smiled. A deep dimple came and went in her cheek. "Leave him be," she said. "He is the queen's own long-robe."

"Ah," the Highlander said. "You would be Macrae, then."

"I am," Duncan said cautiously. The Highlander held out a hand for him to grasp, and after a moment Duncan took it. The man was very young, no more than twenty, with sharp green eyes and a serious manner.

"I am Diarmid Fraser," he said. "We are the MacShimi's tail, just come from Lovat Castle at his request."

A muscle pumped in Duncan's cheek, and a slow flush crept up his neck. Elspeth turned to beam at him, obviously enjoying his discomfiture.

He had tried to rescue her from a pack of Frasers. Damn the whole lot of them, he thought sourly; there were far too many to count. If any clan needed a bond of caution to keep them at home, it had to be the Frasers. He was more determined than ever to get the cursed paper signed and get out of Glenran.

"These are more of my cousins," Elspeth said. "Diarmid you have met. Over there are David, Andrew, Tomas, Domhnall, Iain, James, and Johnnie."

Duncan nodded to each one. "You form your chief's tail?"

"We do," Diarmid answered. "We are his bodyguard at Lovat and ride with him whenever he needs us. He sent word a few days ago, asking us to ride patrol around Fraser territory."

"The patrols are needed to protect our people from the MacDonalds," Elspeth said.

"That clan must be anxious to harass you, to ride out on summer raids," Diarmid said.

"The nights are not nearly dark enough yet for good raiding," Duncan said. "Late autumn or winter nights are always best. They take a chance raiding in this season, even in late summer." He saw Elspeth glance at him in surprise; she obviously did not expect a lawyer to know much about raiding.

"They do," Diarmid agreed. "Ruari MacDonald and his brothers can be sly and mean, but they have never been blessed with wits." Diarmid turned to Elspeth. "Come with us to Glenran." He held out his hand, but Elspeth shook her head.

"I will not, Diarmid," she said. "I have already told you so." Duncan realized with chagrin that they had picked up the conversation that had brought him hurtling to her rescue.

"It is dangerous for you to be out here alone," Diarmid said. "There could be MacDonald scouts in this area."

"Hah! They would not dare to set foot on our land in daylight," she said. "I have promised to visit a friend. I will be safe, Diarmid. You go on."

Her cousin sighed. "Then the long-robe will see you safely where you mean to go." He lifted a brow at Duncan, who nodded.

Diarmid bid them farewell and mounted his horse, then saluted them with a wave of his hand. The Frasers rode away, hoofbeats pounding over the moor.

Elspeth turned and walked past Duncan without a word or a glance, heading up the slope toward his waiting horse. He was reminded of the cool manner in which she had

walked away from him the evening before. He caught up
to her easily.

"We cannot ride—" he began.

"I walk more than I ride," she said. "Perhaps it is different in the south country." She stomped ahead.

"We cannot ride," he repeated in a clipped manner,
pausing by the horse, "because my horse has gone lame. I
will not lead him over a long distance. I would prefer to
lead him back to Glenran before I escort you. How far do
you need to go?"

She turned, her scowl changing to an expression of concern. Coming back toward him, she stroked the horse's
shoulder. "Which hoof?" she asked. He told her, and she
bent to gently lift the front left hoof, examining the
bruise carefully.

"Sasunnach horses are not suited to the Highlands,"
she said.

"This is not an English horse," he said, irritated by her
criticism, and her icy tone. His temper had been tested
today by her half brother, and tested sorely by Elspeth
yesterday. She had thrown a door into his face, had insulted
him, and had riled his temper; and last night she had enchanted him, and had kissed him quite fervently. Now he
had no patience for her changeable temperament.

"Scots may not legally own English horses, though in the
Highlands I doubt that matters," he explained. "Lasair
comes of a strong border breed and has done well enough
in this terrain."

"Until now. You should be riding a garron. They climb
well, and their hooves are tougher for the rocky ground."

"The council did not provide me a garron," he snapped.
He did not need lectures on horseflesh from a girl who
spent more time on foot than in a saddle. "All they gave
me was that cursed document. I brought my own horse
because I had no desire to walk here from Edinburgh."

She did not glance up. "His hoof needs attention." She
rubbed the stallion's glossy black shoulder, murmuring
softly. "What do you call him?" she asked Duncan.

"Lasair."

"A 'flash of fire'?"

"He is fast on Lowland terrain, I assure you."

"He is a beautiful animal." She straightened and looked at Duncan, her eyes a clear, rainwater gray. Drawing her slender brows together as if she considered something, she turned abruptly. "Come this way, then," she called over her shoulder, resuming her walk. "I know someone who can tend to your horse."

"Who is that, and how far?" he asked with barely disguised impatience.

"A healer," she said simply. "And not far."

Duncan watched her stride away from him. If he took the horse back to Glenran, he knew that Elspeth would stubbornly go her way without him. And he agreed with Diarmid Fraser: she was not safe out here alone. The Mac-Donalds were not to be trusted.

Sighing audibly, he tugged the reins and followed her.

They climbed along the gentle shoulders of slopes whenever possible, avoiding the steeper peaks in consideration for the horse. Now and again sunshine broke through the clouds, wide transparent beams that sliced down and disappeared quickly. They walked on in silence; if Elspeth spoke at all, it was more often to Lasair than to Duncan.

She strode ahead, quick and sure, her plaid swinging above smoothly muscled calves. Duncan found this simple action quite pleasurable to watch. Her braid, gold and copper threaded together, thumped rhythmically between her shoulders. Suddenly he longed to flex his fingers in that mass of hair, to loosen it and feel its cool silk again. He wanted to hold her and create a new rhythm for her body in tandem with his own. His heart bounded at the thought, his loins surged, and he sucked in his breath.

Frowning as he walked along behind her, he wondered, not for the first time since he had come to Glenran, at the consistent, complex pull that he felt toward this girl. No matter that she had a brassy tongue that clashed with her delicate silver eyes and spun-copper hair. No matter that she flared his temper. He had been immediately and deeply

attracted to her from the first moment he had touched her
in the stream. And each time he was with her, he wanted
to touch her again, wanted to hear her voice, know her
thoughts. Blinking in amazement at his own thoughts, he
walked on.

That attraction was unlike anything he had ever felt before. A familiar, pleasurable current of lust was created
whenever his strong male body responded to her female-
ness, but there were many layers in his reaction to her. He
could hardly comprehend what he felt regarding her; lust
was only a part of that.

Simply, she fascinated him. He was aware of her presence, of the melody of her light, clear voice. Her professed
ability to foresee the future—his future—touched off his
curiosity, if not his belief. Watching her, he had seen that
she was bold but vulnerable, keenly intelligent but stubborn. He had encountered her delightful humor and her
thunderous temper, and had tasted the sweet touch of her
lips. Elspeth Fraser was by far the most unexpected and
intriguing part of his visit to Glenran.

The compelling bond between them had grown stronger;
he could feel its pull. If she were a lodestone, he would be
cut from that same stone, two pieces cast apart by fortune
and thrown together again. Turned this way, he wanted to
leap away from her; turned that, he was drawn to her like
iron or steel.

The twitch of the girl's braid, her frown, her single dimple drew him in; her loyalty, her bold and earnest character,
held him. Seeking to understand what was happening, he
could not. And each time she looked at him, the lodestone
seemed to turn.

This attraction to Elspeth went contrary to his plans for
himself; he had left the Highlands behind and mapped out
a peaceful, undisturbed life. He had endured enough turmoil years ago and wanted no more. Conquering his temper
and his wilder urges, he had found intellectual sanctuary in
the law. A safe, secure, and fairly predictable way of life,
although only a mild challenge for a man raised amid strife
and action.

He tightened his grip on the horse's rein, his scowl a twin of Elspeth's now. These feelings about the girl were disconcerting and decidedly inconvenient. He intended to collect those signatures and leave Glenran; he certainly intended nothing beyond that.

Elspeth glanced back, frowned at him, and lengthened her stride. Duncan, determined to keep up with her, walked faster, although he had hung back for the sake of the horse.

When he had been as young as these Frasers, a decade and more ago, riding with his cousins the Kerrs, he had enjoyed passionate involvements with young women. One dark-eyed girl he would have married. She had pleasured his body sweetly and had a kind temperament. He had felt an obligation to her, a loyalty more than love. But she had died of a fever, and he had not met a woman after that with whom he cared to spend more than a night or two.

But even with that sweet girl he had never experienced this deep, pounding rush of blood and heart and thought mingled together. He felt swept along by a force he did not understand.

Beside him, the horse nickered and pulled, slowing down.

"Easy," Duncan murmured. He stopped to look at the injured hoof. "Elspeth," he called. Her name, he suddenly realized, was a pleasurable sound on his lips, a soft thrill.

She turned. "What is it?"

"He needs to rest." Seeing a huge old tree near a stream, Duncan led the horse that way. He urged the horse to step down into the water. Elspeth walked over to stand beside him. She patted the animal gently along the nose and spoke softly, helping to keep the horse in the water for a little while.

Duncan walked up the bank to sit down, leaning against the gnarled trunk. He looked up into a maze of branches, heavy with dark green, shiny leaves. This was the largest yew he had ever seen, wide and enormously high, and intricately convoluted at the center of its trunk.

Elspeth left the horse and came toward Duncan, dropping down to recline on the grass and lean back on an elbow. She peered up into the screen of leaves. "This yew tree is said to be thousands of years old. See there, where it has split at the center—a new tree grows out of the old one."

Duncan noticed that the gnarled and twisted trunk was actually two trunks: the original yew tree and the emerging trunk of a much younger tree.

"The new tree grows from the heart of the old," Elspeth said. "That is why the Frasers take the yew for our clan badge."

Duncan picked up a small broken branch from the ground, twirling it in his hand. He recalled what he had heard in childhood about tree lore. "The yew tree regenerates itself," he said. "Just as the Fraser clan has been reborn in these last twenty years."

She nodded. "Hundreds of Fraser men were killed by the MacDonalds at Blar-na-Léine. Like the yew, we are resilient. We will not be diminished by such as the Mac-Donalds." She frowned. "And now the MacDonalds are about to receive news that will not make them more fond of Frasers."

Duncan nodded. "I witnessed the letter that was sent to the MacDonalds. The promise to wed you to Ruari is withdrawn. Hugh sent it out along with his own refusal."

She tilted her head, her braid tumbling down. He saw the shining crown of her head. "Hugh told me that it was your suggestion," she said. "I am glad that it was done."

"You will be able to marry whomever you like. Hugh will surely find you a good husband." That thought cut through him more bitterly than any wind. He lowered his glance and stroked the smooth leaves in his hand, releasing a sharp piney fragrance.

She looked at him, a flash of silver, and then away. "You may have helped me to avoid this marriage, Duncan Macrae, but now you have made yourself some enemies."

"Have I?"

"Robert was very angry. You are the queen's lawyer, and a more powerful man than he. Robert hates to be proven wrong."

"He signed the letter courteously enough. He understands the law, Elspeth."

She shrugged. "I know him. He will seethe for a time. Though he may do nothing, he will not forget this. But you have a greater enemy than Robert, I think."

"And who is that?" He flicked the leaves idly.

"Your signature was on that letter as witness. If the MacDonalds learn that you are here, even though you have been sent by the queen, they may seek some revenge. Ruari has a savage nature. He will be infuriated by that letter."

"The MacDonalds are no new enemy to me, girl." His voice was quiet and hard.

She frowned. "What quarrel could a Lowland lawyer have with Clan MacDonald?"

"I am a Macrae," he answered. "My clan has fought MacDonalds for generations."

Tilting her head, she looked at him for a long moment. "Your heart still hurts, Duncan Macrae, though your body has recovered," she murmured.

"What do you mean?" A chill crept up his neck.

Her eyes were the color of clouds and rain. "There is a discomfort of some kind in your back and your chest. Old pain, remembered pain. You have been injured by the hand of a MacDonald. The wound has healed, but you still hold the hatred and the anger. You lost much that day."

Inwardly he was shocked, though he gave no sign. "Many people in my clan have been hurt by the MacDonalds," he said curtly. He glanced at the horse, who nuzzled on grass beyond the tree. "We should go. How much farther to this friend of yours, this healer?"

Elspeth got to her feet in one lithe movement. "Not far. Up the next hill and down again, to the edge of Glenran." She went over to the horse and took the reins.

Duncan stood, stretched his arms, and stopped. He felt the slight, stiff tug of the scar tissue that ran in a jagged strip across the ribs beneath his left arm. Drawing his brows together, he watched Elspeth as she led the horse up the slope.

He was certain that she did not know of the scar. Although she had seen him without a shirt, both occasions had been in darkness. The original wound had been deep and serious, and had nearly killed him, but its traces were faded now. His frown deepened further.

A MacDonald had given him that scar years ago.

Chapter 10

There's comfort for the comfortless
There's honey for the bee;
There's comfort for the comfortless,
There's nane but you for me.
　　—"The False Lover Won Back"

"Finish your ale, now, and I will look at the lawyer's horse," Bethoc said. Elspeth nodded, sipping cool ale from a wooden bowl, and glanced at Duncan. They sat outside Bethoc's house, seated on a grassy block of turf placed against an outside wall.

Duncan had drained and set aside his wooden bowl, and stood leaning one shoulder against the wall of the house, his arms crossed. He watched Eiric run in the yard with the little dark bog lamb. Elspeth wondered what the lawyer was thinking.

She had taken a moment before they had arrived to mention that Magnus had a small daughter, motherless now, who lived with Bethoc. The lawyer had lifted his brows in surprise, but had said little. Elspeth had noticed that he had a way of listening carefully, in patient silence, whenever the matter was of a serious nature. Though doubtlessly he was trained to listen well, she appreciated the quiet respect showed by his attentive silences. Whenever she spoke, he would fasten his blue eyes on hers, keen and alert. In those moments she felt that he saw only her, heard only her. The feeling was as heady as strong wine.

"This morning," Bethoc said, "my little goat was missing. She was out in the pen by the garden, and I thought she had chewed loose the gate rope and wandered down to the burn, but I have not been able to find her."

"Perhaps the MacDonalds took her," Elspeth said.

"I think it likely," Bethoc replied.

Duncan frowned. "Why would they take a widow's goat?"

Elspeth glanced at Bethoc and saw the woman shake her head to discourage any mention of Ruari MacDonald's earlier visit and his brutality. Bethoc's bruises had already faded, and Duncan would have no clue of trouble.

"They might have taken the goat," Elspeth told Duncan. "And they might have done worse than that. Please, Bethoc, come to Glenran and stay with us. You and Eiric will be safer there."

"We are fine here," Bethoc said with a stubborn tilt of her chin. "I have performed a charm around the croft to keep us safe. I made a cross of rowan berries for over the door. And juniper and lavender grow just there, see, at the edge of the yard, as a protection from strangers."

"None of that protected your goat," Duncan said wryly. "A charm is not much good against MacDonalds who care to go reiving."

Bethoc stood. "Let me look at your horse." She limped ahead of him, her club foot rocking beneath her. Pausing by the horse, she bent down and picked up the injured hoof.

After a moment she nodded. "I will perform an *eōlas,* a healing charm. The swelling will cool and lessen." She went into the house and returned a moment later with a bucket of water and a short length of black yarn.

Kneeling by the horse, Bethoc murmured a steady, lilting chant as she looped the yearn around the leg. "Bone, joint, and sinew," she chanted. "Sinew, joint, and bone, all heal in the name of the Lord." As she spoke, she tied knots in the yarn, pulling each one tight. When nine knots were done, she tied the string around the horse's fetlock.

Elspeth watched, holding Eiric in her arms. Bethoc lifted her hands over the water and made spiraling motions, murmuring another chant. Taking from her pocket a small stone with a hole worn through its center, she dropped it into the water and continued her soft singsong.

Elspeth was familiar with the words and the gestures. Bethoc had taught her much about the ancient ways. She knew the chants for curing, and knew the power of knots tied in lengths of colored yarn, each color with its own power. She knew how to charm water for healing, and knew some of the ancient words and gestures that Bethoc said could raise the powers of earth and air and fire.

She had rarely used these rituals herself, but she knew that none of them were nonsense. Glancing at Duncan, she could tell that he was skeptical of this simple healing charm. Though his expression was mildly perplexed, he remained silent and observant.

Bethoc scooped a few handfuls of water to pour over the horse's hoof. Steam rose, as if the hoof were hot, but the day was cool and the horse had been resting.

Setting Lasair's leg into the bucket of water, Bethoc stood upright and looked at Duncan. "The hoof will need to be soaked. Leave the horse here for the night."

"He does not like to keep his hooves in water," Duncan said.

She smiled. "He will stay in this water, for he knows that it will heal his wound."

Duncan raised a brow at this curious comment. "He will need a few days to heal," he said. "Let me pay you for boarding him."

Bethoc held up her hand. "No coin will I take from you, Duncan Macrae. Your horse will be fine by tomorrow, I think. But you come when you can, for the next few days will be busy for you. You are always welcome here."

Elspeth looked with wide eyes at Bethoc, who smiled and turned to walk into the house, beckoning them to follow.

"Sit there," Bethoc told Duncan. "You have a deep bruise under your eye. I can help it."

Duncan glanced at Elspeth, then sat on a bench by the open door in a thin wash of daylight. Bethoc fetched some clay jars from the wooden cupboard and stood behind Duncan. Murmuring a low chant, she laid one hand over Duncan's left eye and closed her own. The hand healings that Bethoc sometimes did could be very powerful; Elspeth knew she could quickly banish headaches and bellyaches, and heal cuts and bruises in a day or two.

Listening to the steady rhythm of Bethoc's breathing, Elspeth kept a careful eye on Eiric, who sat on the floor with a ball of yarn and a wooden spoon. The child wrapped the yarn around the spoon as if it were a spindle, with a look of intense concentration on her face. When the lamb wandered in the open door, Elspeth quietly shooed her out again.

Turning back, she saw that Duncan sat patiently, his eyes closed, his long, thick lashes black crescents beneath black, straight brows. A slight flush touched his cheeks above the dark sand of his unshaven beard. Dark waves of hair fell past his jaw, feathering along his strong neck. Elspeth remembered how cool and soft his hair had felt beneath her hands last night. Looking at his firm, pliant lips, she remembered their pressure on her own, and blushed.

As if he heard her thoughts, Duncan opened one eye and looked directly at her. Bethoc removed her hand and stood back, and Duncan kept his bright, intense gaze evenly on Elspeth.

She ducked her head, heat staining her cheeks, and turned to Eiric, who was so content with her yarn and spoon that she was oblivious to the others in the room.

Bethoc set a small earthenware jar on the table. "Here, *mo cuachag*," she said to Elspeth. "Apply this to our friend's cheek and nose. Rub in a good amount, gently. I will begin the supper."

"But—"

Bethoc smiled. "The best healing comes from the hand that dealt the blow."

Duncan's eyebrows jumped high at this. Elspeth sighed, knowing how deep the Sight ran in Bethoc. Still, she too was surprised that Bethoc could know this. She came forward, her flushed cheeks growing hotter.

Feeling his gaze on her, she dipped two fingers into the thick brown mixture of comfrey, willow, and birch oil, used for muscle and skin injuries. Smearing the oily stuff delicately over his cheekbone and across the bridge of his nose, she was grateful when he closed his eyes, for his gaze was distracting.

His breath blew softly over her hand as she worked. She could have counted each dark hair of his brows and lashes. His features were precisely made, almost beautiful. She listened to the sound of her breath coming into rhythm with his.

Her fingertips soothed the slick stuff gently over his cheek and up over the bony ridge of his nose, back and forth, a sweet, relaxing rhythm. The ointment grew slippery and warm. Her glance drifted to the firm curve of his mouth, so close to the palm of her hand; his breath drifted over her wrist. A swirl of excitement plunged through her, and she inhaled quickly. She kept recalling, like a flood of sensation, the feel of his lips over hers, the warmth of his hands last night.

Clearing her throat, she scooped up another fingerful of ointment. Behind her, Bethoc moved quietly around the room, building up the peat fire and setting a kettle of water on to heat. Then she went to the door.

"I will fetch some onions from the yard, if you can watch Eiric for a bit," Bethoc said, going to the door.

"We will," Duncan said. Looking at the little girl, he lifted his hand in a brief wave. Eiric stood up, teetered for a moment, and waddled over to him on short, sturdy legs, trailing a length of red yarn behind her.

She solemnly held up the spoon, which she had smothered in a tangle of yarn. Duncan accepted the gift and admired it.

"Ah," he said to Eiric. "You will be a fine weaver one day."

Elspeth smiled. "She may be. Bethoc is the finest weaver in Glenran, and she will teach Eiric well."

Eiric held up her arms to pull on Duncan's shirt, surprising Elspeth with her obvious preference. The child began to climb up his leg, and he wrapped his long fingers around her middle to lift her. He set her on his lap and handed her the yarn-wrapped spoon.

"She likes you," Elspeth said.

"Some women do." He glanced at her, a quick blue gleam.

"Ah," she returned, pinching down a smile. Eiric began to rewind the yarn vigorously, waving the handle dangerously close to Duncan's face.

"Hold, there, *gràdhan*, my little dear, I wish to keep that eye," he said, gently taking the spoon away.

"Eiric," Elspeth said, "be still." She moved her thumb up and over the ridge of his brow in little circles. "Your Gaelic is very good for a Lowlander."

"Mmmmm ..." The low growl in his throat seemed to tickle along Elspeth's spine. "It should be, for I am a Highlander. I did not learn Scots English until I was nearly seventeen." He held the spoon patiently while Eiric wound more yarn around it. "Why does Bethoc call you *mo cuachag*—my little cuckoo?"

Elspeth shrugged. "She has called me that since I was a child. It is a term used sometimes for little girls who sing sweetly." She felt her cheeks pinken again and took her hand away from his face.

"You do sing sweetly. I hope you are not done," he said softly, his eyes closed. "That feels ... quite nice." She hesitated, then began to rub another dab of ointment into his skin with the tip of a finger. The bruised area had grown flushed and shiny as she had applied the nurturing ointment.

Bethoc was right, she thought. The best healing comes from the hand that gave the hurt. Even her own anger and fear, which had simmered ever since Robert's arrival, seemed to be dissolving. Ruari MacDonald seemed less of a threat too, and the tangle of fear and attraction she felt toward Duncan Macrae had eased.

"*Mo cuachag*," Duncan said. "My little cuckoo. A good name for you, I think. You do tend to repeat yourself." He lifted his brow and opened an eye, a starlight blue twinkle. Then he made a soft cuckoo's call in his throat. Eiric laughed, a sweet, happy trill. He did it again, grinning at Eiric. The child imitated him, and he laughed with her.

Elspeth twisted her mouth in a little grimace. "Stop, you. And how is it that I repeat myself?" She lifted her fingers from his cheek.

"You say over and over that I must leave," he murmured, "but I am content to stay, my little bird." Sitting on his knee, Eiric made the cuckoo sound again.

She frowned. "Do not jest with me."

"Never," Duncan said softly. His gaze locked with hers.

"He is a good, fair man, your lawyer," Bethoc said. She stood in the doorway of the cottage, watching Duncan, who had gone outside to tend to Lasair. He had taken Eiric with him, for she had cried so loudly when he went out the door that he had turned back to scoop her up.

Elspeth watched Eiric earnestly help Duncan pour out a bucketful of oats and barley into a small trough. "My lawyer? He is the queen's lawyer."

"He is good with the child. Magnus should show more interest in Eiric. She adores her father, but he does not really see what a treasure she is. Ask Magnus to come back with the lawyer when he comes to get his horse. Magnus will see the love Eiric shows Duncan Macrae, and he will be jealous."

Elspeth smiled at this devious plan and agreed.

"I saw some images when I held the lawyer's head today," Bethoc said. "There is much goodness in him. But there is a deep sorrow too. I saw sharp steel, and men riding at night. There is more in his past than he tells."

"I sensed an old hurt in him too," Elspeth admitted. She glanced outside. She had wanted to tell Bethoc about the strange and disturbing vision she had seen of the lawyer, but she had not yet found a moment. Perhaps now she could speak of it.

Eiric took Duncan's hand and began to drag him happily toward the little burn at the base of the hill. Elspeth knew that Duncan was about to be coerced into Eiric's favorite pastime, watching the fish in the burn. That would provide the time she needed to talk with Bethoc.

"The first day I met him, I had two visions," Elspeth said, turning away from the open door. She sat on a bench, and Bethoc joined her there, listening attentively as Elspeth told her what she had seen.

Bethoc's brow creased in a frown. "You saw his execution?"

Elspeth nodded. "Somehow," she finished, "I feel that I will lead him to the block. But I do not understand how I could become involved in a political death. Perhaps the vision was wrong."

Bethoc continued to frown. "Such visions prove true, given time. You know that. You have never yet been wrong."

"I have tried to warn him," Elspeth said. "If he leaves the Highlands and stays away from me, perhaps he will not come to the block at all. At least he cannot bring me into his death, and so it may change the outcome for him."

"Warn him and say no more. Fate cannot be altered."

Elspeth shook her head. "I wonder, Bethoc. If a seer warns a woman of an accident with fire, and the woman takes such great care that no burning occurs—then fate has been altered. Have we no responsibility as seers to speak out, to save those in danger?"

Bethoc shook her head. "I think God determines these things, and only shows them to us. Take care, girl. Your heart has been hurt already, seeing the death-knowing for someone."

"But if I could do something to help, perhaps Duncan Macrae's death could be averted."

Bethoc watched her steadily. "My daughter's death would have happened even if you had warned us of what you knew. My healing powers, my herbs, my hands—nothing saved her. Her death was meant to happen, for God's own reasons, not revealed to any."

Elspeth looked down. "I only told you that your daughter would have a beautiful baby girl."

"You said only that, though you knew more. You took all the hurt into yourself. But you were wise to hold your tongue." She leaned forward. "Be wise here too. Warn where you can, and keep silent for the rest. If the lawyer is to die, you cannot change that fate."

"I would if I could."

"Accept what the Sight shows you. When you predict a

happy thing, it is a gift. Do not fret over the rest, or it becomes a burden." Bethoc touched her arm. "I know you feel sorrow over this. Let me look into the water. Augury may help here."

She limped away to fill a wide wooden bowl with water, and placed it on the table, sitting down before it. Murmuring softly, Bethoc passed her hands over the water three times and then stared at the still surface. Elspeth waited.

"There is strength and bravery in this man," Bethoc said. "He is stubborn and loyal. And he is a peacemaker ... although he has the devil's own temper." She tilted her head as if she listened to some inner voice, and watched the calm water.

"This man is your destiny," Bethoc said. "He is your heart, and you are his. That is why you want to change this fate for him. You fear to lose him."

"That is not so," Elspeth breathed.

"I see you standing at his left shoulder."

"I saw the same at the stream," Elspeth said. "My face, close to his left shoulder."

Bethoc nodded. "The left side is the position of love and marriage. There is a bond between you, and there will be a pledge. The bond has already begun to form."

Elspeth bit her lower lip and stayed silent.

Bethoc continued to stare at the water. She shook her head slowly. "I feel death around him ... but his end is not shown to me. Death is there, in his past."

Bethoc drew a deep breath and leaned forward. "I see ravens around him, but the birds have been there a long time. Three ravens. Three deaths trouble him from his past."

Bethoc frowned and leaned forward, her gaze focused on the bowl. "The images are gone now. I can see no more for him unless he asks me himself." She sat back, thoughtful, and then looked at Elspeth. "This man faces a great challenge, danger of some kind. Warn him if you will, but his fate is set for him. He can endure what will come, but he must believe that he can endure it."

Elspeth drew her brows together. "He will die, then?"

Bethoc shrugged. "I did not see it. But if you saw it, perhaps it is so. I felt love and comfort between the two of you."

"Love and comfort?" Elspeth stared in disbelief.

Bethoc nodded. "He will offer you marriage. Accept it."

Elspeth stood quickly, stunned. "How can that be? I have warned him away to save him. A wedding between us would surely seal his fate."

"There is love there, Elspeth. The threat comes from elsewhere. The bond I felt between the two of you is a gift that few ever have. Even if your time together is brief, the gift is precious."

"I will not love a man who will be taken from me! A parting by the heading ax is no memory to treasure!"

A shadow darkened the door of the croft. Elspeth looked up.

Duncan stood in the doorway, holding Eiric in one arm. He looked evenly at Elspeth. There was no smile on his lips, and none in his eyes. She looked away, aware that her words seemed to hang in the air of the little house. A swirl of dread told her that he had heard them.

He stepped into the room. "We have seen enough fish for a lifetime, I think."

Elspeth's heart thumped heavily. She watched as he walked past her to sit on a bench. Eiric curled into his shoulder, nearly asleep, and he spoke softly to Bethoc over the child's head. They laughed, something to do with the fish in the burn.

Elspeth looked at Eiric cuddled against him. What a simple, sweet joy to rest so trustingly in that strong embrace. How blissful to forget, even for a moment, the burden of his future.

To forget too what Bethoc had told her: that he was her heart and she was his. She walked over to Duncan and held out her arms to lift the child from him. Her hands trembled.

He looked at her, his eyes a startling blue in the quiet shadows.

"You look as tired as this little one," he said softly.

She shook her head, accepting Eiric's weight in her arms.

"We should leave soon," he said. "It is a long walk back to Glenran."

"Do not go back," she whispered. "Go south. Go home."

He half smiled, a gentle curve of his upper lip. *"Mo cuachag,"* he said. "Little cuckoo, always with the same tune. When will you change that song?"

"Never," she answered, and turned away.

A few days later, Elspeth returned to Bethoc's home, bringing Duncan and Magnus to fetch the horse, as she had promised. Lasair's hoof was completely healed, and had been since the second day, Bethoc had said. Though Duncan expressed his thanks, he could not convince Bethoc to accept any payment. Elspeth had watched with amusement, knowing that Bethoc would never take coin for such work.

"Come with me, Duncan Macrae. I have a gift for you," Bethoc said after the midday dinner. She beckoned to him. Duncan cast a look at Elspeth before he followed Bethoc into the second room of the small house, divided from the main room by a wattle screen.

Elspeth turned to look at Magnus. He sat with Eiric, who had climbed up into his lap. He raised his eyebrows in curiosity at Elspeth. "Bethoc likes the lawyer, then," he said.

"She does," Elspeth said. "Very much."

Elspeth crossed to peer into the weaving room. Magnus lifted Eiric into one arm and followed. Eiric played with her father's blond braids as they watched Bethoc, who showed Duncan the weaving piece stretched on her loom.

Inside the small room, bright afternoon light sliced through a window. A cupboard, a stool, and the large loom filled the snug space. An incomplete piece of tartaned plaid, blocks of dark green and blue crisscrossed with red and yellow stripes, was stretched on the wooden framework.

Duncan touched the taut cloth. "This is where the Glenran Frasers get their fine blue and green plaids, I think," he said.

"They do," Bethoc said. "Woad, for the blue, and broom plant, which gives a fine green color, grow in abundance near here. I use those colors in my yarns." She rubbed her hand along the cloth. "Tartan designs are very simple. Colored stripes and blocks are repeated in the warp and then in the weft." Duncan nodded as she pointed out the pattern.

"Bethoc is well-known for her fine tartan," Elspeth said from the doorway. "The Frasers wear them, and she sells many lengths of plaid every spring and fall at the Inverness market."

"Tch," Bethoc said, "I make enough to give to the Mac-Shimi. He trades it once or twice in the year, and always brings me good soap and salt and wine in return."

"Hugh makes certain that Bethoc has whatever she needs," Magnus told Duncan. "Herbs and plants from England or Flanders, leather shoes, dishes. She will take little from him for her fine cloths."

"He tries to give me silver and gold too, though I have little enough use for coins," Bethoc said.

"You could sell for a higher price in the Lowland markets," Duncan said, fingering the thick, soft wool. "There is a demand for good Scottish wool just now, both raw and spun, and for tartan weaving of this quality."

Bethoc laughed. "I am a weaver, and I take joy in that. I care nothing for profit. Hugh Fraser brings me what I need."

Duncan nodded. Elspeth noted that he respected and understood Bethoc's simple needs. The queen's lawyer had a caring heart, just as Bethoc had told her; though he may have become a Lowlander for the most part, he was not avaricious like Robert Gordon.

Bethoc tilted her dark head and looked frankly at Duncan. "You are a fine, handsome man, Duncan Macrae," she said. "You have a look of my husband to you, with those blue eyes and dark hair, and I wish I was years younger." She smiled. "But I see that you lack a good plaid. I will give you a length of good cloth, but you must promise to wear it."

"He is Highland born and raised," Elspeth said. "So he must have worn the wrapped plaid before."

He swiveled his glance toward her. "I have," he said. "But in the Lowlands, a Highland plaid is no advantage."

"And is it an advantage to wear the trews all day, with no real freedom for the body? Or to wear only the raven's color?" Bethoc turned to the cupboard and opened it. Inside were folded tartan plaids. She chose a thick cloth of dark green, crossed with red, yellow, and brown.

"When you wear the colors of the earth, you invite its protection," she told him, opening the cloth.

Duncan let Bethoc drape the plaid around him, arranging it loosely. "This is too fine a gift," he said. "Let me pay you."

"You will not," she declared. "To refuse this gift would bring you ill luck." She looked keenly at him. "And you have no need of poor luck, Duncan."

He smiled ruefully. "That I do not." He admired the plaid in the light. "This is skilled work. I have not seen a plaid this fine since I was a boy." Grasping a handful of the wool in his hand, he rubbed his thumb over it. "Soft and thick."

"Ah," Bethoc said. "You have been in the south country, where the weavers make thin two-color plaids fit only for wrapping mutton. This is carded wool, which makes a softer and warmer cloth than that combed wool the Lowlanders produce." She smiled, her pride lending a radiance to her handsome face. "I use four and more colors in my tartans, sometimes seven. They are good designs. You will be glad to have one."

"I am that," he said. "My thanks, Bethoc. I owe you much, for the cloth and for healing both my horse and myself." He touched a finger to his cheekbone, which was clear and smooth.

Her green eyes crinkled beneath a slight frown. "You are welcome. I will take no payment from you. I pray that you will return a favor to me, for the day will come when I will ask for it."

Duncan lifted a brow quizzically but only nodded.

Bethoc's ominous words sent a heavy fear through Elspeth. She wanted to see him gone from here, not bound to any of them. The bond of caution would be signed, and he would leave. *Please,* she prayed fervently, *let him leave soon.*

"You look like a fine Highlandman now," Magnus said.

Duncan smiled, and Elspeth looked up at him. He fisted his hands on his hips, and the Lowland lawyer seemed to disappear, revealing a Highlander as wild as her cousins. The plaid seemed to set a cold fire in his blue eyes and lend power and pride to his already strong stance.

She drew in her breath, and realized that she had begun to love him. The sudden thought set her stomach to spinning.

"Soon," Magnus said, watching from the door, "we will go on a hunt. Will you come, Macrae?"

"Surely I will."

"And what do we hunt, MacDonalds?" Elspeth asked, more sharply than she intended.

Duncan laughed and shook his head. "Only the red deer, girl," he said. "Your clan has done enough hunting of MacDonalds."

Chapter 11

"O will ye be a robber's wife
Or will ye die by my pen-knife?"
"O I'll nae be a robber's wife
An' I'll nae die by your pen-knife."
—*"The Bonny Bonny Banks o Fordie"*

"Abab!" Kenneth swore in disgust. He relaxed his hold on the bowstring and turned to glare at Elspeth, who had just sneezed. The light sound had scattered the herd of deer that they had been stalking throughout the morning.

"Sorry," she murmured. Along with Kenneth, Magnus, and Duncan, she lay flat on her stomach in deep, damp heather beneath the wide gray bowl of the sky. From her perch on the hilltop, she glimpsed the white tails as the deer escaped into a thick birch wood. Sighing, she turned to sit up, and another waft of heathery scent tickled her nose. She sneezed again.

"Elspeth—" Kenneth began impatiently.

"The girl could not help it, now," Duncan said. He got to his feet and stretched his arms. "We will find the deer again. And we have been lying here on our bellies for a long time. All of us are tired and stiff and hungry."

"Very hungry," Elspeth grumbled.

"We should have left her at home," Kenneth muttered as he stood up. Elspeth was not surprised to see a near pout on his face. Kenneth was very intense about deer stalking, and had often complained that she was restless on a long hunt and too unwilling to see the deer brought down. Yet he often asked her to come, because she seemed to know where to find the deer.

Her Sight allowed her to sense the deer. Unlike the dull, plodding presence of cattle, the deer felt to her like the western wind, soft, light, and fast. She loved their elegant grace, their earthy coloring, their silent alertness.

And though she did not enjoy hunting, she had come out with her cousins today, and she knew why. Sliding a glance at Duncan, she stood and brushed at the bits of heather scattered over the wool of her plaid.

Since dawn they had been stalking about twenty deer, following the herd over hills and moors on quick, silent feet. Her cousins and Duncan carried long yew bows, with quivers slung over their backs. They had stopped often to watch and wait; hunting required a great deal of lying still in wet heather and hours of tedious silence. Elspeth would rather roam the hills, watching the deer run freely along the moors, than stalk them for a kill.

She scanned the overcast sky. The day had been damp; her plaid was wet, her bare knees were mucky, and her braid was heavy with mist. Cold and hungry as well, she was impatient to be done with the hunt.

Duncan leaned over and murmured to Magnus, who nodded. Elspeth, watching, noticed the handsome, lean lines of Duncan's face, the black slash of his brows, the thick fringe of eyelashes. He spoke again, soft and low, and the deep rumble seemed to tingle throughout her body.

She sighed and kicked at a snag of purple heather. This keen awareness of a man who should not be here, who should be riding his tall horse back to his queen, had been consuming her. Over the past several days she had found herself staring at him frequently. And she had caught many times the quick flash of his blue eyes, the winging down of his black lashes.

She wished that he had never kissed her that night on the fairy hill. Then she wished that he would do it again before he left Glenran. She wanted to feel that dizzying, joyful lift of her soul just once more. An echo of that excitement returned as she looked at him now.

He wore the green plaid Bethoc had given him, with his fine linen shirt beneath; he had borrowed wool knee stockings and a pair of leather brogues. Much better, she thought, than wearing the raven's color while trying to hide

among the hills and heather. Her eyes covered the fine,
long length of him, over his tautly muscled legs and long
powerful back. His hair spread between his shoulders like
a glossy black wing.

Magnus shouldered his bow and turned to Duncan. "If
we do not chase the deer now, we may lose them."

Duncan looked up at the sky. "There will not be much
time left to hunt. Rain hangs in those clouds, and if that
happens, the deer will find cover. We should go now."

"Then I will fetch the ponies to carry the game," Magnus
said, and loped off toward a copse of birches not far away,
where two sturdy garrons were tethered.

While they were talking, Elspeth scanned the birch trees
below, where the deer had run. She could sense them somewhere off to the left, but could not see them.

Duncan came to stand beside her, lifting a hand to shade
his eyes. He watched the forest carefully. "Look there,"
he called to Kenneth. "The deer are just inside the wood,
heading west."

"Come ahead, then," Kenneth said. "We will catch them
now, I think. Elspeth, you wait here."

She looked at him in surprise. "But—"

"I will not lose the deer again. With the rain coming, we
will either find game now or call off the hunt."

"Kenneth is right," Magnus told her, coming back with
the horses. "Wait under those trees. We will be back soon."

She scowled openly at her cousins. Kenneth raised a finger and pointed at the stand of birches nearby. Knowing
that she could listen or not as she pleased, she also did not
want Kenneth to lose his quarry, since it meant so much
to him.

She sighed and shrugged. If she did not feel like waiting
long, she would just walk back to Castle Glenran.

Kenneth waved Magnus forward impatiently. They
stepped over the rise of the hill and climbed downward
toward the birch wood.

Duncan began to follow, then turned to her. "Stay under
the cover of the trees. Those clouds are heavy with rain."

She scowled at him too. He returned a half smile and

followed the others down the hill. They crossed a small burn and entered the wood, and she was able to glimpse Duncan's green plaid as he walked between the trees. Soon she could no longer distinguish his plaid from the tangled screen of birch and alder and fern that filled the stretch of forest.

Plucking a stem of heather, she twirled it in her fingers until the silvery stem and tiny purple bells were a blur of soft color. She felt as turned about as the stem, picked up and cast into a spin. Duncan Macrae had caused it, and she felt almost helpless to stop it. Her attraction to the man was as confusing as it was compelling.

A quick, strong breeze battered her hair and plaid. Glancing anxiously at the ragged gray clouds that gathered overhead, she headed for the birch copse. Where a tiny burn cut through the moor, burbling over rocks, she stopped to scoop up a handful of cold water and drank it. Then she went into the shelter of the trees.

Sitting on the ground, she unwrapped a hunk of cheese that Flora had sent with her and ate it, leaning against a tree trunk. She glanced up at the stormy sky, which gave an eerie grayish green light. The wind was chilly, and she folded her arms over her chest for warmth.

Softly at first, and then more loudly, she began to sing, her voice blending with the rise and fall of the wind. She closed her eyes and listened to her song, thinking only of the warbling sweetness of the tune.

Suddenly she broke off the song and sat up. One hand glided back to touch the hilt of the little *sgian dubh* tucked at her belt. A prickle at the back of her neck told her that something disturbed the peacefulness of the birch copse; she had learned never to ignore such a feeling. Looking around carefully, she saw nothing and slowly sat back again.

Glancing up at the darkening clouds that rolled over the hills, she told herself that she must have sensed the threat of the impending storm, which looked as if it would be fierce. But her cousins and Duncan would return soon.

Resuming her song, she tapped out a rhythm on her knee.

"Lovely," a voice said. She turned her head quickly. A man sat on a pony, silhouetted against the sky. Leaping to her feet, Elspeth reached back for her little knife and slid it free.

"Elspeth Fraser," the man said, stepping the pony slowly toward her. "We must talk."

She angled the blade toward him. He stopped a few paces away and watched her, his eyes wary. A thick shock of reddish hair blew back from his forehead. His red plaid was oddly brilliant in the greenish light.

"We must talk, Elspeth," he repeated. "Come here, girl."

Her fingers flexed on the handle of the knife. "We have no words to share, Ruari MacDonald," she said.

Thunder rumbled in the distance as Duncan and the Frasers left the wood. Kenneth had shot one of the hinds and Duncan another. The animals were now slung over the backs of the two garrons, along with the bows and quivers.

"The quickest path back to Glenran is that way," Kenneth called to Duncan, pointing in an opposite direction.

The wind lifted the plaid at Duncan's shoulder, and blew his hair wildly. "You go on," he called over the wind. "I will get Elspeth." The Frasers nodded and moved off, leading the horses. Duncan began to climb back up the long hill toward the place where they had left Elspeth.

Narrowing his eyes, he looked up. An ominous cloud bank, heavy and dark, moved rapidly across the sky. He felt an uncomfortable prickly sensation, like dread, forming at the back of his neck. The threat of the coming storm must be making him anxious, he thought. Picking his way around the sharp angles of rocks, he took the slope with long steps, wanting to find the girl and get back to the castle as soon as possible.

Thunder pounded somewhere off to his left. He doubted now that they would reach the castle without a thorough soaking. He heard a raw screech and glanced up. Overhead, a raven cut past, its wide wings carrying it away from the storm. Elspeth would not like that omen, he thought wryly. Ravens made her anxious. He watched the bird before he went on. More thunder growled, and a crash of lightning struck somewhere far behind him. The sky was now as dark as at twilight.

Reaching the top of the hill, he saw them almost immediately. A man in a red plaid sat a pony near Elspeth. Their backs were turned away from him. He wondered for an instant if she had found another of her cousins, part of the MacShimi's tail. If so, he would have to be careful to approach more politely this time.

Then, in one fast motion, the man slid from his horse and lunged at Elspeth. Grabbing her wrist, he twisted her savagely as they locked together in a struggle.

Duncan ducked his head down and ran, groping for his dirk, pounding across the moor. His shoulder hit the man's back with all the force of the thunder that slammed overhead.

Elspeth cried out as all three of them went down in a brutal tangle. Throwing one arm around the man's neck, Duncan pressed the flat of his blade to the man's chest and tightened his grasp. Rolling away to free Elspeth, who was caught underneath, Duncan threw his leg over the man's thigh and pinned him securely.

Trapped, the man cursed in a guttural, half choked voice. Duncan did not relax his grip but glanced at Elspeth, who had scuttled away to crouch nearby. She watched them with wide eyes.

"Who are you?" Duncan asked. Rust-colored hair and a red plaid were all that he had seen so far. "What do you want here?"

The man swore and struggled against him, but Duncan gripped hard around his neck and pressed the edge of the dirk against his throat. Although Duncan was the larger of the two, his opponent was compact and wiry, with an iron strength that challenged Duncan's ability to hold him.

"Say your name," Duncan rasped.

"Ruari MacDonald," the man spat out.

Duncan glanced at Elspeth. She nodded. "Get up," she said, her voice quavering. "Please, both of you, get up."

Duncan slid his weight slowly off Ruari, grabbing his arm to pull it behind. Allowing Ruari to get to his feet, he twisted his arm viciously to hold him. With his free hand Duncan pressed the point of the blade to Ruari's throat.

"Why did you attack Elspeth? And may I tell you that I have recently sharpened my dirk," Duncan said.

"I only wanted to speak with her," Ruari said. He was so much shorter that Duncan could easily see over the top of his head. Red hair, the color of old blood, lay in snarls. Ruari turned his head, and Duncan glimpsed red-stubbled cheeks and small brown eyes, flat and angry. Ruari glared at him, and then at Elspeth, who now stood a few paces away. She grasped a knife in her hand, her feet in a wide stance, and glared back.

"You have no cause to speak with her, and you have no cause to ride on Fraser land. MacDonalds have lately been seen reiving cattle and sheep, and harming Fraser kin. If I were a Fraser, your throat would be cut now." He pressed the blade closer for emphasis. "Perhaps I shall let Elspeth do that."

She took a step forward, eyes flashing silver fire.

Ruari flinched. "She is a damnable witch. But my uncle obtained her for my bride, and her brother made the promise good. Gordon has tried to withdraw it now, but the Frasers owe her to me. I saw her out here, and only tried to tell her that I am still willing to wed her."

"If you saw her here, then you have been following her," Duncan said. Ruari said nothing, only slid a glance at Elspeth.

"If you say I am a witch, why do you want me for a wife?" Elspeth demanded.

Ruari looked at her for a long moment. Duncan saw the lust in those flat brown eyes, in the curl of his lip, heard it in the hoarse rasp of the man's breath. He knew why Ruari wanted her. The knowledge sent a twist of rage through his gut. He squeezed the hilt of the dirk in an effort to keep it still.

"The crown has sent word that we must cease our fighting with Clan Fraser," Ruari said. "My uncle wants this marriage made, since you are the MacShimi's cousin." He stared at her, breathing hard. "I need a wife. Once you are away from the evil influence of that old clubfooted witch, you will not practice witchcraft," Ruari said. "Our marriage would help both our clans. Tell the MacShimi that I will still take you to wife."

Elspeth took a sudden step forward and stood face to face with Ruari. "Let him go," she said to Duncan.

He frowned at her. "Elspeth—"

"Let him go."

He released Ruari's arm, but laid the point of his dirk between Ruari's shoulder blades. He waited, watching Elspeth.

She stared at Ruari, who stood only a little taller than she did. Thunder rumbled and leaves rustled in the cold, fast wind.

"If you should visit Bethoc MacGruer again," she said, "you will learn what witchery can do. I will hunt you myself and see you die before my eyes." She struck him in the face with the flat of her knife, raising a thin thread of blood across his cheek. "That is owed to you for Bethoc."

She stepped back. "Get on your horse and be gone from here. I lay a *damnadh* on you, Ruari. You will not touch me or my kin unless you wish to bring harm to yourself."

Ruari uttered what sounded like a low, feral growl. He tried to move, but Duncan pressed the dirk against his back.

"Nor will you harm this man," Elspeth said, her voice clear and hard. "He is Duncan Macrae, the queen's own lawyer. Even you, Ruari MacDonald, must honor this man's authority."

"Macrae!" The word was a snarl. Flaring his nostrils, Ruari slid a glare at him and spat. Duncan watched him steadily, quelling the bitter anger that rose in him. He gave support to Elspeth's warning by his unwavering gaze and the pressure of his dirk point.

With a sudden, powerful wrench, Ruari burst away from

Duncan and began to run. When Duncan leaped forward to pursue him, Elspeth leaped too, pulling hard at Duncan's arm.

"Let him go!" she said. Duncan looked at her with surprise.

Reaching his pony, Ruari vaulted up, lifted the reins, and rode out onto the moor. A sudden explosion of thunder ripped through the tree cover.

Elspeth looked up at Duncan, breathing fast.

"Dhia," he muttered, shoving his fingers through his hair. "We would be safer if the man were dead, girl."

"I wanted you to do it," she said, "but I was afraid."

"Afraid of what?"

"If you killed him, you might seal your own fate. He is John MacDonald's nephew, and you are the queen's lieutenant in the eastern Highlands. You could be brought to trial."

He sighed, knowing this was true. Seeing that she trembled, he wrapped his fingers around her arm to steady her. "Cease your fretting," he said. "No harm will come to me." Thunder rose, wild and loud, and the wind tore at their hair. He looked up. "A bolt of lightning is a much more serious threat now. We need to find some shelter."

Nodding, Elspeth grabbed his hand. "Come this way."

She yanked on his arm and they began to run through the birches and down a little hill. In the distance a stiff thread of lightning spooled to the ground. The first drops of rain began to splash, fat and cold.

"This way!" she shouted over the storm.

Chapter 12

*"I'll grow into your arms two
Like iron in hot fire;
But hold me fast, let me not go,
Then you'll have your desire."*
                            —"Tam Lin"

Thunder rolled through the sky and lightning struck the
moor behind them with a frightening crash. Within moments they were running through a soaking, pounding rain.
Seeing a thatched-roof hut between some trees, Duncan
headed there, pulling her with him.

The door swung open easily, and he yanked her inside,
slamming the door shut. Leaning against it, breathing hard,
only then did he look around to see who stood there, no
doubt surprised by their sudden entrance.

"No one lives here," Elspeth said, breathing fast. "This
is a shieling, used by the herders during the summer pastur-
ing." She wiped her wet face with the palm of her hand,
pushing back the tangle of hair that had slipped out of
her braid. "We can make a fire. There will be blankets
here too."

Nodding, Duncan continued to lean against the door,
feeling wind gusts batter it, and looked around the hut. A
small window admitted stormy light into the dank room; a
stone hearth lay in the middle of the floor, cold and empty.

A flash of lightning illuminated the room. Elspeth walked
over to a wooden chest, opened it, and took out folded
plaids. Blasts of rain swept through the little window. Duncan could feel the cold spray from where he stood.

Elspeth went to the window and closed the shutter, fastening it with a leather loop. In the sudden darkness, cracks
in the door and window admitted only murky light.

With her back turned, Elspeth unwrapped her long plaid. In the dimness her linen shirt was a pale blur, her bare legs a slender, graceful gleam. She drew a blanket over her shoulders and tossed the other toward him, then draped her plaid over the table to dry.

"Your plaid is wet," she said. "Use the other blanket." He moved away from the door and took off his belt, then unwrapped his plaid and removed his boots, to stand in his long shirt. He draped the old blanket, which smelled pungent and musty, over his shoulders, and hung his wet plaid over the table beside hers.

Elspeth sat by the cold hearth, holding two sticks in her hands. Setting one upright against the other, she began to twirl the vertical stick. After several attempts she emitted a little cry of frustration.

"Let me," Duncan said. Slipping his dirk from its sheath, he went over to kneel beside her. He felt the chill in her small fingers as she handed the sticks to him.

His father had taught him how to make a need-fire when he had been a child. With the dirk he sliced into one stick, sharpening the end. Then he set the point into a depression cut in the other stick, and rolled the upright stick patiently between his palms.

Soon he smelled a wisp of smoke. A flame jumped up, a tiny golden light in the dark. With a little tug at his heart, he remembered the wide grin of approval his father would give him whenever he had managed to start the fire.

He glanced at her, and she smiled. The faint gold light revealed the elusive dimple in her cheek. "There are peat blocks in the back corner," she said, and went to fetch them, stacking them inside the stone circle. Adding the flame, Duncan nurtured it, blowing, waiting. The glow caught and spread into the dry peat with a crackle and a waft of musty sweetness. Smoke stung his eyes as it drifted up toward an opening in the roof.

Duncan sat beside Elspeth and held his hands out to the growing heat. They listened to the moaning wind and the steady patter of rain on the thatched roof. She jumped slightly at a loud burst of thunder, followed closely by a crack of lightning.

"The storm will not last," he said.

"I wonder if my cousins found shelter," she said as another growl of thunder rolled past.

"They might have made it back to Glenran before the storm. Ruari, though, was surely caught by this."

She nodded. The low firelight threw a web of amber patterns across the smooth skin of her cheeks, and lent a golden sparkle to the curls that framed her brow.

"You showed courage to face him as you did," he said.

"I was angry," she said. "And I knew that you would never let him harm me."

"Why did you strike him for Bethoc?" he asked.

She looked down. "He hurt her once," she said softly.

He nodded. "You gave him a cut and a damning. He ran from you, not from me," he said, and lifted a brow at her.

She slid him a quick look, her clear gray eyes reflecting flame. "I saw how easily you could have cut his throat. But you held back, though your blade shook with it. I thought long-robes were raised in libraries and fed on ink and paper. But you know hunting and raiding, and how to take a man to the ground and hold him there."

He twitched back a smile. "This long-robe has seen more than libraries and trial rooms. I have lived on both sides of the law. And with both Scots."

She tilted her head. "What do you mean, both Scots?"

"In the Lowlands, the Highlanders are called wild Scots. And they, in turn, call Lowlanders the housekeeping Scots."

"Are you?"

"Am I what?" He relaxed back on his side, reclining on an elbow, sliding his bare feet toward the heat of the hearth.

"Are you a housekeeping Scot?"

"I have rooms in Edinburgh, and a woman to keep them."

She lowered her eyes away from him. "Ah. I see."

He grinned, knowing she did not see, and delighted that

she was bothered by it at all. "The woman who keeps my
house is at least a hundred years old, and related to my
mother's family. Did you think I was married?"

She shrugged. He saw her cheeks ripen in the amber
light.

"Could you not tell that with your Sight?"

"I cannot read you so well, I think," she said.

He nearly laughed at that. She read him better than she
knew. He remembered what she had said about the scar
he had gotten at the hands of the MacDonalds. But he
would keep that to himself. "You foretold disaster for me
fast enough when I first came here. I have suffered your
angry warnings for some time now."

"But you will not listen to my warnings, even now that
I have told you just what I saw for you." She turned wide
eyes to him. "I have no anger toward you, only concern."

He raised an eyebrow. "Concern? Is that why you pulled
a dirk on me in my bed, or cannoned a door into my face?
Is that why you walk ahead of me as if you would rather
speak to a stone about the weather than to me about any
matter at all? Spare me your concern, girl. Enemies would
treat me with more kindness."

She flushed. "I have a temper."

"You do, and it is easily raised. And you have a well of
pride in that red-gold head." He held out his hand, wiggling
his long fingers at her. "Here, take my hand and read me
with your Sight."

She looked at him but made no move. Sighing, he leaned
forward, grasping her hand. "You will find that I will live
a long life. And that perhaps will ease your concern."

She shook his hand free. "I am no teller of fortunes like
the Egyptians that travel through here now and again. I am
a seer. The knowledge seeks me, I do not seek it."

"You do not ask the future with bones and stones, or
some other object?"

"Bethoc has the Sight, but she also looks with stones, or
water, or fire. She has taught me how to do that, but I
prefer to wait for the knowledge to come. Sometimes I can
sense what lies in someone's past, or sense the coming of

danger, or where animals might be. Cattle and deer are like a scent on the wind." She shrugged. "It is difficult to explain. But when true visions come, they come fast and sharp."

"Did you know Ruari would attack you, then?"

She shook her head. "I only felt uneasy waiting there. Not every misfortunate thing is foretold."

"Have you had the Sight all your life?" He sat straighter, listening attentively as he was always careful to do. He could not easily accept the idea of prophecy. But he had to admit, grudgingly, that Elspeth possessed some ability that could not be defined or measured. Because he was curious to know more about her, he was curious about the Sight.

More thunder, followed by the violent crash of lightning, seemed to shake the little house. Elspeth drew a breath and clutched the blanket around her shoulders.

"I was very small when the Sight first came to me," she said. "I saw a young gillie standing by the hearth in the great hall, wet to the skin, holding his hands out to the fire. He looked at me, and his face was pale like ice—" She caught her breath and then went on. "I asked him if he wanted a blanket. He was dripping water onto the floor stones. I called my aunt. She came into the room and said that no one was there, and scolded me for telling a tale."

"The gillie had not really been there?"

She shook her head. "The floor stones were dry. But I saw him, I spoke to him. I still remember his face. The next day he drowned while crossing a river."

Duncan was quiet for a long while. "Magnus told me that your visions are always true ones."

"They are," she said. "I have never been wrong."

"This time you will be wrong." He raised his eyes to hers. The sudden conviction that he felt steeled his glance.

She looked away. "You do not believe in the Sight."

"I do not. This vision frightens you, not me. This time you will be wrong, Elspeth."

"I should never have told you," she said. "No man

should hear a prediction of his death. It is too great a burden."

He took her hand, sliding his fingers over cool skin, small bones. "I am not afraid of this." She would have pulled her hand back, but he held it. "Look at me."

She lifted her eyes. He saw fear in her silver-gray gaze, not of him but for him. He saw hurt there too; if there was a burden here, she carried the weight of it.

Inside him something seemed to give, seemed to open and melt. He wanted to offer her some comfort. She was hurting inside because of what she feared for him; he wanted to give her reassurance that none of this would touch him.

Letting go of her hand, he slipped his fingers along the side of her face. She looked up at him. Beneath his hand the bones of her jaw and her slender neck felt small and vulnerable.

"Listen to me," he murmured. "I am not a doomed man. No vision has power over me."

She gazed at him steadily. "I wish that were true."

"It is. I will not let it happen."

She looked away. Beneath his hand he felt her swallow. "Do you understand? I will not let it happen."

"Bethoc says that when a vision comes like that, it is destined," she whispered. "How can fate be stopped?"

His thumb traced along her cheek. He thought he saw the limpid gleam of tears in her eyes. "Who can say what fate will hold for me, or for you? I feel no fear of this. None."

"I do not want this to happen to you. Before, I did not care so much, but now ..." A tear slipped out, and the warm drop touched his hand.

A force gathered in him, like the pull of an eddy, like the force of a wind that moves the clouds before it. His heart thundered softly as he smoothed his fingers down her cheek, along her jaw. He swore to himself then that he would prove to her that the vision was wrong. No fear swirled in his belly when she spoke of this thing. He wanted to convince her—he needed to convince her—that he was safe.

He would have given anything just then to take the pain out of her gaze. Not since his grandmother had anyone showed so much concern for his well-being. The knowledge that Elspeth did, for no reason but that her heart was giving by nature, stunned him, touched him deeply. She felt remorse and fear on his behalf. He felt an urge to ease it for her, but did not know how.

Leaning forward and tilting her chin up, he lowered his head and kissed her, slow and easy, offering the only tangible comfort that he could.

"I have cheated the raven before," he said. "I will be here a long time, girl."

She made a little sound like a whimper and looped her arms around his neck. The blankets slipped down, hers and then his, and he pulled her closer, spreading his hands along her back.

Through the thin fabric of their damp shirts, he could feel her breasts against his chest, soft and yielding, their tips firm. The sensation quickened and deepened his breath. He met her lips again, and she drew in a long breath, followed by a tiny shudder. She opened her mouth a little, and he tasted the inner moisture there.

He drew his mouth from hers and held her head, tilting it down gently to kiss her forehead. She closed her eyes and he shifted to rest his cheek against hers.

"Elspeth," he whispered. The wind moaned overhead, and new rain burst over the roof. "What happens when I am with you? Do you feel it?"

"I feel it," she whispered. She raised her face to his, and he kissed her, long and slow and gentle at first, until the burgeoning insistence within him changed the nature of the kiss, changed the course of the moment. He knew that she felt the whirlpool along with him, and knew, finally, that they were caught in its powerful flow.

His fingers glided along her throat, over the slight bones of her chest, to the place where the slope of her breasts began. She drew in her breath, and he let his hand glide farther, over the soft, gentle curve of her breasts, over her ribs to her hip, turned and inviting, to the edge of the shirt's hem.

Slipping his fingers under the loose linen, feeling her breathe and shift and stir in his arms, he rested his hand on her thigh. A subtle heat emanated from her body. He sighed against her mouth as the heat of his own body began to resonate with hers. Inhaling sharply, he knew that the lodestone that was her, that was him, had turned again. The pull was stronger than he had felt before. He did not know if he could resist its draw.

His hand hovered on her thigh, and his fingertips caressed the soft skin of her hip. "Ah, Elspeth," he breathed, "do you want this? Do you feel what this is between us?"

"I feel it," she repeated as before. "I want this." He sensed that she felt no fear of this moment. Though she might dread the future for him, she seemed to welcome what burgeoned between them now. He could sense it in her steadily pounding heart, could feel it in her sweet, even breaths against his cheek.

Somehow, he knew that the finest reassurance he could give her would be to share with her the life that flowed within him. Life, not death; love rather than fear. He needed that himself.

He did not believe in prophecy, but he had heard the knell of a death warning and needed renewal. He wanted to replace that drone with the pulse of life, for her and for himself.

She shifted to touch her mouth to his, and he sighed, pulling her to him in a fierce embrace. She tightened her arms around his neck and tilted her head, parting her lips. His tongue slipped inside, where she was moist and sweet and warm.

A spiral of excitement swirled through his gut and plunged into his loins, filling him completely, heating him, demanding more. The urge grew and spun until he lay back, taking her with him, drawing her body over his, pressing her hips against his turgid center. She sighed and wrapped her legs around him, and her soft breath mingled with his. Only a thin piece of fabric separated them. His loins surged, aching with fullness. He might have satisfied himself with a shift and quick thrust, but he held back.

She slid her hands up under his shirt, over his bare chest, over his shoulders. When her hands neared the long scar, he shifted, rolling her onto her back. Skimming his hands up her body, he encircled her breasts. Incredible softness and a sweet, firm weight filled his hands. The warm, tight nubs pressed into his palms, hardening further when he eased his thumbs over them.

She arched her back and her breath quickened. He touched his lips to her breast, taking its silkiness into his mouth, moaning low at the deep, wondrous pleasure. Drifting his lips upward again, he kissed her throat, took her mouth, and slid his hands beneath her, pressing her hips upward with splayed, urgent fingers.

Her fingertips feathered through the soft thick hair over his chest, across his ribs and down, over his belly to where he was hard and swollen. She did not touch him, although his body throbbed with anticipation. She took his tongue then into her mouth and took his breath away.

The wind moaned again, and the walls trembled around them, and the fire flickered in the draft. A crash of thunder startled her, but when a rich gust of rain poured down, he felt the tension drain from her body.

He pulled away from her and drew up the light linen of her shirt, wanting to see the pale gleam of her skin in the dimness. Deep, warm coppery light swirled over her body. Running his fingers down the lithe curving length of her torso, he cupped a hand over the downy cleft, heated and sweet, between her legs. He leaned forward again to kiss her mouth. She shifted, and his fingers slipped inside, so easily.

His other hand circled around her back. Her heart beat fiercely, drumming against his chest, stirring him to embrace her, to bury his face for a moment in the rain-sweet softness of her hair.

His own heart pounded with wild force. He felt the blood pulse through him, felt the muscles harden, felt the heaving, heady flow of his own strength, his own aliveness. Beneath his fingertip, deep within her, she moved, undulating so that her hidden layers opened for him.

Quickening her movements, quickening her breath, she reached for him instinctively, pulling at his shirt. He slid over her, succumbing to the pulsing force between them. He shifted, and she opened to him, and her little cry of momentary fear sounded soft in his ear, so soft that he murmured reassurance with his gentle thrust.

A sigh, and another, and the heated, moist, secret part of her accepted him as if he were her core, some lost part of herself joyously reclaimed. She took him in, soothing, urging, succoring him as if she could envelop his very soul, surround him with love and suspend time.

And he knew then that this was his affirmation to her: that he was vital and alive. He was part of life, part of her life now. Warnings and threats could not touch them here. Time, sight, future or past did not exist here. Only this moment existed, only touch, and warmth, and scent, and the sound of their hearts and their breath.

He followed the heated, throbbing pulses of his body, thrusting deeper into her, wanting her to feel him, to know that he would be here forever, that he would be here for her. And with each breath he took, each thrust he made, he fell deeper into the whirlpool.

Duncan sat by the fire in his wrapped and brooched plaid. Elspeth finished lacing her boots and crossed her legs, gazing into the low flames. She glanced at Duncan, saw him watching her steadily, and glanced away again.

What had happened between them had filled her with a sweet, languid sensation, a keen awareness of her body, of him, of her surroundings. She felt the damp, cool drift of the breeze that came in from the open window now that the rain had stopped. She felt the wool and linen against her skin, and smelled the familiar musty peat smoke and the combined odors of damp wool, and sweat, and rain.

What his hands, his lips, his body, had given her was beyond definition. A precious gift, she knew, and she had returned it in full. When he had reached out to her at first, she had suddenly, urgently, wanted to ease the awful effect of her constant death warnings. Without knowing how it had happened, she had given naturally and generously to him. But she had found ease and solace there for herself too, and had discovered something more, a whirling, fervent joy. She felt as refreshed, as renewed, as the land outside following the thunderstorm.

What had shivered through her body, and what had poured from his hands, from his body, into her soul, had been an intense, magical love. She felt it still, infusing her whole being.

She glanced at him again, and he smiled, holding out his hand. Elspeth took his fingers silently, caught up in her thoughts.

But she felt tentative, unsure, knowing her life would change somehow. For now, Duncan was here with her. The elusive filaments that bound them had become more tightly woven in the last hour. She knew Duncan felt it too. And she knew with certainty that this bond could bring disaster for him.

She drew in a deep breath of fresh, wet air and sighed deeply. Bethoc had told her that Duncan was her heart, and that she was his. Although the fear she had felt seemed muted by the love that had begun between them, Elspeth knew that the vision was still there, unchanged. She wanted to believe what he had told her—that he was in no danger—but she could not.

"Here," Duncan said, reaching into the swath of plaid over his chest. "Flora sent this with me." He handed her a small leather flask. She opened it, smelled the fire of the liquor inside, and sipped. The sweet burn strengthened her. She looked at him.

"You must go back to Edinburgh, Duncan," she said huskily. "I am truly frightened now. We should not be together."

He grasped her hand firmly. "I must stay at Glenran a bit longer. Do you not want that?"

She lowered her head, her loosened braid swinging over her shoulders. "Go soon," she said. "Please."

He sighed. "When the bond of caution is signed, I must take the paper back to Edinburgh."

"Good," she said. "Stay away from the Highlands."

He leaned over suddenly, turning her by the shoulders to face him, drawing her near. "And when I leave here, will I see you again?"

She smiled sadly. "You will wed some court lady and live a peaceful life. If you leave the Highlands."

"Ah," he said, "you are a stubborn girl. Is that another prediction? The ladies of the queen's court are not like you. I would be very bored with no one to say my doom now and again."

"It is no doom to wed a fine Lowland lady," she said.

"Well," he said, taking his hands from her shoulders, "some are quite gracious, I admit."

"They wear no plain woolen plaids but silks, I hear."

"Silk and damask and lace. Jewels, pearls in their hair, fine fragrances." He glanced at her.

"Ah," she said in a small voice, looking away.

"And they are quite learned. Some can read many languages."

"I can read Latin," she said.

Duncan narrowed his eyes and studied the flames. "But I have never met a Lowland lady who would wade barefoot through a peat bog. Nor who would wield a dirk, or ride through the night after cattle. Or face a wild Scot holding only a small knife."

"They must be very beautiful, these gracious ladies."

"They are," he agreed, teasing her affably. "But not a one I know has hair like gold and copper spun together. Or has the voice of an angel. Or the step of a fairy," he added in a loud whisper. She flicked a look at him. "Although Lowland women, I have observed, will kiss anyone."

A surprised laugh bubbled out of her. "They what?"

"Oh, they kiss for hello, and for thanks, and farewell.

They would give a kiss for nearly any reason. Have another joint of roast chicken, here's a kiss."

She looked at him doubtfully. "You tell a tale."

He grinned and lifted a brow. "Do I?"

"Anytime they do this?"

"For any reason. Very pleasant it is." He leaned forward. She smiled, unable to resist, and touched her lips to his.

"Lowland women are very fragrant," he murmured. "And delicate." His lips brushed hers again, and her head tilted fully back, her heart pounding. "They are so soft."

"Soft?" she murmured, breathless. "The Lowland women?"

"Who?" he whispered, and his arms went fully around her. Leaning back in his support, she drank in the long kiss, melting inside like butter slipped into hot *uisge beatha*.

A whooping cry outside the window echoed over the hills. Elspeth jumped, and Duncan got to his feet, stepping quickly to the window.

"There come your kinsmen," he said. She came to stand beside him and saw three men on garrons, riding over the moor.

"They have likely been searching for us since the storm cleared," she said.

Duncan rubbed a hand over his face and sighed. He turned to slant a brow at her. "Does the Sight run in your family?"

She frowned, puzzled at the question. "A little. My Fraser grandfather was well-known for his visions and prophecies."

"Well, then. Whichever of your cousins draws his dirk on me, then we will know that one has inherited the Sight as well."

She scowled at him, too anxious now for teasing. "Do you think they will know?"

He shrugged and smiled. "Do you want them to know?"

She looked way, uncertain how she felt about all of this.

"Come ahead, then." He held out his hand.

She stepped past him, went out the door ahead of him, and walked decisively toward her cousins.

"My father once said to me, never show your fear. He must have learned it from the Frasers, I think," Duncan commented, walking behind her. She threw a disparaging look over her shoulder and marched ahead.

Magnus, Kenneth, and Hugh cantered toward them on their garrons. Expressions of obvious relief were on their faces as they waved and halted their mounts.

"Elspeth, are you well?" Hugh asked.

"I am fine," she said.

"Duncan Macrae, we thank you for seeing her safe," Kenneth said. "I am sorry, Elspeth, to have left you alone."

"Where were you?" Magnus asked. "We went back to Glenran, and have been searching ever since the rain stopped. It has been hours."

"We took shelter in the shieling," she said.

"The shieling?" Magnus asked.

"The shieling all the afternoon?" Hugh asked.

Elspeth shrugged and nodded. She saw Magnus look hard at Duncan and start to say something. Then he closed his mouth and looked away.

Hugh scratched his head and looked at Duncan. "She is fine, my cousin?"

"She is," Duncan said. "Ask her yourself."

Hugh tilted a brow at her. Elspeth huffed an indignant sigh. "I am well and fine, Hugh Fraser, and you need not ask."

"The girl saw to her own safety today," Duncan said. "You should be proud of her courage." His eyes sparkled. "Ruari MacDonald will not be eager to face Elspeth Fraser again."

"Ruari MacDonald!" Magnus said. Elspeth told them what had happened in the birch wood.

Hugh frowned. "It is no true surprise that you met Ruari, then. When we got back to Glenran, we learned some grim news." He looked solemnly at them. "The MacDonalds raided in a part of Glenran last night. We were up and out at the hunt so early that we did not hear of it until now. Several farms were raided, a barn was burned to the ground, and an old couple were injured."

"Well over fifty cattle and sheep were taken," Magnus added grimly.

"We will counter-raid tonight," Hugh said. "I will send out gillies to run the fiery cross through the territory, and whistle in our kinsmen to ride with us. We will meet at the Fraser yew."

Duncan shook his head. "You cannot do that."

"And who will stop them?" Elspeth asked.

He turned to her. "The queen's lawyer."

Chapter 13

Ay through time, ay through time,
Ay through time was he, lady,
Filled was wi sweet revenge
On a' his enemys, lady.
— *"Rob Roy"*

"If we do not retaliate, the MacDonalds will call us old women," Ewan insisted, leaning on both hands and glaring across the table at Duncan.

"We keep our pride if we return this raid," Callum said. "Whether or not we sign your bond, the MacDonalds will continue to harm our people and our livestock if we do not stop them."

Listening, Duncan tugged his gold earring thoughtfully. He had been hearing much the same from the Frasers since they had returned to Glenran after the hunt. He glanced toward Elspeth, who sat silently in the increasing twilight shadows.

The clear gray of her eyes seemed shadowed too, and a slight frown divided her brows. Duncan frowned, a match to hers, and looked back toward the Fraser cousins.

"We will raid tonight," Hugh said emphatically. "You may come or stay, Duncan man, but you cannot convince us that this raid should not be returned tenfold."

Duncan rose from the bench and leaned his hip against the table, looking down at the Frasers from a position of greater height, an advantage he had learned in courts of law. This invitation to join them on the raid was the opening for which he had been waiting. Their acceptance assured his chances of getting the cursed bond signed and delivered to the Privy Council.

The Frasers were angry over the recent raid, and he

would have to convince them to proceed carefully. "I know you want an immediate counter-raid," he said. "But remember that there are legal raids, and there are raids outside the law."

Callum blinked. "I thought they were all illegal."

Duncan shook his head. "Angry counter-raids such as you plan to run go against the laws of Scotland. But deliberate raiding is sometimes within the law." He paused. "Sometimes." His audience, seated on benches around the wide table, grew agitated, shifting and murmuring to one another.

Magnus leaned toward him. "Tell us, man!"

"The Scottish parliament has recently reviewed the matter of raids and counter-raids, which are a constant problem along parts of the Lowland borders. They declared that immediately following a raid, a 'hot ride' is allowable if certain conditions are met. It is already too late for that," he cautioned, holding up a hand. "But if a few days have passed since the first raid, a particular kind of pursuit, called a 'cold ride,' is acceptable."

"Hot or cold, we ride soon," Ewan insisted.

"Counter-raiding in anger," Duncan went on, "without the supervision of the law, and which results in harm to humans or livestock, is never regarded as legal. Do not ride out in a high temper as soon as it is dark enough. You do not need charges of thievery and murder brought against you just after a bond of caution has been written out for your clan."

"Then explain this cold ride," Hugh said. "And remember that we have not signed your bond, and can do what we choose."

"If you ride cold, you will need a warden, a man appointed by the sheriff."

Kenneth groaned. "There is no time to send a request to Inverness for the sheriff to ponder and set aside. I am with Ewan—we should ride now, tonight, hot or cold."

"And risk fighting MacDonalds when the bond has already been issued? That is a quick path to fire and sword," Duncan said. "There is another way."

"He is right," Magnus told the others. "Go on."

"The sheriff of Inverness has lately been renamed. The titular sheriff is now James Stewart, Earl of Moray, the queen's half brother. And Moray is the man who sent me here to you."

Callum whistled low. "We are in luck, I think."

"Perhaps you are," Duncan said mildly. "As the queen's lawyer—and the sheriff's man—I can supervise the raid and make certain that it is legally done."

"We do not care if it is legally done or not," Ewan grumbled. "That is south country thinking. Just see that it is done to good effect."

Magnus looked at Ewan. "South country laws can ruin our clan should the crown send out an order of fire and sword. Listen to Macrae. If we do what he says, we will have the cream from both buckets."

Duncan scratched his jaw as he pondered his next step. "I have seen your raiding style," he said carefully. "There was much of the high and low, the left and right, to it. Silence only if it suits you is not the way to run a good raid."

Judging by the blank gazes returned to him, Duncan realized that the Frasers were unaware that their free, impulsive style of raiding was not the most effective method. Indeed, they looked as if the idea of raiding techniques had never occurred to them. Elspeth too stared at him openmouthed.

Duncan recalled, watching them, that the Glenran Frasers had been raised in a wild pack, with only Lachlann Fraser to guide them; Lachlann apparently had been more scholar than fighter. With so few older men available to teach them hunting, fishing, fighting, and raiding, they had taught themselves, developing their own unique approach—at least in raiding. Duncan sighed, knowing that he could teach them much, given the time to do it. But the Frasers were anxious to get on with the counter-raid.

"You will need experts," he told them. "One or two at least on the MacDonald terrain. Another several experts at the bow and arrow. Trackers, and someone with excellent night vision. Seers will not do," he added, glancing sternly at Elspeth. She scowled at him from her seat in the shadows. Suppressing a smile, he continued. "Gather your best men, those most skilled with claymores, dirks, and lances. Summon your cousins from around Glenran. We will need twenty or thirty men."

They nodded, one or two at first and soon all of them. Duncan went on. "Always send out the man who knows the terrain first, and let him scout the way for you. Send with him someone with sharp sight and keen hearing. Follow them with men who can flow like wind through heather on pony or on foot. Be silent and quick and clean. Always know where you are going and what you intend to do. Do it as fast and as stealthily as you can. And always know more than one way to get back home again."

"How is it that a lawyer knows cattle reiving?" Hugh asked.

Duncan looked at each of them in turn. Deciding to reveal something more of himself, he felt a frisson of discomfort. Trusting cautiously as a rule, he had come to trust these Frasers quickly, with their honest, boisterous loyalty. "I had brothers once. We raided on MacDonalds in the western Highlands. I have cousins too, several of them," he said. "We rode together in the borderlands. My mother's family are Kerrs."

Hugh nodded, his brows lifted. "I have heard the name. The scourge of the Lowlands, the Kerrs. Border raiders. Men who ride outside the law."

"Interesting kinsmen for a long-robe," Callum said.

"Exactly so," Duncan said. The Frasers were looking at him with complete amazement now, as if he were a hearthside dog who had suddenly stood up and spoken with the voice of a man.

"You will act as warden on this cold ride?" Magnus asked.

"More than that," Duncan said. "I will teach you to raid like border reivers."

They rose before dawn and did not sleep until well after dark, and spent most of that time out on the moors and the hills. For three days Duncan divided them into groups, welcoming every Fraser cousin who came to Castle Glenran, summoned by gillies who ran out with the word that the MacShimi needed them.

Some drilled on horseback, galloping on sturdy, fast garrons up hills and down in tight, neat packs, riding through thick, snaggy heather whenever possible to soften the sound. Others set up targets on hillsides and moors and practiced shooting with bows and arrows. Still more paired off to play at sword fighting and lances. Duncan directed them frequently to switch places so that everyone spent time practicing each skill.

When the luminescent darkness of late summer fell each evening, their work intensified. The drills continued as they strove for the same clean perfection in darkness that they had easily achieved in daylight.

During some of the training sessions, wanting to spare his own stallion another injury, Duncan rode a garron pony, a dappled gray with a thick, creamy mane. He had ridden garrons years ago in the western Highlands, and remembered quickly the ease with which these animals could climb steep hills and gallop through snaggy patches of heather. But he doubted, now that he had ridden tall English-blooded horses, if he would ever again feel comfortable having his long legs hang so far down that his toes sometimes brushed over tall undergrowth.

On the third morning, a drenching rain convinced him to gather everyone in the great hall for the afternoon, where he asked them to describe the MacDonald terrain and the MacDonald holdings. Those Fraser cousins and kinsmen who had come from other parts of Glenran, Duncan discovered, had much to contribute to the discussion. When he asked for paper and pen and ink, Flora eagerly bustled off to find some so that he could draw a few basic maps.

Listening as they talked about the MacDonalds, Duncan had sketched the maps, inking in dotted lines to indicate possible routes for the cold ride to follow. As he did so, he had become aware of a deep satisfaction: along with the contentment of a skill shared and taught, he also felt the ice-hard resolve of revenge begun at last.

With each passing hour he thought of his own reasons for wanting to ride out against the MacDonalds. He remembered Ruari's face as he had looked at Elspeth; that alone was enough to stir Duncan's blood to a surging rage, rousing in him a long-buried desire for revenge.

He could never forget that a group of MacDonalds had crossed into Kintail to kill his father and his elder brothers. And he had not forgotten that they had wounded him as well, almost to the death. When he had seen Ruari threaten Elspeth, when he had heard of the latest raid, the wild Scot side of him had begun to grow stronger, responding to this infusion of fresh anger.

True, a different branch of Clan MacDonald harrassed the Frasers. The revenge was theirs, not his. He knew that the Frasers were determined to see the debt paid well. But Duncan had begun to anticipate the raid with a fervor that did not suit his role as the queen's representative. He should be riding along only to see that the law was met. Unable to deny now that he had other reasons as well, he kept that knowledge to himself.

By the fourth day, Duncan had taught the Frasers the basic principles of cautious and clever reiving. He had seen the Frasers quickly apply their fine archery and riding and fighting skills, and apply their deep enthusiasm too to the tasks.

Elspeth had worked as hard as her cousins. She rode faster than the others, being smaller and lighter, and she had a fine, keen hand with a bow. She had no good skill with the broadsword, for each one she lifted was too long for her arms and slender body, and far too heavy, though she would not admit it. Duncan had noted that she stubbornly and consistently tried to handle the broadsword in practice sessions. One afternoon, though, he stepped up to stop her.

"The blade is too long, and you might hurt yourself or one of us by accident," he said, lifting it from her hands.

She pulled the silver handle, resisting, but then relinquished the cumbersome weapon.

"Well, it may be too large for her," Kenneth said, walking up to them, "but I would not come near her if she was holding a small blade in a fit of temper. Elspeth can outdirk any man here."

"Can she, now?" Duncan murmured, his eyes locked to hers. He remembered his first night at Glenran, when he had awoken to the gleam of a dirk in her hand. And he recalled the ferocity with which she had struck Ruari MacDonald in the face with a knife blade. "I will remember that," he said.

"And remember too that if we had time and the coin to have a sword made to fit her, she would soon be our equal," Kenneth said.

Elspeth grimaced triumphantly at Duncan. A smile teased his own lips, and he saluted her with a bow of respect. She passed him with an intriguing and wholly unconscious flounce of her plaid. He smiled again and turned away.

He was well pleased with the Frasers' skills, and with their enthusiasm and ready intelligence. He knew that they were nearly ready to take their newly reorganized skills onto the night moor. But he wanted to be certain.

On the fifth afternoon, six of them rode out to the farthest edge of the marches between MacDonald territory and Fraser land, near Bethoc's little croft. Reaching the crest of a high hill, they surveyed the open lay of the land below them. The spectacular view of misted hills and silver rivers matched well enough the maps that Duncan had made.

Heading back to Castle Glenran, they stopped briefly at a crofter's cottage. The young wife there, her brown skirts kilted high to reveal her bare shins and feet, offered them oatcakes and bowls of cool milk. As he stood sipping some of the fresh milk, Duncan heard Elspeth thank the woman. He turned to see their hostess smile.

Elspeth tilted her head to one side, a curious look on her face. Her eyes in that moment were almost as clear as water, with a deep sparkle. Duncan watched her covertly, fascinated.

"You will have a child before the first spring blooms are through," she said to the young wife. "A healthy boy who will have your fine brown eyes."

The woman blushed a deep rose. "I have not told anyone yet that I carry a child," she murmured. "I just became certain myself not long ago."

"All will be well with you both," Elspeth said. She reached out and laid a hand gently on the woman's shoulder. "This will not be like the first time. You will carry and birth easily, and will do so again."

"Thank you," the wife whispered. "I lost my first child early. But no one ever knew that."

Duncan stared at Elspeth over the rim of his bowl. She flicked her eyes toward his, a direct, open look that sent a shivering warmth down his spine before he lowered his gaze.

Elspeth Fraser astonished him. Did she indeed have some heaven-bestowed gift that allowed her to see into the mind and heart of another? Into that person's future? Duncan frowned; he could not easily accept such a possibility.

Perhaps, being female, Elspeth had seen some bloom in the woman's face to which men were simply oblivious. There had to be some private language of posture or gesture that only women understood.

But she had known intimate secrets that this woman had not spoken aloud to anyone. And she had already guessed, though he knew not how, that he had been seriously wounded by MacDonalds long ago.

He shook his head slightly as he set the bowl down. No one, simply no one other than his closest blood relatives, knew the truth of the scar on his back. He could not explain how she knew a MacDonald had wounded him. That she had predicted his death by execution was an extremely uncomfortable thought—if he accepted her ability.

Trained by the law to deal with logic and clearly defined premises, he found himself challenged to understand this girl. She was haunting, magical, made of contradictions, mist and sunlight, a twist of cool silver and warm gold. He was fascinated, enthralled, and confused.

He knew that she had some indefinable power, but he was not ready to admit that she could foretell his future. To admit that her Sight was true would be to face his own end.

Elspeth spoke softly with the young woman, laughing now. Duncan turned to answer a question from Magnus, who had to repeat it twice.

All Duncan had heard was Elspeth's light laugh, floating up to chime with the wind.

Riding home, Ewan began a song that the others soon joined. Duncan listened, content to enjoy the song, but was soon elbowed by Kenneth, who urged him to sing too. He shook his head vigorously.

Elspeth, riding on his other side, leaned toward him. "If you claim to have a Highlander's blood, then sing with us."

He shook his head. "I prefer to listen."

She tipped her head and smiled, a certain way that often brought out a dimple in her left cheek. "I will teach you the words if you do not know."

Odd and clear, the thought drifted through his head then that he would do anything to please this girl, to see that flashing smile for even the briefest moment. He knew the words; the song was one he had heard many times as a boy. Sighing, not quite believing that he did this so readily, he cleared his throat and joined in with the second verse. He could feel a hot flush stain his cheeks.

Kenneth was the first to turn around with a look of amazement. The flush on Duncan's cheeks grew stronger. Then Callum turned, and Magnus. The bright stain on his face burned like a small fire, and his voice dwindled away on the wind.

Ewan, riding in the lead with his back to the others, stopped singing and twisted in his saddle, frowning as if he were puzzled. "Did you hear a dog howling just then?" he asked.

Kenneth burst out laughing and said nothing. Callum and

Magnus cleared their throats and looked away, snorting with muffled laughter.

"Just a high wind, Ewan," Elspeth said reassuringly. "Just a high wind."

The other cousins grinned and kept their silence. Ewan shrugged and turned back, resuming his song, his voice as rich and mellow as cream blended with *uisge beatha,* everything that Duncan's singing voice was not.

Duncan looked at Elspeth. She tilted her head at him, pinching her lips together in an expression of deep sympathy.

"I have a reason for listening rather than singing," he said, a little stiffly.

"You have," she agreed. "Well then. Perhaps if I spend some time with you, I can help you."

He twisted his mouth wryly. "I doubt you can."

"If you can teach us to reive, I can teach you to sing," she said. "Call it a payment, Duncan Macrae." Her gray eyes sparkled and her hair shone brightly in the sun. Suddenly Duncan thought that he had never seen anyone so fairy-like or so beautiful in his life. She smiled, and he felt as if he had been given his full payment.

He laughed, the humiliation forgotten, and she laughed too, bright and open and airy. He felt a small burst of joy, like a trickle of clear water over thirsty ground.

"Elspeth Fraser," he said, grinning and shaking his head, "you will have a task ahead of you, then." He turned to Kenneth. "Are you rested, man? And you, Callum?"

"Rested? Well enough. Why?" Kenneth asked.

Duncan smiled. "This would be a fine night for a long ride, I think."

Callum grinned, and Kenneth did too. Magnus turned around and nodded. "A fine night to hunt the MacDonalds," he said.

"Perhaps so," Duncan said. "Perhaps so."

Chapter 14

"Haste Donald, Duncan, Dugald, Hugh!
Haste, take your sword and spier!
We'll gar these traytors rue the hour
That eer they ventured here."
        —*"Bonny Baby Livingston"*

Along the silvery track of the river through the deepest hour of the night, thirty riders followed the moonlight. Over rough moors and rocky slopes, through cold, swift burns, they moved on, a silent part of the dark and the wind.

Hardly a word had been uttered since the group of Frasers and Fraser kin had mounted their horses at the old yew tree two hours and more ago. Elspeth glanced at Duncan, who rode beside her, seated tall and straight in his saddle, his plaid a dark swath in the night, his hair lifting like a black wing. He carried a long lance, its wicked point upright. She looked around. Several men carried lances, the steel points like a glittering forest behind her. Many of the riders, including Elspeth, had bows slung over shoulders or saddles.

She drew in a breath and let it out, a little puff of frost that reminded her that the night air was chilly. But she felt warm from the the heat of the ride and the heat of anticipation.

She could sense the cattle now, off to their left. She would have said something, but Duncan veered off in that direction without hesitation, as if he too sensed them. The riders followed him.

She smiled, thinking that he must have a touch of the Sight, for he rode with deliberateness, as if he too knew where to find the cattle, as if he listened to some inner voice. Though the scouts ahead had hearing as keen as the deer, and sight as sharp as a hawk's, Duncan had hardly consulted them. He seemed to know instinctively how fast, how far, and in what direction to ride.

Earlier in the evening, he had asked Elspeth to stay at Glenran. If the MacDonalds discovered the raid, he had said, and found her part of it, she would be in particular danger. She had refused to stay.

"We are joined now, you and I," she had said. "I will not watch you ride away until the day that you must go to Edinburgh."

Looking at her with a hint of sadness, he had reached out to touch her hair. *"Mo càran,"* he said, "my dear one. Come, then."

He glanced over at her now, and though he did not smile, Elspeth felt the caress of his gaze, the steady promise in his eyes. A promise to her, and to all of her cousins.

She had grown to adulthood always equal to her cousins. Now, looking at Duncan Macrae, she felt accepted as his equal as well, but with a depth she had never known before. Riding beside him, meeting his glance, she felt a sense of completion, precious and somehow necessary. She felt stronger, as if she had suddenly discovered another part of her soul, a force that was brave and steadfast. She knew that Duncan brought that to her.

She reached out to him, and he grasped her hand for a moment, then pulled away.

He rode forward alone to catch up to the others who rode far ahead of the group. Kenneth and another kinsman, Tomas, waited for Duncan in the sheltering slope of a hill. The two of them knew the terrain, could predict and recognize the rise and swell of every hill, the angle of every rock, the depth of each burn.

With gestures and low words they consulted together. As Kenneth and Tomas rode off, Duncan turned to wave the others away from the silver band of the river.

Though Elspeth had ridden on several raids, she had never ridden like this. The riders swept through the night following Duncan's silent signals. Striking fast and clean, they rounded up fifteen cattle in one valley, five in another, ten more in the shelter between two high hills. No one challenged them; no one even saw them. They collected cattle and sheep like wildflowers in spring, finding a field of plenty in each new valley.

The garrons churned tough and steady through deep heather that muffled the sound of their passing. The bright moon was faintly obscured by mists, blurring the shapes of the riders. They rode on, gathering more animals as they went.

Arriving at the dooryard of a little homestead, they barred the door from the outside, then opened the pen and let out several sheep, leaving most of the flock behind. An old cow that lowed nervously in the yard was passed over, as were the goats. Duncan nodded as the group herded past him, then turned his horse to head still deeper into MacDonald territory.

Two riders entered the yard of another homestead to coax several more sheep out of a pen, herding them off to join the others, who waited beyond a hill. The sleeping inhabitants were undisturbed by the silent reivers.

In another small glen they took a good portion of cattle from a large herd. Duncan glanced up at the sky, frowning at the increasing mist. He waved the riders toward home at last.

By the time they approached the marches of Fraser land, fog hung over the ground in soft, thick veils. Before dawn they reached a wide but shallow stream, which had been simple enough to cross earlier. Now they found themselves challenged to keep the cattle and sheep moving steadily through the water.

Duncan tried in vain to deal with a particularly stubborn pair of sheep, who could not seem to follow the rest straight through the flowing water to the other side. Finally he leaped down from his saddle and scooped his arms around the fat ewe to drag her back upstream toward the flock.

Chuckling, Elspeth jumped down to help him. Wading through the cold water, she grabbed the other, a hefty lamb, by the scruff of the neck, and pulled him forcibly back to the opposite bank. Grinning at her, Duncan leaped up onto the bank and reached out a hand to pull her up beside him.

"We are on Fraser land now," he told her in a low voice, "but the need for speed and silence is no less important." She nodded and stepped aside to catch the reins of her horse, which one of her cousins had led to the bank.

"Come ahead to the loch," Duncan called softly. Elspeth mounted up and followed, as did her cousins, shepherding the flock and the lowing herd between them.

During the planning of the raid Duncan had advised that the animals be herded into a secure hiding place for a few days. "If the MacDonalds come looking for their animals," he had told them, "no Fraser within miles will have an extra sheep or steer."

Hugh and Callum had suggested a wooded isle in the center of a small, remote loch not far from Castle Glenran. The lochan was well hidden, tucked against the base of a broad hill and shielded by a thick pine forest. The cattle and sheep could be left there for days, for there was plenty of grass on the isle. The forest would both discourage visitors and muffle the sound of the herd.

An hour later, herding the animals with a grim perseverance born of stubbornness and pure exhaustion, they reached the loch. A submerged sandbar linked the shore to the isle. Washed over by water only a few inches deep, the access to the little isle was successfully concealed.

Elspeth soon discovered that guiding the animals along the narrow sandbar required enormous patience. Only two or three animals at a time, in long columns, could be led to the isle. The Frasers walked alongside to prevent strays from leaping out into the deeper water of the loch.

Swiping with one hand at the straggling hair falling over her brow, Elspeth walked knee-deep in bleating ewes, slogging through cold water that soaked her deerskin boots and the trews she wore under her plaid for added warmth. She stumbled once or twice as the soft-bodied animals nearly tripped her.

Thick mist from off the loch drifted over the sandbar

and the isle. Dawn seemed to hang back, although the air was now a paler gray. Ahead, she could just see Magnus's blond head as he ushered several sheep onto the isle.

Nearby, shadowy in the mist, she saw Duncan, who escorted the last of the sheep to the place where the cattle had already been hidden. Although he had not shown the strain of the long night, the subtle droop of his head and shoulders told her that he was very tired.

The raid had been an enormous triumph, and she knew that the Frasers owed their thanks to Duncan Macrae. Soon the MacDonalds would return a raid; they would ride past the lochan with its little wooded isle, and would find none of their own animals on Fraser land. And the Frasers and all their kin would be on guard this time when the MacDonalds came.

She was certain that no MacDonald raid could equal what the Frasers had achieved this night. Such fine reiving earned respect in the Highlands. The Frasers had good reason now to swell their chests with pride; they had humiliated and bested an enemy, and though all knew that the gesture might be returned in force, they could enjoy their triumph for now.

When the last of the sheep had been taken to the center of the isle, Elspeth breathed a deep sigh of relief and sat on a rock by the shore. Thin waves lapped over the smooth brown stones at her feet. Looking around, she saw little beyond vague shapes in the fog.

Emerging from the drifting blur, a few of her cousins sat near her on the pebbled shore. Several of the others had already crossed the sandbar back to the mainland to stay with the horses. Magnus bent over to scoop handfuls of water to drink and then splashed his face, his golden braids dipping into the water. Sighing and groaning, Kenneth and Callum dropped down on their knees to drink and wash as well.

Walking out of the mist, Duncan stood near her. "Go back to Glenran now, all of you," he said. "Send two men back here, fresh for the day, to watch the cattle. I will stay until they arrive."

"I will stay with you," Callum said, and Duncan nodded.

"And I will as well," Elspeth said.

He tilted a brow at her. "You are exhausted."

"No more than you or Callum. I will stay."

He sighed and nodded. "As you wish."

The others left, walking back over the sandbar to mount their garrons. Elspeth could hear the soft, fog-distorted sounds of their departure.

Bending forward, she scooped up some water to drink. Then she fumbled at the fastenings of her deerskin boots, laced up to the knee, and removed the boots. She dipped her toes in the water, easing her feet into the chill. After a moment she dried her feet with an end of her plaid.

"You should have gone back," Duncan said. She glanced up. He stood just behind her, fog swirling around him.

"I would not leave you now," she said quietly.

"What did you say?" Callum asked.

"We should come away from the shore," Duncan said, turning away. He led them deeper into the isle, to an expanse of rocks and grass between two small knolls, the whole edged by pines and ringed by the water of the lochan. The cattle and sheep were grazing in this central, hilly area, their lowing and bleating muffled by fog and pines and water.

The three of them sat down on a hillock. Elspeth yawned and sat back while Duncan and Callum spoke quietly of the raid, of their satisfaction with the evening's outcome. They discussed the number of animals taken, and Callum mentioned a few farmers whom he thought should be given some of the animals.

After a while, Callum yawned as loudly as Elspeth.

"Go to sleep, the two of you," Duncan said. "I can stay awake. But when I am back at Glenran, I may sleep for the rest of the week." Callum removed his plaid and stretched out in his long shirt. He wrapped the plaid over him like a blanket.

Duncan turned to Elspeth. "You as well," he said.

She yawned again and undid the brooch at her shoulder,

then unwound the length of her plaid until she sat in her
long shirt and plaid trews.

She smoothed the cloth flat on the ground and covered
herself with part of it. For the greatest warmth she knew
that she should layer heather sprigs inside the plaid and
fold it double, but she was too tired to bother.

She glanced at Callum. Though only a few paces away,
he was shrouded in mist. But his snores were loud enough
to compete with the lowing of the cattle.

"Dhia," Duncan muttered. "The MacDonalds will be led
straight to us." He reached out with his foot and shoved
Callum, who snorted and rolled over, quieter now.

Elspeth laughed. Duncan turned to look at her. "Rest
now, *mo càran,*" he said. "You have done a good night's
work."

Duncan got up to stroll a few paces away, watching the
herd. In the heavy, obscuring mists Elspeth soon could not
see him. Knowing she could not possibly sleep, she scrambled to her feet, glanced at Callum, and carried her plaid
with her to find Duncan.

He sat on the slant of a knoll, knees drawn up, his face
thoughtful. He watched her silently as she dropped down
beside him and spread out her plaid. Reaching out a hand
to him, touching his arm, she felt the feathery layer of dark
hair, warm skin, and the ripple of hard muscle beneath. He
took her hand in his. A wash of feelings, lush and pleasant,
flooded over her at the simple touch. Tugging a little on
his hand, she wanted him to lie inside the cocoon with her.

"Rest, Duncan," she said. "We are safe here. No one
can see or hear us from the mainland."

"I cannot rest," he said, letting go of her hand. Startled
by his abrupt gesture, she frowned at him.

"What is it?" she asked.

"I must watch." He propped his arm on his upraised
knee and looked away from her.

She sat up, suddenly restless. Her plaid dropped away
and the chilly mist penetrated her shirt, but she hardly noticed. She reached out and put a hand on his back, flexing
her fingers to massage the taut muscle beneath his shirt.

She knew how tired he was, and saw how seriously he took
his responsibility to watch while she and Callum rested.

A shock, like a tiny stab of lightning, went through her
fingertips as she touched his back. She shuddered. When
the vision came, sudden and vivid, it nearly rocked her
over. Images flashed through her mind. Flattening her hand
on Duncan's back, she placed her other hand on the earth
for support.

"We cannot sleep. We cannot stay here," she said.

He looked at her, his brows lowered sharply. "What?"

"I—" She shook her head, confused. "I touched you, and
then I saw a vision. A hand holding a raised dirk, and then
another." She squeezed her eyes shut, fighting against a
rising discomfort, like the ghost of a physical pain, and real,
gut-centered anguish. "Red plaids, several of them, like
some MacDonalds wear. Men moving through moonlight.
Men in a battle, yet silent. There are no screams, but there
is death—death all around you—"

"Stop." His voice was a hard-edged growl. "Stop this."

"Duncan," she whispered. "I saw you stabbed in the
back. You will come to harm if we stay here. The MacDonalds—" She stood suddenly, grabbing her plaid, hastily trying to wrap it around her again. "We have to leave—"

"Elspeth." He stood, swift and tall, to grab her arms.
"Stop." He shook her as she attempted to pull up her plaid.
Her hands trembled. She was breathing too rapidly, but
could not calm herself. The vision had terrified her.

"Elspeth. We are in no danger." He pulled her to him,
hard and fast, holding her tightly, covering her head with
his hand. She grabbed him, pressing her face into his chest,
hearing his rapid heartbeat. "Hush, girl."

"But I saw—"

"What you saw is in the past," he said, his voice low in
her ear. "You saw something that happened years ago."

She raised her head. "What?"

"Men in moonlight, men in red plaids. Someone stabbing
me in the back. It all happened just as you described. But
it happened many years ago." He was holding her so tightly
that she could feel the tremor in his strong arms, could

hear the ragged draw of his breath. "Somehow, when you touched my shirt just over the scar on my back, you saw what caused the wound."

"Duncan. What happened to you, then?" Her voice nearly broke over the words.

He stroked her hair slowly. "It was in the past," he said. "It is over. There is no need to speak of it."

"But—"

"Hush, you," he said. "We are both tired, and such matters cannot ease our minds, or our bodies. Lie down now and close your eyes. Go on." When she did not move, he pushed down on her shoulders.

Stunned, she sat down on the ground and lay on her side. He knelt and tucked the thick plaid around her. She watched him, saw his face as if in a dream, wreathed by mists and the weak light of the dawn.

"Tell me," she said. "I want to know what happened."

Duncan brushed the hair that edged her brow. "Someday I will tell you. But not now." He slid his hand over her head. "I do not understand how you could have seen that. But you did. Somehow you did." His eyes were keen and blue through the fog. "I wonder if you speak the truth in all your visions, after all."

"Duncan." She felt for his hand, and he wrapped his fingers over hers. "I am beginning to be afraid of the truth."

"Mo càran," he said. "Do not worry."

"I only want you safe," she whispered. Fatigue crept over her like the enveloping mist, obscuring coherent thought, dragging her under. She rested her cheek on her hand, closing her eyes.

After a moment she heard his faint whisper as she drifted into sleep. "For you, *mo càran,* I will stay safe."

Elspeth laughed again, a light trill that floated up with the mist and echoed faintly. She let the joyous feeling wash through her, welcome after the unhappiness of an hour earlier. She saw Duncan grin, a grudging smile, and it lifted her heart further.

"Hush, you," Duncan said. "You will wake Callum. A short nap and you are as giddy as a babe. I told you I could not sing."

She smiled. "And I promised to teach you. Listen again, now." She sang one line from a song, a simple, engaging pattern, her notes pure and round.

Duncan sighed and tried to imitate her. His voice strained over the melody and fell flat. Elspeth nodded patiently, and repeated the third and fourth notes. He tried the line, but the tune seemed to collapse in the air.

"The MacDonalds will hear us," he grumbled. "We will lead them right to the cattle."

"If anyone passes the loch in this fog, they will think this isle is haunted and they will run quickly," she said.

"Hah. They will imagine some frightening beast if they hear me sing. But Callum's snores will drown us both out, I think."

She smiled and shook her head. "Listen, and then I want you to sing with me. And sit straighter. Let the breath be open. Then match your notes to mine, only much lower. You can."

He grunted, and she sang, and repeated the phrase. After an awkward beginning he hit one strong note and then another. He lifted his brows in surprise.

"I told you," she said, and sang the whole verse. He went with her, up and down, hitting more sour than sweet notes, but his voice was stronger, deeper, less strained than before.

"Well, then," she said. "Now no one will think something wicked haunts this isle."

He took her hand again. "Sing, and I will listen," he said. "And if the MacDonalds come this way looking for their cattle, they will think a true fairy guards it and will run the other way."

Chapter 15

"How many small fishes
Do swim the salt sea round?
Or what's the seemliest sight you'll see
Into a May morning?"
　　　　　　—"Proud Lady Margaret"

"Ah," said Kenneth, frowning up at the high-raftered ceiling, "what is sharper than a thorn?"

"A dirk," Callum said. Kenneth shook his head.

"A woman's tongue," Ewan said. Elspeth frowned at him.

"Hunger," Magnus said. Kenneth nodded, caught. "Well, then," Magnus said, taking his turn, "what is whiter than milk and softer than silk?"

"Clouds," Kenneth suggested.

"Snow," Ewan said.

"Curds," Callum said. His cousins stared at him.

"Down of a feather," Elspeth said. Magnus nodded at her.

"My turn," she said, sitting forward. Her brow creased as she pondered her next riddle. The others waited.

Duncan relaxed against the high back of a carved chair, listening to the riddles fly back and forth. He drained the last sip of his heather ale and looked around the great hall. Darkness filled every corner, and a peat fire glowed in the central iron basket; though the hour was very late, the Frasers still sat in the hall. Following the raid, they had slept much of the day. At twilight they had gathered in the hall to eat their fill of a large and lavish dinner, including what Flora had announced with delight as MacDonald mutton gracing the stew.

After the meal there had been some singing. Duncan had

declined to join, finally relenting enough to hum; Elspeth had seemed pleased enough with that, he thought. Then the riddling had begun, a pastime that the Frasers obviously enjoyed.

Elspeth cleared her throat now and sat forward. "Tell me," she said, "what is a hoop by day and a snake at night?"

Ewan chuckled. " 'By day like a hoop, by night like a snake, who answers this riddle, I take for a mate.' That is an old one, Elspeth. We all know it. A belt."

She made a quick face at him. "Well, then, try this one. What is never, ever silent?" her cousins glanced at each other, puzzled.

Duncan set down his cup. "The sea is never silent."

"Ah!" Kenneth said. "Duncan answered, and will have to be your mate." Someone laughed.

"Whoever would try to marry me, I would set him a harder riddle than that one," Elspeth said firmly.

"Would you?" Hugh asked. "Would you set a challenge, as in the old tales?"

Elspeth nodded. "I might do so."

"You should have tried that on Ruari MacDonald," Kenneth said. "He lacks the wit for riddles. We would not have had to refuse the marriage offer then."

"But Robert had interfered," Hugh reminded them. "He was still angry when he returned to the south after his meddlesome attempt to give Elspeth to the MacDonalds. Robert may be harmless enough, but it is Ruari we should all beware. He has enough wit to be offended by our refusal."

"Ruari will not bother us again," Elspeth said decisively. "Now then. Duncan Macrae answered my riddle, and he must say one next."

Earlier, watching Elspeth, Duncan had remembered a riddle that his father had taught him many years ago. He did not think she would like it much, but he could think of no other.

"What is blacker than the raven?" he asked.

Elspeth glanced at him, startled.

"Night," Callum said.

"Not in the Highlands," Duncan said wryly.

"Ink," Ewan tried.

Elspeth continued to stare at him; Duncan felt her glance, wide and wary. He turned his head now and looked at her. "Elspeth knows," he said.

"Death is blacker than the raven," she murmured.

"It is," he said. "Have you another riddle?"

"I am done riddling for a while," she said crisply, reaching for the jug set on the table. She poured ale into her cup. When Callum and Kenneth slid their cups toward her, she poured some for them as well.

Hugh reached for another flask and measured himself a generous dram, offering the container to Duncan. Swallowing a little of the amber liquor, Duncan felt the penetrating heat slip down and spread easily through his body.

Magnus asked for another song, and Elspeth nodded, reaching for the *clarsach,* the little table harp. She tipped it toward her and settled it against her shoulder. Strumming the strings with supple fingers, she sang an old song. Duncan recalled hearing it before, the tale of a woman and a blacksmith, both wizards competing to outdo the other in magic. Each time the blacksmith sought the woman's maidenhead, the woman outsmarted him, until she finally decided to lie with him, but on her own terms. The song was quick and witty, and Elspeth sang it with a light, wry tone.

Her voice was as clear as water poured over silver. He studied the fine planes of her face, and the warm gold and copper blend of her hair. He watched her slender fingers on the harp strings, and remembered those fingers laid against his lips, tracing over his body. With an inner shudder that was far more pleasant and warming than the drink, he thought about stroking her body with his own fingers and tasting the sweet flavor of her skin. He would approach the task slowly, luxuriantly, and her clear silver voice would sound his name joyously.

Relaxing back against the chair, he looked at her through hooded eyes, thinking about the delights that they had shared in the shieling. He began to imagine even more pleasures they could share in the near future. Drawing a deep breath, blowing it out quickly, he realized suddenly that there might be no future encounters for them.

He felt he had earned the Frasers' respect and trust in last night's raid. Soon then, he would obtain their signatures on the bond, and he would leave Glenran. Although Elspeth insisted that she wanted this to happen, Duncan was not so certain now that he wanted to go. Every moment that he spent with her seemed to become another reason to stay here, to postpone the signing of the bond of caution, to let time spin out indefinitely.

He could no longer ignore his legal duty. As the queen's lawyer and representative, his duty to the crown must be completed.

But he did not know how to complete what had begun with Elspeth Fraser.

"Six days have passed since the raid," Hugh said to Duncan, on a rainy evening when the Frasers gathered once again to sing and tell riddles. The MacShimi reached for a flask of ale and poured some into his cup. "Six days, and the only counter-raid from the MacDonalds has been one weak foray, when we lost no more than ten head of cattle."

"Ah. We have frightened the MacDonalds into better behavior for a while," Kenneth said, overhearing.

"Perhaps," Duncan answered. "Though we knew that our raid was a gamble. I had hoped, the night we rode out, that the MacDonalds would have already signed their bond of caution."

"Since their only retaliation has been that one small raid, obviously their bond has been signed," Hugh said. "Nothing less would deter them from a full-scale raid against us."

"If so, the MacDonalds must avoid confrontation with your clan." Duncan sat back, swirling the liquid left in his cup. "And now, my friends, it is time to sign your own bond." He looked at them evenly, knowing that the Frasers owed him this favor.

He had delayed this moment as long as possible, not wanting to see the task finished just yet. He could not leave

Elspeth so easily; but he set his jaw and pushed the thought away.

"I must deliver the document to the council," he continued, "before they send someone up here looking for me. I have been gone weeks longer than I had planned. Summer is well past."

"The autumn nights are growing dark and chilly," Kenneth said. "This is perfect weather for reiving."

"No more reiving for Clan Fraser," Duncan said. "I will see you pen your names on that paper now. I must leave for Edinburgh as soon as it is done." He refused to look over at Elspeth.

"I will sign the bond," Hugh said quietly. "With one condition."

Though a brief nod was his only outward reaction, Duncan was surprised—and suspicious—at Hugh's easy compliance. The MacShimi had resisted with fierce determination for the two months that he had been at Glenran.

"And what is the condition?" Duncan asked.

"Marry my cousin Elspeth," Hugh said.

Duncan blinked, his only outward reaction. He wanted to look at Elspeth, but somehow he could not turn his head. He felt her there, near him, an arm's length away, heard her wordless exclamation of surprise, felt her hard silence after.

Around the table a rippling murmur of agreement passed through the Frasers. They obviously approved, nodding and smiling at him.

"Do what?" he asked.

"Marry my cousin Elspeth," Hugh repeated calmly. "There is clearly some feeling between the two of you. My cousins and I have discussed this. We want you to marry our cousin."

"You did not discuss it with me," Elspeth snapped.

Duncan looked at her then. Her eyes glittered like cold silver. She glanced at him briefly before turning to the MacShimi. "How can you do this without asking me?"

"You should marry, Elspeth," Magnus said. "It is time."

"Not this man," she said.

"We have chosen this man for you. Macrae will be a good husband for you. We are concerned for your safety," Hugh said. "Ruari MacDonald has already approached you once. He may do so again, and if he does, he will try more than words."

"I told Ruari not to come back," she said, lifting her chin.

"Do you think he will listen to a woman's warning?" Magnus asked, leaning forward. "You may have angered him more by humiliating him that day. We want you safely wed and taken away from here."

"Taken away?" She sat up suddenly.

"Duncan lives in Edinburgh," Kenneth said. "There you would be safe, away from Ruari MacDonald."

She folded her arms over her chest. "I will never live in the Lowlands. And I cannot marry the lawyer."

Hugh turned to Duncan. "Marry the girl, and we will sign."

"In the Lowlands we call such a bargain black rent," Duncan said in a low voice. While he had strong feelings for Elspeth Fraser, he would not consent to wed her like this.

He could see that she felt the same. Her flashing gaze lanced every cousin who sat around the table, and pierced him too in passing.

"You want the document signed, and we want Elspeth safely away from here," Hugh said.

"I will not barter with you on this," Duncan said.

Elspeth leaned forward. "Listen to the lawyer."

"Marry the girl, and the bond will be honored," Hugh said.

Duncan stroked his fingers along his jaw and glanced around the table. The Frasers looked at him eagerly. He felt like one of the Frasers' trout, stunned and grabbed before he knew what had happened. Caught fast. If he did not accept her hand, Hugh would offer her to another man. Duncan knew that the MacShimi planned to wed his cousin off to protect her from the MacDonalds. Duncan realized that he had no hesitation about marrying her; the choice, suddenly, was no choice at all.

He glanced at Elspeth. A range of emotions struggled across her face. Anger tightened her mouth and flared her nostrils; indignation lifted her slender jaw and throat. But he saw fear too shadowing her clear eyes. He could almost feel it.

"I will marry her only if she wants it," he said.

Hugh turned to Elspeth. "I am your guardian. I say you will marry him and leave Glenran."

She stood, fisting her hands at her sides, her breath heaving beneath her plaid. A warm flush spread across her cheeks.

"This is best, Elspeth. We cannot trust Ruari MacDonald," Magnus said. "Later, Duncan can bring you back to the Highlands. A handfasting for a year."

"Handfasting is not generally done in the Lowlands," Duncan said quietly. "That is a Highland custom."

"Then he will marry you before a priest," Hugh said.

"Unless he follows the Protestant faith," she muttered.

"A priest will do," Hugh said.

Elspeth narrowed her eyes, and Duncan saw something more there now, replacing the fear: a spark of cleverness, a sharp sudden blade of thought that made him wary. "Duncan Macrae must answer my riddle before I accept any arrangement with him."

"No games, Elspeth," Magnus said. "We are serious."

"So am I. Many a maiden in times past took a husband on the strength of a riddle. I will do that also. If Duncan cannot answer it, I do not have to wed him."

"Agreed," Duncan said. His voice, deep and sure, sliced through the rising commentary from her cousins. "Say your riddle, then."

"This is no tale told by a *seanchaidh*," Hugh said. "We want this done."

She ignored her cousin. "No riddle, but a challenge to be answered." Her eyes flashed like cold stars as she looked at Duncan. "Give me an entire sea, all foam and spray, with a bottom of gold and silver, and place it in my hands."

Magnus blew out a long breath. Kenneth and Callum both whistled low, and Ewan stared, wordless. Hugh shook his head slowly.

"Give me a day," Duncan said. "You will have your answer." He stood up. "And then I will say whether we wed or do not."

With a tight smile he bowed and, turning, left.

Tossing in his bed from side to side, punching the pillow, yanking the fur coverlet, Duncan thought about the riddle. Angling first one way and then the other in his thoughts, he finally decided that Elspeth, being quick-witted, had purposefully created a challenge for him that had no firm solution.

The puzzle was vague enough to frustrate a man who dealt in logic. She probably hoped that he would leave for Edinburgh before he could find an answer. But he was determined to think of something. Every riddle had a solution. If he could get the Frasers to sign that bond, then a riddle was a simple matter.

He rubbed a hand over his bleary face, imagining with chagrin his attempt to explain all of this to the Privy Council. Soon sleep began to spin a subtle web, and he relaxed.

He dreamed vividly and awoke before dawn in a cold sweat.

In the dream, he had been standing on the shore of a sea, with darkness all around him. Far out in the water, black as the night sky, he could see a faint, pale shape. Elspeth was in the water, drowning, calling for help, sinking under the waves.

Duncan found himself, in the way of dreams, suddenly out in the water, swimming, struggling to reach her. Each stroke swept him farther away. He heard her cries but could not move closer.

Gold and silver seemed to be everywhere, sparkling in the moon and the stars, reflecting in the water. He scooped up a handful of water and gold coins spilled out of his hand.

Swimming with determined strokes through the dark, glistening waves, he seemed only to tread water. Elspeth

cried out, and a wave took her under. She would die if
Duncan did not reach her in time.

He awoke, jerking upright, pushing against the cloying
covers. The dark silence of the room gradually penetrated
his awareness. Breathing hard, he stared around him at
black shadows and the dim glow of the hearth.

His heart beat rapidly, and his insides felt wrenched from
the intense emotions of the dream. Still caught in the after-
math, he wanted to grab Elspeth up into his embrace and
hold her there safely. But he knew she was in no real,
immediate danger.

He was suddenly totally determined to solve the riddle
and marry the girl. He could not leave her now. He simply
could not ride away from Glenran and go back to Edinburgh without taking her with him. But she would not agree
until he answered her preposterous riddle.

She had asked for the sea, all gold and silver. Looking
around the room, he remembered the dream, and had an
idea.

The quill scratched slowly across the paper, spitting
ink as Hugh wrote out his name, drawing each letter
carefully. Duncan waited, as he had for each of the cousins to add their names to the document. When the Fraser
chief was done, he slid the page toward Duncan, who
sanded the ink, and then signed his own name beneath
Elspeth's signature.

"That is done, then," Hugh said. "And your answer to
my cousin?"

Duncan heaved a deep sigh. He looked around the great
hall, where all the Frasers, including Flora, had gathered
to witness the signing of the document. Now they waited
to hear how he would solve Elspeth's challenge.

Afternoon sunlight poured down in pale, transparent
wedges through the arrow-slit windows along the upper
wall. Silence filled the high-ceilinged space.

"Are you ready to answer her?" Hugh asked.

Duncan looked at Elspeth. Her eyes were huge in her
pale face, her mouth partly open. His heart beat strong and

hard beneath his shirt. Looking at her now, so pure and beautiful, so much what he wanted, he remembered last night's vivid dream. He tightened his fist to keep from reaching out to her.

She shook her head slowly. He realized that she was asking him not to answer the riddle. He looked away.

Before dawn he had dressed and left the castle. Wandering over moors and hills on foot, he had examined all the possibilities in his mind. After an hour or so, the solution had become clear to him.

"I am ready," he told Hugh. Then he walked to the ambry cupboard built into the wall. Earlier he had asked Flora to leave some things there for him.

Reaching into the cupboard, he lifted out a wide wooden bowl, which he had previously lined with gold and silver coins. He placed the bowl on the table where all could see it. Elspeth frowned. Her cousins watched him silently.

Turning back, he took out a jug of ale and a bowl of salt.

He poured the ale into the bowl, quickly enough that it foamed as it sloshed over the gold and silver coins. Then he added a few pinches of salt.

Lifting the heavy bowl, he carried it the length of the table. "Hold out your hands," he said to Elspeth.

"What is this?" she asked in a hollow, thin voice.

He set the bowl in her hands. "An entire sea," he said, "placed in your hands. Brine, all foam and spray"—he leaned forward and blew a little at her, gently—"with a bottom of gold and silver."

"Oh." She stared at it.

"You did not say how large it should be," he said.

"Oh," she said again, her voice a mere breath. She set the bowl on the table, still staring into it.

Behind him, the Frasers murmured among themselves. Someone laughed outright. Duncan looked only at Elspeth.

He saw her swallow, and for one wild moment he felt the fear in her. Although she was apprehensive, he could not regret what he had done, or where it would lead.

Then her wide, rainwater eyes turned upward to his. Her gaze was touched with dread. She was silent, her lower lip trembling, her breath quick. She flattened her slender hands against the table.

Duncan bent forward to speak to her over the happy din of the cousins just behind him, who were laughing and clapping one another on backs and shoulders.

"We are caught, *mo càran*," he murmured. "Like fish in the sea, we are caught."

She blinked and nodded. Then her eyes shifted to a point just beyond his shoulder.

"Duncan Macrae." Behind him, a voice cut through the clamor in the hall, flat and grim. Duncan straightened and turned.

Robert Gordon stood framed in the open door, his black cloak sparkling with rain. Elspeth rose from her seat. Her cousins quieted as they too turned to look.

"Duncan Macrae," Robert repeated. "The Privy Council has sent me after that bond of caution. The Earl of Moray wants to know if the thing has been signed." Robert walked across the room, stripping off his gloves. He flung them down on the table. "If not, they have asked me to see that it is done. Now."

Duncan frowned, his quiet displeasure mirroring the expressions of the Frasers who gathered around him. He folded his arms and leaned against the edge of the table.

"Robert," he said. "Greetings. And how is it that the council sends you after the bond of caution?"

Robert swept off the dark bonnet that hid his coppery hair, and shoved his dampened cloak back over his shoulders. "I lately had business in the royal courts," he said. "While I was in Edinburgh, I met with Maitland, the secretary of the council. When he learned that I had been here, he asked how you fared with the Frasers and the bond of caution. I let him know how much difficulty you were having. Maitland reported to the Earl of Moray, and I was told to ride here and see to the signing of the bond myself. Now."

Robert grabbed up an empty cup from the table and

thrust it toward Elspeth. "Ale, girl," he said. She snatched it from his hand and poured ale into it from a jug, then handed the cup back to him, sloshing some of its contents over his hand. Wiping his hand on the front of his doublet, he slid a dark glance toward her. Drinking the ale swiftly, he set the cup down. "Fetch the document," he said to Elspeth.

She opened her mouth to answer, an indignant glint in her eye. Duncan touched her arm and gave her a warning glance, silent and keen.

"Show me the council's writ of order," Duncan said.

Robert shrugged. "They directed me to see to the completion of the bond."

"If so, then you will have the order in writing, and you will not have been so foolish as to leave it behind. Give it to me."

Robert sighed, almost a growl, and unfastened a few of the loops on his doublet to slide his hand inside, withdrawing a folded piece of paper.

Duncan took the paper and scanned the text. A muscle jumped rapidly in his cheek. He drew a slow breath to master the anger that rose in him at Robert Gordon's arrogant assumption of superiority. The paper was no formal writ from the council; it was not even directed to Robert.

"This letter is from Moray to me," Duncan said. "The council wants the bond signed and delivered back to them as soon as possible. There is nothing here that surprises me." He put the letter aside. "But I thank you, Robert, for acting as Moray's messenger. I will see to the matter, as I have intended all along."

Robert glared at him. "Other council members suggested to me that I see to the signing of the thing myself and bring it back immediately. That is not in writing, for it was a confidence between us."

"Perhaps," Duncan drawled. "As it happens, the bond has been signed already. I will deliver it to the council as soon as your sister is ready to travel to Edinburgh."

"Edinburgh!" Elspeth gaped at him.

"Why should Elspeth go to Edinburgh with you?" Robert asked.

"We are to be married there," Duncan said.

"We what!" Elspeth stepped forward. Duncan slid a look at her, casual and unruffled, and looked back at Robert.

"Married!" Robert turned, his swirling cloak spitting raindrops. "Hugh Fraser, is this true?"

Hugh folded his arms over his chest and nodded. "The queen's lawyer has agreed to wed Elspeth."

"I will not go to Edinburgh!" she said.

"Why should she wed Macrae?" Robert asked Hugh. "There is no advantage to that for any of us—"

"We are not thinking of our advantage," Hugh said, his voice cold and hard. "We are concerned for Elspeth. She will be safest with the lawyer in the Lowlands."

"I will marry her in Edinburgh," Duncan said. "Whoever would attend our wedding may ride with us to Edinburgh tomorrow."

Two swift steps, and Elspeth stood before Duncan. He lifted an eyebrow and watched her narrowed, stormy eyes.

"I will not leave my clan or my home for the Lowlands." She drew a long breath and winged her eyes away from his. "I will not wed you, lawyer," she said.

"We want you safe from Ruari MacDonald," he said quietly.

She shook her head. "Safe for me may be the blackest danger for you." She turned to Hugh. "I will not do this."

"Elspeth, this wedding will take place," Hugh said. "For your good."

"This cannot happen," she said. Her eyes lifted again to Duncan. "I did not think you would answer the riddle so soon," she said. "I hoped that you would have to return to Edinburgh without solving it."

"I know," he said. "But I had to answer your riddle." His glance held hers, steady and deep. "I had to."

"Solve this, then," she murmured. Her breath was fast and high, as if she had been running. "I will not wed you in the Highlands or the Lowlands." She spun then, her braid whipping over her shoulder, and walked out through the open door.

Duncan sighed and glanced at Hugh.

Hugh half smiled. "Ah," he said. "I think I know the answer to that one."

Chapter 16

No time they gave her to be dressed
As ladies when they're brides, O,
But hurried her away in haste;
They rowed her in their plaids, O.
                    —"Rob Roy"

Only a murmur against wood, the knock was enough to rouse Duncan from sleep. He sat up, and the sound came again. Pulling on his trews, he crossed the room and stepped into the deep shadows that surrounded the hidden door.

"Duncan," came a low voice. "Open up, man."

He eased the narrow door open. Callum and then Ewan stepped into the bedchamber, the hilts of their broadswords gleaming in the low light. Duncan frowned, wondering what sent them there, armed and alert, in the depth of the night.

Or were they alert? He narrowed his eyes, noticing a suspicious bobble when Ewan crossed the room, as if he had imbibed a good bit of the water of life, but not enough to sink him.

"Come with us, man," Ewan said. "We gather outside."

"Is it MacDonalds?" Duncan turned back to the bed, where his shirt and plaid lay tossed over the footboard. He dressed quickly.

"Hurry," Ewan said. "The others will be in the courtyard."

"There must be no raids, and you know that well." As he spoke, Duncan belted his plaid, pulled on his boots, and reached for his dirk, which lay beneath his pillow.

Callum stepped up behind him. "No raid," Callum said, "but a wedding."

Duncan paused. "A what?"

"We like you well, man," Callum said. "And we are sorry."

Duncan reached again for his dirk. "Sorry for what?"

He felt something heavy and hard strike the side of his head. His knees buckled as the floor came up to meet him.

"For that," he heard Callum say.

"Elspeth. Open up, girl."

Stumbling from the bed, part of her sleep-numbed mind wondering if Duncan waited for her, Elspeth hurried to the little door. She had left the hidden door unlatched when she had gone to sleep, hoping that he would come to her by the secret stair.

She wanted to talk with him about the riddle, about Robert and the bond, and above all, about this question of marriage. But she also wanted to feel his lips pressed to hers, just once more before he left for the south. She craved the hard, sultry heat of his body along hers. She wanted comfort and forgiveness and understanding, if such were possible between them since her continued refusal to wed him.

Although she knew that she must separate herself from Duncan in order to avert the horrible fate she had foreseen, Elspeth still yearned to see him, to hear his voice, to feel his hands and lips upon her.

Brushing back the tousled hair from her eyes, she opened the door expectantly.

Kenneth put a finger to his lips and stepped into her room. "Get dressed, now," he said, "and meet us in the yard."

"You cannot ride out on a raid! The bond is signed. We have given our promise not to ride against the MacDonalds."

Kenneth shrugged. "Hugh summons us in the night. Come ahead, girl." He stepped back into the dark recess of the stairs.

Elspeth dressed quickly, throwing on her shirt and wrapping her plaid hastily. She took no time to braid her hair, but pulled on a pair of woolen trews against the night chill.

In a few moments she descended the narrow stone stairs and made her way out of the castle, stepping into the moonlit yard.

Magnus, his braided hair silvery in the moonlight, held the reins of a pair of garrons. Beside him, Kenneth sat on his own horse, while Ewan, Hugh, and Callum stood nearby. Her cousins clustered in the yard as if they waited for her.

She glanced from one tall, grim-faced cousin to another. Callum held the reins of another garron; Duncan sat in the saddle, his shoulders oddly slanted, his head fallen to one side. She ran over to him and looked up. His eyes were closed, and Callum supported him with one broad hand.

Elspeth frowned. "Is he drunk?" she asked Callum.

"Drunk?" He stared at her. "Ah, drunk. That he is. Cannot hold the *uisge beatha*." Callum shook his head.

"What is going on here?" she asked. Callum tipped his head and opened his mouth as if to speak, then shrugged.

She whirled to face the others. "Why do you gather tonight? There can be no raids now, after the bond. And why is Duncan like that? I have never seen him drunk before."

"He was sad to leave you," Ewan said. "Very sad. We thought to help him with that. Get on your horse, Elspeth."

"On my horse? Are you all as drunk as he?" Elspeth had an odd feeling, a sense like a heavy turning in her gut, a warning, but too late. She stepped back. "I will go nowhere—"

Quick as the snap of a whip, Kenneth pulled a plaid from a saddle and threw it over her head, catching her like a fish in a net. Struggling, she pushed against the pairs of arms that held her, lifted her, turned her. Cursing loudly, bucking against their grip, she kicked her booted feet into solid flesh. Despite her efforts she was flung over the saddle like a sack of barley.

She was not frightened, knowing her cousins would never harm her. But their action was unexpected, and she sincerely doubted the wisdom of any scheme enacted in the black of night. But why, she thought, would they abduct her like this?

Only one answer occurred to her, and that thought made her kick and struggle frantically.

Someone climbed up into the saddle and held her down. Elspeth screamed angrily, kicking now into empty space. She pummelled with her fists as best she could, but her arms were snugly wrapped to her sides. The feeble blows she managed to land had no effect on rider or pony. The garron surged beneath her as it rode steadily over the swelling moorland.

Her voice was hoarse within moments. The air inside the plaid grew stale and overwarm, and her head hung downward uncomfortably. She squirmed, trying to right her head so that the blood would not pound so painfully behind her eyes.

After a while her cousin—she was certain the man was Callum, for only he had hands quite that large—gripped her upper arms and dragged her to a seated position in front of him. "Sit here, girl," he said in her ear, "if you can behave."

"Behave?" she squeaked through the cocoon of the wool. "Behave? And do any of you show good manners? Let me go! Drunkenness has put you to this!"

"Not so drunk, girl," he said. "We want you to be happy. We take you to be wed."

"Happy?" she shrieked. "Wed? You abduct your own cousin!"

"A fine idea, is it not?" She could hear the grin in his voice, and she elbowed him. He grunted and patted her shoulder. "Now, girl, you will be glad of this later."

"Glad? I will be glad when I can curse you to your face, you *gloichd*!"

"Ah, Elspeth," he said. "Ah, that hurts, to be called an idiot."

"Well, you are," she said. "Take me home."

Callum sighed. "I cannot. The MacShimi orders this."

"Then he is a *gloichd* with you. Did Duncan Macrae suggest this? I said that I would not wed him!"

"But we do you a great favor," he said.

"Give me none of such help," she muttered. Callum

laughed. She turned her head back and forth in agitation, trying to loosen the snug plaid over her face. Finally Callum loosened the fabric, and she felt the fresh air, although he would not lift the plaid away.

They rode on while Elspeth fumed beneath the plaid. She squirmed and swore and muttered creatively about the demise of each of her cousins.

"Hold, now," Callum said finally. "We might deserve such awful fate. But wait. You might name your sons after us."

"I will name a plague on you," she said.

"I am sorry, Elspeth," Callum answered. "But we knew you would not come peacefully. We decided that this marriage had to be made, and we agreed that this was the best way to do it."

She grumbled and leaned back against him as the pony took a steep hill. She was just about to open her mouth to describe some ugly demise for Duncan Macrae as well, the most thoroughly drunken one of the lot that she had observed. Then she remembered, with a grim, dark feeling, that the heading block awaited him.

She gasped and straightened in the saddle. "Callum," she said. "Do not do this. You do not understand what will happen if I wed Macrae."

"We are here," he said suddenly, halting the pony. He bounded out of the saddle and lifted her in his arms. Though the first swift flood of her anger had passed, she continued to kick out, snarling and muttering, determined to make this difficult for her cousins.

She was carried, swathed in the darkness of the plaid, into a large building. Callum had climbed a few steps to enter. Voices echoed all around her, quiet but hollow, and footsteps scraped softly, as if over stone. She cocked her head to one side, trying to listen, trying to discern. The sounds reminded her of the great hall of a castle. But she could hear the high, soft moan of the wind, as if they were still outside. A ruin, she thought, a broch or some other dilapidated stone structure.

She was set down on the floor, and someone knelt to

wrap something snugly around her, binding her arms to her sides. When she swore, she heard a soft voice at her ear.

"Hush, girl," Kenneth said. "Hold your temper. Profanity does not belong in church."

"Church! Take the plaid off me, Kenneth," she said. "Let me see."

"Not yet, *gràdhan*," he said with affection. He patted her head, and she heard the soft scrape of his brogues as he walked away.

Long moments of utter silence followed. She began to panic. The dark, stuffy confines of the plaid clawed at her nerves. Straining against the woolen wrapping, she leaned back and met the cold roughness of a stone wall. Off balance because her arms were bound to her sides, she nearly fell over.

A scrape and a thud close by, and a low groan, told her that someone had sat down beside her. She tried to move, but slid over even farther, until her head and shoulder met the solid warmth of another body.

The groan came again. "Duncan?" she asked. "Duncan?"

"Here," he mumbled beside her, his voice husky. "*Dhia*, my head hurts."

She scowled inside the plaid. "I am sure it does," she said furiously. "And I hope it hurts you till Doomsday."

"Ah," he said. "You think that I—"

"Are these the two?" A voice, trembling with age, spoke nearby, a voice that she had heard before but could not quite place. She heard Magnus answer a loud affirmative.

"Will Elspeth have the man, then?" the old man asked.

"She will," Magnus said.

"She will," Hugh and Kenneth answered together.

"Well, then, I will do it," the man said. Elspeth recognized the voice as that of a parish priest named Patrick. They were surely in an abandoned church a few miles north of Glenran, on the other side of the great loch.

"Father Patrick!" she said. "Father Patrick! Kenneth, Callum—someone take this thing off my head!" She whipped her head and shoulders around, knocking into

Duncan, who grunted and fell over. She floundered on top of him like a landed fish, trying to wriggle out of the enveloping plaid.

"Hold still, girl, my hands are bound. I cannot help you up," Duncan grumbled, his deep voice only a breath away from her ear. She squirmed again and he groaned miserably.

"I expect no help from a drunken *gloichd* who would ask my cousins to help with a marriage abduction," she said through her teeth. She tried now to wriggle away from him, but he turned, apparently onto his side. The movement dumped her over and pinned her, face to face with him, against the stone wall. She felt his hard chest against hers, and sensed the warmth of his breath at her cheek, through the heavy wool over her face. He shifted again, and she rolled more completely on top of him. The gentle, easy fit of their hips and torsos had no appeal for her now. She thought she heard the muffled laughter of her cousins beyond. She twisted, arching her back and bending her legs in an effort to get to her knees.

"Stop your wiggling, girl," Duncan muttered in her ear. "Though it is very pleasant." His words were oddly slurred.

"I will show you pleasant, you—" It took some manuevering, but she made certain that he felt the quick thrust of her fist in his midsection.

"Oof," he said.

"Father Patrick!" she yelled. Duncan winced, and she realized that she had screamed into his ear.

Quick footsteps came near. "Well then. Look at that. These two cannot be wed too soon," Ewan drawled. Someone laughed, and a pair of strong hands hoisted her to her feet. The plaid was removed, though not as fast as she would have liked. The chill of the air felt like a wind from heaven.

She breathed deeply once or twice, and then rounded on her cousins. Magnus bowed his head, suppressing a grin, and walked away. She turned a stormy glance on Ewan, who held her arms.

"How dare you!" She jerked her shoulders. "Let me go!"

"*Gràdhan*, darling, I cannot," Ewan said. "This marriage will be done. We thought that we might have to force you some."

"Hah. Force if you must, you will have no consent from me. Where is Father Patrick?"

Beside her, Callum and Magnus were lifting Duncan to his feet and undoing the bonds that held his hands behind his back. He shook his head slowly, as if he were dazed, and ran a hand through his hair. Kenneth walked up to him, and Duncan spoke, a low, growling comment that she could not hear. Kenneth frowned and replied softly before he moved toward Elspeth.

"This is a mockery," she muttered. "Father Patrick!"

"Elspeth, hush now, and let the priest marry you to the lawyer," Kenneth said.

Father Patrick came toward them, a stoop-shouldered old man, white-haired, shuffling along beside Hugh. The Fraser chief was talking to him in a raised voice.

Until then Elspeth had forgotten that the old priest was partly deaf. And, she recalled with a sinking feeling in her stomach, he was also nearly blind. Likely he had not even heard her call out to him, and in these shadows he would not have noticed that Elspeth and Duncan had been bound and held by force.

"The best priest for the task," she muttered sarcastically.

"Thank you," Ewan said. "He was my choice."

The look that she slid him was sharpened with anger, but he smiled at her. "Ah, Elspeth," Ewan said. "Show us that you accept the husband we have chosen for you."

Elspeth curled her lip and turned away. Glancing at Duncan, she narrowed her eyes, watching him closely for the first time. He folded his arms and leaned against the wall, staring around him with a wary expression that seemed more alert than before. He glanced toward her and slowly nodded.

In the moonlight that spilled through the ruined wall of the old church, she saw a dark circle of dried blood at his temple.

"*Dhia!*" she gasped. "He is not drunk! He is hurt!" She

turned an accusing glance on Ewan, and then on Kenneth beside her. "What did you do to him?"

Ewan looked penitent. "We had to knock him over the head," he said. "He would not have come with us if he knew what we had planned for you. Callum did hit him overhard, but he will be fine."

"You are all idiots," she snapped.

Kenneth bent forward, his long, dark hair brushing against her shoulder. "We want you to marry this man, and you want to be wed to him, I think, though you refuse. We are seeing it done," he said decisively. "He was leaving tomorrow for Edinburgh. Callum suggested that abductions were common enough and easy to arrange. Hugh agreed it was a fine plot and thought of this church. So here we are."

"We just had to abduct the groom as well as the bride," Ewan added. "But this is working out nicely, I think." He grinned and clapped Kenneth on the back as they walked away to greet the priest and Hugh.

She looked again at Duncan, who leaned calmly against the wall. He looked at her again, and she found herself blushing, from a rise of anger or from the sudden, breathless anticipation. He stepped away from the wall and came toward her, and her heartbeat leaped.

She realized that he was fully capable, now that he was recovered from Callum's blow, of refusing this marriage. Yet he seemed willing to go through with it.

"Elspeth," he said. He stood very close to her, leaning forward, his dark hair swinging down. "You know what they mean for us to do here."

"I know." Her voice was low, strained. "But I do not—"

"*Mo càran,*" he murmured. His hand came up to rest against her cheek, a warm slide against her cool skin. "It will be a good thing. I promise you."

"I am afraid." The words came out on a breath.

"I will not take you from the Highlands if you do not wish it."

She shook her head. "It is not that. I fear for your life," she whispered. The steady press of his fingers against her neck was a subtle comfort in the midst of this chaos and

chill. She heard her cousins laugh as they talked among
themselves. She heard Duncan sigh.

"Marriage to you is no threat," he said, and stepped
away.

"Duncan—" she said.

"Here is Father Patrick," Hugh said loudly as he drew
the old man toward the weather-stained, moonlit altar.
Kenneth came to her side to bring her near the priest, and
Duncan stepped close. Surrounded by a tight circle of tall,
determined men, Elspeth tipped up her head to look at
Duncan. He glanced at her, took her hand in his, and
turned to the priest.

Father Patrick was old and deaf and half blind, but he
had a completely intact memory and a nimble tongue for
Latin and Gaelic combined. He intoned the ceremony so
fast that Duncan was asked if he would take this woman
before Elspeth had quite accepted the fact that she was
hearing her own matrimonial vows. She had not even
thought through her answer.

"I will," Duncan murmured.

"He will," Magnus and Hugh said together, rather
loudly.

Father Patrick, his white head bobbing with satisfaction,
asked Elspeth a similar question. She tried to pull her hand
from Duncan's, but his grip was suddenly like iron. She
took a deep breath, planning to protest the vows.

"I will n—" she began. Ewan clapped a hand over her
mouth.

"She will," he said.

"She said she will," Kenneth enunciated loudly. The
priest nodded and smiled. Mumbling desperately, Elspeth
stomped on Ewan's foot. She tore her hand from Duncan's.

Father Patrick blithely intoned the wedding blessing by
rote, his words so rapid that Elspeth could hardly make
them out. He sketched a cross in the air and expressed his
congratulations. Hugh put an arm around the priest's
shoulders.

"Thank you," Hugh called loudly into his ear, and led
the old man away. Ewan dropped his hand from her mouth.

"Ah," Kenneth said with satisfaction, "the thing is done."

Elspeth turned and glared him. "How can you be proud of this?" She whirled and confronted Duncan. "And you are just as proud! Is this a legal marriage?" she demanded suddenly.

He lifted his brows as if he had not considered that issue until now. "I do not know," he said. "A marriage should be registered with the archbishop—Fortrose on the Black Isle would be the place for that. And since the Church has lost power in Scotland, marriage vows said by a priest are questionable. But there are several witnesses here, and that is enough usually in the Highlands."

"He says it is not registered, and the Church ceremony is no longer approved. It is not legal," she said to Hugh, who had walked back to join them.

Hugh smiled down at her. "Legal?" He laughed outright. "Elspeth, this is the Highlands. We saw a wedding, and we say that you are wed." He turned to his cousins. "Let us go home now, with our new cousin, Duncan Macrae, and his wife, our Elspeth. We will share a few drams of Glenran's finest *uisge beatha* in celebration of this marriage."

Elspeth fisted her hands on her hips. "A few drams will likely kill Duncan after that head knock."

Ewan laughed. "When Flora sees you, Duncan man, she will dose you with hot infusions and poultices."

"I am sorry to have hit you," Callum said, peering at Duncan. "But you are wed now, and that is important."

Duncan rubbed his temple. "Just get the horses," he said. "My head aches. I need some rest." He looked at Elspeth and lifted a dark brow. "Will you join me in my chamber, wife?"

She drummed her fingers on her folded arm. "I will join you," she said through clenched teeth, "when all the seas of the earth freeze solid." She looked around her. "I cannot believe that you have done this to me. I said I would not marry him."

Hugh shrugged. "You said that you would not marry him in the Highlands or in the Lowlands. This place is neither, for it belongs to the Church of Rome." He frowned. "Or does it belong to the reformed Church now? I have not kept up with the changes. But then, neither has Father Patrick."

Elspeth made a sound of disgust and glanced around at her grinning cousins. "Abducting your own cousin is a dishonorable thing to do."

"Ah, but we were glad to do it for you," Ewan said.

"It is an honor," Kenneth said. "Macrae is a fine man." He grinned and pounded Duncan affectionately on the shoulder.

"I am not certain if we are even married." She careened her icy gaze to each of her cousins and Duncan in turn.

"Ah," Callum said, leaning toward the lawyer. "Duncan Macrae, you have wed a woman who does not lose her anger easily."

Duncan grimaced. "I am learning that," he said.

"Well, long-robe," she said. "Are we wed?"

"I will consider it later, when I can think more clearly." He rubbed his head. "For now, we are. At least in the eyes of God and of your cousins."

"That is good enough," Kenneth said, and smiled broadly at Elspeth. "You will thank us for this one day, girl."

Elspeth had never growled before, but she did so now, with great flourish, and stomped away to find herself a horse.

The dream came again, although it was slightly different this time. Standing by the same dark sea, Duncan saw the waves rise over Elspeth. He swam with hard, strong strokes, and drew close enough to touch her; grabbing her hand, he lost his hold. The dark, sparkling surface of the water sucked her under. He was calling her name when he awoke.

Sweat dampened his hair and skin, and trickled down his brow. His head ached, a dull reminder of Callum's wedding gift. Several moments passed before he noticed that the room was dark. He had slept from afternoon well into the evening, having succumbed to one of Flora's potent headache infusions.

Pushing back the fur coverlet, he grabbed his trews and pulled them on. The dream still spun in the back of his mind. He wanted to be certain that Elspeth was unharmed. Reason told him that she slept undisturbed in her room above his bedchamber, but he had to see her.

When they had all returned to Glenran just before dawn, Elspeth had gone up to her room and locked the door, refusing entrance to any but Flora, who had come down occasionally to dutifully repeat a little invective for the cousins' benefit. There had been no such verbal messages for Duncan, who had sat in the hall with a foul-smelling poultice held to his head.

Pride, he found, more than the headache, had prevented him from climbing the stairs to knock on Elspeth's door. Kenneth and Callum had gone up once, ready to beg forgiveness if necessary, but she had told them quite succinctly to go away. Duncan had decided, observing all of this, to approach her only when she could act with reason and grace.

Robert Gordon had sat with them in the hall, sharing the *uisge beatha* and watching the activity with a feral gleam in his pale eyes. When Robert raised his goblet in a toast to the day, Duncan was convinced that Robert was acknowledging the turmoil more than his half sister's marriage. Robert had voiced no congratulations to Duncan on his wedding, but had made a point of asking to see the signed bond.

Now the little door creaked as Duncan opened it, and he bent down to enter the narrow passageway. He crept up the cold stone steps in bare feet, feeling his way through the darkness to the small door that led to her room. Pushing it open carefully, he peered inside.

Her room was dark except for the rich orange glow of the peat bricks in the hearth. Stepping soundlessly into the chamber, he stood to his full height. Cool air swept gently over his bare chest, and the wooden floor was rough and cold under his feet as he walked silently to the bed.

She slept, lying on her side. He could hear her breathing,

steady and soft. Placing his hand gently on her bare shoulder, he felt the slight lift and fall of her body.

She was safe. He felt a wash of relief, though he thought it nonsense to need this reassurance. Rubbing his face, he wondered at the impulse that had sent him here like this, as if he obeyed some irresistible instinct. His pride had not relented. He would not beg her forgiveness for the wedding abduction, as her cousins were ready to do. Having committed no offense against her, he would not allow her to punish him with childish anger. He sighed and slid his hand from her shoulder, turning to go.

Elspeth's eyes drifted open, and she saw him in the shadows, as if he were part of some dream. "Duncan?" she murmured.

"Only me, Elspeth," he whispered, standing tall and dark beside her bed. "Sleep, now."

"What are you doing here?" She frowned, trying to think, trying to wake up. The day's events flooded into her awareness then, and she stiffened. Sitting up, she wrapped the linen sheet about her nude body and looked up at him.

"I had a foolish dream," he answered. "I only came to see that you were safe." He stepped away.

Realizing that he was about to leave as suddenly as he had come in, she reached out quickly and touched his arm. He turned and caught her hand in his.

His touch rushed through her body, fast and keen. She tilted her head to look up at his shadowed features. Tall and bare-chested, he seemed to loom wild and powerful over her.

"Do you want me to leave?" he asked.

She shook her head. He let go of her hand and stood, silent, dark, a strong presence that waited for her to speak.

"What was your dream?" she asked softly.

"Foolish, as I said," he told her. "Likely the result of Flora's headache treatment."

"Dreams are rarely foolish," she said. "I have had many dreams that have proven to be true, or have taught me things about myself."

"Did you dream tonight about holding your temper?"

She frowned and looked away. "I was forced to wed you," she said. "My anger is properly deserved. By all of you."

Duncan reached out and grabbed her shoulders, yanking her to her feet. The linen sheet was dragged along with her, barely covering her. Grasping it with one hand, she looked up at him in surprise.

"I have heard enough of your indignation," he said. "I have accepted this marriage, and I expect you to do the same. Your cousins, who love you more than anyone in the world, want it to be so. But you behave like a spoiled child who has not had her way."

"The marriage is not even legal." She glared up at him, masking the hurt she felt at his harsh words.

"I will register it as soon as I can if you are bothered by that," he answered. "Odd for a Highland woman who has reived in the night to moan about legality."

"Odd for a lawyer to ignore it," she retorted. "Perhaps you have been too long with the wild Scots."

"Wild Scots, indeed." His grip tightened on her shoulders. She winced. "Remember that the MacShimi could have let you go to Ruari MacDonald. Hugh considered wedding you into some other clan. Your husband might have been a total stranger to you." His eyes were night-dark blue, intense, and deep. "What your cousins schemed for us may have been brash and youthful, but it was well meant. You are safely wed to me, not to Ruari or some other wild Scot. Am I so poor a choice?"

"I did not want to marry."

"But you are wed," he said, his tone near a growl. "Accept it graciously. You allow your temper to rule you, head and heart."

She scowled at him. The heat of his hands on her shoulders seemed to burn through her skin. Through the nubby linen sheet she could feel the hard press of his chest against her breasts. The distracting pulse of his heart so close to her own undermined her reason. She heaved a half sob of frustration.

"How can I accept a marriage that may bring about your death!" Gasping, she bit her lip, as if she could stop the spilled words.

"I have been patient with you, Elspeth," he said. He raised a brow, a dark slash in the shadows. "But I have my limits. I have told you that the heading block does not worry me. Is there more to this damnable vision? You made no mention of weddings before."

"You will be safe only if you go away from Glenran, away from me. Already you have been here too long—"

"Dhia, mo cuachag," he said. "How well you deserve the name of cuckoo. Stop repeating this warning. I am tired of hearing it."

"I will stop when you listen!" she shouted suddenly. He swore and sat her down firmly on the bed. She sank into the feather-stuffed mattress and grabbed the sheet, holding it against her.

He sat beside her, and his heavier weight caused her to roll against him. Her bare shoulder pressed against his arm.

"Now then," he said. "Speak. If there is more to that vision or whatever it was, say it all. Tell me the entire cursed thing."

"I cannot tell you all of it," she said.

He sighed, a blast of frustration that rocked the rope-sprung bed. "Tell me," he ordered, his voice a low rumble.

Chapter 17

"Your faith and troth ye sanna get,
Nor will I twin with thee,
Till ye tell me the pleasures o heaven,
And pains of hell how they be."
—*"Sweet William's Ghost"*

"Tell me," Duncan repeated, "whatever you have seen. Ravens, phantoms, beasties—none of it will frighten me. But I have had enough of these warnings."

"I cannot tell you. It is an awful thing to hear of your own death." She folded her arms and looked away.

"Dhia," he cursed again. "You are the most stubborn woman I have ever encountered. Your fear of this thing— your fear, not mine, girl—is destroying this marriage union before it has even begun. Never give anything such power over you. Now speak."

He was right, and she knew it. She loved him, and deep inside she felt joy over their marriage, despite her refusal, despite her anger. A hesitant joy, because she feared she would jeopardize him without intention; but she would have given anything just then to be free of this ominous future. She had felt love and joy between them, and she wanted it to flourish.

"Our marriage can be a strong one," he said softly, as if he read her thoughts. "But your fear prevents it from happening for either one of us. Just tell me whatever you have held back."

She sighed, and nodded, and began to speak.

He listened, brow furrowed, gaze fixed to hers through the dark. While she spoke, he nodded occasionally, his hair falling softly along his strong neck, his body warm and solid beside hers. He accepted what she said without comment, without criticism or ridicule. She felt encouraged to pour out what she had shared with Bethoc but so far had kept secret from him.

She described the vision of the ravens that first morning, symbols of death to come; the appearance of the dark man on the horse who, she was certain, was Duncan himself; the vivid and startling image at the streambed, when she saw Duncan with his head bound with a cloth, his shirt pulled down at his neck, the profile of the wooden block behind him.

Some of this Elspeth had told him once, when they had sat on a hillock and spoken of fairies and singing, and had tasted a sweet, deep kiss. Now she revealed more.

"I saw myself at your shoulder," she said, her voice so low that he leaned forward to hear her. "Your left shoulder, the place of marriage. I felt that somehow I would be the cause of your execution." She drew a shuddering breath.

"You could not cause me to come to the headsman," he said.

"But I felt it so strongly"—she inhaled, a half sob—"so strongly that I knew you must leave here and stay away from me."

"Did you feel that we would marry, that day at the stream?" His patient voice was a caress.

"Bethoc told me so," she said. "I did not want to hear it, but she told me it would happen. She saw that, and more."

"What else, then?"

Elspeth lifted a hand to his chest, tracing along the path of the scar that swung in a crescent under his arm, from his heart to his shoulder blade. "I touched you once, here, and saw a vision of men, and dirks, and a terrible killing."

He was silent. Beneath her fingertips she felt the deep thunder of his heart. "Bethoc saw the same for you. Men with dirks and much sorrow in your past. She saw men in steel helmets, riding with lances." She glanced up. "Were those border reivers?"

He lifted a brow noncommittally. She went on. "You will face a great challenge, Bethoc says, but you have the

strength to endure. She said that you were my destiny."
She paused and drew a breath. "She said that you are my
heart, and that I am yours." She felt a blush rise to heat
her face.

Duncan placed his hand over hers on his chest. His
strong heartbeat pulsed through their layered hands.

"Now there is a word of truth," he murmured. "You are
my heart. *Mo cridhe.*" He lifted a hand to cup the side of
her face. She leaned her head into his palm and looked up
at him.

"And did Bethoc also see the grim headsman for me?"
he asked.

"She did not, but says that my vision is a true knowing."
She stroked his chest softly, and let her hand fall to rest
on his thigh. "Now will you believe me and be cautious?
She said you are my destiny."

"That is not necessarily bad, my girl," he said.

Elspeth remembered something. "Duncan, that old
woman near Dulsie who was a seer—what did she tell
you?"

"I remember little. She spoke of danger with the Mac-
Donalds, which anyone could have seen at that time. And
she said something about risking my life for one who is
like a brother to me. It was just prattle; everyone there
knew I had four brothers, and knew we were loyal to each
other. But they are all dead now, and I did not save even
one of them."

She reached out and squeezed his wrist; he took her
hand. "Elspeth." He gave her a keen glance through the
shadows. "Do you know the conditions of a human
pledge?"

"I know that you are the cautioner, and the pledge, for
our bond. You gave your personal promise that the Frasers
will keep to our signed word."

"In part," he said. "A human pledge is held responsible
if the signed party does not honor the bond. This system
works well with the wild Highland Scots, who may have
little regard for the law, but who care deeply about the
well-being of their kinsmen and friends. The Frasers and

the Macraes have long been loyal to each other, which is why the council decided to send me."

"A fine, then, might be asked of you if the bond is ever broken," she said.

"A large fine. And if the council so rules, the human pledge can be imprisoned or executed in payment of the debt."

The words hung in the air between them. "Duncan," she whispered. "I am afraid."

"Ah, girl. That bond will not be broken. And I can easily afford to pay the fine." His voice was soft and deep, like velvet, comforting her. He leaned down, his face so close to hers that she angled gently toward his mouth. His breath brushed along her lips. She leaned closer.

His lips touched hers, and he slipped his hand along her cheek. The feathery graze of his fingers sent a spiraling shiver through her. Their lips clung and held. He traced his lips to her ear. "I am not afraid of your vision," he whispered. "And I want you to dismiss it. Finally."

She slid her arms around his neck and closed her eyes, resting her forehead on his shoulder. "I cannot."

Circling his arms around her, he sighed and stroked her hair. "Before I came here, the council sent word to your clan about my arrival. You might have heard talk of bonds and pledges from your cousins. I think that you put it all together and imagined my execution."

She shook her head, pressed against his shoulder. "I did not imagine it. I am a seer."

He hesitated. "I will admit that you seem to know some things with your seer's mind. Things from the past."

"You admit that?" She blinked up at him.

He nodded. "When you touched my back and described a night that happened years ago—I was startled. But perhaps the past is like a well, from which seers can draw knowledge."

"I see the future as well as the past."

"It is very hard for me to believe that anyone can see the future, Elspeth." He blew out a long breath. "When I first came to Glenran, the lawyer you were expecting, you might have assumed that I would risk losing my head for the bond."

"I knew nothing of pledges and bonds before you came," she insisted. "You do not believe me." She straightened away from him, though he did not release her.

"And even if I believed you," he said softly, "do you think I would run from you to save my neck? You have been warning me away for weeks. Have I gone?" He waited, and she shook her head. "Each time you spoke to me, your voice, your earnestness—some charm about you made me want to stay."

"You did not consider any of my warnings," she said.

He tilted her face upward with his thumb. "There is some pull between us that had been there since the first moment. We both have felt it."

"We have," she said softly. "But—"

"Hush, now," he whispered. "There is nothing to fear. I will not leave you." His face drew closer to hers.

"Duncan—"

"Hush, you," he said. His lips traced along her cheek.

She moaned on a soft, low breath and turned her mouth to seek his. His lips met hers fully, his mouth moist and warm on hers, starting a rapid pulsing deep inside her body. His fingers skimmed along her jaw, down her neck, dusting over her collarbone. Shivers waved through her, delicate, exquisitely tender.

He lay her back on the bed, his lips drifting over her face, along her throat, then upward to find and hold her mouth again. She tasted the heat and moistness of his tongue, sensing the eagerness in him. She eased back her head as he kissed her throat, tracing his lips along the tender underside of her jaw.

The sheet that had been tucked around her slid away. She felt the cool drift of the night air on her breasts, and then his warm hands covered her. Skimming over her breasts, he swept his hand over her abdomen, over her hips, and back up, the light butterfly touch growing stronger. He circled her breasts with his hands, smoothing, stroking, coaxing the center buds to harden. She arched farther and sighed, lifting her arms around his neck.

Spanning her fingers over the firm planes of his chest, she felt the heat beneath the soft hair that cushioned her palms. She felt his heartbeat, strong and steady in the dark, and drew him down to her. His body was warm and hard and solid over hers.

She slid her hands over his torso with growing fervor. She felt suddenly that she wanted something fierce from him, strong enough to drive away the fear that still lurked inside her, like a beast that threatened to devour her happiness.

She wanted to vanquish that fear and replace it with the deep love she felt in his arms. He sensed no doom in his future as she did. She wanted to draw from his strength and surety like water from a well. She wanted to taste his courage, draw it inside her, let it flourish and spring within her.

He kissed her again, and as his hands soothed her, she arched closer to him, wanting to ease the desperation she had been holding inside her heart. In his arms, pressed to his body, her soft curves fitting to his taut torso, she felt a deep quivering begin inside her. His fingers drifted down to feather at the threshold of her body, slipping inside to nurture the sultry spark within her as if he coaxed a need-fire flame.

His lips took one silky nipple, and the lambent sensation within her became a deep radiance, as if a small, hot sun was being kindled at the center of her being. Having taken marriage vows with him, she was bound to him by heart and promise; now the flow of that promise began to fill her. She wanted more from him now, from his hands and his lips, from his body and his heart.

Arching, aching, shifting her hips, she pressed against him, feeling his need for her, hard and alive, igniting her own need. She moaned softly. He understood and shifted then, a luscious, firm slide that brought him into her. She eased over him like glove to hand, a fervent push that took him deeper, and she felt the blood and the heart and the courage that pulsed through him. Here, here was what she sought, and she sighed, and cried out, and took what he offered.

"What," Duncan said, rolling onto his side and wrinkling his nose, "is that?"

"Bog myrtle," Elspeth said, sniffing. "To keep away fleas. And heather. The mattress has recently been re-stuffed with feathers and freshened with dried plants." She lay tucked on her side facing Duncan, and the aromatic filling rustled beneath her as she stirred.

They had dozed a little and awoken, but dawn had not yet come. Duncan rested on his side watching her. His bare chest gleamed in the subtle blue light that flooded through a crack in the window shutter. His hair seemed black, his face shadowed like a beautiful, wild, dark angel.

When she had awoken, she had remembered immediately that her vision still existed, still held power to destroy her life as well as his. But she knew that she had gained a little over the fear now, strengthened by the love and joy that flowed through her.

Bethoc's words came back to her, and she looked at Duncan and knew the truth of that prediction. What she and Duncan would have, even briefly, would be more than others had in a lifetime. Elspeth tried to accept that in place of the infinity of time that she craved with him.

He curved his lip in a lazy, contented smile. She reached up a finger to trace the outline of his mouth.

"I will have to go back to Edinburgh today," he said softly. "The council is waiting for the bond."

She half sat, remembering something. "Duncan," she said. "When you were asleep in the afternoon—after Flora gave you the headache potion—Robert left. He took the signed bond with him."

Duncan sat quickly. "He took it?" She nodded. He shoved a hand through his unruly hair, swearing softly. "I knew he was ambitious. I did not think—" He glanced at her. "Did you speak with him? Did anyone try to stop him?"

"Flora told me after Robert had left. She said that Robert took his leave of my cousins after you had gone to your chamber. They did not realize that he had taken the document with him until after he had gone."

"I must go after him." He swung his legs over the side of the bed. "That bond is my responsibility."

Elspeth grabbed his arm. "Stay," she said. "It is still the dark of night. He will not reach Edinburgh for days yet. You have time. Stay."

He sighed and nodded. "I will leave at dawn, then." He lay back on the feather pillows. Elspeth stretched out beside him and touched his arm. She could feel the tension in him, like a taut bow. Laying a hand on his chest, she felt the hardened muscles and began to stroke her fingers through the soft hair there, wanting to soothe him.

"Robert is anxious for the council's approval to do this," she said. "But you can stop him."

"He is too anxious. I thought it unwise to trust him, but I did not think he would actually take the thing if I was ready to carry it back myself."

"He is only after his own gain. He has ever been that way."

Duncan lifted his arm to circle it around her; she settled against his chest. "I have known men like him," he said. "They are so caught up in their own glory that they do not care who is trampled as they climb up. But only a rare man, even an ambitious one, has a true inclination to be evil. I am not so concerned that Robert took the bond, but I need to appear before the council when the bond is delivered to them. I am the only one who understands the conditions of the agreement we negotiated."

"Robert will say what suits his own purpose."

"I have learned that about him," Duncan said. "And I do not want the Frasers to suffer any injustice, however small, if Robert presents the bond to the council." He rubbed her arm in silence. "I have rooms in Edinburgh, near the castle," he said after a moment. "You will like it there, I think."

A strange sensation plummeted through her, a heavy

dread. "I will not go to Edinburgh," she said. "I cannot live there with you."

"Will you not? And where do you expect a lawyer for the crown to live?"

Elspeth was silent. She felt the tension increase in Duncan, just as it rose in her. She lifted her hand from his chest. "I will not live in the Lowlands. I am a Highlander."

"You are my wife." His voice was low and grim. "You will go with me."

She rolled away from him and folded her arms over her chest. "I have a family here, and I will not leave them."

"They expect you to leave them. They want you to leave them. Hugh wanted our marriage made to ensure your safety. And Ruari MacDonald lives too close to Glenran for me to feel comfortable if I leave you here and ride south."

"I will not go to Edinburgh," she said flatly.

"Where do you think to live with me, then?" His voice was sharp-edged and curt.

A solution occurred to her suddenly. "You have a castle at Dulsie," she said. "We can go there."

"We cannot," he growled.

"Why?"

"It is too far from Edinburgh."

"Alasdair went there," she said, remembering that her cousin Alasdair was married to Duncan's sister. "I can stay there for a while, until Ruari has forgotten his insult here."

He sat up and leaned toward her in the dark. "First of all," he said, his voice so near a growl that she pulled back, "Ruari will not forget this insult, and remains a threat to you. Next, I will not go to Dulsie. So you must come to Edinburgh."

She sat up and drew the sheets around her. "Why will you not go to Dulsie?" she asked. "You have kin there—"

The heavy undercurrent in his silence stopped her.

Suddenly she knew why he would not go. She knew it in his tension, in his silence. "That scar you bear," she said slowly. "You feel responsible for those deaths I saw."

He stared at her.

Her heart beat heavily, almost painfully. Whether or not he answered, she felt the clear ring of truth. Here was the source of the pain that she had sensed in him. "Duncan—"

"Leave it." He laughed harshly. "Your Sight is not welcome in my past."

"Your family would welcome you."

"They would not. Come to Edinburgh."

"I will not leave the Highlands."

"That," he said, "is ridiculous."

She looked away. "I will not go to Edinburgh," she said, "because the heading block is there."

He made a fist and pounded it on the bed. She jumped, and curled her arms around her upraised knees. "That vision has obsessed you!" he yelled. "There are heading blocks in other towns as well. Will you avoid them all your life?"

"All of yours," she said softly.

He blew out a heavy sigh. "I must go to Edinburgh to find your cursed half brother and get back my cursed document. If I do not—" He stopped.

"What then?"

He shook his head. "I must go."

The thought that struck her was sharp and horrible. She gasped and turned to him. "You are the pledge for the bond."

"I am the pledge," he said. "And I must present that bond to the council properly. If I am not there, Robert may say what he pleases. Your half brother could land me on the block."

Elspeth stared at him. *"Dhia,"* she breathed.

"Exactly," he muttered.

Wind blew through his hair, whipping the dark strands, longer than he had worn in many years, across his brow. He lifted his face to the crisp clarity of the autumn wind and rode his horse out of the castle yard, passing beneath the stone gate in the outer wall.

Guiding the horse past the lochan, he thought again of his great disappointment that Elspeth had not come to say

farewell. He had gone to his chamber to dress and gather
the few things that he had brought with him, and when he
had come down to the hall, Flora told him that Elspeth
had gone out. Saying brief farewells to the Fraser cousins
and to Flora, he kept glancing around, looking for Elspeth.

He could still feel the soft touch of her all along his skin.
He had loved her again, fiercely, just at dawn, and though
he had drawn soft, passionate cries from her, he had not
been able to find a way through her stubbornness. She still
refused to come to Edinburgh with him.

Sighing, he resolved to attend to the business of the Frasers' bond and return to Glenran as quickly as he could.

His black cloak blew out behind him as he rode past
the lochan. Trees rustled in the brisk wind, and the steady
shushing sound reminded him of the sea near Kintail. The
air was clear and sharp, showing the autumn colors of the
hills and trees with keen detail. After riding a league or so,
he saw a slight figure standing on a hill. He reined in the
horse and walked his mount that way.

Elspeth waited for him on the rise of a knoll. A wind
lifted her braid from her shoulder, sparkling copper and
gold in the early sun. She moved to face the wind, and to
face Duncan.

The horse took the slope easily. Duncan stopped and
looked down at her. "Is this another fairy hill?" he asked.

"I wish that it were." Her gray eyes were storm-colored;
he saw the burden of hurt there. "We might be caught
and held inside for a hundred years. Nothing could harm
us then."

He sighed and looked away, toward the pewtery flash of
the great loch in the distance. "I must go, Elspeth," he said.

"I know," she said.

"Will you come with me?" He had to say it once more.
She shook her head, looking down.

"Then I will be back for you," he said.

She stepped up to the horse's side and laid her hand on
Duncan's knee. He caught her fingers and held them
tightly. "I do not know whether I will see you again," she
said. "I do not know if this marriage brings safety or danger

to you. My Sight will not show me what I need most to know."

"Our marriage brings safety, Elspeth," he said. "For both of us. How can there be danger where there is love?"

She smiled ruefully. "Love and fear both you brought me the day that you came here."

He reached out and touched her head. Fine-spun silky strands blew over his fingers. He knew that she had a fine, brave heart, and knew that whatever fears she had to face, she would do so and be stronger for it. He wanted her to realize that her fear was the only obstacle, the only threat. He wanted to convince her of his own conviction that he was safe.

Sighing, he looked up, his gaze skimming over the landscape, beautiful and wild. He looked past a cluster of nearby hills and suddenly frowned.

"Elspeth," he said, pointing in the distance, "what is that plume of smoke there? It is too thick to come from some hearth."

Elspeth turned to look. "Bethoc's house is just over that hill."

Just at that moment he heard the rough thunder of horse hooves behind them. Turning, he saw Magnus, Hugh, and Callum galloping toward them, angling their mounts to ride on past.

"What is it?" he called.

Callum reined in his garron as Hugh and Magnus tore past, their faces grim and set. "Fire," Callum called. "At Bethoc's. Hugh saw it from the roof just now." He cantered away.

Elspeth stared up at Duncan, her eyes wide with fear. He held out his arm; she grabbed his forearm and leaped up behind him. Digging in his heels, he urged the horse forward.

Chapter 18

Nimbly, nimbly raise she up,
And nimbly pat she on,
And the higher that the lady cried,
The louder blew the win.
                    —*"Clyde's Water"*

Fire plumed over the roof of the cattle byre, a simple three-walled structure topped with thatch and attached by an open breezeway to the house. As Duncan halted his mount, Elspeth jumped down, running toward Bethoc, who carried a bucket of water toward the byre. Crossing the yard, Elspeth noted frantically that the house was not yet on fire.

Magnus ran toward the house, his expression that of pure terror, and dashed inside. Just as Elspeth reached Bethoc's side, Magnus emerged from the house.

"Eiric! Where is she!" he yelled. Bethoc pointed, and Elspeth and Magnus turned. The child sat beneath a fir tree a safe distance from the house, a tiny dark-haired figure beneath the spreading branches. Magnus nodded with relief.

Elspeth did not take time to ask Bethoc about the fire, but grabbed the heavy bucket of water from Bethoc's arms and threw its contents toward the byre. Behind her, Callum and Hugh and Duncan were fetching water, throwing it, shouting, organizing their efforts. When Bethoc appeared behind Elspeth with another full bucket, she took it without a word. Hugh was flinging water toward the roof, while Duncan found an iron spade and began to toss dirt onto the flames.

Feeling as if she were caught in a nightmare, Elspeth fetched water from the stream at the bottom of the hill and helped to douse the flames. The thatched roof of the byre, made of heather and turf, was already damp from recent rains; creating heavy smoke, the dampness also slowed the progress of the fire. Magnus and Duncan were wetting portions of the house to protect it from sparks.

Finally the fire began to lose its will, and the smoldering byre collapsed like the charred, spent logs of a hearth fire. Wiping her ash-blackened face, Elspeth accepted a drink of cool water from Duncan, who had found a ladle somewhere. She turned to see Magnus walking over to his daughter. He lifted her up in his arms.

"Duncan," she said, "what is the matter with Eiric?"

He turned to look. *"Dhia,"* he swore. Both of them ran.

Magnus turned as they came, his face a mask of rage. Eiric lay quietly in his arms, her dark blue eyes wide, her face swollen with tears and the bruise that darkened the side of her face. One small leg was twisted, wrapped in strips torn from Bethoc's chemise.

"Her leg is broken," Magnus said flatly. "I will kill Ruari MacDonald for this." He covered his daughter's head protectively with his hand.

"Ruari!" Elspeth said. "Why?"

Bethoc stepped forward. "They came just after dawn," she said. "Ruari and his brothers. They dragged us from our bed, they knocked over furniture, destroyed the loom—" She paused, breathing heavily. Elspeth noticed then that all Bethoc wore was a torn shift and a plaid shawl. "They took the animals, herding them away. Just a few sheep and two cows. Before they left, one of them used the spade to toss a burning peat brick onto the byre roof. It smoldered there awhile and caught fire."

"What happened to Eiric?" Duncan asked harshly.

"She got away from me when they took her little bog beast—the lamb Elspeth gave her. She cried and ran. Ruari was standing by the byre then. I saw him kick Eiric away, so hard that she was lifted into the air. She fell against those stones there." She pointed toward a cluster of rocks. "Her shinbone was broken in the fall."

"I will kill the man," Magnus said, his tone dry and factual. Elspeth glanced at him with concern and reached out

for the child. He hesitated, then handed her over. "Who
of you rides with me?" he asked.

"I do," Callum said. He and Hugh had walked up to
hear Bethoc's story.

"And I," Hugh said.

"We ride now," Magnus said.

"The bond," Elspeth said. "Are you forgetting the
bond?" She glanced at Duncan, who watched the Frasers
with a grim, hard look, his face pale beneath sooty swipes.

"She is right," Duncan said. "The bond of caution prevents you from riding out with intention to kill any
MacDonald."

"No bond prevented the MacDonalds from riding in here
and doing this," Magnus growled. "No bond will stop me."

Duncan sighed and rubbed a hand wearily over his face.
Watching him, Elspeth sensed the conflict that he felt. The
same painful desire for revenge wrenched at her.

"He harmed my child," Magnus said. "And raided and
burned out a widow."

Duncan nodded. "I will ride with you."

"Duncan," Elspeth said, clutching his sleeve, balancing
Eiric's weight with one arm. "You are the pledge for the
bond. Your life is forfeit if it is broken!"

He turned. "What would you have me do, Elspeth?" His
gaze was a piercing blend of rage and resolve. "Shall I
leave the Frasers with this and ride to Edinburgh now to
save my neck?"

She looked at him, understanding what he was thinking.
"You could not do that."

"I could not," he said. "The right action here is the
moral one. Not the legal one." He turned abruptly to go
with her cousins. Mounting their garrons, they thundered
out of the little yard. Elspeth stared after them for a while,
and then, holding Eiric securely, walked toward the house.

Elspeth leaned in the doorway of the croft and looked
out over the dark moor, eerie in the pale, cold moonlight.
The smell of charred wood was still strong in the air. She
sighed and glanced inside the dim interior of the house.

Eiric slept soundly now, her tears of pain and fear soothed finally by Bethoc's infusions and Elspeth's softest songs. Beside her in the box bed, Bethoc slept too, exhausted. The silence, in contrast to the earlier chaos, was a relief, but Elspeth did not feel at ease. Sleep was unthinkable just now.

Kenneth and Ewan had arrived at the croft shortly after Magnus and the others had ridden out. They had helped to clean up the mess left by water and soot, making certain that no embers remained alive. A short while ago her cousins had left the croft to ride patrol around the area. Because Bethoc refused to go to the castle, not wanting to move Eiric yet, Elspeth had promised to spend the night. Kenneth and Ewan would return for them in the morning.

She stepped outside, looking around cautiously as she walked through the yard. Tense and uneasy, she needed to be sure, one more time, that all was truly peaceful outside. Uncertain when Duncan would return, she hoped it would be soon.

Hearing a slight noise, she whirled. A small shadow slipped past the house, making a bleating sound. Recognizing the dingy fleece of the bog lamb in the darkness, she ran forward.

"Little one," she said softly, "where did you come from? How did you get away?" The lamb bleated again and trotted past her, heading for the turf block that served as an outside bench, where it began to nibble in earnest.

Elspeth looked around, heart leaping, wondering if Duncan and the others were back and had recovered the lamb. She had heard no approaching garrons.

Turning, she saw a black shadow, shaped like a man, step around the side of the house. She gasped and ran forward.

"Duncan?"

Hands reached out for her, yanking her nearly off her feet. She was dragged into the fierce embrace of two strong arms. One hand held a gleaming dirk.

"Let me go!" she cried, struggling.

"Easy, girl," Ruari said. "And I will not harm you."

"You have done enough harm here already," she said.

"I brought back the lamb," he said, clapping a heavy hand over her mouth. "For the child. I did not mean to hurt her. She surprised me, running up behind me."

Elspeth's reply was muffled by his hand as he dragged her away. Alarmed, unable to break free, she wrenched off the bronze brooch she wore on her plaid and dropped it in the dooryard.

Moments later, another man stepped out of the darkness and raised his arm. Something heavy struck her head and sent her thoughts spinning into oblivion.

Trussed by the plaid that was wrapped around her torso like swaddling bands, stiff and sore from riding at the front of Ruari's saddle, her head aching, Elspeth had endured endless hours of rough travel in a fog of half consciousness. Now, more alert, she was aware of Ruari's wide chest and slight paunch pressing against her back. She struggled to sit straighter.

This ride was like a cruel mockery of her marriage abduction; with that thought came an irresistible urge to elbow Ruari. She did, nearly throwing herself off balance for the pleasure of the blow.

"Stop that, girl," he growled in her ear. He righted her with a shove. "Strike at me once more and I will show you how well I can thrust at you. But perhaps you would like that."

The suggestion, not the first such that she had heard from him, made her feel ill. Biting back a sharp reply, she glanced at his brother Niall, who rode beside them. He was a broad-shouldered, heavily muscled man, whose dull brown hair and ragged beard looked as if they had not been washed in months. Niall had not uttered more than a few words the entire time that she had been with them. Whenever he had looked at her, she had sensed a dimness there, as if he were a half-wit. She wondered if he could even speak a full sentence. She watched him for a moment and then turned her gaze toward the mountains.

Studying the purple slopes, she realized how far they were from Bethoc's croft. The mountains were closer here, not so distant as in Glenran. Purple heather mingled with dun grasses on the steep slopes to produce a swirled effect, like oil and water. An eagle soared overhead, and the cold wind cut like steel.

The last two days had passed in a daze of headache and fatigue and numbing fear. Riding league after league, hardly comprehending what little was said to her, hardly taking in where she was or how much time had passed, she had struggled little. Night had come, and dawn, and hours of blazing sunlight. Then night again, and dawn; this was the third day.

They had rested only briefly now and again, stopping to sleep or to share a meal of dried beef, oatcakes, and cold water. Some of the time she had barely been conscious and could only vaguely remember the journey so far.

But now her head had cleared, and she was furious. Anger powered her like water over a mill wheel. She ached to elbow Ruari again, but wisdom—what little penetrated the heavy mist of her anger—told her to hold back. Instead she turned her energy to assessing her situation.

Ruari and Niall had taken her through MacDonald territory, riding west. They had passed through the green and beautiful valley where she and her cousins had often raided. This part of the Highlands was wilder, fiercer land, dun and harsh, overlooked by precarious slopes made of black rock and rough scree.

The chief of Clan MacDonald had his castle in the west, she knew. Perhaps they rode there; she was unsure what Ruari meant to do with her. He could not wed her, although he had made that suggestion earlier; she had not told him yet that she was already married.

She slid a glance behind her. Ruari MacDonald had the jaw of a warthog, she decided; it had a dull jut to it, peppered with a rust-colored beard. His brown eyes squinted at her, with a better intelligence than his brother, though he lacked a keen edge to his wit.

"Not much farther," he said. "Have you ever seen the sea?"

She nodded. During occasional trips to the Inverness

market, she and her cousins had gone to see the wide, magnificent expanse of the ocean. She frowned now, realizing that Ruari must mean the western sea, which she had heard was wild and cold.

Ruari said nothing more, and Niall never spoke at all until they halted the horses by a wide, shallow stream. Twilight by that time had spread indigo across the sky.

Ruari lifted her down from the saddle and led her to a wide-branched alder tree. She said that she must attend to herself. Ruari hesitated, then undid the plaid that bound her.

She went to the shore of the stream, sipped water from her hands, and then found a high bush behind which she could relieve herself. Ruari waited on the other side of the bush. When she came out, he grabbed her arm and led her back to the alder, shoving her to sit. The plaid that had bound her lay on the ground. She took it up and wrapped it around her, for the night air was chilly and Ruari did not look as if he meant to build a fire; there had been no fire the previous night.

Niall sat beneath the tree. Glancing at her with disinterest, he leaned back against the trunk.

"What do you mean to do with me?" she asked. "My cousins will ride after you."

Niall looked at her and grunted. He reached into his plaid and pulled out a cloth packet, unwrapping a few scraps of leathery beef. He began to chew slowly.

"Offer the girl some food, Niall," Ruari called.

Niall had begun to put a piece in his mouth, but stopped and held it toward Elspeth. She looked away in refusal.

Ruari had seen to the garrons, and now sat beside her. "No one will follow us," he said. "We heard that your cousins signed a bond of caution that keeps them from riding after MacDonalds."

"We had heard the same of you," she said.

"Ah. My uncle, the chief, signed some document from the crown that mentioned Frasers. But my brothers and I did not sign any paper." He smiled, a gleam of dingy teeth and a surprising hint of a dimple. "We cannot read or write."

"My cousins and my husband will find you," she said. "Count up your days, Ruari MacDonald."

He stared at her. "Husband?" He leaned forward and grabbed her arm through the thick plaid. "Who is your husband? When did you wed?"

"He is Duncan Macrae, the queen's lawyer," she said proudly. "He will see that your heads are taken for this. You have broken the MacDonald bond and must pay."

He glowered at her. "Macrae? The queen's lawyer who signed Robert Gordon's letter is your husband now?"

Niall spat on the ground and eyed her flatly, still chewing.

"He is a Macrae of Dulsie, in Kintail," she said, lifting her chin.

Ruari jumped to his feet. "Holy blood," he muttered, "you tell me this with pride, that you have wed a Macrae of Dulsie?" He yanked her to her feet, grasping her by the arms. "Do you know nothing of MacDonalds and Macraes to say this to me?"

She stared at him, confused. "What do you mean?"

"Are you a fool?" He leaned forward, breathing hot in her face. "The Macraes of Dulsie and the MacDonald clan are old, bitter enemies. Is this the son of Douglas Macrae?"

"That was his father's name," she said slowly. Ruari swore and dropped his hands from her, turning away, turning back, swearing again.

"Douglas Macrae had five sons," he said. "The Five Brothers of Kintail, they were called, since Dulsie Castle lies beneath the mountains called the Five Sisters. Douglas and two of his sons were killed by men of our clan several years ago."

"What happened?" she asked.

He snorted as if she were stupid. "The whining curs were defeated, of course. They were caught in a raid. Our clans have been feuding for generations." He folded his burly arms over his chest and looked at her on an eye level; he was hardly taller than she, though he weighed nearly two of her.

"I was a child then, but I heard the tales," he told her. "How the sons of Douglas Macrae were like wildcats after revenge, attacking any MacDonald they could find. They raided day or night, burned homes, stole animals, killed as many men as they could find."

"Is that wrong?" she asked. "You and your brothers do that to our clan often enough. We have come to expect your visits."

He slid a dark glance at her. "The Macraes raided alone, just the three sons who were left, lads they were, fifteen, sixteen, hardly older. But they did as much damage as twenty men. They were unstoppable. They were legendary after a while. My mother used to tell us that the wild Macraes would get us if we did not behave." He shook his head. "They did stop after a year or so. One of them was killed then. Another died a few months ago. We had heard that the third son went to Edinburgh." He looked at her. "And this is the man you have married?" he said incredulously.

"Wild Macrae," Niall said, nodding. "Get you."

Listening to all of this, Elspeth knew that it was true. A cold shiver went through her. She remembered Duncan's scar and the images that had come to her when she had touched it. Pain and anger lingered in that scar, and she had tapped into the hurt as if it were a vein. Now she knew what Duncan held inside.

She drew a breath and faced Ruari. "My husband is one of the wild Macraes of Dulsie," she said, "and he will come after you for taking me."

Ruari muttered incoherently and stepped toward her. She stumbled back, but he grabbed her by the plaid as if she were caught in a sling. He yanked her forward roughly.

"You were to marry with me," he snarled. "I took you away from the witch's home to see it done. But now—" He flung her away with a hoarse, angry curse.

She fell awkwardly over a large rock. Ruari's leather-covered feet stepped near her face as she lay in the dry autumn grass. "But now you have wed a man who is a legendary enemy to my clan. I think, Niall," he called, "that we have found a way to avenge the wrong done to our clan by the wild Macraes."

Niall grunted. "Revenge," he said, sounding as if he savored some rich flavor.

Ruari ripped the borrowed plaid off her. Then he reached down again and tore her own wrapped plaid, pulling so hard that she rolled with the drag. Lying on the ground in her long, rumpled shirt, in trews and deerskin boots, she hardly dared to move.

"But first," Ruari said, "I will have what the Macrae has had. It is my right."

The night was cold, the moor black as hell's own path, barely lit by cold, thin moonlight. Duncan rode beside Magnus, both grim and intent on their ride. Listening to the thunder of their horses' hooves, Duncan felt the sound echo in his heart.

The wind tore at his hair, blowing it back like wings, filling the plaid he wore. He gripped his knees to the garron and pushed onward, tireless, having no need for sleep or food or drink. He felt such rage and steel-hard determination that he could feel no discomfort. He had no need but revenge.

Two nights ago, they had returned to Bethoc's croft after a futile search for Ruari and his brothers. Hugh and Callum had gone on to Castle Glenran, but Duncan and Magnus had decided to stay the night at Bethoc's. Exhausted, not wanting to disturb Bethoc or the child, they had lain down beneath their plaids in the yard. They slept like great rocks, without movement or awareness. Just before dawn Bethoc had come out of the house to push Duncan's shoulder anxiously.

She had awoken, she said, to find Elspeth missing.

Signs of a scuffle were faint, but Bethoc soon found Elspeth's brooch. Conclusions came quickly, especially after Bethoc held the brooch quietly and then announced that Ruari had the girl, and no doubt of it.

Bethoc had looked at him with dark, knowing eyes. "They ride west," she said, "for the sea. Here is the favor

you owe me, Duncan Macrae. Ride and find her. Bring her
back. She is not safe."

"No favor," he had told her, "but my own pleasure to
do it."

Duncan remembered, and still felt, the anguish that had
sliced through him. He had stood in the small house and
stripped off his black cloak.

"I have left my fine plaid at Glenran," he told Bethoc.
"I would ask the loan of another from you."

Bethoc had brought him a folded tartan cloth of deep
blue and dark green, the colors the Frasers favored. He
had wrapped it around himself silently, his face grim, his
heart beating with a purposeful thud, a warrior's rhythm.
He had felt the fierce blood, the wild Macrae blood, course
through his veins like fire.

Bethoc had opened a wooden chest to lift out a claymore
wrapped in wool. "My husband's," she had told him, hand-
ing it to him. "He died with the Frasers at Blar-na-Léine.
He was a fine Highlandman. Like you."

Duncan had belted on the heavy, sharp blade and left
the cottage to leap onto his horse. Magnus, after kissing his
small daughter, had mounted to ride with him. There was
no time to go to the castle for the others; Bethoc would
see to it that they learned what had happened.

They had ridden at this pace for two days and nights,
hardly stopping except to rest briefly and to rest the horses;
Duncan marveled at the tireless perseverance of the Highland garrons. Only a few words had been exchanged between him and Magnus each time they had stopped to
share the food and flasks of *uisge beatha* that Bethoc had
sent with them. There was little to say and much riding to
be done.

Magnus had found the tracks of two horses, one carrying
a heavier load than the other, the burden of two riders.
Bethoc had been right in divining that Ruari headed west.
Duncan surmised that they would go to the clan chief's
castle on the wild western coast.

He knew the place; it was not far from Dulsie. Now each

passing league brought him closer to Dulsie. Closer to Elspeth.

His wife. The thought nearly rocked him from his seat: his wife, as fragile in appearance as a fairy's child, and as strong as steel hidden beneath a layer of gold. He knew that she had the will and the wit to hold her own against Ruari. She would have to until he and Magnus could find her.

Clenching the reins more tightly, he rode on.

Chapter 19

O they rode on, and farther on,
And they waded through rivers aboon the knee,
And they saw neither sun nor moon
But they heard the roaring of the sea.
                    —"Thomas the Rhymer"

"Lay a hand on me, and I will curse your soul to the depths of hell," Elspeth said. She rolled to her feet and cautiously stood, legs wide apart, hunched down, a fighting stance that her cousins had taught her.

Ruari moved toward her, and she skirted back. Niall still sat beneath the alder tree, chewing his food and watching them. Elspeth fixed her gaze on Ruari, who balanced the dirk in one hand.

"Come here, girl," he said, almost mildly. "I will not hurt you. We can warm each other through this cold night."

"Warm yourself in hell," she said.

"Elspeth," he said, "you were promised to me first. I have a right to do with you as I please."

"You have no rights to me." Flicking a glance behind her, she backed toward a cluster of trees and bracken. She would be able to run through there more nimbly than Ruari, she knew.

Ruari advanced toward her. "Come here, witch," he said.

Then she realized that she had a powerful weapon if she knew how to use it. Ruari's own fear could help her.

She straightened and stood still. Taking a deep breath, she rolled her eyes back and spread her arms wide. Ruari moved forward, grinning widely, apparently pleased with her compliance.

Then Elspeth began to murmur words that Bethoc had taught her, a lilting chant in an ancient language. She lifted her face to the night sky and sang out the chant in a clear voice. She drew a symbol overhead. The spell was one that asked favors of the air spirits. She only needed its ruse, and repeated the chant, sliding a quick glance at Ruari.

He stopped and tilted his head suspiciously. Elspeth ended the chant and looked at him, extending her arm to point at him.

As if she had summoned it, a wind rushed through then, icy and strong, lifting Ruari's plaid about his knees, whipping his hair. He opened his mouth and stared at her. Behind him, Niall stood and moved forward.

She pointed and began to speak. "Do not touch a seer in the midst of a vision, Ruari MacDonald," she said, "or you will see the same sight yourself." She rolled her eyes back and shuddered for his benefit.

Ruari stepped close, but did not touch her. He motioned to Niall, who came to stand beside him. She could smell their unwashed odor.

"I see the ravens overhead," she said. Ruari looked up at the night sky; she glanced at him and rolled her eyes back up. "Ravens who bring me news of your clan's demise. Of your own doom. Leave this place."

"Stop this," Ruari muttered.

She drew a deep breath. "I see the death of your clan," she said. She closed her eyes, and her breath suddenly quickened. A shiver coursed through her from the top of her head to her toes, a piercing jolt. Her knees nearly buckled at its surge.

The vision was real now, and she was caught. She saw men lying on a snowy field in a wide glen, edged by high mountains. Gasping, butchered, the men dragged themselves across the moonlit snow. She saw women with them, and children, all dying. Dark crags, vicious slopes, overlooked the horrible scene. She wanted to look away but could not. She wanted to scream. Then the words came.

"The MacDonalds will trust those who cannot be trusted," she said. "Tragedy and devastation will follow." She raised a trembling hand to her head, her senses spinning now. The awful images still swirled through her mind.

"You lie!" Ruari grabbed her shoulder hastily. His eyes grew wide, and Elspeth realized dimly that he saw a glimpse of the vision.

"Stop!" he shrieked, leaping away from her. "Cursed witch!" he said. "I saw the mountains—Glencoe, it was. People were dying there. This Sight comes from the devil!"

"Glencoe," she said dully. The vision had faded, and she felt sick, drained. "That night will not come for more than a hundred years. You are safe from that death, Ruari. But not from another." She stumbled to her knees and nearly fainted, holding herself up with her hands flat on the ground.

"Ruari not die. Witch," Niall said. He stepped forward and pulled her up. "Witches die."

As he began to lift her, a surge of blackness filled her sight, and she fainted.

When she awoke, she was restrained in the warm swaddling of the plaid once again, and had been flung over the front of a horse. She saw the night-dark ground rushing past. She closed her eyes, afraid she would be sick.

She lost consciousness again. Awareness came back when Ruari dragged her from the horse and began to carry her. Hearing an insistent rhythm, a loud shushing noise, she lifted her head.

The wind whipped damp and cool, and she could smell the salt in it. Ruari carried her along a cliff. She tried to struggle but could not move her arms or legs. Beyond the cliff she saw the wide, dark gleam of water, touched with white foam. A thick fringe of trees and rocky hillsides rose all around the water, enclosing the narrow end of it.

"This loch runs to the sea," Ruari said. "The tides sweep in here as high as in the ocean." He stomped down a slope with her in his arms, and headed out across a pebble beach. Reeds clustered at the water's edge, and waves rushed at the shore, loud and powerful. The loch was like a small sea, its waters sliding out toward a gray-blue horizon.

Realizing that he meant to take her into the loch, Elspeth twisted furiously. He set her down on her feet and back-

handed her, and she reeled with the blow. He caught her
and slung her over his shoulder, knocking the breath
from her.

For all that Ruari had done against her so far, he had
not shown Elspeth the same overt violence that he had
shown too often to Bethoc. Until now. A chill crept over
her. She suddenly sensed the depth of his cold hatred, mingled with fear and ignorance. She knew that he meant to
do her real harm.

"We have no tolerance for witches here," Ruari said as
he walked on. "And we have a particular punishment for
them."

"Witch," she heard then. Niall was somewhere behind
them.

"Macrae will kill you if you harm me," she said.

"He will try to kill me no matter what I have done,"
Ruari said. "I am a MacDonald, and he is one of the wild
Macraes. He needs no excuse to come after me. But now
I will kill him in his soul before I kill his flesh. And help
to avenge my clan."

"What do you mean to do?" she asked.

"Niall and I mean to drown a witch and wife to a Macrae," he said mildly. "Niall thinks it is the best thing to
do. Eh, Niall?"

"Kill the witch," Niall said. Elspeth raised her head and
glared at him. He moved away from her.

Ruari crunched across the beach with wide, purposeful
steps. Elspeth had never felt so helpless in all her life:
trussed and bound, she was in the keeping of a man whose
small mind prevented him from understanding that her
Sight was no threat to him. In trying to outsmart Ruari,
she had only convinced him of her witchery and had
trapped herself. And his intense hatred toward Duncan Macrae had endangered her further.

He stepped into the water and waded out a long way,
shallow water swirling around his legs. Niall plodded after
them. As Ruari set her down, cold water seeped knee-high
through the binding plaid. Looking around, she saw a high

rock jutting up behind her, black as ebony in the gray light
before dawn.

"This is the only way to destroy the evil in you," Ruari
said, holding her up. She twisted in his grasp.

He took out his dirk. "I thought that you were only
under the influence of the witch of Glenran. I hoped that
you would be redeemed once you were taken from her.
But that vision you had was an evil thing. You are a danger
to my clan.

"There was a reason," he went on, angling the long,
gleaming blade toward her, "that God prevented me from
marrying with you. Your choice of husband shows your evil
nature." He glared at her. "You and Macrae are both the
devil's own."

He slit at the confining plaid, pulling it off her. Cool air
hit her arms and chest through the thin cover of her linen
shirt. When he freed her legs, she tried to leap away. Niall
grabbed her then, holding her firmly.

Ruari tore narrow strips from the cloth and tossed the
long plaid away, where it caught on the rock. He tied her
hands in front of her, then tied her ankles.

"I will give you a chance. If the devil is your master, he
will welcome you to his hell below the loch. But if God
watches you—which I doubt, for they who have the Sight
are one with the devil—then you will be safe." Lifting her
high in his arms, Ruari set her on top of the rock.

Niall held her there while Ruari tied a long strip of torn
plaid around her, binding her to the rock. "I will come
back after the tide has risen," he said, stepping away. "If
you are still alive, I will take you to the shore. And we will
wait for your Macrae to come."

He turned, and he and Niall waded back to shore. Elspeth called and struggled, but they did not turn, fading
into the shadows along the beach.

The water rushed below the rock, cold and dark in the
dim light. Though a faint mist gathered above the surface
of the water, Elspeth could see seagulls dip and soar. Dawn
infused the mist with pale color. She looked down again;

the tide was swift. Already the base of the rock, which had been visible when Ruari had left her here, had disappeared.

Wedge-shaped and pointed like an upright dirk, the rock had a narrow shelf at one side, where Ruari had set her. Huddling against the rough, slick surface, tied fast to the rock, she stretched out her stiff legs and rested her tied hands in her lap. She pulled desperately at the woolen strips that bound her, but the knots were tight in the wet cloth.

A cold wind tore past, beating her head and shoulders, chilling her through to the bone. The tattered plaid that Ruari had flung away was still caught on the rock like a red banner, flapping noisily. Water swelled and lapped over her feet and ankles. At least her legs, encased in woolen trews and high deerskin boots, were somewhat protected from the cold water.

She watched the strong tide currents and bit back tears. Stunned at first that Ruari had done this to her, she had remembered what Bethoc had once told her: that the sisters and brothers of the Sight would someday be persecuted because people like Ruari were unable to understand that the Sight was not an evil thing. Seers were not necessarily guilty of witchcraft.

Water splashed over her feet and ankles. Watching it, she realized that, even tied and helpless, she still had a chance. A deep, high tide might cover the rock, but if the smallest part of the rock remained exposed, she could survive. Perhaps a fisherman would see her. And even if Ruari returned for her and took her to shore, she would still be alive when Duncan came.

With utter certainty she sensed that Duncan was searching for her. Since the first day that she had been taken, she had felt his presence, like the compelling lure of a lodestone. He was here, somewhere, in the west. She knew it, and it heartened her.

Ruari had told her that Duncan had been relentless in his pursuit of the MacDonalds years ago, after the death of his father and brothers. That same inexorable will would drive him to search for her without stopping.

She watched the foaming swirl of the seawater. Duncan might ride west in pursuit of Ruari MacDonald, but how could he find this remote place before the water engulfed the rock?

Fear swelled and surged through her then. The water slid relentlessly up the face of the rock, spilling over her knees to pool in her lap. The seawater did not feel as cold, as unforgiving, as she thought it would. Her tears dripped into it, salt into salt.

He could have razed whatever lay in his path. Surges of anger ripped through him, waves of savage, icy fury. Each thought was forged by blazing anger. He rode onward, eyes cold and hard, jaw set, his hair whipping like raven wings, his plaid blowing back.

"Duncan," Magnus said, riding beside him. Duncan turned and glowered at him. "We must stop, man, or ruin the horses. I am just as determined to find her as you are, but we are exhausted."

"Not much farther to the castle of John MacDonald," Duncan said. "We still stop there and ask if Ruari has been seen."

"You expect them to answer that?"

Duncan shrugged. "What choice is there? Their track is no longer obvious. We know they have gone west. The clan chief will have to offer us hospitality, since I am the queen's representative. We will go to the MacDonald stronghold unless we find some track before that point."

"You would go to the chief of your clan's greatest enemy?"

"And yours," Duncan growled.

Magnus nodded. "There is some of the devil in you, Macrae," he said. "But the horses do not have your endurance."

Duncan began to slow his garron. "You are right. We should not ask of the animals what we ask of ourselves," he said.

They dismounted to take shelter within a circle formed by several fir trees. Sharing what little food they had, they soon rolled up in their plaids. Magnus fell into an exhausted sleep.

Duncan lay down and pulled his plaid over his head, but he could not calm his thoughts. He knew that he had slipped into a kind of rhythm of revenge, without thought, without reason. Magnus, although driven by his own anger, had possessed the sense to insist that they rest.

A bitter rage flowed through Duncan. He realized that he had succumbed to the same blood anger that had caused him to fight hard, ride hard, and hate so fiercely years ago. Now he rode after a MacDonald once again; the irony of the situation had not escaped him. Though he knew that he was on the verge of breaking the Fraser bond himself, somehow he did not care. The fine could be paid. The satisfaction of catching this MacDonald would be worth the price.

Riding through dark, craggy terrain that he had not seen for years, he had remembered, too vividly, what had happened sixteen years ago, when he had lost part of his family and, he was convinced, part of his soul.

He had never seen the faces of the murderers. He did not even know who had driven a dirk into his own flesh. But he had lived when his father and two eldest brothers had not. And so it had fallen on him, more than the rest of his family, to seek vengeance, to take responsibility for what happened later, the brutality, the hatred. He had thought the debt paid, the wound assuaged. Then he had come to Glenran, to deal indirectly, he thought, with MacDonalds again. Now his own wife had been taken by one of that clan, and the old wound had been opened.

He felt uneasy, sleeping out here in the open beside Magnus, two men rolled in plaids. But sleep finally came, descending suddenly and deeply. He did not know how long he slept. Then the vivid dream woke him like a plunge of icy water, as it had twice before.

This time Elspeth sat on a rock in the middle of the sea. Mountains rose on two sides of the expanse of water. A huge wave rushed over her, sweeping her away. Swimming in the cold water, Duncan lost sight of her.

But he heard her light, sweet voice calling his name. He tried to answer, a desperate mumble as he woke.

In a cold sweat, his heartbeat hammering in his ears, he sat abruptly. He wrapped and belted his plaid, brooching it with Elspeth's pin. Pulling on his boots, he stood quietly, touched Magnus's shoulder, and then turned. He walked away from the campsite toward his horse, knowing that Magnus would follow.

He knew now where he must go.

The water surged past her waist, soaking her shirt, floating her breasts, rocking her body. She was shivering, and the taste of salt was on her lips. She could hardly feel her arms and legs for the relentless chill.

Not long ago, as the water rose, she had been able to pull enough on the long strip of wool around her chest to stretch it. Rising slowly to her feet on the narrow shelf of rock, she had slid the binding upward with her, until it had slipped off the pointed wedge behind her.

Then she had turned to catch her bound wrists on a protruding angle of the rock, trying to anchor herself against the higher waves that could sweep her into the rolling sea. If she had fallen into the swift water with her wrists and ankles both tied, she knew that she would flounder and drown. This, at least, would keep her safe a little while longer.

Clinging there, striving to keep her feet steady on the shelf beneath her, she had grown more and more angry.

Angry at Ruari MacDonald for his ignorance. Angry that he thought her a witch, that he thought Bethoc evil as well. And she was annoyed with Duncan and her cousins for not finding her before this. She felt a vague, undefined, churning rage that she turned on everyone, including herself. She cursed out loud, wishing that she had never set foot outside Bethoc's croft that night. She should have sat through the night, dirk in hand to guard against Ruari, and waited for Duncan to return.

Now, as the water lapped coldly around her ribs, she began to cry, deep, gouging sobs that were soon spent. Fear had a firm, fierce grip over her. Then she remembered what Duncan had once told her: never give anything such power over you. *I cannot let the fear destroy me*, she thought; *I cannot.*

Raising her head, she took deep breaths of the salty, damp air until she felt the clawing fear gradually lessen its hold. She had been afraid before, and had lived through to the hope on the other side of it. And she had never had patience with her own despair. There was a way to survive the incoming tide. There had to be, and she would find it.

She reminded herself that she had been raised to be tough and brave, a part of Clan Fraser's unique legend. The only course open to her was bravery. To accept the defeat and humiliation of this predicament was weakness. Her cousins would not expect it of her. Duncan would not expect it of her. He had seen her face Ruari MacDonald with pride and courage.

She could not give this victory to Ruari.

Elspeth had felt courage before, knew its heady stir in her heart and her blood. With her cousins at her back, she had reived and ridden in the night; she had faced the MacDonalds too, although never in battle as her cousins had done. And she had felt the courage that flowed deep in her husband. She could not hurt him by giving in to this.

She faced this battle alone. The sea was her enemy now, this rock her only salvation, its strength supporting her, as had her cousins, as had Duncan. She thought of Duncan, of how much she loved him, of how much she wanted to be with him, for however long they would have. Gradually, she began to feel courage well inside her, from a source as boundless as the sea, from the love she held for him.

She lifted her chin and gazed out at the foaming gray sea, at the thin mist, at the endless clouds that filled the enormous bowl of the sky. Dawn washed through the clouds, a breath of pale color. Light moved through the darkness as if it were some calm, sustaining hope.

Straightening, planting her feet firmly on the rock, she pulled against the sodden woolen strips that bound her wrists. She tugged, wanting to be free at any cost. If she

could get her hands free, she would take her chances in
the sea; she was a strong swimmer and could make it back
to shore.

She tugged again. The sky brightened, a wash of water
rushed up over her chest, and she pulled all of her weight
on the saturated plaid strip. The cloth bit painfully into
her wrists.

And stretched. She pulled, and the strip tore a little.

She watched the dawn's glow, watched the roll of the
next wave come toward her, and yanked again.

Chapter 20

"O haud your tongue, my dearest dear,
Let all your follies abee;
I'll show you whare the white lilies grow
In the bottom of the sea."
                                        —*"The Demon Lover"*

Duncan stood on a cliff and gazed down at the loch. Dawn brightened the sky and shed a glowing light on the misted water and stony beach below. He saw a deserted shore and a narrow sea loch filling with the morning tide, swelling around the jutting tips of a few black rocks. The water near the shore was carpeted with golden reeds. The wind was up, salty and cold.

He had come here because he had seen this place in his dream. Upon waking, he had remembered where he had seen the strong, unique slant of those mountains, rising so close to the shoreline. He and his brothers had been to this loch years ago.

The same insistent gut twist that had always told him where to ride on a raid, how far, in what direction, had told him that Elspeth was here at this place. He had followed that instinct unquestioningly, as he had always done in his reiving days.

Now he sighed, despondent. Elspeth was not here. Uncertain what he had expected to find, he felt an empty disappointment. He shook his head at his own folly.

Magnus stood behind him, silent, looking over the cliff at the surging water below. The wind whipped their hair and plaids, but they stood motionless. Duncan watched gannets gliding over the water, dipping their white wings down.

Duncan stepped away from the cliff edge.

"What is that, out there?" Magnus said. "A seal?"

Duncan turned. Magnus pointed toward a black rock far out in the water. The faint mist obscured details, but something waved and fluttered in the water. A long snag of kelp, Duncan thought, but then noticed that it was red and patterned. Something else was there too, a coppery smudge moving away from the rock, through the waves and the thin veiled mist.

He looked again. The snag was not kelp but red plaid, floating on the waves. The copper-colored smudge was part of a moving body. A seal? Too small, too pale and graceful. He blinked in astonishment.

For one wild moment he thought he had seen a mermaid.

He burst into motion, running down the slope of the cliff toward the beach. Surely he had seen a head, a face, with floating, bright red-gold hair, swimming toward shore.

He stripped off his belt and sword, his plaid, his boots as he ran across the stony beach. He hit the water, diving into it so fast that he had no time to feel the slam of the cold seawater. Sliding beneath the waves, he came up again, looking around, treading water with his arms.

He saw the angle of the rock jutting up. He glimpsed her pale face above the surface, her hair floating out.

"Elspeth!" he called. He struck out diagonally, long, strong strokes, pulling through the fast current of the tide, losing only a little ground as he went. He saw her disappear beneath a crashing wave, saw her bob back up again, and go under.

He swam, and neared her, but was carried back again by the current. Pulling harder with his arms, driving with his legs, he swam close enough to touch her.

She reached out, her hand grasping his arm. He slid an arm around her waist and pulled her toward him to help her swim the distance to the shore.

A few long moments more, and he was able to stand in the shallows, holding her up. Elspeth collapsed in his arms, and he lifted her, uncertain if she was still conscious. As her cousin waded out toward them, Duncan carried her to the beach, dropping to his knees, laying her down.

Magnus knelt too, smoothing the wild tangle of hair out

of her face, murmuring to her. Duncan eased his hands up her back to coax water out of her lungs. His heart lurched with sudden gratitude when she coughed and sputtered. He held out his hand, like a command. Magnus put a dirk into it, and he sliced through the sodden cords that bound her ankles together; then he cut off a scrap of red wool around one wrist.

Lifting her gently, he turned her into his arms. She coughed again and circled her arms around his neck wearily.

"I knew you would come," she said, resting against him.

"I had to find you." He pressed his lips to her hair and fought back the sob that clawed at his own throat. He held her to him, and she clung.

Taking her face in his hands, he looked at her. He felt as if he could not take in enough of the sight of her face, her wet red-gold hair, her wide gray eyes. He lowered his lips and touched hers, a strong, moist, warm pressure, tasting salt, sensing the heat of life within her.

Magnus approached, having gone to fetch Duncan's discarded plaid, and laid it over Elspeth's shoulders. Shivering, she smiled up at her cousin and leaned her head against Duncan's shoulder. Feeling her tremors, he slid an arm around her and pulled her closer, hardly feeling his own chill.

"How did you come to be in the sea loch?" Magnus asked.

Duncan frowned as he recalled something long ago forgotten. "Did Ruari strand you on a tidal rock?" he asked her.

She nodded, sniffing. "He did, but I broke loose." He nodded, hardly surprised; he knew how capable she was, how much courage she had. He knew she had not waited for the sea to swallow her, and his heart filled with pride to have her so much a part of his life.

"Why would Ruari strand her on a rock?" Magnus asked.

"It is a punishment for witchery, done in some coastal areas," Duncan said. "An accused witch is tied to a rock and left to drown in the oncoming tide. I should have thought of this earlier," he said. "I should have realized that Ruari could do something like this."

"But you did know," Magnus said. "You rode straight here, as if a demon were at your heels."

Elspeth looked up at him then, her eyes questioning, curious. "How did you know to come here?" she asked.

He hesitated. "I saw it in a dream," he finally said. They stared at him. He smiled, a faltering, embarrassed smile.

Magnus glanced at his cousin. "I think he means it."

Elspeth nodded and looked at Duncan. "Tell us the dream."

"I saw you in the sea, drowning. I tried to save you. And I recognized this place." He shrugged. "So I came here."

She frowned. "Did you have the dream just once? Recently?"

"Three times," he said. "The last just over an hour ago."

Elspeth was silent, staring at him; her eyes were all that he saw, pale gray, like the mist that hung over the loch.

Then Magnus cleared his throat. "You have the Sight, man," he said with a tone of respect.

Duncan shook his head. "It was just a dream. But it gave me an idea of where to find her. I know the area. This was a logical place for Ruari to bring her if he thought her a witch."

"But you did not know he would accuse her," Magnus said. "That was more than a dream."

Duncan scowled at him. "Perhaps it was good reasoning," he said, feeling distinctly uncomfortable.

"Duncan," Elspeth said, laying her hand on his arm, "three times you had this dream. It was a true vision. You are a seer."

"Not me," he said, shaking his head. "Not me." He did not want to hear any more of this. The Sight could not exist, not in truth—not in him. He had not yet explained Elspeth's odd bits of knowledge, but he would find a way. And his dream had been just a dream.

Just a dream, but it had led him straight to her when she

needed him. He had swum out to her, as had happened in the dream; he had seen these mountains edging the shore.

Standing abruptly, he walked away, bending down to swoop up his shirt, his belt, his claymore thrown down on the stones. He yanked on his shirt and sat to pull on the boots, aware that the others were staring at him. Belting his wide, loose shirt over his wet trews, he shoved the heavy sword into place and stood.

Fisting his hands on his hips, he stared back at them.

"Come ahead," he said. "We have to get back home again now that we have come all the way out here."

Magnus rose slowly and put his hand on his dirk. Elspeth sat on the stones, as pale as if she would faint. Alerted by their wary expressions, Duncan turned cautiously.

Several paces away, Ruari MacDonald advanced over the pebble beach. A large man loped beside him.

"Hold, Duncan Macrae," Ruari called, drawing his long claymore from its scabbard. "Hold while I slice you like a carcass. The MacDonalds want to feast on your bones."

Duncan put his hand to his sword and began to pull the blade free.

Ruari rushed at him then, roaring, running like a wild boar, plunging at Duncan with his claymore raised to strike.

Elspeth struggled to her feet, but her legs were weak and faltered beneath her. She sank to her knees on the hard beach, raising a fist to her mouth as she watched the four men fight with dirks and broad-bladed claymores. Every thrust, every arcing clash of the steel blades, made her flinch.

She had never seen true bloodlust before. But she saw it now in Ruari, who rushed at Duncan with brutal fury on his face, savage power behind each swinging blow. A roaring, raging animal, Ruari's extreme fury made him careless, and his swings went too wide, too fast, too wild.

Duncan sliced, quickly and viciously at Ruari. Blood welling from his upper arm, Ruari roared and swung. Duncan slid to the side, forcing Ruari to whirl and strike again furiously. Then Duncan leaped to the side with powerful, easy grace, so much more agile than Ruari, with his short, stocky body. The loud clash of their broadswords echoed across the stones.

Niall came at Magnus with plodding efficiency, a strong opponent lacking quickness or cleverness. When Niall rushed forward and overbalanced on his thrust, Magnus rolled with him to the stony surface of the beach.

Elspeth gasped and glanced back at Duncan anxiously. A grimace of rage passed over his face as he swiped the heavy blade at Ruari, beating him back. Ruari stumbled over the uneven rocks that littered the beach and fell, losing his grip on his sword.

Biting her knuckles as she watched, Elspeth waited for the bloody thrust of Duncan's weapon. He stood over Ruari, staring down, his breath making his chest heave. Ruari stared up at him, both men still and tense.

Duncan touched the tip of his blade to Ruari's chest. Then, with a growl, Duncan turned his back in an utter and humiliating dismissal. He walked away.

Elspeth knew that he could have easily thrust Ruari through in the chest or belly, but he had not done it. She could hardly believe what she had seen, did not understand why Duncan had held back. She rose to her feet as Duncan walked across the beach. Elspeth glanced quickly at Magnus and Niall, who still struggled, and turned back to watch Duncan and Ruari. The tension between them was palpable. Her gut knotted with dread.

Ruari got to his feet and ran after Duncan, head down. Before Elspeth could even cry out, Ruari pulled his dirk from his belt and cannoned into Duncan.

Hardly glancing behind him, Duncan bent and slid to the side in one smooth movement. Ruari rolled over Duncan's back, stabbing his dirk into him as he went. Elspeth watched as Ruari flipped and twisted grotesquely, crashing headfirst onto the stones, pulling Duncan with him.

Elspeth covered her mouth with shaking hands and screamed. Neither man moved. Blood saturated Duncan's sleeve.

Then, after a moment, Duncan shifted and came to his

knees. Elspeth ran to him, nervously eyeing Ruari's still form.

"I am fine," Duncan rasped out as she touched him. He raised a knee and leaned on it, looking at Ruari. *"Dhia,"* he said. "I think he is dead."

"How could that be?" she breathed.

Duncan poked Ruari's body with the hilt of his dirk. Ruari's head rolled unnaturally. "His neck is broken."

She gasped, and would have spoken, but a terrible, gut-deep roar behind her caused her to whip around.

Niall had gotten away from Magnus and came toward them, head and arms hanging down as he shrieked. Elspeth jumped back.

Falling to his knees, Niall roared again, with such anguish that Elspeth felt tears burst in her eyes. Duncan stood, dirk in hand, but Niall made no move to attack him. He only knelt, and screamed, and covered his brother's body with his own.

"Niall—" she said hesitantly.

Then Niall looked up, his dark eyes reflecting fear and pain. He looked at Duncan. "Killed Ruari!" he bellowed, and stood. Duncan stepped away cautiously, raising his dirk.

Gripping his own dirk, Niall rushed at Duncan, who easily sidestepped him. Niall came at him again, but this time the heavier man knocked Duncan to the ground, trapping his dirk hand. Elspeth saw that blood flowed freely from Duncan's arm as he struggled against Niall's strength.

Ruari's sword lay on the beach, and she ran toward it, noticing then that Magnus had not gotten to his feet. Hesitating, she took a step toward him; when he moved, she ran for the sword. Hefting it in her hands, she whirled and ran back to Duncan.

The claymore was the heaviest she had ever held, although the blade was shorter than those used by her cousins. She lifted it, her slender wrists, wobbling with the effort.

Niall and Duncan rolled on the beach as Niall held Duncan's throat in a crushing grip. Duncan held him back with his weakened arm, while he tried to angle his dirk to stab Niall.

Elspeth, watching, saw that Duncan's wounded arm could not take the strain much longer. She saw Niall angle his own blade toward her husband. She stepped forward, raised the claymore, and brought it down broadside on Niall's head.

A suspended moment, and then Niall slumped. Duncan pushed him away. Elspeth watched Niall anxiously, and saw with relief that he still breathed.

Duncan rose to his feet, shoving his hair out of his eyes. Blood seeped from the wound in his arm. Elspeth reached toward his arm, murmuring concern.

"Leave it," he said. "I am fine. I see that you learned how to wield a claymore after all."

"Well enough to be of help," she said. He nodded, still catching his breath, and glanced over at Magnus, who lay prone.

A few quick strides, and Duncan reached Magnus, kneeling beside him. Elspeth ran too, dropping to her knees beside her husband. Magnus struggled to sit up, his hand clutched to his belly. When she saw the blood dripping between his fingers, Elspeth touched his shoulder gently. "Let me look."

He took his hand away, and she suppressed the gasp that rose in her throat. The wound was wide and deep, a vicious puncture that entered just under Magnus's ribs.

Elspeth bit her lip, knowing that a deep wound, just there, could kill a strong man in a few hours. Magnus was already visibly weak. With careful, gentle hands she pulled the long tail of his shirt out of his plaid, peeling it away from the wound. At her soft word Duncan tore a length of the shirt and handed it to her to wad against the wound. He tore another length and helped her wrap the linen around Magnus's ribs.

Elspeth spoke softly to Duncan. "We must take him somewhere to rest and be tended," she murmured. "We cannot go back to Glenran now. If he travels far, he will die."

Duncan nodded. He looked toward the mountains that loomed over the loch. "I know a place."

"Take us there, then," she said.

"We will have to travel for two hours or more. Do you think he can do it?"

"He will not die," she said. "We will not let him."

Duncan nodded. She took his arm and began to roll his sleeve up, the cloth reddened with blood from a deep cut in his upper arm. He pulled away at first, but she sent him an insistent scowl. Sighing, he held his arm out for her to tend. She wrapped the wound with a torn piece from Duncan's own shirt.

"Where will you take us?" she asked.

He gazed at her, his eyes a somber blue, like a deep loch. "We will ride to Dulsie Castle," he said.

A twisting pass took them upward, closer to the wild mountain peaks that rose dark and desolate to the east, their treacherous rocky rises coated with mosses and pierced by spouts of falling water. To the west lay steep downward slopes covered with dry grass and dying heather. Far below lay a blue maze of sea lochs and inlets.

Duncan bent forward against the cold, brisk wind, shivering without his plaid, which he had given to Elspeth. He rode the garron at an easy pace through the pass, reaching out an arm now and again to support Magnus, who sat his garron behind Elspeth, leaning heavily against her back. Duncan wished he could take the burden from her, but the garron could not carry two full grown men.

Magnus shook his head wearily when Duncan reached out. "I can ride, man," he said, his voice hoarse.

Duncan looked at him suspiciously, noting the gray pallor in Magnus's face. He admired his endurance and stubborn pride. Magnus had held himself upright and had kept conscious despite pain and blood loss. "Not much farther, man, I promise you," Duncan said.

Elspeth turned her head to look at Duncan. "Where is Dulsie from here?" she asked.

"Less than a league away now," he said. "The pass will narrow and climb downward, and there we will see Dulsie."

She nodded, and he watched her for a moment, saw the wild glint of her coppery hair, noted the tired curve of her shoulders. He wanted to reach out to her, but his own heart was heavy and held him back. The closer he got to Dulsie, the more tense and withdrawn he had become.

The price he had paid at the sea loch weighed on him like a great stone. The bond of caution was broken, and by his own action. A MacDonald was dead. He drew a deep breath and sighed deeply, and looked at Elspeth.

"At Dulsie we will be able to eat and sleep," he said, trying to smile. "I know that you are tired."

"You as well," she said. "I will sleep and eat only after Magnus is seen to. Will there be a garden at Dulsie where I can find herbs to treat Magnus?"

He nodded. "My sister Mhairi, Alasdair's wife, will be there to help you. My other sister, Kirsty, is too young yet to be of help, I think. And my grandmother is knowledgeable," he said. "She will know what to do, and will have whatever you need. She treated my back wound when my family thought I might die of it—" He stopped.

"Duncan," she said, "why have you stayed away from Dulsie?"

He shook his head and glanced away. There was much to tell her, but he had no desire to begin now. Soon enough he would see those walls, would ride through that gate, would face his past.

He looked around him. The morning mist had cleared to a bright, crisp day, and cloud shadows floated over the hills. The air was cold and keen, just as he remembered. He breathed it in, and a muscle pulsed in his jaw as he thought of how much he dreaded, and wanted, to see Dulsie Castle.

Although Magnus's condition required it, Duncan knew now that it was time he came home. A steep blue mountain rose ahead of them, its peak ringed with soft clouds. His heart thudded at the sight, for Dulsie Castle was harbored at its base.

"Dulsie. *Tull-sìth*," Elspeth said, in that way she had that often echoed his thoughts. "Why is it called the fairy hill?"

"There is a legend from long ago," he said. "The hill on which the castle sits was once inhabited by fairies. The first Macrae to build on that hill fell in love with a fairy woman. She wed him and bore his children. He went away to sail the sea and was lost in a storm. But his wife had given him a magic net of silver thread to take with him.

"The fairy woman went out every night and called her husband's name, holding a long silver thread in her hands, the same as the thread she had used to weave his net. She pulled the thread through her hands and sang out for him.

"One day the laird came walking back to Dulsie. He greeted his wife, and said that although he had been washed overboard, the net had floated him to shore, bringing him back to her."

"That is a lovely tale," Elspeth said.

"It is said," Duncan went on, "that the lairds of Dulsie will always return if they leave, no matter the reason."

Elspeth glanced at him. "And you are the laird of Dulsie now," she said, "coming home."

"I am, since my last brother's death a few months ago." He returned her gaze evenly.

Duncan led them down the last part of the twisting, slanted pass, and they struck out over tufted, rough moorland. "There," he said, "is Dulsie."

His heart pounded at the sight, so familiar and yet so strange. Unchanged in sixteen years, it looked somehow new to his eyes. Gray stone, constructed in a square, bold tower, had faded to a soft color that blended harmoniously with the rich greens of the fir-clad mountain slopes behind the castle. A high stone wall encircled the tower house, and a narrow river, rocky and turbulent, rushed around the curve of the fairy hill like a natural moat. A long causeway of the same gray stone crossed the rapid torrent, linking the castle to the moorland.

They crossed the moor, and soon the garrons' hooves were clattering on the stone bridge. Pausing halfway, Duncan waved toward the parapet atop the tower house.

"I am Duncan Macrae!" he called. "Duncan Macrae, bringing two Frasers!"

After a surprised shout, someone called out an order to open the gate. He rode through, aware that the three of them looked ragged and exhausted. He saw that Magnus, in spite of his wound, sat tall behind Elspeth, and Duncan knew that came from sheer pride and determination.

Duncan slid from his horse and turned to help Magnus dismount. Elspeth nudged him and he looked around to follow her gaze toward the castle yard. A few servants stared openly at him. Two Highlanders, Macrae cousins whom he recognized immediately in spite of the passage of years, began to walk toward him.

He greeted them tentatively. They clasped his hand with cautious acceptance, and then turned to help steady Magnus, who was too weak to stand alone.

"Duncan!" He turned to see Alasdair running toward him. Throwing his arms around Duncan, Alasdair clapped him on the back. Wincing as his arm was jarred, Duncan returned the embrace.

He drew back. "Alasdair, may I present my wife?"

Alasdair's eyes popped wide. "Wife! You two have much to tell! Come here, cousin!" He held out his arms and Elspeth came into them.

Duncan looked around to see two young women standing nearby. One was tall and brown-haired with a sweet face, whom he did not recognize. The other one, slight and dark, held a baby wrapped in a plaid that matched the shawl over her gray dress. Two small boys stood behind her, staring up at him. A delighted smile lit the woman's face.

"Welcome home, *bràthair*," she said, and stepped forward into his arms.

"Mhairi," he breathed, wrapping his sister in his arms. The baby kicked out between them. Duncan laughed and looked at him.

"James," she said, "ready for his nap. And here are Douglas and Farquhar. Greet your uncle, now." The boys, both blue-eyed with black hair, stared solemnly. One of them bravely stuck out a hand for Duncan to grasp, and then the pair ran off together.

He glanced at the other woman, who, he now saw, was much younger than Mhairi, near Elspeth's age. She smiled at him shyly, her rich brown hair and serene face reminding him of someone. He drew in his breath. She looked like his mother.

"Kirsty?" he asked. "Is this little Kirsty, grown to a beauty? You were but three when I left."

"Duncan." She smiled and came forward to kiss his cheek.

Alasdair asked the Macraes to carry Magnus up the outer stone steps into the tower house. Magnus protested, but no one listened closely. Kirsty turned to lead the way, calling to a servant to fetch hot water and cloths.

Duncan turned Mhairi toward Elspeth. Bouncing the crying child, Mhairi smiled and took Elspeth's hand in hers. "Welcome," she said. "And thank you for bringing Duncan home again after so long. We have missed him."

"Mhairi," he said, "where is—"

She nodded toward the tower. He turned.

A woman stood at the top of the long flight of stone steps that angled up to the tower entrance. Her hair was as white as soft clouds, her eyes as blue as he remembered them. She was tiny, her stooped shoulders wrapped in a plaid over a brown kirtle. The woman watched him for a long moment.

Duncan moved forward. He glanced back at Elspeth, motioning her forward with him. Pausing at the bottom step while Elspeth stood behind him, Duncan looked up the long flight.

"Grandmother Innis," he said, "I have come home."

"Duncan." Innis Macrae looked at him for a long time. He grew nervous under her resolute stare. "I had heard from Alasdair that you were in the Highlands." Her voice was older, tremulous, her face more gaunt than he remembered. He wanted to mount the stairs toward her, but her eagle's stare kept him where he was.

"You have brought a wife?"

He remembered that she had never missed any detail; age had not dimmed her sight or hearing. "I have," he said.

"I tell you, Duncan Macrae," she said, "if your pride had kept you away from here longer, I would have ridden to the Fraser castle myself to fetch you." She beckoned him forward. "Welcome home."

Chapter 21

Come lay me soft, and draw me near,
And lay thy white hand over me,
For I am starving in the cold,
And thou art bound to cover me.
                    —"Love in Despair"

Duncan leaned against the bedpost and looked at the bed where Magnus lay beneath a pile of fur coverlets. Innis stood nearby, her small blue-veined hand on Magnus's brow. Beside her, Kirsty leaned forward to apply warm, wet herbs over the stitched wound, then gently wrapped a folded cloth over his bare abdomen. She drew up the sheet and stood back.

"He has no fever," Innis told Duncan. "He will sleep like the dead on that potion we fed him, and he will wake feeling stronger. But he must stay in bed for a long time to let those stitches heal. What is damaged inside, I cannot say, but he has a better chance of healing inside and out if he lies still."

"We will stay as long as necessary," Duncan said.

Innis looked at him strangely. "You are the laird of Dulsie. Of course you will stay."

He sighed and was silent. Innis moved closer, a wraith-like woman who did not reach his shoulder. Her head bobbled slightly as she looked up at him. She had aged, and he felt sudden regret that he had not been here for those lost years.

"The lairds of Dulsie always come home," Innis said.

"I have a home in Edinburgh, and duties there," he said. "I am a lawyer for the queen and her council."

"I know that. But that Lowland place is no home for you. Your kin are here."

He sighed. "I cannot stay here just now," he said. "And Elspeth is a Fraser. She is not ready yet to leave her home."

"She is your wife. Her home is here with you."

He was silent, feeling his grandmother's steely stubbornness still in evidence. She appeared delicate, but he remembered that iron will hidden behind her fragile exterior. That, at least, had not changed. He glanced at Kirsty, who shrugged calmly.

He expected his grandmother to express more of what she thought, and waited. Innis Macrae had never held back her opinions; that had been one of the problems between them years ago. But Innis only sighed and turned away, walking to the door.

"I am an old woman," she said, "and I need my rest. I will come back later to watch over your friend. Kirsty will stay for now. She is a capable girl." She laid her hand on the door latch. "We will talk, you and I, later. For now, you also are wounded, and very tired. Mhairi showed your bride to your old bedchamber a while ago. I will expect you both to sleep through the day tomorrow. Then we will talk." She nodded to him and pulled open the door.

He looked at Kirsty after the door had closed. "She has not changed much," he said.

"More than you know, Duncan. Your absence these years has been a lesson in humility to her."

He glanced at her quickly. "Humility? I never meant—"

"But that is how she views it, and has told Mhairi and me that many times. Go to bed, Duncan," she said, touching his sleeve. "You look as if you barely have the strength to stand."

He smiled wearily. "Little Kirsty, grown so tall and lovely. You have a fine mothering way about you. Are you wed?"

"Not yet," she said. "Innis needs me here."

"Ah," he said softly, feeling a pang of regret that he had not been here for these people, his family, out of his own stubbornness.

Magnus groaned and rolled onto his side. Kirsty moved

to pull his shoulder back. "I stitched his wound myself," she said, adjusting the covers over him. "He is a strong man, your friend. He took the pain of the stitches without complaint. A wound such as that, and the ride you made, might have killed another man."

Duncan nodded. "You will have the devil's own time keeping him to his bed when he wakes up."

"Well," Kirsty said, looking down at Magnus, "he is a fine, strong man, but he will have a devil of a time getting past me." She flashed a smile at Duncan.

He laughed, shaking his head. "Innis said you were a capable girl. Quite a compliment, coming from her."

"I am that. Now go to your bed, Duncan Macrae. I will watch this Fraser, and all you need to do is rest yourself."

He nodded, hugged his youngest sibling, and left the room.

Entering the bedchamber in which Elspeth slept, he moved across the rush-covered floor with quiet steps. The room was fully dark, the window shuttered. In the hearth, a banked peat fire sent out a soft, dim glow and waves of heat. He paused by the bed.

Elspeth slept, her breathing soft and even, her shoulder upturned, her hair spread out over the pillow. He watched her, feeling weary but restless. Wanting to lie down beside her and gather her softness against him, he steeled himself and walked past the bed. There was too much rushing through his mind; he could not rest. He had to think.

He went to the window, recessed in a deep niche above a stone bench, and sat heavily on the cushioned seat. His wounded arm, cleaned and bandaged, ached dully. Blowing out a tense sigh of frustration, he leaned forward and shoved his fingers through his hair.

He, the queen's lawyer, the human pledge of the Frasers' bond of caution, had broken that bond when he had ridden after Ruari MacDonald. He had allowed his temper to overtake him, as it had years ago. His temperament, inherited from generations of wild Macraes, had ruled him once

again, as it had ruled him in his youth. He had thought his
wild nature conquered, tamed, and dispirited for good.

That broken promise, which had resulted in a death, now
directly endangered his life. Once the council heard of
this—and they would, he was certain, for the MacDonalds
themselves would waste no time in reporting it to the
crown—he would be arrested and brought to trial.

He had brought himself to the edge of his own doom by
his own actions. In trying to reassure Elspeth that he was
in no real danger if the bond was ever broken, he had
not been entirely truthful with her. There existed a strong
possibility that he could be accused of treason. Not only
was he the lawyer and the pledge for the bond, he was
responsible for breaking the Frasers' signed word. The
council might demand more than a fine.

The situation was much graver than he could ever reveal
to Elspeth. Cursing softly, he thumped his fist against stone.

He had told himself, and told Elspeth often enough, that
there was no truth in visions. He knew now that her vision
was no scheme, as he had once thought. Although her Sight
eluded his ability to explain it, he began to realize, with a
startling sense of dread, that she might very well be right
after all.

He could not even explain his own dreams, which had
led him to find her in a remote place. How could he hope
to explain, in some logical way, why Elspeth believed that
he would face an execution? Now that he had brought himself, by his own thoughtless actions, to that same precipice,
how could he doubt that the Sight existed?

He sighed, cursed again under his breath, and shook his
head in the dark. He had more pressing problems to solve
than that one. Whatever had brought this situation about,
he had to find a way out.

Turning, he lifted the iron hook that held the window
shutters together, opening one side. A cool, damp breeze
ruffled his hair as he looked out. A brilliant sunset flooded
the skies, sparking some hope in his dismal thoughts. He
was in the Highlands, far away from the council and the

Lowland courts. He had time to ponder this dilemma, and time to decide what must be done.

Red and gold clouds towered above shafts of glittering, transparent light. Below lay the black silhouettes of mountains and the gleam of a long sea loch. He had looked upon such sunsets countless times as he was growing up, yet it seemed as if he had never seen the wild beauty and power in them the way he did now.

"I have never seen a sunset like that," a soft voice said behind him.

He started and turned to look at Elspeth. She wore a simple white shift, probably borrowed from Mhairi, and her loosened hair flowed around her shoulders. In the reflected light of the sunset, her hair looked like golden fire.

She moved into the wide niche and sat beside him, turning to look out the window. Her knee brushed his.

"Only in the western Highlands will you find sunsets like these," he said. Though he looked at the sky, he felt her gaze on him.

"These Highlands are your home," she said. "You belong here. Your family has missed you."

He shrugged.

"Duncan," she murmured, "why have you stayed away from Dulsie so long?"

"You are tired," he said. "Go to bed."

She sighed and stood. He looked at the floor, at her bare toes beneath the hem of the white gown. The cloth blew softly in the breeze. "Duncan—"

"Go to bed." He turned away.

She reached out and touched his back through his shirt. "I have felt the pain you hold here. Tell me what happened."

He was tired and his wounded arm ached. He did not have the strength to explain it all to her now. Closing his eyes, he shook his head slowly.

Her finger traced the scar hidden beneath his shirt, brushing over it as if she knew its track by heart. "You were wounded here by the MacDonalds. That much I know for myself. Tell me the rest."

"These matters are in the past. They are done." He heard the harshness in his voice, heard the pain beneath the surface, and wondered how much longer he would be able to hold it at bay. Her fingers stroked the scar, and rested at the spot just under the shoulder blade, where the scar had its source. Like the spring of a river, his anguish, his anger, flowed from that spot. He trembled with the effort to hold in his feelings.

"These matters are not done, not for you. Duncan, please—" He heard her long intake of breath. He felt her fingertips grow hot through the linen of his shirt. The heat spread along the arc of the scar.

"I see a lad asleep, in the dark. He is tall, thin, dark-haired. I know this is you years ago." Her voice went on, a soft murmur. "Men come, they raise their dirks. Blood drips, black in the moonlight . . ." She paused. "I see a man who sits up and tries to defend himself. He is older than you are now, but he has your face, broader, thicker. He is killed through the heart."

"Stop!" he shouted, and stood up to tower over her. "What good is this to you or me?"

She leaned back slightly to look up at him, her eyes clear and luminous in the sunset glow. "This pain will destroy you," she said. "Let go of it."

"Leave it be, will you, girl," he growled.

"Ruari told me that MacDonalds caught your father and brothers reiving, and killed them. He said that you and your remaining brothers went wild in revenge, harassing his people without mercy."

"It is a cursed lie," he said, and grabbed her shoulders. "And why do you ask me? Witch that you are, you have seen it for yourself. Look again and know the rest. Leave me be."

Tears slowly formed in her eyes. He knew his words had hurt her. He could see it in those gray depths; he could sense it through his fingers on her skin.

She blinked and spilled one tear. He began to speak, could not form the words. Dropping his hands, he turned away from her.

"If you will not share your pain with me, I will not beg it from you," she said. He heard her soft steps as she walked away.

Something made him turn. She stood near the hearth, her arms folded over her chest, her white gown diaphanous where the low light glowed through the thin fabric. Her hair streamed down like liquid copper, hiding her face, flowing over her rounded breasts and slender arms.

She looked so vulnerable, childlike, ethereal, an angel caught by the harshness of this world. And he had hurt her with unthinking, unkind words. She was no witch, far from it.

He sighed and walked over to stand behind her.

"We were sleeping," he said, his voice hushed. "We had been out on a hunt in our own territory. Several men came into our camp that night. They murdered my father and my brothers. My father woke and tried to fight, but was killed through the heart. My brothers never woke up at all, I think."

"And you?"

"I woke and tried to reach my dirk, but I made a noise. One of them turned and cut me down to the bone, from the shoulder around to the chest. He thought me dead. Then they took our horses and ran." He felt a pressure in his chest like an iron band squeezing his breath. His voice was flat, hard. "I lived. I tied a shirt around my wound and half dragged myself to a farmer's croft for help. When I recovered enough to ride, my remaining brothers and I went out on the first of our raids."

Elspeth bowed her head, her hair swinging down, a soft gleam. He wanted to touch it, to wrap it around his sorrow.

"The MacDonalds were the reivers, the murderers that night," he said. "I want you to know that."

She nodded. He lifted a hand then to touch her hair, sliding his fingers down its soft silk. "Now what will you do with this pain?" he asked. "It has no use for you."

She turned her head and pressed her cheek against his hand. "I would take it from you if I could," she said.

He laughed, a harsh, grating breath. "Take it? I would

not give this burden to anyone. It is too bitter. It has been mine to carry for all these years." He sighed. "I did what I could to avenge them, but it was not enough."

She spun around and laid her hands on his chest. "Not enough? You could not help their deaths." She rubbed her fingers over his chest. "Let it go, Duncan."

"I never saw the murderers' faces. I did not wound even one of them that night. They all got away." He felt a return of that old fury, never satisfied. As it roiled in him, heavy and dark, he craved, suddenly, a release from its weight. He drew a long breath and blew it out. He placed a hand over hers, on his heart, and felt the steady thump through their fingers.

"Duncan," she whispered, "your father and brothers only needed vengeance once. Do not carry this grief around in you."

Raising his hand to her cheek, he slid his fingers into her soft hair. "I avenged their deaths many times over, until I left Dulsie, and I never once felt the satisfaction of it."

"Your anger chains you to that day, like iron fetters," she said. "I know what it is to carry a burden like that. It is hard to make yourself set the weight down and be done with it."

He watched her, so earnest, her clear gaze filled with love. "What burden do you carry, then?" he asked softly.

"I have watched you face your own death," she whispered. He began to speak, but she placed a finger against his lips and went on. "And before that I saw the deaths of others. My uncle, my aunt. Eiric's mother. And each time the weight of the knowledge felt as if it could crush me. I did not speak of what I knew. I was unable to help them."

"You spoke of my death quick enough," he said, his tone lighter. He smoothed her hair, slid his hand down to her slender shoulder, kneading his fingers there. "Those death visions you have had," he said, "they have all come true?"

"All so far but yours."

He nodded and pulled her closer. She rested her head against his shoulder, and he held her. "To see such a thing and not speak of it—except to the queen's lawyer—that is a heavy burden, *mo càran*." She nodded, and he sighed and held her tightly.

A rare fear rose in him, a cold, spiraling chill. In breaking the bond, he had begun to move toward what Elspeth had seen for him. He was loath to tell her his true situation; he wondered if she had realized it yet.

Too late now to accept her seer's warning. If he had listened earlier, would he have broken the bond so impulsively? He squeezed his eyes shut at his own intense thoughts, and sighed into her hair, blowing the fine strands. Her arms circled around his back. With utter certainty he knew that he would have broken the bond again and again to ride after Elspeth. He would have done anything, dared anything, to have her now as he had her, safe in his arms.

But he had not listened to her warning. And now he wondered if he had the courage to live with the knowledge that his death approached.

He felt a sudden, fierce urge wash through him, rinsing through like a heavy wave of the sea, taking with it the pain, taking with it the fears of death, of the past. He wanted only to taste and feel and immerse himself in this moment, in the love she offered him so freely. He wanted that intense wave of feeling to flood the past from him.

"No more pain, *mo càran*," he murmured against her hair. "No more talk of death and forebodings." He slid his hand over her back, over her shoulders, and caught a handful of her hair, pulling gently until she tilted her head back. "We are both so tired that we have forgotten the great gift we have been given."

"Gift?"

He kissed her cheek. "There is love between us. That should replace all this fear, all this talk of doom."

Her tiny answering sob was lost into his mouth as he kissed her lips. Tightening her arms around him, she kissed him fiercely, pulling his head down to hers, her lips wet with the tears that glazed her cheeks.

He groaned softly against her lips, and her mouth opened for him. He explored her lips, the delicate line of her teeth, the soft inner heat. His loins swelled with a deep need that

no kiss could soothe, igniting a spinning heat that was
barely controlled in him.

Sweeping her up in his arms, he reached the bed with a
few quick steps. She was avid now, greedy, her mouth on
his, her hands all along his neck, his shoulders, his chest.
He laid her on the bed and she pulled at his shirt insist-
ently. He undid the leather thong that snugged his trews at
the waist, and she pulled at his garments until he stretched
out nude beside her. Gathering her into his arms, he
smoothed his hand over the light linen shift and down her
back, her buttocks, her thighs.

She slid her hands along the planes of his body, a quick,
light touch, grazing over the flat muscles of his belly. Fan-
ning her fingers there, she paused. He burgeoned and grew
hard, waiting for her still fingers to move, wanting her gentle touch.

"Ah, girl," he said, and rolled her onto her back. "This
is what we need, you and I. This . . ." He traced his fingers
down the length of her torso, between her breasts, feeling
the incredible softness of her skin, sliding his hand over the
hard cage of bone below her breasts, sliding down over her
firm belly, her pubis, feathered, downy, waiting.

She arched and moaned, and her hand on his abdomen
moved down to fondle him until he sucked in his breath
and moved his hips away, not ready yet, too ready.

He kissed her deeply and swept his hand down her legs,
catching the thin linen in his fingers, sliding the cloth up
her thighs, over her hips, over her breasts until he pulled
it from her. Flesh on flesh now, warm and soft, her body
pressed to his.

Rolling, she nudged him until he turned to lie on his
back. She slid over him, catching him between her legs,
moving like the sea over him. She kissed him, and the taste
of her tears was salty on his lips. He held her head in his
hands and opened his mouth over hers, sharing that
warmth, that moist heat.

She arched and he caressed her breasts until the tips
were tight buds beneath his palms, and then he took one
and then the other into his mouth. She cried out and flung

herself forward, her hair waving over him like cool silk,
like fine-spun gold reddened with fire.

Following a deep, soothing rhythm, she moved over him,
her breasts skimming over his chest. When he could bear
it no longer, he took her hips and shifted her. She opened
her legs over him and he entered, sweet, easy, plunging
into her welcoming, gripping heat. Enclosed, he began a
rhythmic pursuit of that elusive feeling, an intense, spinning
vortex, something more than physical. Here in her arms,
nurtured inside her, he could renew; he could find life and
forget the past and the future.

Her body, her love, washed over him like the sea, rinsing
away deep-buried pain. What was drained in him was re-
plenished; what was hurt began to heal.

She arched, and he groaned softly, pulling her closer, the
heat and softness within so intense that he could not form
words, could not see a thought to its end. He only felt: the
heat, the moistness, the exquisite, blissful infinity within
her.

She cried out. He held her hips fast against him and
thrusted, giving himself into her like flame blends into
flame. He felt as if the edges that defined his body from
hers had begun to dissolve. One being was created and
existed while the stroking rhythm of heart and breath and
pounding blood overtook them, bound them together, and
then released them.

He sighed, and slowed, and drew her head down to his
chest, stroking her back, feeling both her heartbeat and his
own through her slender body. She kissed his shoulder, and
he kissed her head. He glanced toward the window.

The sunset had faded into indigo, and the stars winked,
cold and bright. He thought of the fairy wife of that long-
ago Macrae laird, and knew that a similar magic had been
spun in his own life by the loving woman who lay in his
arms.

He only hoped that the bond, the silvery web that netted
their hearts, would be strong enough to pull him home
again once he left here.

                    *   *   *

"I want to go back to sleep. I am so tired, my bones hurt," Elspeth said, and groaned. "My feet hurt. My back and my neck and my—"

"Hold, hold," Duncan said. He chuckled softly in the deep shadows. He had slept for a long time, and had risen from the bed a short while ago to shut the window; he had forgotten it earlier, and a brisk wind had awakened him.

Noticing that dawn edged the sky, he had come back to bed to climb into the warm cocoon of the deep, soft feather mattress, with its fat pillows, fur coverlets, and woolen curtains. Elspeth had woken up when he sank into the bed.

"Come here," he said, "and I will ease your hurts." She rolled ungracefully, dropping her arm across his chest with a loud sigh.

"You cannot ease these hurts," she said, "they are too much. I am one ache from head to foot. I have lived my entire lifetime in two days. I feel like I am a hundred years old. Let me sleep."

He rubbed her neck and shoulders, making small circles with his fingertips. "You do not look a hundred to me," he murmured. "You are young and strong, and clever enough to escape from the doom of a tidal rock."

"That was a long swim. No wonder I ache," she answered, and stretched her neck so that he could knead her stiff muscles. "How old is your grandmother?" she asked.

"I do not know. A hundred." At her quick gasp he laughed. "Seventy, eighty years, perhaps. Very old."

"She is formidable and yet somehow adorable. So tiny and white, like a wise fairy."

"She is all of that," he said. His hand moved down to rub her lower back, the curves of her waist and buttocks soft and wonderful beneath his hands. "And she told me that she does not expect to see either of us until late in the day. You shall get all the sleep you want."

"Shall we sleep all the day, then?" Her sleepy voice was infused with humor.

"Not all, I think, though we might keep to our bed," he murmured, and spread his fingers over her face to tilt her lips to his in the darkness.

"Duncan," she said a moment later. "Did you quarrel with Innis Macrae when you left here?"

"I thought we were done with that," he said softly.

"I want to know the whole of it, why you left, why you stayed away so long."

"There were five of us, the Macrae brothers of Dulsie," he said, wanting to share his past with her. "When I am with your cousins, I am reminded of my brothers. I was the youngest. It astounds me to think that they are all gone now but for me." He lay back on the pillows. "We were a scourge, the three of us who were left after the MacDonald raid. Uncontrollable, wild. My mother was sick with grief and had no authority over us. But my grandmother has always been a strong, willful woman, and she let us all know that she thought our wild raiding was foolish."

She laid a hand on his chest, a comforting warmth. "I was barely past boyhood," he went on. "The Highland way is honor and pride, but my brothers and I thought we should demonstrate that by strength at any cost. We returned savagery for savagery. We were relentless, and we were wrong, but it took me years to learn that."

"You were clever at those raids, I heard, and a legend after a while. Ruari told me that. His mother would frighten her children with tales of the wild Macraes."

He smiled ruefully. "We took a great deal of MacDonald cattle and hid it well. We killed only those men who confronted us—we did not murder them in their sleep, and we did not do harm to women or children. We were after men only. After months of this, another of my brothers was killed. I quarreled with my grandmother when she insisted that we stop. The Macrae chief, and the chief of the Mackenzies, with whom our clan is allied, sent word to cease. So I left Dulsie in anger.

"My mother had died of her grief, and I went south to tell her family—she had been a border girl, a Kerr, sent by King James's council to wed a Highland laird. My mother's cousins took me in. They were border reivers, among the cleverest of the lot, and so I carried on there in much the same way." He flexed his shoulder, feeling an uncomfortable stiffness in his wounded arm. "I learned more about reiving and burning and murdering than a man should ever know in the time I spent with the Kerrs."

Her hand came up to stroke his chin, rasping her nails over his beard. Her fingertips played with his earlobe, with the golden circlet there. "How did you come to wear an earring?"

"My cousins and I decided to become pirates one night. We stumbled, drunk and full of ourselves, into a tavern where an old woman punched our ears for us. But we sobered and never went to sea. We liked reiving too much. Did you know that a sailor wears a bit of gold in his ear so that if his body is washed up on some shore, he at least can supply the price of his coffin?"

She smiled. "Highland lad, pirate, reiver—how did you ever become a sober lawyer, dressed like a humorless raven, and full of logic and righteousness?"

He cast her a wry look through the dark but answered. "My father always felt that education was needed if Highlanders were ever to advance themselves beyond poverty and warfare. He had decided on the law for me, and had paid my way at St. Andrews before I was even twelve years old. Once I realized that my wild life was gaining no good for me, or for the memory of my father and my brothers, I took leave of my cousins and went to St. Andrews. I earned my way through the rest of my education by clerking for solicitors, among them William Maitland. He is now on the council, and has ever been a friend to me, although he is a formidable man himself. May he and my grandmother never meet."

"Ah. We did wonder, when the queen's lawyer knew reiving better than a pack of Highlanders," Elspeth said. She touched his chest, her hand moving gently under his arm. "When I first touched this scar, I felt so much anger in you," she said. She flattened her hand and was silent for a moment. "But now no images come, only echoes and tremors, much milder."

"I have let go of some of that rage, I think," he said. "I have learned much about anger and loss, but never more than in the past few days." He sighed. "When I came to Glenran and had to face MacDonalds again, all the past churned up inside me."

"You were fully aware that you went against the council's wishes when you organized our raid."

"I was. And I did relish that ride against the MacDonalds."

"A raid can be a challenge, a good game," she said. "No true harm done but cattle and sheep exchanged back and forth. This is the game we played that night with you, and we enjoyed it. Ruari was the one who made it turn ugly later, not you, or us."

"When Ruari took you—and even earlier, the day of the hunt when he threatened you—I was ready to kill him."

"But you did not. You walked away from Ruari when you had the chance to kill him."

He sighed. "I did not want to take another life. I have taken too many without right."

"The law has taught you that?"

"The law showed me that there are other ways to deal with feuds and murderers and thieves."

"The law saved your life, I think."

"In a way."

"I know that Scots laws mean little in the Highlands," Elspeth said. "The Highlanders still obey the wild, unwritten laws of kin and honor above all. Feuding only destroys lives, takes parents from children, and siblings away. But feuds will not end, no matter what the crown does to stop them, unless the clans decide to stop." She shrugged. "And I think that will not happen for hundreds of years."

He glanced at her. "This from one of the wild Frasers? Remember that you talk to your queen's representative."

She tilted her head. "I understand what you did when you were young, Duncan Macrae, and I understand what you are now. And I love you, Highlander, Lowlander, lawyer or reiver."

He kissed her, the cool, delicate tip of her nose, and the full, soft lips beneath. "I love you as well, Fraser, seer, reiver, my wife."

"I have one question of you before I sleep," she said, snuggling against him.

"What is that?"

"Do you truly think me a witch?"

He smiled in the dark. "You have a way about you that is neither earthly nor rational," he said. "But I would call you fairy or angel before I would ever call you a witch."

"Again," she reminded him.

"Before I would ever call you a witch again," he said, corrected. When she sighed and began to breathe in a sleepy, satisfied rhythm, he knew that his apology had been accepted.

Chapter 22

"To dream o ravens, love" he said,
"Is the loss o a near friend;
And I hae killed your brither dear,
And for it I'll be slain."
　　　　　　　—"Young Johnstone"

"Last night I dreamed of a raven again," Innis Macrae said. "As I used to when you were younger."

Duncan nodded and sipped the contents of his cup, *uisge beatha* mixed with cream and honey. His grandmother had insisted that he drink some every day to keep up his health, though he detested the sweet concoction. He tried to please her, especially when her sharp eye was upon him, waiting for him to finish the drink. He sipped again and set the cup down on the table. She had ordered a pine fire built in the great hall, and its light and heat, in the middle of a stormy autumn day, was welcome.

"And what did the raven tell you?" he asked patiently. He remembered that his grandmother's dreams had often been a source of discussion when he was a boy. She had always tried to follow whatever her dreams told her.

Now he understood why. He had a new respect for the substance of any dream. He waited for her answer.

"A raven and a dove came to sit on my windowsill. They told me their wishes, as if I were a witch to grant them," she said. "The dove wished for wings of gold and silver. And the raven wished for you to be its master."

He stared at her. "Was I to train it to hand, like a hawk?"

Innis shrugged. "I do not know."

"Did you grant these wishes?"

"I told them I had no power left in me, for I am old. I

sent the dove to fly off to Elspeth. And I told the raven
that it could find you in the Highland hills. I told it to ask
politely if you would be its master, and if you declined, to
leave you in peace."

He looked at her for a long moment, knowing that Elspeth regarded ravens as a sign of coming death. "Well,"
he said, "I am sure you said the right thing to this raven."

"Indeed I did," she declared. "I shall ask Elspeth what
it means. Alasdair says she is gifted with the Sight."

He hesitated, then shrugged. "Ask her, then. She was
with Magnus earlier, though I do not know where she is
just now."

"She is with Mhairi and the babes. Magnus is much
stronger, though he is not yet healed. He thinks he is ready
to travel back to Glenran, though it has been hardly two
weeks."

Duncan hid a smile as he sipped his drink. "Have Kirsty
speak to him. I think that he might do whatever that girl
says."

"I have noticed that she has a firm way with the lad,"
she said. "Magnus has been arguing with her, but she has
a way of getting what she wants." She peered at him, and
he thought he saw a curious twinkle in her blue eyes. "And
do you do what Elspeth bids you?"

He lifted a brow. "Me? Do what I am told?"

Innis half chuckled. "I thought not. You never did that.
But I see that you have changed, Duncan Macrae."

"I am a man. When you last saw me I was a boy."

"A stubborn, angry boy with a heart of stone."

"I have many regrets over those days, grandmother
Innis."

"Tch. I am an old woman now, and I have struggled with
a high temper all of my life. Peace comes, after a time,
when an angry heart softens. I gave you my forgiveness
long ago, and hoped you would return. But years went by,
and you did not come back. I knew the Dulsie legend
would bring you home, but I thought that I would go to
my deathbed without your forgiveness."

He swirled the liquid in the cup. "I was afraid to come home for many of those years," he said softly.

"Afraid of me?" Innis looked pleased, Duncan thought. She smiled and leaned against the high back of her chair. "Well, I see now that you have learned to soften your temper. And at a much earlier age than I ever learned it."

"I have had some lessons in that lately," he said.

"This girl you have wed. She has a fine knowledge of healing, and I understand she is a seer as well. And she is a Glenran Fraser. Macraes and Frasers have been allied clans for generations. Your father would have approved."

"He would. She is a unique girl."

"I like her well." There was an elfin gleam in her blue eyes. "Does she have the fairy blood in her ancestry as do the Macraes of Dulsie?"

He frowned. "Why do you ask that?"

"She must have some deep magic. To bring you home when your stubborn temper kept you away for nearly half your life. To soften your heart and teach you to love. I can see that you love her, very much. It shines in your eyes and glows on your cheeks." She reached over and pinched his cheek.

He laughed. "That is your fine *uisge beatha*."

"Not all of it," she answered. "Not all of it."

The door of the room opened, and Alasdair strode in, his face flushed. He sank down onto a bench and sighed deeply.

"What troubles you, lad?" Innis asked.

"I cannot stand the shrieking any longer. Pass me some of that *uisge beatha*. I cannot bear to know that a great man has been brought so low."

"What are you talking about?" Duncan asked. He poured liquor into a cup and handed it to Alasdair.

"Magnus. He roars with pain. Can you not help him, Innis?"

"*Ach*. He is not in pain," Innis said. "Kirsty roped his hands to the bed when he was asleep, because he got up too often. He is yelling at her in a rage. When last I was in there, she told him that she wanted his solemn promise

to keep to his bed another three days before she would
undo the ropes." She shrugged. "That girl has the sweet
face and healing hands of an angel, but she is willful as
a wildcat."

"I knew a great man had been brought low," Alasdair
muttered. "Do something, Duncan."

Duncan held up his hands. "Not me, man. When Magnus
heals, let him do something about it."

They looked at Innis. She smiled sweetly at them. "Indeed, let Magnus teach the girl a lesson," she said. "He
looks the man to do it, I think."

Elspeth had never climbed as high as this, up to where
the golden-grassed mountain slopes grew bare and rocky,
where spouts of water burst from crevices, foamy white
against the shining dark face of the rock. She had never
climbed high enough to see the soft, fleecy undersides of
the clouds, like rings of heaven settled over the mountain
peaks.

She was there now, beside Duncan. He turned to smile
at her and held out his hand, his fingers warm and strong
as they wrapped over hers. He pulled her higher, his footing sure on rock shelves eons old. Grass and mosses formed
a thick, tough carpet between the rocky outcroppings, cush-
ioning their booted feet as they moved upward.

Elspeth let go of his hand to pull herself up, holding onto
a jag of rock and stepping onto a flat, peaceful spot high
above the lochs and hills. Cold wind beat against her face
and her hair, pushing against her with remarkable strength.
Glittering sunbeams warmed the rock surfaces, leaving the
shady undersides cold and mysterious.

She looked at the world below, at the long autumn-gold
slopes, at the unchanging gray of the rock; at the wide,
towering expanse of the sky, a tapestry of clouds and sun
shafts; at the lochs and rivers, shifting blue glass poured
out over the earth.

Breathtaking power and wild, high isolation surrounded
her. Sitting down on a crag, she watched the world and felt
as if she were suspended between heaven and earth. Be-

yond the realm of the everyday, she felt as if she could almost touch the raw power and the sublime grace that infused this place.

"I wanted you to see this," Duncan said as he sat beside her. She smiled up at him, breathing in the clean, sharp air. The winds blew back her hair and beat at the red and black plaid she wore, borrowed from Innis Macrae's cupboard, which was filled with plaids belonging to Duncan's brothers. She dangled her booted feet out into open space and leaned against Duncan, feeling his solid form at her back.

"Below, there, at the tip of that loch," he said, pointing to a long stretch of water, "is the fortress of Eilean Donan. A cousin of mine keeps it as constable for Clan Mackenzie." The tiny fortress below looked like a fairy castle carved out of the landscape, an integral part of the harmony of water and mountain, rock and sky. The saturated blue of the loch was the color of Duncan's eyes. She smiled and nestled against him.

"This place is beautiful," she murmured. She watched a pair of golden eagles glide downward, their shadows skimming the rocks and slopes. "Did you come here as a boy?"

"My brothers and I came here often," he said. "We hunted for eagles' nests, and dared each other to climb the heights." He chuckled at the memory and rested his arm on her shoulder, pointing downward. "Beyond that small mountain tarn—that tiny loch, there—is the place where my father and my brothers are buried, with generations of Macraes." They looked there in silence.

"I miss them," he said after a moment. "They were good men, kind men. My brothers were no older than your cousins when they died. My father was a warrior. He loved to laugh, and he loved to fight. And he loved his sons." His hand gripped her shoulder, and she laid her fingers over his. Quick tears stung her eyes.

"You belong here," she said. "Not in the Lowlands, or even in Glenran, but here, among this power and beauty. This is where you are happiest. Your losses have made you stronger than you know. This place is part of you."

He did not answer, but she felt his agreement in the

press of his hand. Then he stood, the wind catching his hair, billowing his wrapped plaid; his long, muscular legs were spread in a wide stance. She looked up at him and saw a Highlander, his source of strength the earth and the mountains, his source of joy the winds and the water.

"Never leave here, Duncan. Dulsie is your heart."

He looked down at her. "You are my heart," he said, holding out his hand. "And we belong here together."

She rose to her feet and reached out to take his hand, high above the earth and just below the heavens. The first shiver began to plunge through her then, and her eyesight filled with a golden haze that spread like a glittering sun shaft. Her breath quickened as the vision seized her.

Duncan had taken her hand, unaware that a vision had begun its shining course through her mind. She tried to pull away, wanting to protect him, but could not move. *Whoever touches a seer at the moment of a vision will see the same*, she tried to say, but could not speak.

Up the side of the mountain, surrounded by a shimmer of golden light, a young boy climbed toward them, his dark hair gleaming, his legs lean and quick. He lifted his head and laughed, but did not see Elspeth and Duncan on the rock shelf above him; they were not of his time, nor he of theirs.

She saw that his eyes were gray, like silver, like stone. And she knew this boy was her son. Duncan's son.

The shimmer clouded to a haze, and the boy disappeared as if in a mist. She turned to Duncan. His face was pale, his gaze piercing.

"I saw him," he said. "I saw him. Our son."

She nodded, a tear spilling down her cheek. "He will be strong and happy. He will love to laugh, like his grandfather before him. And he will love this mountain."

Duncan held out his arms, and she went into them.

"I do not want him to grow up fatherless," she said.

"He will not," Duncan said, pressing his lips into her hair. "He will not, I swear to you."

*   *   *

When they had climbed down the mountainside, Duncan tugged on her hand and led her toward Dulsie Castle, over rolling hills deep with silvery heather stems and brown fern.

"Come this way," he said, and led her down a shaggy hillock, where a burn cut deeply through the ferns and grass, its brown, peaty water flowing over mossy stones. He leaped over the burn, but when she went to come with him, he gestured for her to stay.

"Stand on the other side of the stream, just there," he said. He bent down and rinsed his hands in the burn. "Now do the same."

She leaned down to wash her hands in the cold water. "What are we doing?" she asked, and stood again, wiping her hands on her plaid. He reached over the water and grasped her hands in each of his.

"This is an ancient custom in the upper Highlands," he said. "A pledge of love and faithfulness should be made across a running stream. As long as the stream runs, our love will hold true. It is an old, old form of a marriage vow, I think, before the Christians came to the Highlands."

She held his hands and closed her eyes. The light burble of the water, the shrill of the wind, the rustle of the grasses, and his murmuring words blended together. She repeated his pledge, swearing to give her love and faith through time, and opened her eyes.

Duncan smiled and leaned over the stream, kissing her. "I have not yet registered our marriage with the Commissary Court on the Black Isle, but I will do so. In the meantime we have had a Catholic rite and now a pagan one. We are fast wed, and none can put it asunder."

"None," she said. He tugged her hand, and she leaped the stream to climb up the hillock after him. At the top, he halted suddenly, still holding her hand.

"Look there," he said. Elspeth glanced down at the base of the hill, and saw Magnus striding through the grass as strong and fast as she had ever seen him. She gasped in surprise and took a breath to call out to him.

"Hush," Duncan said. "He may not want our company just now."

Running ahead of Magnus, Kirsty cut a quick path through the long grass. Elspeth frowned; it looked as if her cousin was chasing the girl. And she could see the glower on his handsome face from where she stood.

Magnus shouted and began to run. Kirsty stopped, whirled around, fisted her hands on her hips, and called back some angry taunt. Then she raced ahead, with Magnus in pursuit. A few moments later, Magnus closed in on her and called out again. Kirsty ran on. Then Magnus leaped forward and took her down with him into the ferns.

Elspeth could hear their shouts from where she stood at the top of the hill. She watched them roll over a time or two, saw the gleam of Magnus's golden head and the dark burnish of Kirsty's, and turned to Duncan.

"Do something!"

"They are fine," he said. "Magnus owes this to her, I think. He did not approve of her method of healing him."

"Well, he is healed now, apparently, from the looks of this," Elspeth grumbled. "He was as stubborn as an old goat last week. I would have tied him to the bed as well. He gave her a devil of a time. She kept telling him that getting up could tear open his stitches. He would not listen."

Duncan cast her a wry look. "He has pride. And Kirsty has too much will."

"Hah! He pouted like a babe because a woman out-smarted him." She folded her arms and huffed indignantly. "Magnus has always thought himself invincible. Even after his wife's death, even with the responsibility of a small daughter, he has remained aloof, above his emotions. Kirsty has brought something out in him that no one else could. I never thought to see him behave like this." She felt a smile growing and hid it from Duncan. "It may have been very good for him to meet a woman as strong-willed as Kirsty."

"Kirsty has grown up to be a strong-headed woman, and no doubt. I remember that her temper, even as a babe, was legendary in our house. No one crossed little Kirsty."

"Well," Elspeth said, "someone just did."

Magnus stood in the deeps ferns and grasses, and hoisted Kirsty over his shoulder. She kicked her legs and pummeled his back. Duncan chortled in delight.

"Stop laughing," Elspeth said stiffly, scowling at him.

"If a woman catches a man's temper like that, it is as good, sometimes, as catching his heart. I would wager they are both caught fast. Look there."

She looked, and blinked. "He is kissing her."

Duncan laughed again. "And she is kissing him. Magnus is teaching her he will not be tied down unless he wants to be, I think." Elspeth elbowed him.

"I think she is teaching him that there are some things stronger than Magnus Fraser."

"Come away, now, and leave them to their lessons," he said, pulling her down the hill in another direction.

"You are a wise man, Duncan Macrae," she said, grinning.

"How so?"

"You brought Magnus here when he needed healing. And look what he has found."

He smiled. "I am no seer, to predict a marriage."

"It takes not much of a seer to know that a good, strong marriage may very well come out of that kiss back there."

Seated at the table in the great hall, Duncan leaned back in his chair and grinned at Alasdair. They had been chuckling over the story of Magnus's courtship. Little more than a week had passed since Duncan and Elspeth had seen Magnus and Kirsty out in the hills. Magnus was smitten so hard that he had already asked the girl to marry him. She had agreed readily. Duncan recalled his grandmother's delight when she had heard that Magnus wanted to bring Kirsty back to Glenran with him after the marriage ceremony.

"She is disappointed to lose the girl, I know, but she knows Kirsty will be happy, and that pleases her most," Alasdair said.

"And she was overjoyed to find that she already has a

granddaughter," Duncan said. "She has made them prom- ise to bring Eiric to visit in the spring."

"Innis thinks that now you and Elspeth will be living here. Have you told her that you intend to return to Edinburgh?"

"I do not know if Edinburgh is the best place for me anymore, Alasdair," Duncan said. "There is a serious mat- ter that I must attend to there, but if I can speak to the members of the Privy Council, I can clear it up. Then I will spend a few weeks closing up my law cases and come back to Dulsie. Elspeth wants it. And I want to be here, I think."

Alasdair nodded and would have commented, but a sud- den shout from one of the Highlanders keeping watch on the rooftop caught their attention.

Duncan and Alasdair went to an open casement to look outside. A group of riders, plaided and armed, came across the moor toward Dulsie Castle at a fast pace.

"Frasers," Duncan said after a moment. "And others."

"How did the Glenran Frasers know you were at Dulsie?"

"I sent a running gillie to them to tell them that Elspeth was fine, and that we would all be here for a while. I did not expect them to ride here."

"There are only three Frasers, but several others with them. They look like a tail—" Alasdair paused and swore. "Robert is with them, and he brings a tail of his Gordons."

"Ah," Duncan said. "Now I know why they have come." The group reached the stone bridge and clattered across. His heart thudded as strongly as that forceful rhythm. He had hoped it would not come to this. He sighed deeply and turned away.

Alasdair frowned. "Why does Robert bring his Gor- dons here?"

"To arrest me," Duncan said quietly.

"The Privy Council has put you to the horn, Duncan Macrae." Robert watched him through pale blue eyes, hooded like a hawk's. He pulled a folded paper from inside his doublet, snapped the page open, and slid it the length

of the table toward Duncan. "You are outlawed for breaking the bond of caution signed by the Frasers, and by yourself, as their cautioner and as their pledge. I told the council
that I would fetch you. If you do not come peaceably with
me and my escort, I must place you under arrest."

Duncan nodded calmly. His glance took in all those who
stood in the great hall listening. His wife and his family,
both Macraes and Frasers, had gathered to hear the message Robert had brought. Elspeth stood near her cousins,
her face pale, her gaze fixed on him. He saw the fear in
her eyes, and saw the firm love there as well.

He was glad that Elspeth was holding onto his grandmother's arm, for the old woman looked her age in that
moment. Her slight shoulders slumped beneath her plaid
shawl. Mhairi and Kirsty were just behind Innis, watching
him with expressions of shock. He looked away.

He perused the document, written in a cramped legal
hand and signed by three members of the council. Leaning
against the edge of the long plank table, he thoughtfully
scratched the beard shadowing his chin and passed the page
to Alasdair.

"This document lacks the signatures of the full council,"
he said to Robert.

"They were not all available. Those that signed speak
for the rest," Robert answered. "It is legal."

Innis Macrae stepped closer to the table. "Why has Duncan been put to the horn?" she demanded, glaring at
Robert.

Robert tilted his head politely. "He had a direct hand in
breaking the bond of caution that he and the Frasers
signed. As the pledge, and as a lawyer, he knows the pen-
alty for that."

Innis turned to Duncan. "Who is this Robert Gordon?"

Robert smiled coldly. "I am Elspeth's half brother, lady."

"You are related to this sweet child? Then your other
half must be the spawn of the devil," Innis snapped. Robert
raised his brows at this, but turned away without comment.

Alasdair swore and looked at the three Frasers, Callum,
Kenneth, and Ewan, who had ridden in with Robert and

his men. Duncan had noticed that they bore the grime and exhaustion of their journey with sober dignity. He had not missed the flashing anger in their eyes whenever they looked at Robert.

"Explain what has happened here," Alasdair said to the Frasers. "Robert is no trustworthy source."

Callum stepped forward and began to speak, cutting past Robert's blustering protest. "Duncan's gillie came a week or more ago, and told us all was well enough here. We were prepared to wait for Elspeth and Duncan and Magnus to return to Glenran in their own time. Then Robert arrived, surrounded by his men. He demanded to see Duncan. We said he had gone home to Dulsie—"

"Not knowing then that you had been put to the horn, Duncan," Kenneth interrupted. "We would not have said where you were so quick had we known what Robert wanted."

Callum nodded. "We would have sent Robert off to look in some other corner of Scotland, and come to warn you, man."

"My thanks," Duncan murmured. Robert, hearing their low exchange, glared at Callum, who ignored him. Duncan recognized that as a supreme act of control, knowing how Callum and his cousins disliked Robert.

"When Robert set out to ride here," Callum continued, "we decided that some of us should come too. But first Hugh offered to pay part of the fine, saying he would try to raise the rest."

"Hugh offered to pay the fine, and Robert refused to wait?" Alasdair asked. Duncan lifted a brow, knowing that the fine should have been asked of the Fraser chief first before the horning was declared. Robert had obviously hastened the legal proceedings, with the council's help.

He wondered why, and wondered how it had gotten approval.

Robert stepped forward. "I explained the situation fully to the members of the Privy Council. They were well aware that Hugh Fraser could never raise the fine stated in the bond."

"You made certain the council knew that well ahead of time," Callum interjected angrily. "So that they went straight to the horning of Duncan."

Alasdair leaned over toward Duncan. "There has to be some way out of this," he murmured. "You did not actually kill Ruari MacDonald, from what you said. Niall was only wounded. And they did abduct Elspeth and burn Bethoc's barn."

"They will have me on charges of manslaughter, by what is named here." Duncan tapped the paper on the table. "Niall MacDonald told his uncle, who passed the word to Edinburgh as fast as he could. And there is a charge of high treason, which is more serious than the treason of breaking a bond. I do not understand that at all. I must go with Robert."

"Duncan—" Alasdair began.

Duncan held up a hand and turned to Robert. "I will go with you and talk to the council myself. This matter can be cleared up. The Earl of Moray, James Stewart, the queen's half brother, sent me to the Frasers. Moray's signature is not on this page. Nor is Maitland's. Both of those men will support me, but I must speak with them."

"Neither of them are in Edinburgh just now," Robert said smoothly. "But you can attempt to contact them after your trial. If you can get word to them from your prison cell."

"Prison cell!" Elspeth stepped forward. "What is going on here, Robert? Why are you doing this? Duncan is my husband. He is kin to you now. No Highlander betrays kin."

"Elspeth," Duncan said quietly. Seeing her pale, anxious expression, he knew what she was thinking. He moved to take her hands, small and cold, in his. "This will be a formal proceeding only. It will not take long," he murmured. "There are two powerful men to whom I will appeal. They will help me."

"Prison," she murmured. "He said prison."

"That will not happen if I can reach Moray and Maitland."

"You must not go to Edinburgh," she said, and turned to Robert. "You cannot take him there. It will be his doom."

Robert raised his eyebrows. "Is that some sort of prophecy?" Duncan realized that Robert knew nothing of Elspeth's vision. "If Macrae stays here, it will be his doom for certain," Robert said. "The Privy Council has put him to the horn. We have the right to take his life here and now if he refuses."

"You are a heartless beast and no brother of mine."

Robert frowned. "Now, girl. Watch your tongue. Have you not recently been accused of witchcraft? Should the council have someone look into that?"

"What is it, Robert?" she said. "Why do you hate my husband so? He is a fine lawyer, and has achieved the regard of the queen and her closest advisers. He was asked to handle the matter of the Fraser bond when you were not. Is that why you seek to destroy him? Out of jealousy? Are you so small a man?"

Robert's face became a pale stone mask. His eyes slid around the room. Then he turned away from Elspeth as completely as if she no longer existed.

"Duncan Macrae," he said. "Will you come with me and my Gordon escort, or shall we take you by force?"

"I will come," Duncan said. Elspeth squeezed his hand, and he gripped her fingers. "But I will speak in private with my wife now." He pulled on her hand and drew her steadily beside him, past Robert, past the Fraser cousins, past his own family. He opened the door of the great hall and held it while she crossed the threshold ahead of him.

"We will depart within the hour," Robert called toward them. "It is early in the day, and we can make good progress."

"Why is he in such a hurry to take you away from here?" Elspeth said as the door closed, leaving them alone in the corridor.

"I think he does not want to spend the night here, even with the guarantee of Highland hospitality," Duncan said. "Your cousins look as if they would happily murder him."

Elspeth raised a shaking hand to her brow. "I had even

begun to hope that my vision could be wrong after all. I thought you would stay here as laird of Dulsie and never go south again. I thought we were safe."

"Listen to me, my love," he said, placing his hands on her shoulders. "We are safe, both of us. But I broke the bond by my own action, and I must speak to the council. Would you have the blame laid on your cousins? I chose to ride out, and only Magnus went with me. The council does not care how Ruari's death came about just now; he died fighting with me. None of this has been conduct for a queen's lawyer." He gazed evenly at her, his heart thudding as he tried to keep his expression calm, hiding the tumultuous doubt and fear that now roiled inside him.

"When we went reiving after the MacDonalds' cattle, you said that it was a cold ride, a legal one, with you present as the queen's man. This last ride with Magnus must have been a hot ride. It was a legal pursuit," she insisted.

He shook his head. "It was not. Only Magnus and I rode out, without witnesses. I did not think this last time, Elspeth. I had no plan. I acted out of anger, out of a need for revenge. And murder was done. Niall believed that Ruari was murdered, and he made sure that his uncle knew."

"If I had killed Niall myself with that sword—"

"Hush. That would not have helped anyone. I broke the bond. And I must answer to the council."

She broke his grasp and began to pace. "The Frasers should pay the fine, with no harm to you. What was the fine?"

"Seven thousand pounds."

She began to breathe quickly. He knew the amount shocked her. Few Highlanders, even chiefs, had that kind of coin. "We will raise it somehow. It is only a bond, after all," she said. "Do not go to Edinburgh, but send word to your friends Moray and Maitland. State what happened. You do not have to go with Robert. He is no threat to you with my cousins here."

"Elspeth."

"Surely your friends on the council will pardon you and

then arrest Robert for his shameful betrayal. He is your kin, though I am sorry to link you to him in that way—"

"Elspeth, stop." He took a step toward her.

She twisted her hands together frantically. "We will ask for time to pay the fine. Coin rules in government, does it not?"

He grabbed her shoulders. "Stop." Wrapping his arms around her, he rested his chin on top of her head. "I must go to Edinburgh. If I do not, worse trouble will come to the Frasers. Fire and sword will be declared, and the outlawing of the entire clan for the breaking of this bond."

She pressed her forehead into his shoulder. "But there has to be some way to explain to the council what happened. They would not execute a man for protecting his wife."

"They will interrogate me, but they will not execute me."

"Duncan—"

"No one will harm me," he said. He took her by the shoulders and looked into her eyes, knowing her greatest fear, wanting to eliminate it.

"Duncan," she whispered. A deep sob burst from her. He caught her within his arms again and held her.

"You have been put to the horn because of what happened to me. I have led you to this." She raised her head and looked at him, tears glistening in her eyes. "The vision—I knew that I would have a hand in your fate. I felt it that day."

"Hush," he said. "You had no hand in my fate. I led myself here by my own actions. And I would choose the same again, and ride after you again, Elspeth Fraser, to keep you safe."

"But you placed your life in the balance when you rode out."

"Your life was already in the balance. Should I have done nothing because of a bit of paper?"

She smiled then, a wobbly, tearful smile that took his breath away. "For a long-robe," she said, "you sound very much like a Highlandman."

"I am a Highlandman, and proud of that." He smiled into her hair. "Very proud."

She sniffed. "I will come with you to Edinburgh. We will fight this together."

"You will not," he said. "Stay here at Dulsie."

"And not know for weeks, even months, what has become of you? I cannot bear that, Duncan."

"I will send word to you. Stay here. If you are here"—he drew a deep breath—"then my heart is here, and I know I will return. Remember the Dulsie legend, the fairy's silver net."

"The lairds of Dulsie always return," she breathed.

"The laird of Dulsie will return," he said. "Believe that, if you will believe any prophecy."

Chapter 23

The fetters they are on my feet,
And O but they are cauld!
My bracelets they are sturdy steel,
Instead of beaten gold.
                                   —*"Johnie Scot"*

His dreams were as dark as his days, as black as his nights. Even in sleep he could not escape the enveloping blackness. No images came when he slept out of exhaustion, no respite, no hope. Whenever he woke, it was to the same cold darkness.

Only a tiny opening in the wall provided light and air in his prison cell. He often looked up at that chink, a few feet above his head. Sometimes when the shaft of light cut through the dark, he would pass his hand through the transparent, pale light that flowed down.

At other times, amber light glowed through the small grate set in the thick iron-bound wooden door. He could hear voices, distorted by the narrow stone passageways beyond his cell. He heard the scrape of heavy boots and the clink of pikes and swords. But those voices were rarely directed at him, and the firelight was not always there.

He was in a cell in Edinburgh Castle, on the south side below the palace apartments. He knew exactly where he was, having visited prisoners here himself. But he had never spent more than an hour here before. Now it was going on three weeks, perhaps four. Though he had tried to observe and record the cycle of light and dark in the tiny shaft of outside light, he was not certain of his count.

The cell was small, a pacing of eight one way, ten the other. The floor was well below the level of the door, forming a kind of dark pit. At night the cold was piercing, and he would burrow under straw for warmth. There were no furnishings, unless he considered the covering of straw and filth on the floor to be his bed, his table, and his chair. Twice a day a bowl of gruel and a hunk of bread was handed down to him, and every few days the guard would bring in a bucket of fresh water.

Adequate accommodations for a condemned man, he thought. Most prisoners sentenced to death received less than this, unless the man was of very high rank and could offer better bribes to the guards. Duncan had offered what coin he had on his person, and had traded his boots for fresh water.

He had plenty of funds elsewhere, but no way to get more coin unless a friend was to contact him. To the guards he was only a man doomed to die in another week or so. Without more coin for bribing, his status as a lawyer or a Highland laird was of no importance here. For now water, bread, and gruel would come his way. He doubted that the straw would be changed.

He sighed and slid to the floor. The iron fetters around his ankles bit unless he sat a certain way. Heavy chains joined the sets of iron bands around his wrists and his ankles. The chains were long enough to allow movement and heavy enough to challenge his strength. He had spent hours lifting and lowering the chain methodically and pacing the cell.

His legs and arms were nearly as strong as they had been when he had been thrown in here. He would not die a weak man. He ate every morsel of the gruel and bread each day, drank the stale water, and began to understand why some prisoners ate the mice and rats raw when they could catch them. He preferred his meat cooked, and so he let the creatures nibble the straw undisturbed.

Most of his time was spent thinking of alternatives to the sentence of beheading that the council had passed down to him. He had had few visitors since the day of the trial, that swift afternoon of justice mocking that Robert had somehow arranged. Swift and sure, for Duncan had not been entitled to counsel at the trial due to the harsh Scots laws concerning high treason.

Robert had come once but had not entered the cell, and had only passed through the grate a document requiring his signature. Duncan's house servant, a dour old woman, had visited to inquire if the rooms Duncan kept should be rented out to another. He had asked her to keep them at least until he was gone. Then he had asked her to send word to William Maitland, the secretary to the Privy Council, who was away from Edinburgh, to inform him of the situation. He had asked too that word be sent to the Earl of Moray, the queen's half brother, who was also away. The serving woman had seemed intimidated by the two great names he uttered in the dark prison cell. She had left, and Duncan had little hope that she would contact either of those men.

So each day he slept, and ate, and lifted his chains for strength, and watched the dusty beam of light that divided his cell. Helpless to affect his situation, he waited for a miracle.

On the twenty-seventh day, by Duncan's count, Robert Gordon came again. The key grated in the lock, the door swung open, and Robert jumped the length of the drop to the cell floor. Cloaked from head to foot, he tossed back his hood. The door swung closed, but Duncan knew a guard waited in the corridor.

He would gladly have throttled the man who stood a few feet away from him. He considered taking that moment of pleasure in exchange for his life, knowing that the guard would surely kill him if he even attempted to kill his visitor.

But he decided, rationally and coldly, to wait. Curiosity, if nothing else, rose in him as Robert stood in the deep shadows.

"What do you want?" he asked in Gaelic. He hardly recognized the rasp of his own voice.

"I have received word from Elspeth," Robert answered. "Your wife rides here with her Fraser cousins."

Duncan stood slowly, all of his senses tingling at the mention of her name. "How does she know I am here? I have not sent word to her, though I promised. I had no means to do so."

Robert shrugged. "A gillie arrived yesterday with the message that Elspeth knew you were in trouble and needed her. Perhaps she assumed you were in difficulty and decided to make the trip before the winter snows close the passes to the Highlands."

"Perhaps." Duncan stepped forward into the beam of light that sliced through the darkness. He knew how he must look, a bearded wild man, but he knew too that the steady gleam of hatred in his eye kept Robert standing nervously by the door.

"I informed the council that an appeal might be presented. They told me to come down here and tell you, since it is your right to be aware of such proceedings. But I would not hold out hope for an appeal. Especially from a girl dressed like a wild Scot. She will make scant impression on the council. And the Frasers are not in favor with the council just now."

"Nor are the Gordons." Duncan took another step forward. Robert inched back. Sliding his bare feet in their shackles, Duncan advanced again, just for the pleasure of seeing Robert shrink back toward the door. "You have told the council much, Robert."

"It is my duty, I believe."

"Your duty? Was it your duty to arrange that cursed marriage offer with Ruari MacDonald months ago? And when you could not carry that off, was it your duty to make certain that the council knew the bond had been broken? You are Elspeth's half brother. Where is your loyalty? Where is your bond with your own kin?"

"My kin are Gordons," Robert snapped. "Elspeth is only half-blooded to me. I felt an obligation to see that she was well married. Beyond that—"

"She is well married, Robert. To me. But you have ensured that she will be a widow. Who will you try to wed her to now? Someone else who will advance you in the council's esteem? Another MacDonald? Opinion of them is low now, but a gesture at Highland peace might be worth it for you. A Gordon? Marrying your sister to a Gordon would not gain you any favors now." Duncan tapped his chin in a pretense of thinking hard. "Your better course might be to wed her to someone of power. Some widowed judge who could benefit you, perhaps. How about a lawyer for the queen, Robert?" Duncan nearly shouted that.

Robert reached up to knock at the door. "Open up." The guard who had been outside either had stepped away or was very hard of hearing. "Guard!"

Duncan crossed the cell, chains screeching over stone. Robert backed against the door, knocking again. An idea had occurred to Duncan a few days earlier; he decided to give it an airing.

"Clan Gordon greatly desires to rise to their former power," he said. "Whoever took part in their downfall risks their revenge, I think. Are you self-appointed, or did some Gordon of rank ask you to interfere with my life?" Duncan grabbed a handful of thick wool cloak and lifted Robert to his toes. He knew as he breathed into Robert's face that his breath alone could have brought a man to his knees. He liked that thought just now.

"You are a cousin of the dispossessed George Gordon, earl of Huntly. And a lawyer into the bargain," Duncan said. "And I am one of the lawyers who brought George Gordon to trial. I am the man who interrogated his son John Gordon before he was condemned to die. And my signature was among others on the document that declared George Gordon guilty of high treason, even in his putrid, decaying state of health, or death, as it were."

Robert stared at him, his breathing a rhythm of wheeze and pant. "My kinsmen asked me to go after you—it was not I—"

"Not you, never you, is it, Robert? It was not petty jealousy of your sister and the Frasers that brought you after me when the bond was broken. You and your Gordon kin saw a chance for some revenge when you learned about the Frasers' bond of caution. You saw a chance to break one of the lawyers who broke John Gordon."

"Guard!" Robert croaked out.

Duncan opened his hands and let go of Robert's cloak. Then he slammed the chain linking his wrists against Robert's throat, pinning him to the cold, slime-coated wall. "I have little pride left to me, and I will gladly commit murder. These chains are long enough to choke a man."

Robert's eyes rolled wildly. "The council sent you to the Frasers with the bond of caution," he said. "I should have been given that privilege. So I decided to promise Elspeth to Ruari MacDonald. I thought that the marriage would seal the truce. I thought your bond would become unnecessary."

"You lack a subtle understanding of Scots law, then, even for a lawyer. Go on." Duncan tightened his grip. "What then?"

"You humiliated me with that letter sent to John MacDonald," Robert said. "I spoke with my Gordon cousins. We decided that you had earned some humiliation yourself. I came north with the intention of taking the bond. Then you married Elspeth nearly under my nose. When I heard that Ruari MacDonald had taken your wife, I hoped that the Frasers would break the bond. I never dreamed such luck when you broke it yourself." He grinned, a feral gleam in the shadows. "Guard!" he bellowed.

Duncan's glance flickered up toward the grate. No movement there yet. As long as this piece of luck held, he would use the time to question Robert. If he was to die, he would at least die knowing the truth.

"And the trial?" he asked. "With yourself as sole witness, you pushed those charges through: breaking the queen's peace, countenancing with the Frasers under the bond of caution, undergoing Catholic rites. Spying and high treason. Where did you get those letters, Robert? Who forged them for you? I have never written to the French in my life."

Robert managed to shrug. "Notorious charges, were they not? With your friends Moray and Maitland away, this was the time to bring your trial about. The other Privy Council members are men who enjoy wielding their own power in

Moray's absence. The Lord Justice Clerk, Bellenden, is always willing to condemn anyone who breaks the queen's peace. James McGill of Rankeillor is a raving Protestant, and so I emphasized the charge that you underwent a Catholic rite recently with your marriage."

"That was particularly low," Duncan snarled.

"But that alone was enough to get you tossed in the dungeon. A sentence of beheading was easy enough once they believed that the letters were real, and once they realized that they could make an example of you. The dire consequences of ignoring the council's wisdom, breaking bonds of caution, and corresponding with the French. Notorious."

"When Moray finds this out, I will be pardoned. He may fine me for the bond, and I will gladly pay. High treason. Hah."

"Moray knows nothing of this, and you cannot get word to him. Every friend that you have in Edinburgh is either too frightened to be associated with you or has been turned away at the prison door. And your wife will not be allowed to visit, should she come. I have left word of that already."

"Do not bring Elspeth here," Duncan growled.

"Never. You might give her a message to carry out. And if she and her bunch of cousins arrive here, they may be charged with breaking the queen's peace themselves."

"You are a snake," Duncan said, "and easily throttled." He pressed the chain into Robert's neck, his arms trembling with the effort to control himself. He felt a need, a physical urge, to kill this man. Hatred pounded in his gut, raw and heavy.

"I am a Gordon," Robert said slowly, his voice strained by the pressure of the chain at his throat. "And my clan will have its revenge on you, Duncan Macrae, for aiding in our disgrace."

"Your kin disgraced themselves," Duncan said.

"Is everythin' fine wi' ye, Master Gordon?" came a throaty Scots voice at the grate.

Duncan heard the scrape of the key in the lock. He saw

the triumph in Robert's pale gaze as he reluctantly lowered the chain. The door creaked open.

"That man attacked me," Robert said to the guard as he scrambled up to jump out of the cell.

"Sorry, sir, I wasna here, I dinna see it," the guard said.

"God have mercy on your departing soul," Robert said to Duncan. The door slammed shut.

"And on yours," Duncan growled, and spat on the floor.

The guard returned a few moments later to stand by the grate. "Did ye attack Master Gordon?" he called down.

"I did," Duncan said in Scots English. "And gladly."

The guard chuckled. "I heard ye talkin', an I says, there's twa men that want a moment tae work things out atween 'em. So I left, ye ken, an' came back, but ye hadna killed the wee worm. Did ye want more time, then?"

Duncan frowned and then began to smile. "That is a voice I have heard afore," he said slowly. "Hob? Hob Kerr?"

"Greetings, young cousin Duncan," Hob answered. "Nice to see ye again, though I am sad to see ye in that cell, a fine long-robe like yerself, and one o' the finest reivers we ever knew." Duncan looked up to see grimy fingers shove through the grate and wave at him.

"Hob! How is it ye are here in the castle?"

"Man-at-arms now, for steady pay. It pleases me wife more than reivin' in the night. I heard ye were here, and asked for this duty, and just got it. What can I get for ye, Duncan man? A blanket? Some ale and meat?"

"I ken one or twa things I would like," Duncan said. "Unless, as a guard, you prefer to remain true to your duties. In that case, a blanket and food would be welcome."

"I am a Kerr, man. Scots laws are a bairnie's playthings to us." Hob dropped his voice to a whisper. "I dinna ken how I might set ye free, though, unless we both flee to France—"

"I can get free myself, with a little help."

"Ask what ye will o' me, man. I will do whate'er I can."

Edinburgh was unlike anything Elspeth had imagined, a dramatic citadel above teeming streets. She saw a soaring

wedge of rock crowned by a silhouetted castle, and the
sloping city beneath, hung with a blue haze of smoke. A
single broad street with a maze of cobbled side streets lay
below the castle. The city was crowded with tenements and
people—thousands of people, it seemed, wherever Elspeth
looked, walking along the streets, leaning in doorways and
staircases, hanging out of windows. Many of them eyed the
Highlanders as Elspeth and her cousins rode past on their
short, sturdy horses. Even in Inverness she had never seen
such a conglomeration of people. Unaccustomed to such
crowds, she tensed her hands on the reins and rode on
behind Alasdair, who led them along the High Street.

Nor had she anticipated the sneering laughter when they
had entered the city. Silent and wary, she and her cousins
heard the hoots and guffaws of Lowlanders who seemed to
find Highland dress quite amusing. Her cousins wore
wrapped and brooched plaids over linen shirts, with deerskin vests and plaid trews added for warmth in the cooler
autumn air. Their bonnets were stuck with sprigs of Fraser
yew while Hugh wore the three eagle feathers of a chief.
Swords and dirks gleamed at their wide belts. Elspeth
thought they looked like fine, strong young warriors. She
was proud to ride among them and could not understand
the mockery.

She also understood very little of the words that were
called out, for the language was Scots English. But tone,
gesture, and expression were accurate translators.

"Do not be concerned, girl," Alasdair murmured as she
pulled her horse even with his. "There has been strong
sentiment against Highlanders recently. You are seeing
some of that. Ignore it." He smiled at her, and she nodded.

"Where do we go," he continued, "now that you have
brought us here? Shall we look in Duncan's rooms for
him—he rents a floor of a house just down the way here—
or shall we inquire if he is at the castle? He may be with
Kirkcaldy of Grange, who is the captain of the castle, or
with members of the council."

Elspeth shook her head. "He is in the prison. I feel it is
so. He needs us. Where would the prison be?"

Alasdair frowned. "Prisoners are kept in the castle dungeon, or in the city tolbooth. A prisoner of Duncan's rank would be in the castle. If he has been incarcerated at all."

"If Elspeth says it is so," Hugh said, riding behind them, "then we will assume it is true."

"Take us up to the castle," Callum said.

Alasdair nodded, looking from her to the cousins who flanked her. Lifting her chin proudly, Elspeth followed him, with her cousins close behind.

The sun beat on her shoulders in spite of cool breezes, and she felt weary, the same insistent weariness that had been affecting her lately. She had ridden as hard as her cousins, and had eaten little; even the thought of food was sometimes enough to roil her stomach of late. She knew that she was exhausted, but she fought it, just as she had fought it these weeks since Duncan had been taken away.

Alasdair insisted first that they stable their horses in the town. Then he led them to an inn, where they ordered cool ale, fresh bread, and meat pies. Elspeth found that she was suddenly ravenous. They ate, sitting on benches inside the dark, cool interior. Then they went with Alasdair along the High Street, and walked up the long incline of the castle rock to where a tower housed the gate.

Gaining admittance when Alasdair explained to the guards that Elspeth was the wife of a council lawyer, the Frasers entered the citadel, leaving their weapons with the gatesman. They walked to a building on the south side of the palace yard, which, Alasdair explained, held both the royal apartments and the dungeons.

At a door in one inner corner, Alasdair spoke to a pair of guards in steel breastplates and helmets. Hugh, who understood the Scots tongue, went with Alasdair, asking questions himself. Waiting anxiously, Elspeth heard Duncan's name several times, and Robert's name as well.

Beside her, Callum, Ewan, and Kenneth stood, solid and steady. She looked at them, and a rush of emotion flooded her heart. Her cousins were men, with little trace of the lads she had always known.

Hugh, standing with Alasdair, was serious and stern,

though she knew the gentleness layered beneath; Kenneth and Callum understood loyalty so well that she knew they would willingly give their lives for her or Duncan; Ewan had the soul of a bard and the heart of a warrior, and would fight for Duncan if the need came.

Now more than ever before, she saw a deepening maturity in her cousins. Loyal and calm, they stood beside her now, at her back like any fine Highland tail. She knew they would support her in trying to help Duncan. They would see the end of this nightmare with her, no matter the outcome. She closed her eyes briefly, grateful for the blessing of all of these men in her life. Then she opened her eyes to see Alasdair and Hugh turn away from the guards at the door and walk back toward her.

"There has been a trial," Alasdair said. Elspeth nodded, hardly surprised, her gaze fixed on his face. Though she dreaded hearing the rest, she knew that she must.

"Charges were brought against Duncan by the Privy Council through trial by witness—a fast method, with Robert as the sole witness to Duncan's crimes. He was found guilty of disturbing the queen's peace, countenancing with a clan under bond, and agreeing to a Catholic rite. And there is a charge of high treason and spying. But no one would explain the charges in detail to us."

"Dhia," Elspeth said. "Where is he now?"

"He is here in the dungeon, just as you said he would be. But we may not see him. Only Robert and a few others have been allowed in on the queen's business. The guards have orders that his wife and kin are not to be permitted to see him."

"Why? What is the harm?" Elspeth's heart began to pound heavily. She felt Hugh's hand on her shoulder.

Alasdair looked away and looked back again, his brown eyes sober. "He has been condemned to a beheading in four days."

She wanted to close her eyes, wanted to stop thinking, stop feeling. But she could not allow herself that. Taking a deep breath and then another, she faced Alasdair. Hugh gripped her shoulder. She felt Kenneth's hand on her back, and knew Callum and Ewan stood beside her.

"I want to see him," she said.

"He is denied visitors," Alasdair said gently.

"I will see him," she said, fisting her hands. "Only Robert is allowed into his cell?" Alasdair nodded in answer.

"And where is Robert?" Kenneth asked. "It is time we dealt with the man." Callum and Ewan muttered agreement.

"The guards do not know where he is staying," Hugh said.

"Take me to Duncan's rented chambers," Elspeth said. "I know where Robert may be."

Alasdair frowned, perplexed, and then led them out of the castle and back down the incline to the High Street.

"Here," Elspeth said. "Regard my half brother Robert." She turned slowly around, spreading wide the black cloak that covered her from head to foot. Her cousins, crowded into the little antechamber that fronted Duncan's rented rooms, looked at her with amazement.

An hour earlier, Alasdair had used a few coins to convince Duncan's house servant to admit Macrae's wife and her kinsmen and depart. Then Elspeth had set about going through Duncan's cupboards and chests. She had found a silk shirt, black trews and a padded black doublet, a black bonnet and the long cloak.

Trying on the clothing, she had paused once to hold the silk shirt to her face, breathing in the ghost of Duncan's own scent. A subtle trace of leather and spices, blended with an elusive drift of maleness, made her catch her breath. She had held in a sob, swallowing it, refusing to allow herself to break. *Not yet,* she had repeated to herself, *not yet.*

No matter that the garments were too large. Tucking and pulling, tying and rolling, she achieved a semblance of fit. She found a pair of leather soft-cuffed boots, too large, and stuffed them with silk torn from the shirt to fit her feet. Tucking her red-gold hair up under the bonnet, letting some strands hang down, she had stepped into the outer room.

Now, as her cousins perused her critically, she waited for their pronouncement. Standing as tall as she could, she looked at them with a sour, pinched expression.

Kenneth suddenly burst out laughing, followed by Ewan and then Callum. Elspeth grimaced in a way that only Robert would do and rolled her eyes disdainfully. Hugh and Alasdair smiled.

Alasdair shook his head. "We have somber troubles, and the girl takes to jesting."

"This is no jest," she said. "I mean to get into the dungeon this way."

"Well, you have no hope of getting in any other way," he replied. "And this folly may get you thrown into the cell beside your man."

"A fine idea," she said firmly.

"We had better go at dark if we can," Hugh said. "She looks like him in her coloring and slight size, but she would not fool too many for long. We must hurry her through somehow."

"I will—" she began.

"Elspeth," Alasdair said, "do not speak. You have a sweet girl's voice and no command of the Scots tongue."

"Master Robert Gordon to see the prisoner Macrae of Dulsie," Alasdair said. His tone was so authoritative that Elspeth felt a wave of admiration. Keeping the hood of her cloak over her head, she nodded perfunctorily at the guard. He glanced up briefly as she passed through the dark doorway. Behind her, the Frasers and Alasdair were suddenly detained.

She had not expected that. Heart beating rapidly, she resisted the urge to look back at them. Another guard approached her, a burly man in steel and leather, carrying a sputtering torch. She followed him along the narrow rough stone passageway, trying to lope in the manner of her half brother.

"Yer back again, are ye, Master Gordon?" the guard

asked. His tone was sly, but Elspeth did not know what he had asked.

She grunted. He did too.

They came to a wooden door, reinforced with iron bands. The guard fitted a large key into the lock. "Duncan Macrae of Dulsie," he called out.

The door screeched open, and the guard stood back. She cast him a nervous glance and stepped into the blackness.

And fell through the dense shadows, smacking hard on her hip against cold stone. The floor of the cell, she realized, was well below the corridor level. Robert would have known that.

"Oof," she said, sitting up. *"Ach."*

"Would ye like a light, there, Master Gordon?" the guard asked mildly.

"What in the name of—Hob!" Duncan called. "Leave that torch!" As she heard his voice in the dark, Elspeth's heart began to hammer. Then she heard an odd sound, scraping and clinking, as Duncan came near. She noticed too that the air was redolent with unpleasant odors emanating from old straw and slimy walls.

The door creaked again, and Elspeth looked up. An amber glow filled the small cell as the guard bent through the doorway holding a blazing torch. She got to her feet.

"Jesu," Hob said, peering at her. "A wee lassie, is it?"

"My wife," Duncan drawled. *"Mo céile,"* he translated for her benefit. She nodded hesitantly and looked at the guard.

"Jesu," Hob said again. Grinning, he handed her the torch.

"Thank you, Hob," Duncan said. When the door squealed shut, he stepped forward into the light.

Elspeth gasped. He was dark and gaunt, long hair past his shoulders, his beard black, his eyes shadowed. Around his wrists and ankles hung wide iron bands with attached chains. Despite his shocking appearance he stood tall and proud, gazing at her with a deep frown.

"Duncan," she breathed.

He remained motionless. "What are you doing here?"

She stepped forward. "I knew you were here, I felt it, and had to come. My cousins are with me. How can we help?"

"You can leave," he said, turning away. "I have no need of your help. Leave here quickly."

Elspeth stood there, holding the torch, watching his back, wide and muscled beneath the thin shirt he wore. She came forward and placed one hand on his shoulder. He tensed, and in that instant she felt his strength as well as his misery.

Tears stung her eyes. She wanted to hold him again, feel his arms around her, his warmth, his solidness. But he had put up a cold wall between them, invisible but real. That shield hurt her deeply, a wrenching ache. She feared that he hated her both for predicting his death and for leading him to it.

"Ah, Duncan," she murmured. "I know you are angry with me. I am the one who brought you to this. I am sorry." She choked back a sob. "I will do whatever I can to get you pardoned. I will make an appeal to the council."

She felt the tension in his muscles. "Do not go to the council. They will not listen to you," he said. He drew a deep breath. "Go away from here and do not come back."

"Ah, *Dhia*," she said. "Please forgive me."

"There is nothing to forgive," he said softly.

"Hold me," she whispered.

"I cannot," he said. "I am chained."

Gasping back tears, she leaned her head into his back, circling one arm around his waist. They stood silent for a long moment. She felt tension ripple through his body.

She heard a gruff sound, and he turned. His hands, restricted in the iron cuffs, grabbed her waist through the thick cloak and overlarge doublet. She balanced the torch and held onto him, her body trembling.

"I am sorry," she said. "So sorry. The vision—"

"Hush, you," he said, his voice hoarse. "You have done nothing. This is between me and your half brother."

"What do you mean?"

"Pay it no mind," he said. "Only go. You endanger yourself and your cousins by visiting a condemned man." His beard brushed her forehead.

"I will appeal to the council. Alasdair will help me. Tell me what to do. Please."

He sighed. "Stubborn girl. Listen to me. If the council learns that the Frasers are here, they may have your cousins up on charges for breaking the queen's peace."

"What of Moray and Maitland? Where do I find them?"

"They are both away from Edinburgh. But the guard, Hob Kerr, is my cousin, and he has smuggled out my letters to them. That is the most that can be done now." He pushed her gently from him. "Go, now."

"Do not send me away," she whispered.

"Elspeth." His voice swept over her, soft and deep and comforting. "*Mo càran.* You look like an angel come down from heaven into this piece of hell." He pushed her again, gently but firmly, and stepped away, ankle chains dragging. "Leave now."

"Wait—" She began to tug at her well-padded doublet and pulled out a flattened loaf of bread, a wrapped cheese, and a flask. Holding the torch, she set the items on the floor. "Alasdair said you would need food. And this—" She tugged again and pulled out a small, heavy bag of coins. "We found it in your cupboard," she confessed.

Duncan nodded, half smiling. "Thank you. The coins will buy some handsome bribes."

"You will need these too—" Bouncing around, she pulled off the cuffed boots. "They are yours. And take the cloak against the cold." She undid the cloak and tossed it to him. "We have been in your rooms."

"I see. Whatever is there is yours, Elspeth."

"I will bring clean clothes and more food."

His steady gaze burned like blue fire. "Do not come back. It would not be safe for you."

She sighed deeply. "Duncan. The day of that cursed vision, I said that your death would be mine. I know what that means now," she said. "I cannot bear it if you are not with me. You are my *anam*, Duncan. My soul." The soft words echoed through the dark chamber.

"You will survive this," he said. "You are strong. Remember the child in the vision we shared. Our son. Are you—?"

She had not thought about it until the moment that he asked, but she suddenly knew that it was true. The fatigue and the odd bouts of illness and hunger suddenly made sense. "I think so," she said. She held out her hand. Duncan slowly stretched his hands forward, linked by the heavy chain. His fingers gripped hers hard.

"All the more reason for you to go, then," he said softly.

"I will not leave Edinburgh. We will get you out of here somehow. I swear it."

He shook his head. "If you and your cousins submit an appeal to the council, it could make matters worse for all of us. There is a way out of here, Elspeth. I know there is. Just wait, and it will happen. Do not lose hope, *mo càran*."

"I pray that you are right," she said.

"So do I, my love," he said softly. "So do I."

She took a step forward, wanting to feel his arms around her again. He let go of her hand and stepped back, fetters *chinking*.

"Go, now," he said. "You should not be here."

"I cannot leave you here like this," she murmured.

"You must. All we can do now is wait for word to come back to me." He looked at her, tilting his head in the shadows. She felt a tug on her heart, as if a silvery cord pulled between her heart and his. She would have stepped toward him again, but he turned abruptly away.

"Go now, Elspeth," he said. "Before you tear out my heart."

Chapter 24

There is a fancy in my head
That I'll reveal to thee,
And your assistance I will crave
If ye will grant it me.
                    —"The Twa Knights"

Climbing out of the dark cell, Elspeth handed the torch to Hob. After he had locked the cell, she laid her hand against the door, pressing her forehead to the rough wood. Her breath came in a shallow rhythm. She felt numb, suspended in a dark void without emotion or sensation. She was afraid to feel, knowing how much it would hurt when she did.

Hob set a large, gentle hand on her shoulder. She turned and followed him down the corridor. In her stocking feet and without the cloak, the stone passageway was chilly and damp. But she did not care; she hardly felt the discomfort.

Hob approached the guard who had admitted her when she had entered as Robert Gordon. The man gave her a startled glance, but Hob murmured something that made him laugh softly.

She walked past them in a daze, going out to where Alasdair and the others waited in the dark courtyard. Kenneth rushed to her, taking her arm. Behind her, she heard Hob speak in hushed Scots to Alasdair and Hugh. When she turned, Hob gave her a kind nod before going back inside the bleak darkness of the prison.

"The man is Duncan's cousin," Alasdair said, coming near. She nodded. "He wants us to meet him in a tavern tomorrow," Alasdair continued. "And he spoke of you, Elspeth."

She frowned at him. "What did he say?"

"He wanted me to tell you that you remind him of a

young woman whom he much admires, a very great and beautiful lady who has hair the same color as yours, and who has courage to match yours. She too dresses in men's black hose and doublet from time to time. But she does it for amusement. What you do here is no game. He says he understands your wish to save your husband's life, and he will do what he can to help you."

She nodded. "Who is the lady he mentioned?"

"Mary the Queen."

Elspeth sat and waited as her cousins finished an early midday dinner of meat pies, bought in a town shop. She had eaten some bread, light and fine-textured, unlike any she had ever tasted, and had taken a little watered wine, but her churning stomach could not tolerate meat just then.

At first she had thought that the strong lethargy she had felt, and her unreliable appetite, had been due to overwhelming distress. But when she had spoken with Duncan, she had realized that a child drew on her strength. She had told her cousins most of what she and Duncan had said in the dungeon cell, but that bit of knowledge was precious, and she kept it to herself.

She had slept much of the morning, having agreed to wait in Duncan's rooms while her cousins went out to meet Hob Kerr. Alasdair had said that a woman dressed as a Highlander in public would only attract attention to them. Now she was impatient to know what had gone on during their meeting.

Alasdair swallowed the last of his meal and wiped his fingers on his plaid. "Hob does not know if Duncan will gain the pardon he wants," he said. "He has smuggled out two letters for Duncan, to the secretary Maitland and to the Earl of Moray. But Moray is at Stirling, not far from here, and Maitland, who knows Duncan best, is in England. Hob does not know if the letters will reach them before the date of the execution. And who knows what either man will decide to do upon receiving word."

She nodded. "Has the date been set, then?"

Alasdair quickly exchanged a glance with her cousins. "Two days from now," he said.

She drew in her breath sharply. "We must do something. Duncan said an appeal would go nowhere, and might endanger our lives as well as his. But we must try—"

"Hob agreed with what Duncan told you," Hugh said. "There is a rumor that the council members have declared that any Frasers who appeal Macrae's case will be subject to imprisonment themselves."

"Well, I know what I will do," Alasdair said. "Robert Gordon is in Edinburgh somewhere, and I will find the man. He needs to explain himself to us, I think."

Elspeth nodded. "Find him. What does Hob suggest we do?"

"He says that there is one who might listen to us. He says that you, Elspeth, should go to the palace of Holyroodhouse. If you can get an audience, Mary the Queen might be sympathetic."

Elspeth stared at him. "The queen?"

"Remember when I met her last year at Inverness?" Hugh asked Elspeth. "She liked me well. She will remember me and my Fraser Highlanders, I think. I will go with you."

Ewan grinned and clapped Hugh on the back. "Hugh is anxious to see the queen again. He wonders if she would consider wedding a wild Highlander. She is only two years older than our handsome MacShimi, and is in need of a strong husband."

Hugh blushed. "I did offer her the services of the Frasers in fighting the Gordons. But I would not presume to woo her. That bold idea lost the Gordons their standing."

Elspeth watched them doubtfully. "She is a queen, with no time for such as us. Why would she grant us an audience?"

Alasdair shrugged. "Hob seemed to think she might. Duncan is one of her lawyers, after all."

"You can only try, girl," Kenneth said.

"Try," Hugh said. "We will go with you."

She smiled wanly. "A fine tail of Frasers at my back. How could I refuse? We will go, then. For Duncan."

"For Duncan Macrae," Hugh said softly. The others repeated the same, and they raised their hands, joining them together.

Elspeth laid her hand over theirs. Tears stung her eyes.

The great hall at Holyroodhouse, richly decorated and filled with pale autumn sunlight, fascinated Elspeth. She had had a good deal of time that afternoon to study the paneled and painted ceilings, the expanses of whitewashed plaster walls hung with elaborate tapestries; she had smoothed her hand carefully over the polished oak furnishings, and had examined the heraldic carvings on the fireplaces and above the doors.

The Frasers had been left alone in the great hall for much of the afternoon. A clerk had come in once to tell them that the queen was considering their request for an audience. He had directed a servant to bring them wine and had left. Since then they had been waiting for further word from the queen.

Elspeth glanced through the tall windows on one side of the long room, which overlooked a garden. The painted glass windows were placed above iron bars, as if the palace were some elegant prison. To keep a queen in, she wondered, or to protect her?

Looking at the bars, she thought of Duncan in his prison cell. While she waited in this elegant room on the whim of a young queen, Duncan paced the confines of a black cell. Tomorrow he would face the heading block, face what she had foreseen for him months ago. Elspeth felt a wrenching need to do whatever she could to free him. She could not give up.

Bethoc had told her once that fate could not be changed, that seers were shown what God had already decided. She shook her head as if in protest. Why had she ever been shown that moment from Duncan's future? What good was a warning if the outcome could not be altered?

Now that the time for warnings was past, she could not

surrender to fate. She would ask the queen to spare her
husband's life. And if that failed, she would find another
alternative, and yet another, until the moment the ax was
lifted. If she had to, she would hold back the final blow
with her own strength.

For so long she had steadfastly warned Duncan against
his coming death. Time and again she had succumbed to
her fear. But Duncan had not believed her, had not shared
her fear. Instead, he had told her that this time her Sight
would be wrong. He had said that he would come to no
harm, and that he would live a long life. She wanted desperately to believe that now.

His words had become a beacon to her. His courage, his
certainty that he would live, helped to vanquish her fears.
When she had seen him in the prison, he had maintained
that brave belief despite his circumstances. His resoluteness
was like a shining beam of hope for her now. If she thought
he had given up, she might have given up as well.

She resolved to believe in Duncan, to believe that the
love that existed between them would not be lost to fate.
Stronger than the rush of the sea, hope burgeoned in her.
She strove to hold on to it. It was just as precious and real
as the tiny child that had begun inside her.

She rubbed a hand over her eyes and turned at the sound
of her cousins' voices raised at the far end of the room.
They were looking out one of the windows. Hugh turned
and beckoned to her.

"Look here, girl," Kenneth called. She crossed the length
of the room. They were gazing out at the neatly designed
garden, a maze of hedges and flower beds and fruit trees.
A few people moved about in one corner, three or four
ladies in elegant black dresses, and two men, cloaked and
gowned like officials.

"There," Hugh said. "Queen Mary Stewart."

Elspeth stood on her toes and leaned forward to look.
Hugh pointed toward a slender young woman, taller than
the other ladies, wearing a shimmering black gown and a
little cap with a long veil of white lace. The queen laughed
and clapped her hands, leaning back, her long, lithe body

graceful and animated. Her hair glinted red-gold, a little
darker than Elspeth's own hair, beneath the pretty cap.

"She is just a girl," Elspeth said, slightly surprised.

"And she is a beauty," Hugh said.

"And you would do anything for her, lad," Ewan said,
and grinned.

"I would," Hugh said. "I will always be a queen's man."

"She is lovely, Hugh," Elspeth said. "I pray that we will
be allowed to meet her." Hugh nodded.

Callum looked out. "They are going inside now. Perhaps
she will summon us soon."

Another half hour passed. Then a door opened at the
far end of the room. The Frasers jumped at the light sound.

The same clerk who had come before entered now. "Her
Grace will see you," he said. Hugh translated the words
for his cousins. "Come this way."

They followed him through corridors, up a turnpike stair,
and along another corridor. Finally they were shown into
a small room brightly lit by tall glassed windows. The paneled walls were hung with tapestries, and the ceiling was
elaborately painted with thistles and roses.

Two men stood near the doorway, both dressed in black
robes and bonnets, one with a long red beard. Both were
middle-aged, and of fearsome expression and appearance.
They stared at the plaided Highlanders with barely disguised disdain. In a corner sat two ladies wearing black
gowns and delicate lacy caps. They stopped their light chat-
ter as the Frasers entered.

A wooden dais supported a high, elaborately made chair.
Tall and graceful, her black skirts spread wide, Queen Mary
rested her long-fingered hands in her hap, as if she waited
patiently for the Highlanders to take in the small room,
sumptuous by their standards. Sunlight spilled gently over
her, glinting gold over her reddish hair, giving her complex-
ion a warm glow. Stiff white lace at her throat, and framing
her high forehead, highlighted her perfect, translucent skin.
Her eyes were a clear, sparkling brown, keenly intelligent.

The queen inclined her head, and the Frasers knelt. The
clerk who had escorted them murmured a few words of

introduction and stepped back. When her cousins stood
again, Elspeth straightened with them, blushing as she
glanced at the queen.

She felt embarrassed by her wrapped plaid and linen
shirt, by her deerskin boots and single thick braid. She had
never longed for silks and laces before, but now, in the
presence of this elegant, beautiful creature, she felt clumsy
and plain. The other strangers in the room, the ladies and
the men, seemed to fade; Elspeth saw only the young
queen.

Mary Stewart looked at her and smiled. Then she turned
to Hugh and greeted him in Scots. Her voice was light
and sweet, and the warm tone told Elspeth that the queen
remembered Hugh Fraser with affection. A rosy tint
stained Hugh's cheeks as he spoke with her.

Kneeling again, Hugh spoke earnestly for several moments. Mary Stewart listened, then glanced at Elspeth and
asked Hugh a question. Hugh shook his head and spoke
again, and Elspeth heard Duncan's name. The queen nodded and then motioned Elspeth forward. She advanced to
kneel beside Hugh.

Hugh spoke again, his voice strong and decisive. Mary
Stewart answered him at length. Then Hugh turned to
Elspeth.

"The queen wants you to know that she understands how
deeply frightened you must be for your husband. She says
that she does not know the details of the case and can do
nothing until she learns more. She knows Duncan Macrae,
and his conviction on such charges surprises her. Pledges
are not usually treated in such a manner until all else has
been tried. She promises to inquire into it, and would prefer to talk to her half brother James Stewart. One of these
two gentlemen here"—he nodded toward the black-robed
men standing on the other side of the room—"is a member
of the Privy Council. He is not happy to see us here. The
queen has given us protection by agreeing to see us. But
an inquiry is all she can do for now."

Elspeth turned to the queen and bowed her head. "Tell

the queen that I offer myself as a pledge in my husband's place."

Hugh stared at her and shook his head. "Tell her," Elspeth insisted. "I will be the pledge."

He sighed and spoke in Scots. Queen Mary looked sharply at Elspeth and spoke again.

"Her Grace the queen apologizes for her lack of Gaelic, and wants to know if you speak French or Latin," Hugh said.

"I have some Latin. All the Glenran cousins can read the words of the Church," she said. She turned to the queen and bowed her head. *"Salve regina."*

"Good," the queen replied in Latin. "We may speak directly. I cannot sign a remit of execution without good reason if the council has condemned your spouse."

"Your Grace, I believe my husband is innocent," Elspeth said, her Latin phrasing awkward but understandable. "I offer my life for his. I beg you to tell the council that I will be the Frasers' pledge for their good behavior under the bond."

"And if the council transfers his death sentence to you?" the queen asked. "Will Duncan Macrae then ask for your pardon?"

"I believe that the council will not take my life, Your Grace," Elspeth said. "I am with child."

Behind her, she heard her cousins gasp; their Latin was at least as good as hers. Mary Stewart nodded, and her hands, so exquisitely graceful, folded and refolded in her lap.

"I cannot promise to save your husband. But I know that he is a fine man, and I will do what I can," the queen said. "I admire your courage, Elspeth Fraser."

Elspeth looked at Mary Stewart, and a shiver passed through her. An image flashed, an impression only. "Your Grace has great courage," she said, sensing the truth of that. "Far more than I will ever have."

The young queen smiled. Elspeth saw a fleeting sadness in the clear depths of her eyes. "Come back tomorrow," the queen said.

*   *   *

The dungeon of Edinburgh Castle was thoroughly encased in rock, but Duncan imagined that he heard the hammers of the carpenters in the town building his scaffold. The beam of light from the tiny opening in the wall showed daylight still. Time enough to finish the platform before dark.

He assumed that they would set the thing up in the square in front of St. Giles' Church. He had attended a few executions there, one by the ax, one by hanging, and another that employed the Maiden, a grisly and efficient device that sent a heavy steel blade swooping down a framework to remove the head of one recalcitrant papist.

He wondered which would befall him tomorrow morning.

He rubbed his hand absently across the back of his neck and stopped. Then he slammed his fist into the wall. The pain gave him a momentary outlet for his frustration and misery.

Hob had come with the news that the council had sent down the warrant for his execution. The time was set for tomorrow at mid-morning. No word had come back yet from either Moray or Maitland. Duncan had penned new messages with paper and quill brought by Hob, and he had given Hob gold coins enough, from the cache Elspeth had brought, to hire men and fast horses to deliver the letters as quickly as possible.

Hours had passed since Hob had taken those missives out, precious hours that meant life or death for Duncan. He had paced in this black pit, willing the letters to reach their destinations. If either Moray or Maitland heard of his situation, they would act on his behalf. He was certain of it.

The proceedings at his trial had not been entirely legal. The council had decided to make a quick and severe example of him, taking advantage of Moray's and Maitland's absence to do so. Robert had presented false evidence, letters written by powerful French noblemen regarding secret Scottish matters, all addressed to Duncan.

Those papers were forgeries. He had never had dealings, legal or otherwise, with the French. Those lies had ulti-

mately been far more serious charges than the breaking of
the Fraser bond. The forged letters had brought the death
sentence to him.

This had been a triumph for Robert Gordon. Duncan
was astounded that the man's taste for revenge ran quite
this deep. And he was not satisfied that he understood why.

Moray and Maitland would know he was innocent. The
cases he had handled had come directly from them; they
knew him well, and would know that he had no interest in
dealing with the French and nothing to gain from it.

He thrust his fingers through his hair and sighed loudly.
Overturning the empty water bucket, he sat down. The
coins Elspeth had left had enabled him to pay for extra
water. He had drunk his fill and then washed as best he
could. Washing after all this time, even without soap, had
been a simple but immensely pleasurable experience. At
least he would not go to a public execution as a complete
wretch. He had some dignity left.

He frowned again and considered his last recourse. He
had tried to convince Hob to take the rest of the cache of
gold and escape with him to France. So far his loyal cousin
had resisted, claiming, quite reasonably, that going to
France would only prove Duncan's guilt in his accuser's
eyes, making it impossible for him to ever clear his name.
But Duncan was beginning to feel desperate. When Hob
returned, he would discuss it with him again.

With so many matters to occupy his mind, he forgot the
faint banging noises outside, and neglected to even watch
the turn of the light from dusk to dark. He thought deeply,
wanting to know why Robert had set him up for this severe
sentence, and wanting to find a quick solution to his
predicament.

He did not want to die. Every fiber of his being resisted
that. There had to be a way out, and he was certain that
he would find it.

And yet Elspeth had foretold that the day of his execution would come about.

Every possible explanation for that, even the most ridiculous, had occurred to him. He had no explanations left.

Logic and coincidence did not apply. His own recurring dream, which had led him to find Elspeth in the sea loch, had finally convinced him, although he had resisted it for a long time, that the Sight was an undeniable and real phenomenon. Man's brain was not the limit of man's experience after all. There was more to the relationship of God and man than the humanists had thought. The philosophers had some work yet to do.

He smiled bitterly as he sat in the dark cell. His thoughts had finally turned to the deep mysteries of life. He was acting like a condemned man about to face God. He nearly laughed as he leaned his shoulders against the cold stone wall.

He had always trusted logic, trusted his own measures of the world around him. Man can do all things if he will, Duncan had been taught; man is limited only by himself. The writings of the humanist philosophers had given him a basis for his faith in himself above all else. God existed, of course, and no one could doubt that. But he had thought that seers and prophecies were the stuff of medieval superstition.

Yet Elspeth Fraser could map out a man's life from birth to death, past and future. She had the ability to touch a scar and feel the long-buried hurt trapped in it. Such inexplicable talents were better accepted with a large dose of faith.

But faith would not get him out of this situation. He had once had supreme control over his life. Now he sat in a dark, cold prison cell with his worldly possessions and rank taken from him, where clean water, light, a pair of boots, were luxuries. And he realized that his controlled intellect had turned him away from the deep pulse of life.

Elspeth had shown him wildness again, had shown him passion and joy and impulsiveness. Because of her, the wilder part of himself, whose power he had tried to deny, had stirred inside of him. The first impulse was so powerful that it had overtaken him and landed him in prison.

Now that wild side within him gave him the strength to

rebel. He would fight this with his heart, with his mind, and with his fists. He would not go easily to the block.

He doubted that Elspeth had seen that in her vision.

A long time later, sitting in the dark pit, he heard Hob's voice at the door. "Visitors for ye, Duncan," Hob said as the door opened.

Duncan stood and gaped in surprise. Five men, cloaked and hooded, entered his cell. They dropped to the lowered floor with quick, agile movements, all but the last man, who was urged in by the toe of Hob's sturdy boot.

As the hoods fell back, Duncan saw the Fraser cousins, Hugh, Callum, Kenneth, and Ewan. The last man was Robert Gordon.

Duncan tilted his head. "Welcome, lads," he said.

Kenneth grinned. "Duncan, man, we have brought you a gift." He pushed Robert forward. "Alasdair found him in a tavern, boasting that he had brought a dangerous spy to justice. So we collected him and brought him to you."

Duncan eyed Robert warily. "And what am I to do with him?"

Ewan stepped close. "Well," he muttered, "we wondered if you would like to have him take your place on the scaffold tomorrow."

All of Duncan's senses were alert. He snapped his gaze from one cousin to the other. "Take my place?"

"The man is a disgrace, a true snake," Ewan said, speaking from the side of his mouth. "We thought you might like to land your fist in his face. And we have found no better way to get you out than to leave him here in your place."

"Ah. Has he agreed to this?" Duncan murmured.

"Not exactly," Ewan muttered.

"Stop that mumbling," Robert said. "What are you saying?"

"Only that it is time you confessed to your crimes," Ewan answered. "Callum will help you."

With a swift movement Callum grabbed Robert and lifted him off the floor. "Tell us all what you have done,

Robert. We want to hear why you made false charges against Duncan Macrae."

"Hah. Not false. I brought a spy and a treasonous bastard to justice. I found corruption in the heart of the queen's own men and exposed it."

Duncan stared, his chains weighing heavily on his wrists and ankles. "Lies," he said wearily.

"Indeed, lies," Hugh said. "Callum—?"

"With pleasure," Callum said. He knocked Robert against the wall. Robert's head flew back, and he dropped to the floor.

Kenneth called to Hob. A set of keys dropped suddenly through the iron grate.

Hugh scooped up the keys and bent down to unlock Duncan's iron fetters. "Elspeth left you a cloak," he said. "Put it on, and we will leave. Ewan is not as tall as you. He will pass as Robert. Hob will pretend to know nothing."

Duncan had a choice. He could wait for the message from Moray that he hoped would come, or he could grab this chance, however risky, that had miraculously come to him. He nodded and grabbed up his cloak from the floor, swirling it around his shoulders. He felt suddenly invigorated, lighter of the weight of the chains and iron cuffs. He was ready to quit this place and worry about the consequences later.

Duncan stepped toward the door just as a dark whirling shadow fell heavily at the Frasers. Robert gave a frenzied yell as he slammed into them. They all went down in a surprised, chaotic tumble, as if a cannon had landed in their midst.

"I have him!" Callum said. "Oof—"

"But I have him!" Ewan called. "*Dhia!* And he has a knife!"

Duncan spun around, but the darkness was so complete that he could not tell one cloaked cousin from another. All of them, Frasers and Robert, rolled about in the filthy straw, arms and legs flailing. Duncan heard the ugly sound of punches landing. He hunched down to dive in and help, but he was not sure which one was Robert.

Scant moments later, the writhing mass on the floor began to separate into four men who stood up, panting heavily.

"I have him," one of them said. "He is killed. Go!"

Duncan knocked, the door opened, and the Frasers scrambled quickly out of the cell. They leaped into the corridor and ran past Hob for the entrance.

Duncan paused to look at Hob. "My thanks, cousin. I owe ye my life."

Hob grinned. "Och, ye're a fine kinsman, an' I wish ye well. Go now, man." He shoved him after the others.

Duncan ran to catch up to the Frasers, who slowed to file sedately past the guards who had admitted them. The guardsmen paid them such little attention that Duncan realized that money must have changed hands earlier. He had never been allowed that many visitors before. His face hidden beneath his large hood, he too passed the guards at the entrance, then stepped out into the courtyard with the others.

The air stunned him. There was so much of it, chill and misty and damp, and so very sweet. He pulled in great lungfuls of it as he walked across the yard.

The Frasers ran ahead, a cluster of dark robed men in the moonlight. Duncan had not realized how late it was; the guards must have required a hefty bribe to allow visitors at such an hour. But the night before an execution, they might be expected to show some leniency for the condemned man.

He drew in another deep breath of fresh air and smiled. Walking through the gate, he left the castle just behind the Frasers. He saw Hugh lift a hand and wave to the gatesman. Somehow they had cleared their way in and out. No questions were even asked.

Only gold could open gates that quickly, Duncan knew. He began to wonder how much was left in his coffers at home. Apparently the Frasers had been quite free with his coin. He smiled, not grudging them a pence. Then he walked briskly down the incline toward the town, fog settling over his shoulders.

They were well along High Street before Duncan realized that one of them had run on ahead. "Lads," he called softly. "Where are you headed?"

Hugh turned. "Back to your rooms for now."

Duncan shook his head. "When they discover Robert in the cell, they will send up a cry and begin to look for me."

"Hob will delay them as long as he can," Hugh answered.

"Still, it is best I leave the city. Go on to my rooms and take care of Elspeth. If men-at-arms come there, say that you know nothing of my whereabouts. I will ride to find Moray."

"Hugh," Callum said. "Where is Kenneth?"

"He ran ahead," Hugh answered.

"That was Ewan," Callum said.

"I am here," Ewan said. "I thought Hugh ran ahead."

Callum stopped in the road. "Where is Kenneth?" They looked at each other, puzzled, and looked around through the fog.

Duncan felt a shiver go up his spine. "The one who ran ahead was a smaller man than Kenneth," he said slowly. "I thought he was Ewan."

Ewan swore and broke into a run. The Frasers followed, with Duncan in their midst. Feet pounding on the cobbled street, they raced through the town. Seeing the swirl of a dark cloak, Duncan pursued it around a corner and through a maze of side streets, where the mist floated and curled eerily.

He caught up with Robert on the steps of a multilevel tenement house. As Robert ran through the door and up a flight of stairs, Duncan followed. He thrust his shoulder into a half-open door and grabbed Robert before he could close the door in his face. The Frasers pounded up the steps behind him.

"Where is Kenneth?" Duncan growled.

"I knifed him and left him in the cell," Robert panted back. "Kill me if you will, but he will die of his injury. And you will be brought to justice for escaping."

Duncan slammed him against a wall. The Frasers came

into the room behind them and stopped. He landed a strong blow to Robert's jaw, another to his belly. Robert gave him an odd look of shock and crumpled to the floor.

Duncan turned around. "Tie him up," he said. "He will go with us to the block in the morning."

"I thought you were riding to find Moray," Hugh said.

"If Kenneth lives, he may be taken to the block in my place," Duncan said. "When my absence is discovered, and a Fraser is found in my cell, he will be quickly condemned by the council. Hob will not be able to do anything to stop it. His own life may be in danger over this escape. And since we will not be able to go in and get Kenneth, we will have to wait for them to bring him out. And they will," he said, frowning. "The council seems anxious to behead someone before the people."

The Frasers applied their attentions to the task of securing Robert with whatever they found at hand. Leather belts found in a cupboard provided sturdy fetters.

"These are the rooms Robert had been renting while he has been here," Duncan said. He began to sort through the cupboards. Finding sheaves of papers in a small wooden casket, he sat down to look through them. "*Ach*. These are not quite what I had in mind," he muttered, tossing them down.

"Duncan," Hugh said. "How will we get Kenneth off the block in the morning?"

Duncan thrust his fingers through his hair and looked up. "I do not know," he said. "But for now we have some time left to us before the guards discover him. We have a task here in these rooms." He spun in a slow circle, eyeing the cupboards, a trunk, and a few small wood and leather boxes. "Look for papers, lads," he said. "Any kind of papers."

Chapter 25

"O gentle death, come cut my breath,
I may be dead ere morn!
I may be buried in Scottish ground,
Where I was bred and born!"
     —*"The Demon Lover"*

In the great hall at Holyroodhouse, Elspeth watched the rain through a tall window. She and Alasdair had returned to the palace early that morning, walking the short distance through a chill fog and a drizzling rain. She shivered in the spacious hall, which was cool despite a fire in the enormous hearth.

"They never came back last night," she said to Alasdair. "They went out late and did not return. What happened?"

"Stop fretting, girl," he said. His sigh revealed his own concern. "They took Robert after I had found him and went to the prison. I do not know what they meant to do there, though Hugh had some purpose in mind. Perhaps they were allowed to see Duncan and sat the night with him."

"Well, I hope that they meant to take Duncan out of there," she said quietly. "Hob would have helped them if they had tried such a thing. Is an escape possible from that place?"

"That may be the only way to help Duncan now," he whispered. "An escape sometimes happens there, especially if enough coin is passed around."

"We have heard nothing. There might have been trouble."

Alasdair nodded grimly. "It would have been dangerous for them to try anything, no doubt about that."

Elspeth frowned and bit her lip. She turned to look out the window at the mist-shrouded gardens.

A few moments later, a door at the other end of the room opened. The clerk who had come to fetch them for their audience on the previous day entered and cleared his throat loudly.

"Her Grace the queen is not here," he said. "You may leave."

Alasdair murmured a translation. Elspeth gasped, running toward the man as he turned to go. The clerk frowned with an expression of disapproval at her earnest barrage of Gaelic. She turned to Alasdair, who stood beside her.

"He says that the queen has ridden into the town to have midday dinner at the Lord Provost's house," Alasdair said.

"But the queen told me to come back today! She was going to inquire into the matter of Duncan's sentence. Alasdair—" She grabbed his arm. "He will be brought to the block today!"

Alasdair spoke to the clerk again, who answered, shrugged, and then walked away, closing the door firmly behind him.

"This cannot be the end of it," Elspeth said. "It cannot."

Her cousin placed a hand on her shoulder. "We will go to the provost's house. I asked the clerk where it is. Come ahead."

She followed, feeling suddenly exhausted as they left the palace and crossed the extensive grounds. Walking alongside Alasdair, she had the odd sense that the brief walk back to the town would be the coldest, longest journey she would ever take.

They were still on the abbey grounds, approaching Canongate, leading to the city, when she pulled on Alasdair's arm. "The scaffold has been set up in the church square. Duncan may be there already if we were wrong about what my cousins intended last night—" She faltered, nearly stumbling. "I do not want to see the scaffold. I do not have the strength."

"Come ahead," Alasdair said gently. "We must try to see the queen again. It is not far to the provost's house."

She nodded, knowing she must go on, no matter how tired or how terrified she was. Duncan's last chance could

depend on how quickly she gained another audience with
the queen. She would beg Mary of Scotland to grant Duncan a remit of execution.

The rain splashed around her in a steady rhythm as she
walked forward. Pulling up the edge of her plaid to cloak
her head, she glanced at the muddy road.

And stopped. The hovering mist seemed to gather and
change, as if shapes formed from the fog and the rain. A
cold shiver went through her. She sucked in her breath
sharply as a golden light filtered through the fog. Beside
her, Alasdair seemed to fade. He spoke, but she could not
hear him.

As if it lay before her in the road, she saw a wooden
platform, a scaffold. It was not outside a church, but
seemed to be inside a room, for she saw a large hearth
with a blazing fire. On the scaffold stood a tall, elegant
woman gowned in black, with a cascading white veil; she
recognized Mary Stewart, but older, more mature than the
young woman Elspeth had met yesterday.

Elspeth was unable to move. She watched the woman's
image shimmer in the air and change, like a ghost taking
shape again.

Now the queen wore deep red, like dark wine. She knelt
and folded her hands in prayer. A woman, weeping silently,
wrapped the queen's head and eyes in a white cloth. Mary
Stewart stretched forward and laid her long neck across a
wooden block.

Elspeth gasped and fell to her knees in cold mud. The
golden haze dispersed, and the vision vanished. She raised
a trembling hand to her brow.

"Ah, *Dhia*," she whispered. "This queen has such
courage."

"She is a fine lady," Alasdair agreed. "What is wrong?
Did you see something?"

She looked up at his kind, concerned face. Alasdair was
a queen's man through to his heart, as was Duncan, as were
her cousins. She too shared their love for this young queen.
What she had just seen lay years in the future.

There would be time to think about this vision, time to

speak of it if she decided to do so. But deep inside she
knew that her small warning could not affect this event,
a destiny constructed on a scale far greater than Elspeth
could imagine.

Perhaps some visions, after all, were better kept in silence. There had been something deeply poignant and pro-
foundly reverent in the way the queen had faced her own
death. Mary Stewart had shining courage, indeed.

Elspeth sighed. "I saw the mist," she said. "Only shadows in the mist."

"Come ahead," Alasdair said gently. "Do not stop now.
I have never known you to give up. Duncan needs you."

She nodded and got to her feet, her knees trembling. A
moment ago she had seen a vision of true courage, of splen-
did resolve. Witnessing that, she could not allow her own
resolve to drain away from her.

This was not over, she told herself. Duncan was still alive,
and she loved him. Where there was love, there was always
hope. Where there was hope, there was a chance.

She walked on. Alasdair had to run a little to catch up.

The crowd was thin, Duncan thought, pulling the hood
of his cloak forward over his brow. Cold rain and wind had
discouraged the usual crush of spectators. He glanced
around the square. Callum, Hugh, and Ewan were milling
through what crowd there was. They had left Robert neatly
bound and gagged in his rented room only a few streets
away from the church square where the scaffold had been
built, and they had come here to wait for Kenneth to be
brought forward.

Duncan breathed in the keen odor of fresh wood and
looked at the newly built scaffold. A block of wood, old
and scarred, dripping with rain, was set in the center. A
bench for the officials had been placed at the back. The
executioner's ax lay on the floorboards, covered with a
cloth. Duncan could see the wicked edge of the blade. He
flared his nostrils and turned away.

Clearly an execution was planned for today. The guards
would have discovered Kenneth in the cell by now. Hob

would have denied knowing anything, but probably faced punishment as the guard on duty at the time of the escape. Even if Kenneth had survived the knife wound that Robert had given him, he would not have been able to explain who he was or what had happened; the lad spoke no word of Scots.

Kenneth was alive, he was certain of it. By now at least some of the council members would be aware of the whole notorious mess. Duncan was sure that they would decide to execute Kenneth in his place. The executioner would not have left his ax there if the beheading had been canceled. Likely the headsman was somewhere nearby, Duncan thought, probably praying inside St. Giles. A heavy burden of sin, to take a man's life in cold judgment.

He walked away from the scaffold and passed Hugh. "Go back and fetch Robert. I think they will bring Kenneth soon."

Hugh nodded and slipped away, beckoning to Ewan. Nearby, Callum looked at Duncan, nodded once, and turned away.

Good men, these Frasers, Duncan thought, feeling a sudden, fierce wave of emotion rush through him. Loyal and brave, the sort a man should always have at his back.

He thought of his own four brothers, and of his father. Brave and loyal men all, and he had not been able to save any of them. But he had a chance now to save Kenneth, who had become like a brother to him. Perhaps he could make up, some, for those long-ago losses.

He took a step forward and stopped. He suddenly remembered what the old crone had said to him so many years ago. She had said that he would risk his life for one who was like a brother to him.

He smiled, a bitter, rueful smile. So that old woman had been right, after all. Shaking his head in wonder, he moved on.

He glanced around the crowd and wondered again, as he had all morning, whether Elspeth would come to the square. Unaware of his escape as yet, she and Alasdair would think that the scheduled execution would be about

to proceed. He had wanted to find her as soon as he had
left the castle; he had wanted to hold her in his arms, and
then flee the city with her by his side.

Although he hated knowing that she had to endure this
waiting time without knowing the truth, he had purposefully sent no word to her yet. There had been no time last
night, and Hugh had said that she and Alasdair planned
to go to Holyroodhouse early to seek an audience with
the queen.

A wash of pure, stirring love filled him at the thought of
Elspeth making that effort for him. The loyalty and tenacity
of all these Frasers took his breath, touched him deep inside. Hardly feeling that he deserved the devotion they
showed him, he knew he would return the same a hundred-
fold for any of them.

And the need for that was now. Kenneth's life was endangered because of him. As long as the lad was held,
Duncan could not feel free. All the stakes had changed the
moment the lad had taken his place in the prison cell. Best,
then, that Elspeth knew nothing of his escape; he would
not give her false hope. What he faced now would deter-
mine his true fate.

He did not know what would happen here, but he felt it
coming, as cold and real as the chill mist in the air. The
plan he had in mind was the greatest risk he would ever
take. But it was the only way he could free Kenneth and
clear his own name.

He hoped that Elspeth would be delayed at Holyroodhouse. He would not want her to see this.

"Alasdair," Elspeth said anxiously. "The platform is
there, in front of St. Giles. Can we not go behind the
church somehow?"

Being much taller, Alasdair peered ahead and gave her
a gentle nudge. "I see no one on that scaffold. Nothing is
happening. A good sign, I think. And the most direct way
to the provost's house is through the square. Just keep your
head down and do not look. Duncan is not there, girl."

Biting her lip and bowing her head, Elspeth walked on-

ward into the crowd. Someone jostled her, and she stepped
aside and kept moving, seeing only feet, legs, cloaks, never
looking up. She did not want to see the scaffold. She did
not want to see the faces of the people who had come to
watch Duncan die.

Nearing the scaffold, she moved on, smelling the piney
odor of the wood, hearing the gentle hiss of the rain on
the cobblestones. Someone bumped into her again and
she turned.

A pair of feet in cuffed boots walked past her, beneath
a long black cloak, and disappeared into the crowd. She
walked on.

And turned back suddenly. She had seen those boots
before, had worn them herself only days ago. With a quick
intake of breath she looked up and scanned the crowd.
Strangers, unknown to her, a blur of faces in the rain—

And a tall man in a black cloak. She shoved forward
through the crowd, hearing Alasdair's exclamation as he
turned to find her gone. Dipping her shoulder, she edged
between two large women. The tall man, cloaked head to
foot, had his back to her as he walked through the crowd.

Her heart pounded in her chest. She knew the rhythm
of that walk, knew the set of those shoulders. Shoving forward again, she pushed through a gap with a desperate sob
and reached out.

She touched his back, grasping his cloak. He stopped
suddenly, and a jolt went through her. He turned. Beneath
the hood Elspeth saw a flash of blue like a Highland sky.

"Duncan," she whispered. "Duncan."

"Dhia!" The word was soft as a prayer, but she knew he
swore. He opened his arms and the cloak folded around
her like wide black wings. She caught a sob in her throat
and pressed against him, feeling the solid warmth of his
body, circling her arms tightly around him under the cloak.

"What are you doing here?" she asked, her cheek against
his chest. "How is it you are free?"

"Hush," he said, and pulled her with him through the
crowd, moving quickly. He drew her into an alley and ran

with her to a dark corner. There the wings of the cloak enveloped her again.

His lips met hers with a fierceness, a passion that she had thought taken from her life. She held onto him and opened her mouth and felt him there, on her lips, against her body, real and solid and hard, one hand on her back, the other smoothing along her jaw, tilting her face to his.

"Duncan," she breathed, "tell me what happened."

He kissed her again and laid his cheek against her hair. "Your cousins," he said. "They brought Robert and freed me from the prison. But when we thought to leave Robert behind in my place to make his explanations, he tricked us in the dark. Kenneth was left instead. And now he will be brought to the block."

Her trembling knees nearly gave way beneath her. "Kenneth? They would not kill him!"

He pressed her closer. She felt the rasp of his beard on her brow. "They would, *mo càran*. He helped me to escape, and so they can declare his life forfeit. But there is a way to stop it." He drew back and looked at her. "I want you to go back to my rooms. Stay there until someone comes for you."

"I will not leave you," she said.

"Elspeth—"

She scowled up at him. "I will not. Now that you are free, I will not let you out of my sight."

He sighed. "Then you will have to be very strong if you will stay. I do not know what will happen."

"I am strong. When you are with me, I am."

He gave her a curious look, a dazzle of blue touched with darkness. She was chilled by that glance and stepped back. He smiled and touched a finger to her chin. "You have a fine will in you, like hard steel. Rely on that now. Promise me."

"I promise." The chill spiraled down to her feet. "But Duncan, you are free now. The vision was wrong."

"Believe that, my girl, if you believe anything," he murmured. Then he took her hand and walked back to the square.

The rain had lessened, and cold fog had settled in to obscure the castle rock above the town, veiling the church, the empty platform, and the crowd in a gray murk. Within moments Duncan found Alasdair and the rest of her cousins, and murmured to them in quick, hushed tones. They kept turned away from her, and Elspeth could not hear what they said.

Duncan came to Elspeth and took her hand in his, warm and strong, holding it beneath the cover of his cloak. Hugh and Callum ran off through the crowd and left the square. Ewan faded into the crowd, and only Alasdair remained near her.

"Perhaps they will not bring Kenneth after all," Elspeth said. "It is past the noon hour now."

"There." Duncan put his arm around Elspeth. "Walking down the slope from the castle. The mist hid them until now."

Several guards and two black-robed officials advanced along High Street. Elspeth raised up on her toes, straining to see the party as it entered the church square. She recognized the red-bearded man from the queen's audience room the previous day.

Kenneth walked at the center, easily the tallest man in the group, dressed in his Highland wrapped plaid and torn linen shirt. His long hair, braided like dark ropes, swung about his face and shoulders. As they came closer, Elspeth gasped. Deep bruises darkened his temple and cheek, and blood stained his shirt at the shoulder. He was chained and fettered in iron.

But he walked tall and straight between the guards, his face a set mask of pride and courage. The party divided the hushed crowd as they passed through the square. Beside Elspeth, Duncan pulled his hood lower and stepped back.

The guards and officials mounted the platform with the prisoner. Elspeth watched as they forced Kenneth to kneel on the pine boards. From the church behind them, two men dressed in black emerged, a kirk minister and the executioner, who wore an eerie black mask over his upper face.

They joined the others on the platform and spoke in low voices to the two robed officials who had come down from the castle. There seemed to be some confusion among them, gestures and arguing, but at last they seemed to agree, and they turned toward the crowd.

Elspeth did not understand the words, but knew that one of the officials spoke a pronouncement of guilt. Alasdair muttered to her that they claimed Kenneth had forfeited his life by helping a condemned man to escape. The minister uttered some prayers on Kenneth's behalf and read a passage from the Bible.

She glanced at Duncan, who had turned away to scan the crowd with a furrowed glance. Then she noticed that one of the officials held up a white cloth, meaning to tie it around Kenneth's head. The executioner stepped forward.

"There must be something we can do," she said, turning to Duncan. "There must be something!" She laid her hand on his chest, and felt his pounding heart beneath her fingers.

He bent down to her. "Elspeth," he said softly in her ear. "Know that I love you always. Never doubt it. Never forget it."

She looked at him in confusion as he laid his hand on the side of her face and caressed her cheek gently. His touch sent shivers all through her. She stared up at him.

He let go and stepped away, nodding to Alasdair. The wings of his black cloak swept wide through the crowd as he strode forward.

Elspeth moved to follow him, but Alasdair reached out to hold her back. She pushed against his grip in sudden fright when she saw Duncan approach the platform.

"I am Duncan Macrae of Dulsie!" he called out. "I am the man you want. Let this lad go."

Chapter 26

"O see ye not yon narrow road,
So thick beset with thorns and briers?
That is the path of righteousness,
Tho after it but few enquires."
          —*"Thomas the Rhymer"*

Elspeth shoved Alasdair desperately, but he would not release her. "Hold, Elspeth," he murmured. "Hold and wait."

She sobbed and struggled against him, her gaze fixed on the platform as Duncan mounted the steps. His presence had caused an immediate uproar not only among the crowd but among the officials and the guards on the platform. Kenneth stared at him in disbelief as Duncan strode across the pine boards to bend down and raise Kenneth to his feet.

Duncan turned then and spoke to the officials. Elspeth did not understand the Scots words he used, but no one needed to tell her what he said. No one needed to explain what he planned to do. Tears streamed down her cheeks as she watched.

The red-bearded man, obviously indignant, gestured and shouted. Three men-at-arms stepped forward to grab Duncan. Another two guards grabbed and held Kenneth.

Duncan spoke out again, addressing the black-robed officials. The mellow, deep tone of his voice was calm and certain. Elspeth watched him through distorting tears, her breathing fast and erratic.

She hit Alasdair's chest in frustration. "What does he say?" she asked, sobbing.

"One of the long-robes, that red-bearded one, is Kirkcaldy of the Grange, the captain of Edinburgh Castle. The other is a lawyer. Duncan has just told them that he and Kenneth are both wrongfully accused. Now he asks to be allowed to present new evidence to the Privy Council."

Kirkcaldy stepped forward and snarled an answer.

The guards shoved Duncan down to his knees, so roughly that Elspeth cried out. The kirk minister came across the platform and began to tie the white cloth around Duncan's eyes. Elspeth felt the world begin to spin slowly around her. A swirling haze, made of cold fog, closed over the platform.

When the mist drifted back, she saw the scene that she had been dreading all these months.

Duncan knelt by the block, his cloak gone, his shirt pulled away from his neck. The white cloth hid his face from view.

Her heart beat a dull, heavy thud in her chest. Somehow she found the strength to push Alasdair, but he held her fast. "This will not happen," she said. "This cannot happen!"

"If you would help him," Alasdair suddenly hissed, "stand forward now with the Frasers."

Turmoil had begun to churn through the crowd when Duncan had mounted the scaffold. Now their shouts, and the sound from those who had begun to chant Duncan's name in unison, suddenly quieted. The crowd split apart and drew back. Elspeth looked up.

Striding through the center of the square, a group of men approached the platform. Elspeth saw her cousins Hugh, Ewan, and Callum come forward, a tall, brawny escort for Robert Gordon. He walked slight and cowed in their midst, his hair lank and brassy, his face a thin sneer. Callum gave him a shove. Robert's hands, she saw, were tied behind him.

Her cousins came through the crowd and paused before the scaffold. The four tall Highland warriors stood out amid the Lowland crowd. Long braided hair and wrapped plaids, steel dirks and claymores, strong stances and unwavering gazes marked them as men of the earth and water, hills and wind.

Elspeth stepped forward then, with Alasdair at her side. They joined the Frasers to flank Robert Gordon and face the officials on the platform. She squared back her shoulders and stood at the front. Standing with them, she realized that the attitude of the Highland warriors, united and strong, as well as their wild and somehow foreign appearance, had stunned their onlookers into silence.

Duncan rose to his feet and shook off the guard who grabbed his arm. He tore off the blindfold and looked at Elspeth. His intense blue gaze seemed to reflect a clear and shining power. She drew in her breath, knowing that he would have given up his life for Kenneth.

She knew in that moment that he possessed more courage than any man she had ever known. He had offered his life to protect her and her kinsmen, not on a battle impulse but as part of a careful decision. Wildness was there too in his gaze and in his stance. Bearded, his long, dark hair blowing in the mist, his shirt billowing out, he wore no plaid, but Duncan Macrae was as strong and magnificent as any man the Highlands had ever produced. He was as fierce and wild and indomitable as the Frasers who stood at her back.

Duncan looked at her and nodded. She stepped forward and mounted the platform steps, her cousins and half brother behind her. Walking toward Kenneth so that he could stand with them, the Frasers faced the officials.

Hugh came forward. Elspeth listened in surprise as he addressed Kirkcaldy and the lawyer in Highland Gaelic, leaving it up to the Lowlanders to find a translator.

"I am Hugh Fraser of Lovat, chief of Clan Fraser. We are here to support our kinsman Duncan Macrae of Dulsie in his claim of innocence. Neither Duncan Macrae nor our kinsman Kenneth Fraser deserves to die today." He looked at Duncan and stepped back. "Now let Macrae tell you what he would say."

Duncan turned to the officials and translated Hugh's words. They nodded warily and waited.

Alasdair was beside Elspeth, murmuring quiet translations when necessary. Although Duncan spoke in Scots, he repeated much of what he said in Gaelic for the Frasers on the platform.

"I admit that by my own actions, I broke the bond of caution that was signed between the Frasers and the crown," Duncan said. "No one else broke the bond. But I abetted disorder only by attempting to rescue my wife, who had been cruelly taken by two members of Clan MacDonald. That clan had also signed a bond."

Duncan turned and held out his hand. Elspeth came to him, and he wrapped his fingers around hers. "Any man would have done the same in my place. I plead innocent of murder charges. The man I am accused of killing fell and broke his neck when he attacked me. My wife is a witness to that, as is her kinsman, Magnus Fraser, whose injury at the hand of a MacDonald prevents him from being here. He will send written testimony if you so require it."

Kirkcaldy bent to mutter to the lawyer. They watched Duncan with doubtful expressions. The lawyer shook his head.

Elspeth turned to Alasdair. "They will not listen to him. One of us should run to the provost's house. The queen is there!"

"Hush," Alasdair whispered. "The queen has no stomach for executions, and will not come near this place. Duncan is on his own here. Hush, now. He has their attention, at least."

"No other should be punished for breaking that bond but me," Duncan continued. "But the document states that a fine is to be exacted from the pledge before a life would be taken. I will pay the fine."

The two officials frowned and muttered again, turning away. The lawyer motioned for Duncan to continue, and Kirkcaldy nodded.

"The charges of spying and high treason, which brought about the sentence of beheading, were falsely made and maliciously created," Duncan said. "One man accused me, and one man was witness against me. Counsel is denied the defendant in cases of high treason, but that accusation was wrongly made against me. I would speak now, since I was not allowed to defend myself at the trial." Duncan looked over at the Frasers. Callum and Ewan shoved Robert forward and stood beside him, holding onto his arms.

"Robert Gordon accused me of spying and treason. But his own evil turn of mind created those charges."

"These are lies!" Robert shouted. "This man will say anything to save his neck! He is a spy, and I proved it at his trial!" He struggled against the Frasers who held him.

Duncan turned away to face the officials. "Robert Gordon has resented the disaffection of Clan Gordon. He has sought revenge against any who brought that shame about for his clan. As you are aware, I was one of the lawyers involved in the trial of George Gordon, earl of Huntly. I also took part in the condemning of John Gordon. When I married Robert Gordon's half sister, he sought his revenge."

Kirkcaldy and the lawyer consulted, and Kirkcaldy turned to Duncan. "You must have evidence of this," he said.

Elspeth, watching, saw the raw hatred in Robert's face as he looked at Duncan. She drew in her breath sharply. Robert turned his gaze to her then, and she had to look away from the acid blue of his eyes. She felt sick.

Duncan turned to the Frasers and held out his hand, palm up. Callum stepped forward and handed some folded papers to him.

"Robert Gordon had strong reason to seek revenge on me," Duncan said. "He hoped, by accusing me of treason, to save his own neck and hide his own crime." Duncan passed the papers to Kirkcaldy, who looked through them in silence and handed them to the lawyer.

Alasdair's murmured translations filled the silence that followed as the officials looked over the papers.

"Some of these were presented at your trial," the lawyer said. "But these are addressed to Robert Gordon."

Duncan nodded. "The ones you saw at my trial were copied from these original letters. My name was falsely added to the copies. Two of the letters were written to Robert from his Gordon kin, detailing their hopes to bring power back to their disaffected clan." He waited while the men found these pages and read them.

"You will find that the other letters are from members

of the French court, commending Robert for the information he passed on to them regarding the secretly planned uprising of the Gordons. They mention too the money they have sent for this purpose, and the amount they paid Robert for his trouble."

Robert now struggled in earnest. "These are all lies," he called out desperately. "This man hates me. He hates the Gordons. He will say anything—" Hugh pulled out his dirk and touched it to Robert's throat, effectively silencing him.

Kirkcaldy watched this with a flat lack of sympathy. He gave a curt nod of approval when Hugh's blade appeared, and then looked back at Duncan, raising an eyebrow.

Duncan continued. "Robert spied on his own kin and then sold that information to the French. He found it convenient to blame me for that betrayal."

The lawyer nodded. "No doubt the French would like to see the Catholic Gordons rise to power again, since that would strengthen the Church's hold in Scotland." He shuffled through the papers. "According to this, they paid Robert Gordon well for the news." He looked up. "Master Robert Gordon, we shall investigate this."

Kirkcaldy snapped an order, and three guards came forward to grab Robert. Hugh lowered his dirk and the guards led Robert away. Elspeth watched as they escorted her half brother down the steps and through the crowd to take him back to the castle dungeon. Robert had tried to arrange Duncan's death to cover his own crimes. The cowardice of his actions astonished her. She turned away, trembling.

The muttering between the officials now grew to a sharp discussion. Kirkcaldy flapped the letters and spoke loudly to the lawyer, who nodded again and again.

Another order was barked out, and a guard went over to Kenneth and unlocked the iron fetters that joined his wrists.

Elspeth understood none of the Scots words, and Alasdair's hurried translations had given her only a part of what had gone on here. But she knew from Kirkcaldy's tone and his gestures, and from the joyous thud of her heart, that Duncan had proved his innocence.

A murmuring arose in the crowd. Elspeth turned to see a man running toward the platform, shouting and waving a paper over his head. He climbed the steps to the platform and spoke to Kirkcaldy in an agitated tone. Kirkcaldy beckoned toward Duncan. He went, bowing his head to listen to what they told him.

The paper that the man had brought was passed from hand to hand. Elspeth saw a red wax seal and ribbons dangling from the paper's edge. She glanced at her cousins.

Alasdair looked pleased. Then he grinned. Hugh smiled too. Puzzled, Elspeth looked from their elated faces to Duncan.

He turned then, looked at her, and held out his hand. She ran the few steps toward him, and he gathered her into the circle of his arm.

"What has happened?" she asked. "What is that paper?"

"It is a remit of execution, Elspeth," he said. He grinned and held out his hand for the page, which Kirkcaldy handed to him. "The queen has sent her pardon. She was at the provost's house this morning when Moray sent word to her. He received my letter yesterday and acted immediately. The queen read Moray's note and sent this clerk to deliver the remit to the captain of Edinburgh Castle." He opened the page for her to look at it. Though she could not read the Scots, she saw the signature "Marie" at the left side of the page.

Duncan laughed. "The clerk said when he arrived that the queen hoped it would not be too late."

"Too late!" she said. "You got yourself free before this arrived."

"I could not have done anything without your cousins to help me," he said. "The remit, though, comes in time to keep me out of prison altogether. They were going to hold me on the other charges until all was decided. But the remit clears up all of that and asks only that the fine be paid within a year."

Alasdair came over to join them, grinning widely. "God bless that sweet face, as the people here say of our queen."

"God bless that sweet face," Duncan murmured as he

smiled down at Elspeth. He reached up a hand to touch her cheek lightly. "The queen would not have acted so quickly if you had not gone to her yesterday, *mo càran*. That was a brave thing, and I thank you for it."

"Not brave," she said. "I have seen true courage today, in you and in my cousins. And in our queen."

He looked at her, perplexed, half smiling. The crowd began to cheer, and Duncan turned to wave at them. Elspeth wrapped her arms around his waist and hid her face in his shoulder as he turned back to her.

"My vision was wrong," she said. The relief that flooded through her was a rush of pure joy. "It was wrong."

He pressed his cheek to her hair. "I told you long ago that I believed that I would not die." He sighed. "But, Elspeth, the vision was right."

She drew back and looked at him in alarm. "What do you mean? I thought you were free." She glanced anxiously at the officials, who were still muttering between them.

As she looked back at Duncan, she suddenly realized what he meant. Her vision had indeed revealed Duncan's blindfolded face, his bare neck, and the rough curve of the heading block.

She had never seen his actual death.

"Duncan," she said. "The vision happened just as I saw it. But nothing beyond that."

He nodded. "Perhaps my death was never destined at all." He tilted her chin upward. "I do not know what is destined. But I do know that we are meant to be together, *mo càran*. There is nothing that can ever separate us. I will always be with you. Always, Elspeth."

A tear spilled softly down her cheek. "Is that a prophecy from one who has the Sight?"

He smiled and took the tear with his fingertip. "It is," he whispered. "Believe it, for it will be so."

Epilogue

Then I'll grow in your arms two
Like to a savage wild;
But hold me fast, let me not go,
I'm father to your child.
                    —*"Tam Lin"*

The late spring wind blew softly around his face as Duncan climbed the rock-studded hill. Pausing, he inhaled the fresh odor of new grass and looked around him. Wildflowers and bright tufts of grass sprang up between chunks and boulders of gray rock. Just above him, Elspeth sat perched on a bare shelf, her copper and gold hair a shining, warm light against the rocks.

He swore under his breath and walked up the slope. The way was not steep here, and he climbed easily toward her. She waved at him, but he only scowled at her and swore again softly.

He stepped onto the wide shelf she occupied, and stood over her, hands fisted on his hips. "And how did you get up here? They are half mad below looking for you."

She smiled and shifted to the side, making space for him to sit beside her. When he stood there still, glaring down at her, she patted the rock. "Come now, Duncan Macrae," she said. "You will not grudge the little freedom left to me, will you?"

He sighed and sat, dangling his legs beside hers over the rock shelf. "Your freedom should have been curtailed before this. You could have come to harm, coming all the way up here by yourself."

"*Ach*, I did not come far. You fuss like an old woman. Your grandmother does not fuss at me the way you have lately. And remember, you brought me here yourself just two weeks ago. I like it up here," she said, leaning back against the support of the rock behind her. The solid bulk of her belly was round and smooth beneath the shapeless woolen gown she wore. A plaid of Fraser blue and green covered her shoulders and full breasts. Her slender bare legs and feet swung out beneath the hem of the gown. "Although this will be the last time I climb here for a while. I do not have the balance that I used to have."

He grunted at that, rather than laugh and risk upsetting her. He had learned to tread carefully through her high and low moods lately, though Innis had assured him that this would pass with the birth of the child. "You should have at least asked me to come with you. I would have taken you a little way up."

"A little way only," she said. "As if I were a feeble thing. I am strong, Duncan. There are at least two months left before he will be born. I came as far as I felt safe. The first time we came here, you led me much higher." She pointed behind them, where the grassy slope became a rocky, challenging climb, where cloud rings hung suspended. "I had to see this today. The air is clear and sweet up here."

She swept her hand wide, and he looked with her over green hills dusted with yellow and white mountain wild-flowers. Below, he saw Dulsie Castle, its square-cornered stone tower nestled on the green fairy hill. The long slope of the mountain at its back was carpeted with a dense tree cover.

He looked down the hill on which he and Elspeth sat, and saw five plaided Highlanders climbing the long slope toward them. He waved, and waved again, seated at the edge of the rock. Soon one of them saw him—Ewan, he judged, by the deep gleam of his dark red hair—and waved back. Magnus was there too, his blond braids pale golden ropes. Duncan waved again, and the Frasers stopped, hands on hips, heads tilted back to look up the slope.

Elspeth waved now and called out as they climbed closer. Then Kenneth grinned and waved and turned away, his dark head a burnished gleam in the sun. Hugh and Callum went with him, running ahead. Magnus and Ewan followed, and the Frasers headed back toward the castle, satisfied, no doubt, that Elspeth had been found.

"I came up here to think," she said, watching them go. "My cousins are a noisy lot. Singing and dancing until deep in the night."

"It is broad day. And you enjoyed all that music last night, if I remember well."

"I did. But the sounds of their *céilidh* last night still ring in my ears. I was thinking," she said, "about brothers. About yours, and mine, and about my cousins."

He frowned. "What of your half brother?" he asked.

"Robert has been living in that same black cell that held you. What will happen to him, Duncan?"

"I had a letter recently from Maitland. Robert Gordon's friends on the council are deeply embarrassed about what happened. They are trying to avoid an execution, though many think he deserves one. But the whole matter makes them look like simpletons who lost their senses when Moray and Maitland left town. Robert will probably be exiled as quietly as possible in order to save their dignity. They would like to see the whole matter forgotten." He drew a deep breath and looked out over the bright slopes. "Maitland asked me to return to Edinburgh. There are some cases he would like me to take on."

Elspeth turned to stare at him. "Will you go?"

He did not look at her. His gaze scanned the green hills, the blue sky, and soft, deep lavenders of the mountains beyond. A pair of golden eagles swooped down from the mountain behind them, gliding together toward a sparkling blue loch far in the distance. He watched them for a long time before he answered.

"I have already written my reply," he said. "Tomorrow I will send my gillies to run it south to Edinburgh." He turned to look at her then. "My place is here. My heart is here, where you are."

She let out a slow breath, a sigh of relief, he thought. She leaned into him, pressing her arm to his, and the warmth of her body seemed to flow through him.

"You do belong here," she said. "It is a good place to be."

He nodded. "It is that. What else did you think about here on this rock? More about brothers?"

"I was thinking that you lost four brothers and your father, and gained my cousins, who consider you better than a brother to them. And I was thinking too that I have had cousins all my life who are brothers to me. I gained you as well. There are so many men in my life," she said, turning earnestly to him. "Fine, strong, brave men. I love and admire all of them so much. And we will have sons, Duncan," she said. "A new group of Macrae brothers, four at least, I feel, and one daughter."

He raised an eyebrow. "So many? A lot of names to choose."

"Not so hard," she said. "We will name them for your brothers, I think."

"Ah. Iain, Gillean, Lachlann, and Conor?"

She laughed, tilting back her head, the sound of her delight rippling through the mountains—and through his heart. "Those are wonderful names," she said.

"And the girl?"

"Mary, of course."

"For Mhairi?"

"For Mary the Queen," Elspeth said. The smile left her face, and her eyes deepened in color. "We will name her for a woman whose courage and beauty will be a legend in a future time. And our girl will find her own courage somewhere in her life." She looked away. Duncan thought he saw the soft gleam of tears in her eyes. She sat still and silent, and he reached over and touched her shoulder.

"Come, girl," he said gently. "My grandmother has been asking where you had gone. She sent us all out to find you."

She nodded. "Innis will understand that I had to get away. Besides, she has little time to think of me, with all the visitors Magnus and Kirsty brought back with them from Glenran."

Duncan laughed, a short chuckle. "It seems as if Castle Glenran has moved to Dulsie for the spring."

Elspeth nodded. "Everyone came with Magnus and Kirsty. Flora has promised to stay longer, to be here for the birth of our child. Will Innis mind that, do you think?"

"Of course not." Duncan smiled. "Innis thrives on a household full of people. And she has been completely enchanted by Eiric, I think. The child loves her new greatgrandmother well, and has hardly left her side."

Elspeth laughed. "I am glad. Eiric has a warm little heart, and gives her love and devotion freely. She loves Kirsty, and Innis, and Mhairi too. And she is very happy to have three little cousins to play with. Bethoc is wonderful to her, but she is not much of a playmate."

"Well, Eiric will have a playmate soon enough, when Kirsty gives birth. The child is due just after ours, she said."

She nodded. "Last night I had a dream, Duncan."

"What was that?" he asked. "No ravens, I hope. My grandmother is still talking about that dream she had. The raven that wished to have me for its master, whatever that means."

She took his hand in hers. "Death, my love," she murmured. "Did you not know? I think that the dream told her that you would conquer death somehow."

He slid a doubtful glance at her. "Well. I avoided it, at least. What was your dream, then?"

"I dreamed that Kirsty gave birth to twin girls. They were blond like Magnus. And in the dream they grew older and chased our son up the slope of the mountain. He laughed as he climbed."

Duncan smiled and turned her hand, twining her fingers in his. "That dream I will believe," he said softly. "We saw the boy climb up here once."

"We did. And he will be here soon. But not too soon. He likes to take his time, this one. He is patient like his father. Magnus and Kirsty's girls are anxious little ones and may be here before our first son."

"And what will our son have of his mother?" Duncan

asked. She looked at him and shrugged. "I think he will have his mother's gift for song," he continued. "At least I hope he has it from his mother and not his father." She laughed.

He stood then, helping her up. When she stood, he pulled her back against his chest and wrapped his arms around the warm bulk of her middle. Something stirred beneath his hands. He smiled and rested his cheek on the cushion of her bright head.

"Once, long ago, I never thought to be happy at Dulsie ever again in my life," Duncan said. "But now I am grateful for so much."

Elspeth laid her hands over his, over the mound of their child nurtured within. She smiled. "Ah, but have you not heard the legend? A fairy cast a spell in the form of a silver net long ago. The lairds of Dulsie will always return. You could never have stayed away from here all your life."

"I have heard that legend," he said.

"It brought you home safely, Duncan Macrae of Dulsie."

"It did. Or was it my own fairy wife who brought me safely home again?"

She laughed and stepped away from him, taking his hand to draw him down the slope. "That fairy wife only said your doom now and again, if I recall."

"Laid curses on me left and right at first, she did."

"Hmm, at first." She looked back over her shoulder, and her eyes were the color of rainwater, her hair a rich sheen. She seemed to glimmer in the sunlight, precious and exquisite, full of radiant strength and life.

He stopped and pulled on her hand, drawing her toward him, wrapping her in the circle of his arms. "Come here," he said. "You are more beautiful than any fairy."

She laughed, a soft, sweet trill, and her hair shone like copper spun with gold. She placed a finger gently over his lips.

"Hush, you," she said. "The fairies might be listening."

"Let them listen," he murmured. "They will learn something about happiness." He lowered his lips to hers and kissed her, the fullness and depth of the kiss taking his breath.

The whirlpool spun, and he went with it. The laird of Dulsie was home at last.

Author's Note

Each chapter in this novel is headed by a verse from an old Scottish song specifically chosen to complement the story. Most of the verses date back to or just before the sixteenth century. A few are from a bit later because while reading through these wonderful old lyrics I could not always resist their poetic phrasing or meaning on the basis of date.

Sixteenth-century Highlanders spoke Gaelic almost exclusively, and the Loch Ness area was no exception. I wanted to create the cadence and sense of that language in the dialogue rather than use Scots English throughout. Gaelic, which is still spoken in more remote areas of Scotland today, is a poetic, breathy, complex language, and I have tried to honor that.

Lowlanders, then as now, spoke Scots English. This is not considered to be a dialect, but rather a form of English in and of itself. In consideration for the reader, the Lowlanders in this novel speak a conservative version. Anyone interested in a pure Scots English may wish to read works by Sir Walter Scott or Robert Louis Stevenson.

Whenever possible, I tried to remain true to Gaelic and Scots traditions. However, English rather than Gaelic names are used for the main characters: Elspeth, Duncan, Kenneth, Ewan, and Hugh are more agreeable, over a few hundred pages, than Ealasaid, Donnochadh, Coinneach, Eòbhann, and Uisdean, if less authentic.

No matter the language, I hope you found *The Raven's Wish* very agreeable.

Don't miss
MAGIC AT MIDNIGHT,
the sizzling new time-travel
romance
available in June. . . .

Kathryn could still see her own hazel eyes behind those of
the green-eyed stranger, as if she were trapped inside. A
terrified numbness settled over her. She was two people at
once! But that was impossible, there *had* to be a logical
explanation. The reporter in her told her so. She was
dreaming! Yes, that was it, she'd never really awoken and
left the bed. But as she continued to look at the glass, her
own eyes faded, and there were only those of her new
self—wide, clear, and expressive.

The initial confusion began to disperse, and new knowledge flooded in its wake. She suddenly knew the identity
of this dream self! Her name was Rosalind, Lady
Marchwood. More than that, she was married to Sir Dane
Marchwood, one of Regency England's most feared gentlemen, and she'd gone back in time to perhaps the most
famous Regency year of all, 1815, the year of Napoleon
Bonaparte's final defeat at Waterloo. But Lady Marchwood
felt little joy at the great victory. She was too frightened to
be happy, because she was an adulterous wife and her husband was a very dangerous man to cross.

But how could she know all this if it was a dream? Her
glance went to the table, where the glow of the candle
shone on her wedding ring. For an illusion, the flame
seemed very real. She felt that if she reached out, she
would feel its heat. And yet she was *sure* it was a dream.
Yes, for what else could explain it?

Suddenly she realized there was someone else in this most vivid of dreams, for a man appeared behind her.

"Rosalind?" He touched her naked shoulder softly as he said her name. "You must leave Dane and come with me, somewhere he'll never find us. We were meant to be together, and all we have to do is go to my plantation in Jamaica. He doesn't even know I've purchased it." His voice was very English and refined, reminding her of Lawrence Olivier in the old black-and-white *Wuthering Heights* movie. He was twenty-seven or twenty-eight, of medium height, with tousled brown hair and warm, dark eyes. His clothes were fashionable, a sage green coat and cream cord breeches, with a pearl pin in his starched neckcloth, and he had about him a hint of the same anxiety that pervaded her.

Oddly, in spite of his dark coloring, he reminded her of Richard, although she couldn't have said why. She knew who he was. Thomas Denham, Rosalind's lover, the man she'd risked everything for, and the reason she'd set her wedding ring aside for a few stolen hours tonight.

She knew he was waiting for her to respond, but she didn't know what to say. In a situation as incredible as this, the cat had more than gotten her tongue!

Her silence perplexed him. "Did you hear me, Rosalind?"

"Yes. Of course." Her accent was no longer that of modern New York, but British. But it *was* her voice!

"Then why don't you answer?"

"I-I can't."

He turned her to face him. "Can't answer, or can't leave him? Rosalind, I will not believe it to be the latter, for you don't love him. How can you when you so eagerly break your vows with me? We've lain together this very night while he dines barely two hundred yards away with the bishop and other worthies. You wouldn't do that if you felt anything for him." Thomas searched her face in the candlelight. "Yours was an arranged match, pure and simple, and you should never have gone through with it. The two years since you went to the altar have been misery for you because he can't put his first wife's memory to rest. Every time he touches you, he still touches Elizabeth."

The first Lady Marchwood had died ten years before giving birth to Dane's only son, Philip, who now attended Eton and was at present staying with friends for the summer vacation. Kathryn felt dizzy from the potent mixture of knowledge and confusion swirling through her. She knew so much about Rosalind, but was aware she hadn't completely taken on this new self. Inside she was still Kathryn Vansomeren. That was why she was sure it was all a dream. She must have read all this in one of the historical romances she couldn't get enough of, or maybe seen it in an old movie, and now her subconscious was recalling it in this weird dream.

Well, whatever it was, she had to go along with it, for it was real enough until she awoke. That meant getting a grip on herself, like deciding what she felt right now. The real Rosalind was deeply and irrevocably in love with Thomas Denham; Kathryn Vansomeren in Rosalind's clothing most certainly wasn't. The real Rosalind went in fear of Sir Dane Marchwood, but her dream alter ego was curiously intrigued about him. For the moment he was a shadow on the edge of her consciousness, and she couldn't bring him forward into the light, but hearing his name caused her a shiver of illicit excitement.

Thomas put his hand lovingly to her cheek. "Dane will still mourn Elizabeth ten years hence. To him you'll never be anything more than the wife he took to oblige his father's long-standing friendship with your father. You're his property, but to me you're everything in the world."

"I-I know." She was aware he was speaking sound common sense when he urged her to run away with him, but there were disconcerting gaps in her knowledge, as if her subconscious couldn't quite recall the entire plot of whatever book or movie this came from.

Thomas smiled. "Please give the answer that will make us both happy. Nothing binds you to him anymore, but a great deal binds you to me. After what you've told me tonight, it's plain we have to leave before things become obvious. We've played with fire and are about to be burned."

Now she definitely didn't know what he was talking about. He might know what was soon going to be obvious, but she certainly didn't. She almost wanted to laugh aloud in her frustration. Was this the place she'd skipped a chapter, or switched the channel? Whatever the reason, she had no idea at all what Rosalind had just told him.

He took her face in his hands. "I know you're afraid, my darling, but I'll take care of you. Just say yes, and I'll make all the arrangements. We can take passage from Bristol for Jamaica within days."

She had to stall, she didn't know what else to do. "I-I'll give you my answer soon."

"How soon?" he pressed.

"I don't know. Just soon."

He looked swiftly into her eyes. "I don't understand why you're so hesitant. After what you've told me tonight, we *daren't* delay. To stay here now will be to deliberately court disaster. Dane isn't renowned for his sweet temper, and on the three occasions he's called men out, he's extinguished them all, including my brother. As for his valor on the battlefield, well, you and I both know how many times he's been mentioned in dispatches. He could never be accused of a lack of courage. I have little doubt that the army was the ideal setting for a man of his disposition, and I only wish he'd elected to stay where he was instead of resigning his commission in order to come home once and for all. You've admitted it's been a relief his army career has kept him away for most of your marriage. Well, he won't be away from now on. He'll be here, demanding his conjugal rights."

Suddenly she was sure of her facts again. She knew all about Dane's decision to leave the army. She also knew that the two-year marriage had been wretched because Rosalind had always loved Thomas, but the part of her that was Kathryn Vansomeren felt a perverse desire to defend Sir Dane Marchwood. "Dane may be many things, but he isn't quite the black-hearted villain you paint."

Startled, Thomas released her. "Rosalind, I *know* him for a black-hearted villain! My brother William didn't do anything to warrant being called out at dawn. His only crime was to be a Denham."

"I concede that Dane doesn't like your family any more than they like him, but even so there must have been more to it than that. Not even he would call your brother out simply for being a Denham." She didn't know what caused the fatal quarrel between Dane and William Denham, but this was because Rosalind didn't know either. No one knew why the challenge had been issued, not even Thomas. The only one alive to tell was Dane, and he'd never uttered a word.

Thomas found her attitude bewildering. "Why are you behaving like this? I admit that a simmering dislike had always existed between Dane and my family, but the only time it ever erupted into a public quarrel was over that miserable parcel of marshland on the boundary of Marchwood. Surely you aren't suggesting that was why Dane chose to call my brother out. No, of course you aren't, because the truth is that Dane takes pleasure in dueling, and the temptation of indulging that pleasure and eliminating a Denham at the same time was simply too great to resist. I warn you, if he finds out about us, he'll have a much better reason for calling me out than he ever had William!" Realizing he'd raised his voice slightly, he swiftly took her hands. "I'm sorry, but I'll never forgive Dane for William's death. None of my family will."

His touch disturbed her. The real Rosalind would have trembled with delight, but Kathryn was unmoved, a fact he'd surely perceive at any moment. She began to pull away before he realized, but he slipped an arm around her waist and drew her close to press his parted lips over hers. It was a passionate kiss, meant to dispel what he saw as her inexplicable reluctance to take the wise way out of a deep scrape, but she found everything about him suddenly so eerily like Richard that she might almost have been with her blond, blue-eyed New York husband instead of this dark-eyed Englishman from an earlier century.

Suddenly the dream took on a much more sensuous tone. His mouth moved over hers, and she felt the flick of his tongue between her lips. He stroked her breast through the thin stuff of her gown, teasing her nipple between his fingertips. Part of her wanted to respond to the memory of happier days with Richard, but the greater part held back. He pressed her body tightly against his, and she could feel him becoming aroused. They'd already made love tonight, but he was ready again, pressing eagerly toward her.

To her relief, another voice interrupted them, an elderly female voice, frail and heavily Gloucestershire, so not that of a lady. "Sir Dane will be here in a few minutes."

Kathryn turned quickly. An old woman had just entered the room. She was bent and gnarled, with a wizened face and hands like claws, and she walked with the aid of a stick. There was a knitted shawl around the shoulders of her simple gray linen gown, and she might have been taken for any old woman if it hadn't been for her eyes, which shone like those of a quick and clever raven. She was Rosalind's beloved old nurse, Alice Longney, and the wisdom of ages seemed to wrap around her like a cloak.

Alice addressed Thomas. "You must go, Master Thomas, but not by the front way, for you may encounter him."

He nodded, and then looked at Kathryn again. "Please give me your answer now, my darling," he begged.

"I'll tell you at the ball tomorrow night. There'll be many opportunities for us to speak then," she replied. The ball entered her head as much without warning as everything else. It was to be held at the Royal Well ballroom in Cheltenham to celebrate the victory of Waterloo. She was back to the original book or movie storyline again, for how else would she know about the ball? Or the Royal Well ballroom!

He gave her a curious look. "At the ball? But you know I'm not going."

For a moment she was blank, but then remembered he'd already told Rosalind he couldn't attend the ball because of a prior dinner engagement. Why had she made such a blunder? Hastily she tried to smooth the moment over. "Forgive me, I-I'm so worried about everything I can't think properly. I'll send word to you soon, I promise."

He searched her eyes. "Rosalind, there's no time to delay, not after what you've told me tonight. I wish to God you'd told me before, but there's still time. We dare not tarry if I'm to make the necessary arrangements to sail from Bristol. Every hour you delay means we run the risk of Dane finding out, and I don't relish the prospect of being the second Denham to die at his hands."

Alice was increasingly anxious. "Please, sir, you must go now! If Sir Dane should actually catch you here—!" She couldn't bring herself to finish.

He took Kathryn by the arms and gazed urgently into her eyes. "If we remain, you may be sure it will mean shame and ruin for you, and death for me." Then he was gone, striding swiftly past Alice to the narrow landing.

His steps sounded on the staircase, a door closed, and there was silence. Almost immediately the sound of a carriage disturbed the night, and Kathryn saw it pull up at the end of the lane. It was a gleaming maroon vehicle drawn by four grays, and its lamps shone brightly through the darkness of the poorly lit street. The door was flung open, and two gentlemen stepped down.

Both were in their mid-thirties, dressed in formal evening clothes. One was short, with red hair that shone in the light of the carriage lamp as he clapped his companion amiably on the shoulder and then walked swiftly away toward the cathedral. Kathryn knew him to be Dr. George Eden, who came from a wealthy local family and possessed an elegant town house facing the cathedral. He was a much respected man, and one of the few who could count Sir Dane Marchwood among his close friends. It was Dane from whom he'd just taken leave.

Her gaze moved to Rosalind's husband. He was tall and arrestingly handsome, with thick black hair and a penetrating glance she could perceive even from a distance. His lean, athletic physique was perfectly suited to the fashions of the day, and few things could have become him more than his close-fitting black velvet coat and superbly cut white silk breeches, except perhaps the dashing military uniform he'd so recently set aside forever. The jewel in his lace-edged neckcloth caught the lamplight as he turned to speak to his coachman, and Kathryn's heart tightened within her as she gazed at him, for the feelings that surged through her now were unlike anything she'd ever known before.

He walked toward the courtyard, and the closer he came, the more clearly she could see his eyes. She knew they were gray, and that there was something in them that hinted at dark secrets, something immeasurably exciting. He was the perfect hero, with looks to melt the hardest female heart, and a satanic air she found both arousing and frightening. Each step he took brought desire and hazard nearer, and the blend was exhilarating. On the one hand, she found him more sexually attractive than any man she'd ever seen before. On the other, she could sense the alarm the real Rosalind would be feeling now on being so nearly caught with her lover. But the latter feeling was only fleeting, for Kathryn Vansomeren found him devastatingly desirable, a man in an entirely different league from the dull and rather ordinary Thomas Denham, and certainly a world away in every sense from someone like Richard, or even Harry Swenson, for whom she'd so briefly but tellingly thrown caution and common sense to the winds. Everything about Sir Dane Marchwood drew her like a pin to a magnet.

He reached the courtyard and seemed to sense she was at the window, for he halted and toyed with the spill of lace at his cuff as he looked directly up at her. The hint of latent power surrounding him was like a beacon in the darkness, and when their eyes met, she couldn't look away. She was conscious of the electrifying spell of his gaze. It was as if he knew her thoughts, and therefore must know all about the affair with Thomas Denham.

But it was Alice who knew what she was thinking. "No, Kathryn, as yet he only suspects."

Kathryn glanced swiftly around. "You know my name?"

"Of course."

"Ah, but this is a dream, so you would, wouldn't you? I know this is all some old plot I've read or seen, and that it's all mixed up with the real me!" Kathryn declared this almost triumphantly, like she'd just scored a winning point.

"I don't understand you."

Kathryn was suddenly less sure of things. Something about the intensity of the old woman's eyes conjured thoughts of sorcery and ancient magic. No, that was stupid. This was still a dream, probably brought on by jetlag, stress, and British food. Why couldn't her subconscious light on a story she remembered properly? If she'd turned into someone like Jane Eyre or Scarlett O'Hara, she'd know what happened next.

Alice smiled. "Don't look for answers now, my dear, for the rest of tonight could bring you more passion, excitement, and gratification than you've ever known before. Sir Dane Marchwood is the lover you've always longed for, and he's within your reach because for this one night you are his wife."

"If I am, I'm supposed to want Thomas Denham," Kathryn pointed out swiftly.

"Then let me put it another way. For this one night you are Kathryn Vansomeren in Lady Marchwood's body. Dane suspects his wife of infidelity, but he doesn't know for certain, and if you wish to enjoy his caresses, you must convince him of your faithfulness and love."

"Lie to him, you mean?" Kathryn replied flatly.

"No, my dear, for although Rosalind has betrayed her vows to him, you haven't."

Kathryn had to look away as Harry Swenson came to mind again.

Alice smiled. "Oh, I'm not talking about your fleeting affair before you came here."

"You know about that, too?" Kathryn gasped.

"Yes, and when I say that Rosalind has betrayed her vows to Dane but you haven't, that is precisely what I mean. You, my dear, have never betrayed Sir Dane Marchwood, and that's what matters."

"You're talking in riddles."

"Am I? It's very simple, Kathryn. Do you want to lie in Dane's arms tonight?" Alice asked quietly.

Kathryn glanced down into the courtyard. "Yes."

MAGIC
AT
MIDNIGHT
by
Sandra Heath

Have you read
a Signet Regency
lately?